A PLUME BOOK

RASHI'S DAUGH
BOOK II: MIRI

MAGGIE ANTON was born Margaret Antonofsky ... ...
Raised in a secular, socialist household, she reached adulthood with little
knowledge of the Jewish religion. All that changed when Dave Parkhurst
entered her life, and they discovered Judaism as adults. That was the
start of a lifetime of adult Jewish education, synagogue involvement, and
ritual observance. This was in addition to raising their children, Emily
and Ari, and working full time as a clinical chemist.

In 1997, as her nest was emptying and her mother was declining with
Alzheimer's disease, she became intrigued with the idea that Rashi, one
of Judaism's greatest scholars, had no sons, only three daughters. Using
techniques developed while doing her family's genealogy, she began to
research Rashi's family, and the idea of a book about them was born.

Eight years later, the first volume of *Rashi's Daughters* was finally
complete, making Maggie Anton a Talmud maven and an authority on
medieval French Jewish women. She retired from the lab and spent the
next two years researching and writing *Book II: Miriam*, in addition to
lecturing at over a hundred synagogues, JCC's, and Jewish women's or-
ganizations.

Maggie lives in Glendale, California, with Dave, her husband of
thirty-six years, where she is working on *Rashi's Daughters, Book III:
Rachel*, as well as a translation of *Machzor Vitry*. You can follow her blog
and contact her at her website, www.rashisdaughters.com.

Rashi's Daughters

Book II: Miriam

MAGGIE ANTON

A PLUME BOOK

PLUME
Published by Penguin Group
Penguin Group (USA) Inc., 375 Hudson Street, New York, New York 10014, U.S.A.
Penguin Group (Canada), 90 Eglinton Avenue East, Suite 700, Toronto, Ontario, Canada M4P 2Y3
(a division of Pearson Penguin Canada Inc.)
Penguin Books Ltd., 80 Strand, London WC2R 0RL, England
Penguin Ireland, 25 St. Stephen's Green, Dublin 2, Ireland (a division of Penguin Books Ltd.)
Penguin Group (Australia), 250 Camberwell Road, Camberwell, Victoria 3124, Australia
(a division of Pearson Australia Group Pty. Ltd.)
Penguin Books India Pvt. Ltd., 11 Community Centre, Panchsheel Park, New Delhi – 110 017, India
Penguin Books (NZ), 67 Apollo Drive, Rosedale, North Shore 0745, Auckland, New Zealand
(a division of Pearson New Zealand Ltd.)
Penguin Books (South Africa) (Pty.) Ltd., 24 Sturdee Avenue, Rosebank, Johannesburg 2196,
South Africa

Penguin Books Ltd., Registered Offices: 80 Strand, London WC2R 0RL, England

First published by Plume, a member of Penguin Group (USA) Inc.

First Printing, August 2007
1   3   5   7   9   10   8   6   4   2

Copyright © Maggie Anton, 2007
All rights reserved
Map illustration by D. G. Parkhurst

℗ REGISTERED TRADEMARK—MARCA REGISTRADA

CIP data is available

ISBN 978-0-452-28863-8

Printed in the United States of America
Set in Adobe Garamond

PUBLISHER'S NOTE
This is a work of fiction. Names, characters, places, and incidents are either the product of the author's
imagination or are used fictitiously, and any resemblance to actual persons, living or dead, business estab-
lishments, events, or locales is entirely coincidental.

For Aaron
for Ray
and for all the other modern-day Judahs

acknowledgments

AS IN THE FIRST BOOK of my *Rashi's Daughters* trilogy, most of the characters in *Miriam* are real historical figures. Again, I've spent years researching how Jews and women lived in medieval France so I can share my knowledge with my readers. Again, there will be plenty of Talmud woven into the story, as taught by the master, Rashi, himself.

On the subject of Talmud, I want to thank Dr. Rachel Adler of HUC-JIR in Los Angeles for introducing me to this amazing holy text almost fifteen years ago and for suggesting what later became the theme for this volume on Miriam. I fell in love with the Talmud at first sight and have been passionately studying it ever since.

That brings me to my second acknowledgment: Rabbi Aaron Katz of the Academy of Jewish Religion. My study partner and dear friend, Aaron has taught me so much that there aren't words enough to thank him. This book would not exist without his assistance. I am also grateful to Rabbi Tsafreer Lev, Zachary Hepner, and Cantor Philip Sherman, who spent hours explaining every intricacy of the circumcision procedure and the training required to become a mohel.

I want to thank my agent, Susanna Einstein, and my editor at Plume, Ali Bothwell Mancini, for her enthusiasm and her encouragement to take *Rashi's Daughters* to the next level. Also many thanks to Beth Lieberman, for editing advice that turned this book into the one I wanted it to be, and to Sharon Goldinger, who shepherded this naive author into becoming a successful one.

My friend Ray Eelsing and my daughter, Emily, spent many hours critiquing my early drafts. Each brought their own unique talents to the task and their comments were invaluable. Last, but certainly not least, I offer my thanks and love to my husband, Dave, who listened patiently to far too many stories about Rashi and his daughters, who gave me excellent advice about how to improve my first drafts, and who could always think of the right word when I couldn't. Without his support I would have given up long ago.

timeline

1040   Salomon ben Isaac (Rashi) born in Troyes, France, on February 22.
(4800)

1047   Count Etienne dies; his son Eudes III inherits Champagne.

1050   Invention of horseshoes and padded collars enable horses to plow fields much more efficiently than oxen.

1054   Salomon goes to Mayence to study with Uncle Simon haZaken. Under Pope Leo IX, a split develops between Byzantine/eastern and Roman/western church.

1057   Salomon marries Rivka, sister of Isaac ben Judah. Leaves Mayence to study at Worms.

1059   Joheved born to Salomon and Rivka in Troyes.

1060   Philippe I becomes King of France; Henry IV is Emperor of Germany, Nicholas II is pope, Benedict X antipope.

1062   Miriam born to Salomon and Rivka.
Count Eudes III found guilty of nobleman's murder; Uncle Thibault takes over Champagne and forces Eudes III to flee to Normandy where he takes refuge with his cousin, Duke William (the Bastard) of Normandy.

1066   Salomon studies in Mayence with Isaac ben Judah.
Duke William of Normandy becomes King of England (the Conqueror).

1068   Salomon returns to Troyes.

1069   Rachel born to Salomon and Rivka.

Joheved becomes betrothed to Meir ben Samuel of Ramerupt.
Isaac (Troyes' parnas) becomes winemaking partner with Salomon.

1070   Count Thibault marries second wife, Adelaide de Bar, a young
(4830) widow.
        Salomon founds yeshiva in Troyes.

1071   King Philippe marries Bertha.
        Count Thibault and Adelaide's first son, Eudes IV, is born.

1073   Hildebrand, a Cluniac monk, is elected Pope Gregory XII.

1075   Pope Gregory announces excommunication of married priests,
        suspends German bishops opposed to clerical celibacy, and
        threatens to excommunicate King Philippe.

1076   Thibault and Adelaide's third son, Hugues, born.
        Pope Gregory excommunicates German King Henry, appoints
        Rudolph as new king.

1077   Isaac ben Meir born in Troyes.

1078   Daughter Constance born to King Philippe and Bertha.

1080   Samuel ben Meir (Rashbam) born at Ramerupt.
        Archbishop Manasse of Rheims is deposed by Pope Gregory; a
        blow to King Philippe.
        King Henry of Germany appoints Clement III antipope.

1081   Prince Louis VI born to King Philippe and Bertha.

1083   King Henry attacks Rome, Saracens plunder city, Pope Gregory
        flees.

1084   Fire in Mayence attributed to Jews; many move to Speyer.
        Count Thibault's oldest son, Étienne-Henri of Blois, marries
        Adèle, daughter of William the Conqueror.

1085   Pope Gregory dies in Salerno.

1087   King William of England dies.

1088   Smallpox epidemic begins in winter.
        Count Thibault becomes ill, son Eudes IV takes over as ruler of
        Champagne.

1089   Isaac haParnas and Count Thibault die in epidemic.
        Champagne goes to Eudes IV. Blois goes to Étienne-Henri.

1092   Epidemic of infant meningitis in Troyes.
        King Philippe repudiates Queen Bertha and marries Bertrada,
        wife of Count Fulk of Anjou, enraging Pope Urban II.

1093   Eudes IV dies on January 1. Thibault's son Hugues becomes
        Count of Champagne.
        Count Erard of Brienne starts war with Hugues.
        Solar eclipse in Germany on September 23, followed by famine.

1094   Pope Urban II excommunicates King Philippe over Bertrada.
        Terrible drought in summer in Champagne.

1095   Count Hugues marries Constance, daughter of Philippe and
        Bertrada.
        Spectacular meteor shower in early April.

1096   Crusades start: Four Jewish communities in Rhineland attacked
        between Passover and Shavuot. May 3, Speyer; May 18, Worms;
        May 27, Mayence; May 30, Cologne. More than 10,000 Jews die.
        Lunar eclipse in early August.

1097   Jews converted during crusade permitted to openly return to
        Judaism.
        A comet is seen for seven nights in early October.

1098   Robert of Molesme founds Citeaux Abbey and Cistercian Order.

1099   Crusaders take Jerusalem.

1100   Jews return to Mayence.
(4860) Louis VI becomes king-elect of France.
        Paschal II is pope, Theodoric antipope.
        Discovery of alcohol by distillation is made in Salerno medical
        school.

1104   Assassination attempt made on Count Hugues.

1105   Salomon ben Isaac dies on July 17; Samuel ben Meir heads
        Troyes yeshiva.

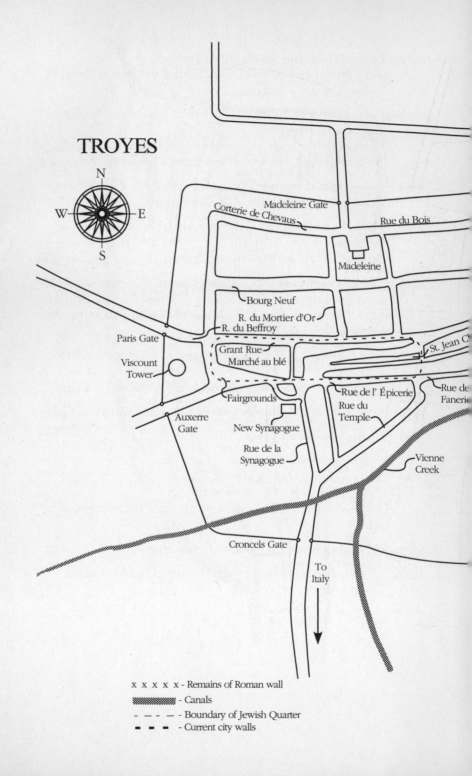

TROYES

N
W   E
S

Madeleine Gate
Corterie de Chevaus
Rue du Bois

Madeleine

Bourg Neuf
R. du Mortier d'Or
R. du Beffroy

Paris Gate

Grant Rue
Marché au blé
St. Jean C

Viscount
Tower

Rue de l' Épicerie
Rue de
Faneri

Fairgrounds
Rue du
Temple

Auxerre
Gate

New Synagogue

Rue de la
Synagogue

Vienne
Creek

Croncels Gate

To
Italy

x x x x x - Remains of Roman wall
▨▨▨▨▨ - Canals
- — — - Boundary of Jewish Quarter
▪ ▪ ▪ - Current city walls

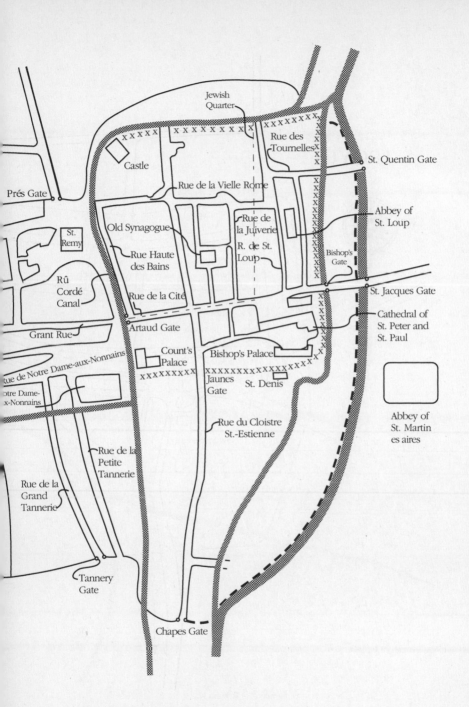

Jewish
Quarter

x x x x x   x x x x x x x x x
Castle   Rue des
                               Tournelles x
Prés Gate   x   St. Quentin Gate
                                                 x
St.   Rue de la Vielle Rome   x
Remy   x   Abbey of
       Old Synagogue   Rue de   x   St. Loup
                         la Juiverie   x
       Rue Haute   R. de St.   x
       des Bains   Loup   x   Bishop's
                                                 x   Gate
Rû   x
Cordé   x   St. Jacques Gate
Canal   Rue de la Cité   x
                                                 x   Cathedral of
Grant Rue   x   St. Peter and
           Artaud Gate   x   St. Paul

           Count's   x
Rue de Notre Dame-aux-Nonnains Palace   Bishop's Palace
                        x x x x x x x x x x x x x x x x x x x x x x x x
otre Dame-   Jaunes   St. Denis
x-Nonnains   Gate

                                         Rue du Cloistre
                                         St.-Estienne   Abbey of
                                                                  St. Martin
          Rue de la   es aires
          Petite
          Tannerie

Rue de la
Grand
Tannerie

       Tannery
       Gate

           Chapes Gate

Ben Zoma said: Who is wise? One who learns from everyone. As it is written (Psalms 119:99), "From all my teachers I have gained understanding." Who is strong? One who conquers his yetzer. As it is written (Proverbs 16:32), "One who is slow to anger is better than the mighty and one who controls his spirit than one who captures a city." Who is rich? One who is content with his portion. As it is written (Psalms 128:2), "You shall eat from the labor of your hands; you shall be happy."

—Mishnah Tractate Avot, chapter 4

prologue

FOR THE JEWS OF NORTHERN FRANCE, times had never been better than in the second half of the eleventh century. Relations with their Christian neighbors were tolerant, even amiable on occasion, since the Church was too busy rooting out heretical sects and implementing Pope Gregory's controversial reforms to concern itself with the Jews. European society was entering 150 years of advances in political organization, economics, scientific pursuit, and education, in what is now called the Twelfth-Century Renaissance.

Under the feudal system, the Jews' social status was high, equal to that of knights. The Jewish trader was a welcome visitor to French estates, bringing news of the outside world, buying their surfeit produce, and selling them imported goods. Jews were moneylenders much as department stores and gasoline companies are today; if their customers received the bulk of their income at harvest time, for example, merchants extended them credit until then.

As Christian Europe's resources grew, Jews bought wheat, wool, wine, and steel, and then transported it to the Muslim East, where they sold it for a profit. In return they acquired silk, cotton, spices, and jewels, which they brought back to the West, sold for another profit, and began the cycle again. Everyone prospered.

The Jews of Troyes benefited greatly from this commercial success. Under the enlightened sovereignty of Count Thibault, the great fairs of Champagne attracted merchants from throughout the known world, many of them learned in Jewish Law. Credit was extended from one fair to the next, in this infancy of the modern banking system. Since local middlemen collected a percentage of every sale, the Jews of Troyes became so affluent that even the poorest families had servants.

In 1068, one of these families was that of twenty-eight-year-old Rabbi Salomon ben Isaac, who would be known and revered centuries later as Rashi, one of Judaism's greatest scholars. After fifteen years studying in Germany's finest Talmudic academies, he was forced to return home to manage the family vineyard, which had fallen into decline due to his mother's senility. With no sons, and desperate from having to give up his yeshiva studies, Salomon broke with tradition and secretly began teaching Talmud to his daughters, Joheved and Miriam.

But Salomon did not lack male students for long. Isaac haParnas, the leader of the Jewish community, saw an opportunity to attract more Jewish merchants to the fairs in Troyes by establishing a Talmud academy there. He offered Salomon a generous salary to teach his grandsons, and other boys soon joined them, forming the nucleus of a new yeshiva. To ensure that Salomon had sufficient time to teach, Isaac haParnas partnered with him in the wine business, which finally lifted the vintner's family out of poverty.

Salomon also had time to begin writing his twin commentaries on the Bible and the Talmud. His Bible commentary is so authoritative that today it is studied in every rabbinic school. Yet his extraordinarily clear and concise commentary on the Talmud is his true magnum opus. Since the Talmud was first printed in the fifteenth century, his words have filled the inside column of every page of every copy. Today more Jews read Rashi's words than those of any other Jewish scholar.

Not surprisingly, Salomon's daughters found their fiancés among his students. First Joheved was betrothed to Meir ben Samuel, a lord's son from nearby Ramerupt. Miriam, however, enjoyed a love match with Benjamin ben Reuben, son of a vintner in Rheims. Her initial compassion for the homesick youth blossomed into a deeper feeling as they worked together in Salomon's vineyard. Joheved, terrified that Meir would discover that she knew Talmud, tried to hide her learning from him. But Miriam suffered no such fears with Benjamin, and the two of them would often study Salomon's lessons together.

Over the next several years, Salomon's yeshiva thrived as more and more foreign merchants studied with him during the semiannual fairs, and then sent their sons to him during the year. His family grew as well when his wife, Rivka, gave birth to another daughter, Rachel. Miriam was so helpful during the delivery that the midwife, her Aunt Sarah, began training her as an apprentice.

Miriam learned to grow her own midwife's herbs and to find the others she needed in the local forest; she helped deliver Countess Adelaide's baby during a complicated childbirth, thereby saving both the countess and the child; she prepared and administered an abortion potion for Catharina, an unmarried childhood friend; and she successfully delivered Joheved's first child.

All this time, Miriam and Joheved continued to study Talmud with their father. When their grandmother died, they took over her position leading services for the women in synagogue, and though they didn't seek it, they were on the way to assume leadership in the community of Jewish women. But Miriam gave no thought to the future of Troyes' Jews or her possible role in it. At seventeen years old, she was focused on her own future as she and Benjamin eagerly prepared for their wedding.

Part One

one

Troyes, France
Late Summer 4838 (1078 CE)

Miriam silently took her place on the bench she shared with Benjamin. As soon as her father finished blessing the bread, she casually let her hand drop below the table so her fiancé could take hold of it. They'd been betrothed five years, ever since she was twelve, and now their wedding was less than three months away. She blinked back tears of joy. Soon she and Benjamin could be alone together whenever they wanted, could kiss without worrying that someone would catch them. She gazed wistfully at her older sister, Joheved, sitting opposite her with baby Isaac on her lap, and gave Benjamin's hand a gentle squeeze. Next year, Le Bon Dieu willing, she'd be holding a baby too.

Benjamin turned to Miriam and smiled. She reached up to smooth her hair into place and realized that she'd left her veil upstairs. Today, however, she was lucky; none of the scholars joining Papa for *disner* were strangers, so she did not need a head covering. Mama, of course, always covered her hair and neck, no matter how hot the weather, even when she was just eating breakfast with the family.

Miriam sighed with relief when Aunt Sarah walked in late from visiting Yvette, who had given birth two days ago. But her relief disappeared when her aunt whispered something to Mama, who immediately frowned in response.

Sarah turned to Miriam. "I don't think I can go to Ramcrupt today, dear. I'm afraid that Yvette may be developing a fever, and I want to look in on her every couple of hours."

"She was fine when I checked her last night," Miriam said, half rising from her seat.

"And she's probably fine now. I expect that she's only sweating this afternoon because of the heat, but you know we can't be too careful where the demon Lillit is concerned."

Miriam nodded. "I suppose I can collect the alkanet leaves by myself."

Salomon ben Isaac interrupted the heated discussion he was having at the men's end of the table. "Absolutely not," he said, shaking a piece of bread at Miriam. "Until Count Thibault catches the highwaymen who've been accosting Troyes' fairgoers, my daughter is not riding alone in the forest."

"But Papa, those merchants were robbed at the beginning of the Hot Fair. Surely the thieves are far away with their loot by now." She wasn't a little girl who needed his protection anymore. "New mothers really need the alkanet salve, Papa, and it's best picked now before the weather cools." If she were going to be a midwife like Aunt Sarah, she had to be able to obtain such medicinal herbs when they were available.

"*Non, ma fille.* Not alone." Salomon noted his normally dutiful daughter's expression—part disappointed, part resentful. "If you need the stuff that badly, maybe your sister can go with you."

Nine-year-old Rachel looked up eagerly, and he added, "Your older sister."

Joheved stifled a yawn. "Not today, please. Little Isaac's back teeth are coming in, and I spent most of the night trying to comfort him. Mama has generously offered to watch him this afternoon so I can take a nice long nap." She handed the baby to her husband, Meir, sitting next to her, and cut them more bread.

Benjamin quickly swallowed his mouthful of chicken stew. In just a few days he'd be returning to Rheims to help his family with their wine harvest. Then the next time he'd see Miriam would be after the festival of Sukkot, on their wedding day. "If you can spare me from the vineyard today, Rabbenu, I'll go with her."

"But you don't know alkanet from foxglove." Rivka's eyes narrowed with suspicion.

Benjamin turned to address his future mother-in-law. "I'm sure I'd be better protection against thieves than Joheved," he said. "And once Miriam shows me what the alkanet plant looks like, I can pick leaves as well as anyone."

"You're welcome to take my horse, Benjamin, I won't be needing her." Meir said with a wink. It wasn't long ago that he had been desperate for time alone with his bride before their wedding.

Sarah put down her wine cup and faced her brother-in-law. "The alkanet grows fairly close to the Count of Ramerupt's castle," she said. "I can't believe any criminals could hide in such a well-patrolled place."

Salomon stroked his beard while everyone at the table waited for him to speak. "I suppose so," he finally announced. Then he shook his finger at Benjamin. "Make sure that Miriam is never out of your sight."

"Don't worry, Papa. Benjamin and I will review today's Talmud session while we ride," Miriam said, her happiness vanquishing her mother's frown of disapproval.

Rivka had never forgiven Salomon for teaching their daughters Talmud. It didn't matter that he was rosh yeshiva of Troyes' Talmudic academy, and therefore no one in the Jewish community would dare challenge his decision. And it didn't matter that both Joheved and Miriam had found excellent matches among his students despite her insistence that no man would want to marry a woman more learned than himself. Hens didn't crow and women didn't study Talmud; it would only lead to trouble.

Rivka found a way to vent her displeasure. She pulled on one of Miriam's braids until her daughter was facing her. "And I don't care how warm it is, a betrothed woman doesn't go outside without her veil."

Within an hour the delighted couple was riding through the forest north of Troyes. It was a beautiful late summer day. While most of the foliage was still green, here and there some dazzling red or golden leaves gave a hint of autumn's future splendor. Birds twittered overhead, seemingly adding their opinions to Miriam and Benjamin's discussion of the Talmud.

She sighed with pleasure as his golden brown curls bobbed each time he nodded excitedly at an argument she made. "Benjamin, would you mind not cutting your hair until after our wedding?" She smiled at him. "I know it's silly, but I want to run my fingers in your curls."

"Ever since that morning when you tried to cure my homesickness by pretending to be my sister, I've wanted to be with you whenever I could."

She chuckled. "Joheved got so angry every time I made her take me to the vineyard while you were working there. She was sure something terrible would happen."

"She was right. You ended up betrothed to a poor vintner's son instead of a rich Talmud scholar like Meir." The grin he flashed made Miriam burst out laughing. He wasn't what most people would call handsome, but he could always make her laugh.

"Remember what Ben Zoma teaches in Pirke Avot," she said.

"Who is rich? One who is content with his portion."

She smiled back at him. "Then I am the richest woman in Troyes."

"And once we're married, I'll be the richest man in the whole world." This time Benjamin's voice was serious.

Miriam was too happy to speak. Just thinking about their upcoming wedding made her feel that her heart would burst.

Soon she heard sheep bleating in the distance, which meant they were approaching Meir's family's estate. Suddenly Benjamin's horse shied. They both slowed to see what had spooked the mare and noticed a putrid smell wafting by on the breeze. A sheep carcass blocked the path ahead.

"Should we tell Meir's parents there's a fox attacking their flocks?" Miriam called to Benjamin as they made a wide detour.

He paused to let her catch up with him. "I don't know. If we drop in on them, they'll insist on offering us hospitality, which will only delay us."

"Not only that," Miriam said, a shy smile lighting her face. "If Marona hears we're out to collect alkanet, she'll probably want to come with us."

Their gazes locked. "Perhaps we could stop by on our way back?" Benjamin said, and Miriam nodded.

They eventually found some alkanet bushes and Miriam began to fill her bag with leaves. "Strange, but there don't seem to be as many plants as before. Would you mind searching for more?"

"I'll see what I can find." Benjamin headed back the way they'd come. There was something odd about that dead sheep, and he wanted to have a closer look at it.

He made increasingly wider circles around the area, keeping in mind the location of several alkanet bushes he passed, until he reached the downed animal. *That's odd, there's nothing bitten out of the carcass.* In fact, he couldn't even see where the sheep had been attacked. Wrinkling his nose at the stink, he got down and examined the body.

Foxes hadn't killed this sheep. Its throat had been slit and a leg cut off. Whoever did it apparently lacked the strength to move his ill-gotten gains alone and had merely carried off the leg, probably intending to return with help.

Mon Dieu, they could be back any time and I've left Miriam alone. Benjamin hurriedly remounted Meir's horse. The next moment, he heard her scream.

It seemed an eternity before he reached her. If he lived forever the tableau before him would remain etched in his mind. Clutching a knife in his right hand and advancing toward Miriam was a fellow so skinny and filthy that he obviously neither ate nor bathed regularly. He was staring at her with undisguised lewdness.

Benjamin's rage flared and his immediate reaction was to drive Meir's horse straight into the villain. But then, realizing that the mare might be stabbed, some semblance of prudence tempered his fury. He grabbed his own knife and jumped down.

"Get away from her, you filthy scum!" Benjamin positioned himself in front of Miriam and yelled to her, "Quickly, ride to Ramerupt castle and alert the guards."

"But Benjamin, he's got a knife," she pleaded as she climbed onto Sarah's horse. "He hasn't harmed me. Please just ride away with me. He won't be able to catch us."

"So the girl's little brother is here to rescue her." The rogue sneered at them, showing a glimpse of yellow and brown decaying teeth. "Go on, little boy, listen to your sister and ride home to your mama."

Benjamin's burning anger flared. What an idiot this fellow was. He could have easily stolen Sarah's horse and left Miriam alone. But no, he had let his lust rule him. Then, when their riding off would have allowed him to escape, he had stupidly insulted Benjamin, essentially challenging him to a fight, which would mean certain capture if he lost.

"I have a knife, too," Benjamin responded. "In fact, I've got two." He reached down and pulled one of his father's pruning knives from its secret sheath in his boot.

Miriam could see that further talk was useless. She wheeled her mount around and galloped into the forest. There were few horses faster than Aunt Sarah's, and she prayed that she could reach the castle in time.

Benjamin and his opponent circled each other warily. Amazed at his calmness, he realized that he'd soon find out how much remained of the proficiency with knives that the Romanian convert, Samson, had taught him. The rogue seemed surprisingly cautious until he suddenly made a run for Meir's horse. However, Benjamin forestalled him by slapping the mare's rump, sending her running, and was rewarded with a shower of curses.

Now they both knew that the villain had no choice but to attack, otherwise they would keep staring at each other until the castle guards arrived. Benjamin tried to remember what Samson had taught him about deflecting and parrying an enemy's blade. He shouldn't even try to apprehend the fellow; all he needed to do was defend himself until help came.

"You know what's going to happen to you; they'll probably hang you for killing a lord's sheep." Perhaps he could delay the inevitable charge by talking.

"Not a chance, little boy." The man's smile revealed that besides being decayed, several of his teeth were missing. "I'll have killed you first, and then I'll be safe with my friends."

"You're right, you won't be hanged. You'll be given to Count Thibault's men and tortured until you tell them where your hideout is. Then they'll throw what's left of your body into a dungeon until you rot."

Was this man a member of the gang that had been attacking the fair merchants? Benjamin suddenly realized the danger he was in. What if other criminals were nearby? Surely it would take two men to move the dead sheep.

His opponent lunged. Benjamin felt his sleeve rip and resolved to pay better attention. For a while there was silence between the two, punctuated with heavy breathing. The man attacked again, but this time Benjamin dodged the blow and stabbed his knife into the man's thigh.

Benjamin began to feel confident; he was barely scratched, but his foe was limping badly, favoring his bloody leg. Then a look of desperation came over the outlaw's face, and he attacked Benjamin straight on. Benjamin jumped away, but not quickly enough. The man's knife grazed his forehead, and the wound began bleeding into his left eye. Now he could barely see. Inwardly cursing his bad luck, Benjamin tried to wipe away the blood while parrying his opponent's thrusts.

Just when he was sure he would receive a serious wound at any moment, two dark-haired youths with swords ran up and disarmed his foe. Soft linen was wrapped around Benjamin's forehead, and he looked up to see Meir's father, Lord Samuel, astride Meir's horse, staring down at him anxiously. Benjamin had been so intent on the battle that he hadn't even heard them.

Samuel dismounted and began to examine Benjamin's wounds. "Are you all right?" he asked. Benjamin could only nod in reply; he was too shaken to speak.

Apparently satisfied, Samuel turned his attention to the two young men. "When you've tied this fellow securely, search the forest for his companions."

Then he put his arm around Benjamin's still shaking shoulders. "Of course we feared the worst when my son's horse showed up at the manor's gate without a rider. I immediately mounted the mare, called my squires to accompany me, and followed her trail back here."

Benjamin had barely begun expressing his thanks when he heard a rider approaching. Hoping it was Miriam, he was taken aback when Meir's mother, Marona, rode into the clearing, clutching her medicine box. Her veil had slipped down, allowing her two long grey braids to flap behind her. Her already frightened expression turned to horror when she saw the blood on Benjamin.

"Where's Meir? What happened here?" Her gaze darted frantically around the clearing.

"Meir's safe in Troyes." Samuel helped her down from her saddle. "Benjamin was riding his horse."

Marona's terror dissipated when she realized that Benjamin was relatively unharmed. After tucking her hair back into place, she carefully cleaned and applied a healing ointment to each of Benjamin's wounds. As she did so, he recounted the afternoon's events, yelping once when Marona removed the squire's makeshift bandage from his forehead in order to properly deal with the laceration under it.

As they waited, Benjamin began to worry about Miriam. "I hope she made it to the castle all right."

Samuel smiled reassuringly. "We must expect some delay. After all, a strange woman can't just ride up to the gates, cry for help, and then ride off again with a few men-at-arms," he said. "If she mentions her relationship to me, I'm sure my knights will aid her immediately, but if not, the sergeant may want to question her."

"Your knights?" Benjamin's eyes widened in surprise.

Samuel looked up at Marona and shook his head. "Apparently there are some subjects Salomon doesn't teach at his yeshiva." He turned back to Benjamin and sighed. "As Count André of Ramerupt's loyal vassal, I am obliged to provide him with two knights to serve as castle guards. Of course, I'm not about to go myself or send my sons, so I hire a couple of landless knights. If I provide them with armor, weapons, a horse, and a small income, they are agreeable to serving in my place."

"Are your squires training to become your knights?" Benjamin was glad for the small talk as Marona tended his wounds.

"Not exactly," Samuel replied. "Alain and Pierre—excuse me for not introducing my squires, but I didn't want to delay their search. As I was saying, their fathers sent them to me to train for the knighthood. For several years they will live with me and learn estate management, at the same time receiving their physical training at the castle. If they prove adept, they may attain the position of steward to a landed family, which would allow them to marry."

Benjamin's jaw dropped. "Knights don't get to marry? I thought only monks stayed single."

Samuel shook his head in sympathy. "*Non*, most knights don't get to marry, either. Only the eldest son, heir to his father's lands, may take a bride. Occasionally a younger son finds an heiress to marry, particularly if he impresses her family with his skill at tournaments. But usually he ends up either in the church, where he can live unmarried to a ripe old age, or among some castellan's guards, where he's lucky to live past thirty."

"Which obviously leaves quite a few unwed young women as well," Marona added archly. "I believe they must choose between being a lady-in-waiting or a nun."

Benjamin pondered this new information. How could the Edomite lords be so sinful as to prevent all but a few of their number from being fruitful and multiplying? No wonder knights had such a reputation for lechery. A man without a wife would be unable to resist temptation.

"There." Marona interrupted his reverie by standing up and wiping her hands. "You're all bandaged now. Be sure and make the *gomel* blessing at services tomorrow—you're a lucky fellow to have such trifling injuries."

Suddenly he heard horses approaching. Was it finally Miriam or just Samuel's squires? Benjamin's heart leaped as Miriam rode into view, followed by two knights with swords drawn. She jumped off Sarah's horse, eager to make sure Benjamin was all right. The knights also dismounted, albeit in a more dignified manner, and walked over to address Samuel.

"My Lord." One of them had a scar on his cheek and he bowed deeply. "I apologize for our delay. There was some confusion at the castle when this distraught young lady first appeared, but as soon as we learned she was one of your relations, we came immediately."

"It's all right, men. Alain and Pierre were able to capture this villain before he could do any serious damage." Samuel indicated the man on the ground. Then he introduced the knights; the scarred one was Colon and his companion was Faubert.

"We have already encountered Alain and Pierre, my lord, which is how we were finally able to find this place," Faubert said. "They told us they have discovered only one brigand, whom they apprehended."

No sooner had the knight spoken than the two squires rode into the clearing, a foul-looking fellow tied behind Alain's horse. The man being reluctantly pulled along immediately began to curse his comrade on the ground, accusing him of betraying them.

With great effort, Miriam had restrained herself from showering Benjamin with an immodest amount of affection. Watching the two thieves arguing, her frustration combined with fury at the villain who'd threatened her, and she vented her feelings by kicking him as hard as she could in his bloody leg. He let out a yelp of pain, followed by a string of obscenities.

"Get these disgusting sons of whores out of my sight," Samuel ordered his knights. "Take them to the castle and let André's experts make them reveal what he needs to know. If Thibault offers a reward, divide it among the four of you."

"Count Thibault will be furious that the bandits attacking his fairgoers have been living right under the nose of his vassal, Count André," Marona said. "And the best way to allay that displeasure will be for André to hand the entire gang over to Thibault before the Hot Fair ends."

They tied the injured man face down on the back of Colon's horse and attached his accomplice's rope to Faubert's. The two knights set off at a brisk pace, obviously pleased at their captives' discomfort. Samuel directed his squires to dispose of the sheep carcass and, after Miriam and Benjamin insisted on remaining behind to find more alkanet, he settled himself on his wife's horse, just behind her. He put his arm around her waist, and the looks the couple exchanged suggested that they expected their ride to be as pleasurable as the criminals' would be miserable.

As if waking from a dream, Miriam and Benjamin found themselves alone in the forest again. Sunlight glinted through the trees, a gentle breeze rustled the leaves, and birds resumed their songs. Except for the small bandage above Benjamin's left eyebrow, everything seemed the same as when they first discovered the alkanet bushes hours earlier. They stood in silence, waiting for the sounds of Samuel's horses to disappear. Then they bolted into each other's arms.

"Oh, Benjamin." Miriam hugged him fiercely and began to cry. "I was so frightened."

"It's all right now." He cradled her head against his chest and stroked her hair. "At least you weren't hurt."

"I was frightened for you." Miriam squeezed him even tighter and began patting his back and arms, as if to assure herself that he was indeed uninjured. "I was terrified that we'd get here too late, and . . ." She couldn't say what she feared most.

"Don't worry—I'm perfectly fine. Marona fixed me up as good as new." He was more than fine. Miriam's caresses were having a most salutary effect.

"You can't imagine how I felt when we got back and I saw you sitting there, chatting with Meir's parents as though nothing had happened. And that horrible man tied up on the ground." As she talked, she felt her tension spilling out along with her words. "I wanted to run over and kiss you."

"So what's stopping you?" Benjamin's *yetzer hara* spoke for him.

"What?" Miriam had been babbling and she wasn't sure exactly what she had said.

"What's stopping you from kissing me?" His voice was husky with desire.

She stared up at him and began to get lost in his gaze. Then she closed her eyes and slowly lifted her face toward his.

He kissed her with almost bruising intensity, and she returned his kisses with equal ardor. Previously she had kept their lovemaking within careful bounds (except for Purim, when they were too drunk to remember what they had done). He could kiss her whenever he wanted, as long as nobody could see them. And if he managed to get her alone for a decent period of time, long enough for her breathing to quicken, he might be emboldened to fondle her breasts through her chemise and feel her nipples harden under his touch.

But this time there were no limits. She allowed, even encouraged, his hands unchecked license under her chemise while her own roamed freely under his. She couldn't get enough of his kisses and caresses; they were the reassurance she needed to prove that he was still alive. Entwined in each other's arms, they sank down to the soft forest floor.

"Take me, Benjamin, make us one flesh," Miriam whispered with a soft moan. "Make me your wife now."

He struggled to remove his *braises*, while she lifted her skirts and pressed her hips up against his. Then she heard a rustling sound coming from the bushes. The squires said that they searched the area, but what if they missed one of the robbers?

iriam felt as though somebody had doused her with cold water. She looked down and realized that she and Benjamin were lying in a pile of leaves, naked from the waist down. Averting her eyes from his exposed flesh, she pulled her chemise down, just as a ewe and her twin lambs broke into the clearing.

Miriam and Benjamin stared at the sheep and burst out laughing.

"I'm sorry, Miriam. After everything that happened today, I got carried away."

"You don't need to apologize, it was my fault too."

That they had nearly consummated their marriage before the wedding didn't bother her. The Rabbis taught that a woman couldn't conceive the first time, but, even if she had gotten pregnant, they'd be husband and wife in a few weeks—nobody would know the difference. Miriam had seen enough of Salomon's responsa, verified by several of the women whose births she'd attended, to know that other betrothed couples did it. After all, once a man and a woman were betrothed, only death or divorce could end their union.

Upon returning to Troyes, they told a mesmerized audience about their adventure, leaving out, by unspoken consent, the final part of it. The next day the fairground was buzzing with rumors that the brigands had been caught in Ramerupt, but that Count Thibault was seeking the fence who had helped them dispose of their loot. Some Edomites suspected a Jew, since the captured Jewish merchants had been ransomed while non-Jews were killed.

Salomon was adamant that Jews couldn't be involved. "Of course the Jewish merchants were left alive," he explained as his family shared their midday meal. "Any thieves sophisticated enough to elude capture by Thibault's men would know that Jews always redeem each other. Why kill a Jewish merchant when it's more profitable to ransom him?"

Miriam offered her support. "Besides, no Jew in Troyes would handle goods stolen from other Jews," she said, slicing a piece of roast lamb onto her bread trencher.

"I suspect that some might be willing, if it were only a matter of violating Jewish law," Salomon said. "But the penalty of *herem*, being expelled from the Jewish community, is too great a risk. You'll see. The fence won't be a Jew."

Benjamin had his doubts, but Salomon was correct. The trader in league with the bandits was an Edomite from Burgundy. When Benjamin set off for home with the Rheims merchants, they passed by the town scaffolds, where ten other bodies were hanging along with the man who had attacked him and Miriam.

"You can't imagine how glad I am to see these thieves executed," one of the merchants confided to Benjamin. "My brother and I were captured on our way to the fair and I was loath to return home with the fugitives still at large."

"Wait!" his comrade cried out. "Driver, stop the carts!"

Several of the merchants got out and spit on their captors' bodies. Then the caravan began moving again, and as Benjamin watched the town walls receding behind them, he sighed. This year's vintage would be the last one he'd be helping his family make. But that sad thought was immediately replaced with an exultant one: the next time he saw those walls, it would be his wedding day.

"If you feel the slightest light-headedness," Salomon's tone was severe, "leave the vat immediately and breathe deeply until the sensation passes."

No sooner had the Hot Fair concluded than the wine harvest began. But a heat spell made treading grapes during *bouillage*, the wine's stormy fermentation, unusually dangerous. Each morning, Salomon exhorted his workers to be constantly vigilant, both for themselves and for the others in the vats with them.

"I want continual conversation among you, the taller workers making sure that everyone replies." He paused until everyone nodded. "Never leave anyone alone in the vat."

"Do we have to talk, Papa?" Rachel asked, her eyes wide. "I mean, can we sing instead?"

"*Oui, ma fille.* You may sing instead." His voice was filled with affection for his youngest daughter. "But you must stay in the vat with me, so I can watch you."

When Salomon realized that hot weather would likely continue for the entire *bouillage* period, his first reaction was to forbid Rachel from treading the grapes. But she was nearly as tall as Miriam now and had been eagerly looking forward to her first vintage.

Salomon shook his head and sighed. It never ceased to amaze him that he and Rivka had produced such a beauty. Not that Joheved and Miriam were unattractive, but they resembled him too much. Rachel, with her dark curls, perfect oval face, and deep green eyes, had somehow managed to combine the ordinary features of her parents into something exquisite.

A father shouldn't favor one child over another, but he couldn't help it. Joheved and Miriam were dutiful daughters, fine vintners, and excellent students, and Joheved had provided him with a grandson, but he had been away studying while they were growing up. It was different with Rachel; he'd returned from Mayence just before her birth, and there had been a special bond between them ever since. Her first word had been *papa*.

By afternoon, the air was sweltering and Rachel, dressed in one of her sister's old chemises, couldn't wait to cool off in the vat of grape juice. Salomon and Miriam were already inside, and Rivka helped her climb up to the top. Rachel looked down, then blanched and hesitated. The must of fermenting grapes seemed alive as it foamed and hissed, and she imagined she was stepping into a pot of cooking soup. But Salomon held out his hands and coaxed her, and she jumped into his arms.

It was difficult to remain upright in the liquid's constant movement. Stems seemed to reach up and encircle her legs with every step, and she tried not to think of snakes. But Salomon held tight to her hand as she jumped up and down in the must, and Miriam starting singing a merry song. Rachel soon forgot her fears in the excitement of making wine and relaxed enough to enjoy the pleasant feeling of the bubbles rising past her legs as they sang together.

Suddenly Miriam interrupted their song. "Papa, I think I feel dizzy." She clumsily made her way to the side of the vat. "Is it all right if I just sit here on the edge, or should I get out altogether?"

"You may sit on top until you feel better." He helped her climb up and then turned to Rachel. "How are you doing, *ma fille?*"

"I feel fine, Papa." To prove it she began to sing again.

But moments later, Rachel's voice began to waver, and before Miriam's horrified eyes, her sister tottered and slipped into the must. Immediately Salomon reached down into the liquid, pulled his daughter up, and, flinging her over his shoulder, climbed out of the vat. Safe in the court-yard, Rachel coughed, took in several gulps of air, and began to cry.

Rivka came flying out of the kitchen to find her youngest daughter, covered in squashed grapes, weeping in her husband's arms. "What hap-pened?" she demanded, glaring at Salomon.

"Don't worry, Rivka." Without lying, he explained, "Rachel isn't in-jured, she's only frightened. You see, she lost her balance and fell into the wine."

Rachel stifled her sobs. "I'm all right, Mama. Really I am." She snug-gled closer to Salomon. "Can I go back in the tank with you, Papa?"

"You've spent enough time with the vintage this year," Rivka an-nounced. She grabbed Rachel's arm and tried to pull her toward the well, but Rachel clung to Salomon.

"I'll see that she's washed," he told Rivka. He lifted up Rachel's chin and looked her in the eye. "Let's get you cleaned up now, and we'll see about you helping in the vats tomorrow."

Miriam couldn't help but notice her mother's sour expression as the pair headed toward the well, Salomon gently pulling bits of grapes and stems from Rachel's hair. Mama and Papa had never gotten along well, probably because they'd been strangers when they wed and spent most of the next ten years living apart in different cities. Miriam said a thankful prayer that the Holy One had blessed her with a love match.

Under Salomon's watchful eye, the *bouillage* ended without further incident, and the wine was left to complete its fermentation over Rosh Hashanah and Yom Kippur. Finally Sukkot was upon them and the wine safely casked in the cellar. Miriam was beside herself with happiness; her wedding clothes were finished, and one of Aunt Sarah's bedrooms had been redecorated for the newlyweds. In recognition of her niece's maturity, Sarah decided that Miriam could handle the simple nighttime births alone. Sarah's night vision wasn't what it used to be.

Miriam's first opportunity began as usual, with an anxious servant knocking at Sarah's door early one evening. The mother, Muriel, had easily borne several children, so Miriam grabbed the midwife's basket and kissed Aunt Sarah good-bye, confident that she would return before midnight.

But when the courtyard's roosters woke Sarah just before dawn, Miriam had still not returned. Leaving breakfast untouched, Sarah rushed to the laboring woman's home. Once in the lying-in chamber, Sarah could see that Muriel was struggling to push the baby out.

"I don't understand it," Miriam whispered, her voice heavy with fatigue. "The baby is in the proper position but refuses to be born. I've tried pepper and agrimony, and some other herbs too, but none of them made any difference."

Sarah examined Muriel while Miriam explained, "I massaged her belly, and I even reached inside to pull the baby out, but nothing helped." Miriam was near tears. "I don't know what else to do, and the poor woman has been pushing for hours."

"The cord may be wrapped around the child, holding him back." Sarah's calm voice masked her concern.

Under Sarah's guidance, Miriam reached up into Muriel's womb, where, sure enough, she found the cord wrapped several times around the baby's neck. Once this impediment was undone, the child was delivered easily. But the infant was dead, strangled by its umbilical cord.

Miriam's hands shook as she delivered the placenta, and she blinked back tears of grief and shame. Sarah quickly whispered to her, "I know you didn't want to disturb me, but you need to ask for assistance when it is warranted."

"My baby, my poor baby," Muriel sobbed.

Sarah patted the distraught mother's shoulder. "I'm sorry, so sorry."

Wishing she could be anywhere else, Miriam silently cleaned the baby's body and wrapped it in clean linen. Sarah continued to comfort Muriel, never letting on that the outcome might have been different if she had been called earlier. But Miriam knew. Because of her incompetence, a child was dead.

As the sky began to lighten, the two midwives walked home in silence, Miriam wishing Aunt Sarah would chastise her further so she could apologize and be forgiven. The bells were ringing for Prime as Miriam wearily climbed the stairs to her bedroom, said her morning prayers, and got into bed. It was long after the bells were quiet when she finally cried herself to sleep.

Accompanying her husband and father to synagogue, Joheved knew nothing of Miriam's travail, only that her sister had spent all night with Muriel. As she climbed the stairs to the women's section, she could hear voices discussing the stillbirth, with several of them blaming Miriam. Conversation ceased abruptly when Joheved appeared, but she had heard enough.

Poor Miriam, this will be hard on her. But stillbirths happen all the time; it's not necessarily the midwife's fault.

Joheved tried to keep her *kavanah* focused on her prayers, and when services were over, she left quickly to escape the gossip. But Salomon and Meir were deep in conversation with two strangers. She stopped at the bottom of the stairs, reluctant to interrupt what was clearly a serious talk, but Meir motioned her to join them.

It was only as she got closer that she could see the tears in her father's eyes, and when Salomon introduced the men as Benjamin's brothers, Simeon and Ezra, she looked questioningly at Meir, who shook his head sadly. Joheved could think of only one reason for Benjamin's brothers to travel to Troyes: two witnesses to verify a death.

Joheved clutched Meir's hand. "It can't be, not just before the wedding." She turned from one brother to the other, but there was only painful silence. So she murmured, *"Baruch Dayan Emet"* (Blessed is the True Judge), the first words a Jew says when learning of a death.

Mon Dieu, Miriam will be devastated. And if Benjamin's death wasn't bad enough, Miriam was now a childless widow, required by Jewish law to marry one of his brothers in order to produce a child to carry his name. But Simeon and Ezra were already married, forcing them to perform a special ritual, *halitzah*, before Miriam would be free to marry someone else.

"I don't know what happened," Meir whispered as they solemnly walked home. "Some sort of accident. Your father thought it best if they explained only once, with Miriam there."

By the time they entered the kitchen, Joheved was nearly shaking in dread of her sister's reaction. Rivka and Salomon, knowing this to be a parent's burden, went upstairs to wake their daughter, and she soon arrived in the salon, bleary-eyed and terrified. With increasing horror, she listened to the men's story.

"We're sorry to bring such news," Simeon began. He paused to sniff back tears. "Our brother Benjamin died nearly a month ago." His chin began to quiver and he could say no more.

Ezra put his arm around Simeon's shoulders, but before either of them could speak, Miriam let out a shriek.

"Non! Not just before the wedding." Her body began to shake and she would have collapsed if her parents, standing on either side of her, had not reached out to support her. "How could this happen?" she demanded.

"It was late at night and our whole family had been working on the vintage for days without much rest." Simeon hesitated and then added, "We don't have as many Jews in Rheims to help us as you have in Troyes. Sometimes there's only one person in a vat at a time."

"Why are you telling me about winemaking? Tell me what happened to Benjamin." Miriam was almost shouting.

Simeon stared helplessly at Ezra, who took a deep breath before speaking. "Benjamin insisted on treading grapes alone even when the *bouillage* was most vigorous. One night he remained in the vat too long, succumbed to the fumes, and drowned."

Miriam's family looked at each other in horror. Then, tears running down her cheeks, Miriam asked the question they were all thinking. "You mean to tell me that in a family of experienced vintners, nobody was aware of the danger, nobody watched out for him?"

"Of course we knew of the danger, and we know how to be careful. But Benjamin didn't care about danger; he wanted to get the vintage finished as soon as possible." Ezra sounded angry, his fists clenching and unclenching as he spoke. "We try to keep an eye on each other, but it was dark. I told him I was exhausted and we should get some sleep, but he said he wasn't tired, that he'd work awhile longer. By the time we realized he hadn't come to bed, it was too late."

Miriam remembered the nights that Benjamin had spent alone in the forest with the honey tree and how he had attacked the robber rather than run away. "*Oui*, Benjamin never cared about danger."

Salomon patted her arm. "We shouldn't blame ourselves." Miriam must not think that Benjamin's hurry to return to Troyes had caused his carelessness any more than his brother should feel guilty for not being there to rescue him.

Simeon gave Salomon a grateful look. "It was a terrible accident."

Rivka quietly directed their maidservant Anna to make a strong tisane for Miriam from chamomile and wormwood, and when the maidservant returned with the drink, Miriam was asking more questions.

"What day did Benjamin die? Who found him?"

"It's enough that we know Benjamin is dead." Rivka's voice was both soothing and a warning. "We don't need to hear the details."

"But I need to know," Miriam said.

"He died a few days after Selichot." Simeon looked away from her. "Our father discovered his body just before dawn."

"It was an evil day, Tuesday the twenty-fourth of Elul." Ezra shuddered. The even numbers two and four were unlucky enough, and such a Tuesday, under the baleful influence of Mars, would have been particularly malevolent.

"Papa, do you think Benjamin suffered at the end?" Miriam asked, trying to recall what she had been doing on the twenty-fourth of Elul. Undoubtedly working on the vintage, but the days had all blurred together.

"*Non, ma fille.* He would have been unconscious already when he fell below the surface."

"I can tell you that Benjamin's final days were probably some of the happiest of his life. He was so looking forward to the wedding . . ." Simeon trailed off as Miriam broke into renewed sobs.

They were all still sniffing and wiping their noses when Salomon motioned Meir to come closer. "A childless widow isn't permitted to perform *halitzah* until it's been three months since her husband's death."

Meir looked surprised. "But why? Miriam was widowed from *erusin*; we don't suspect that she's pregnant."

"That's the law," Salomon replied.

Meir surveyed the two grieving men. "I hope it won't be a hardship for one of them to return in two months."

Rivka's sedative tisane was working, so she and Joheved helped the increasingly drowsy Miriam stumble back up the stairs.

"There must be some mistake, Mama. Benjamin can't be dead," Miriam moaned. "When he went outside . . . in the moonlight . . . last year after Sukkot ended . . . his shadow wasn't headless . . . he told me so." She was so sleepy she could barely get the words out.

"*Ma fille*, I don't know." Rivka shook her head and sighed. The Book of Life was sealed on the last night of Sukkot, and for those whose moonlit shadows lacked heads, the coming year would be their last.

Joheved helped her sister undress. Maybe Benjamin had experienced a seminal emission on Yom Kippur; that too was an omen of death in the coming year. But she said instead, "May you be comforted among the mourners of Jerusalem." At times like this the traditional words were best.

For the next two months, Salomon's family tried to be sympathetic and patient with Miriam. When her daughter picked at her meals instead of eating, Rivka restrained herself from complaining about the wasted food. When Joheved found that little Isaac had managed to climb to the top of the staircase while her sister sat oblivious at the dining table below, she held her tongue and resolved not to leave Miriam responsible for her son in the future.

Salomon merely sighed when his bereaved daughter refused to drink any wine, protesting that it reminded her of Benjamin's death. Even Rachel, who had the most cause for complaint because her sleep was interrupted several times a night by her bedmate's sobbing, kept silent and reminded herself that the nights were so long this time of year that she still ought to get enough rest. They all hoped that Miriam's melancholy would diminish after she performed *halitzah*.

To Salomon's relief, and Miriam's dread, Ezra and Simeon returned on the appointed day. Since a *beit din* for *halitzah* required five judges, none of whom were related to the man or the woman, Meir went to fetch Isaac haParnas, his son Joseph, and three other leaders of the community, while Anna's husband, Baruch, gathered a minyan of ten men to meet them at the synagogue. Miriam sat softly crying in her mother's arms, while Benjamin's brothers huddled on a bench, their hands twitching nervously. Ezra stood up immediately as all the men entered and the judges announced, "We have gathered at this place for *halitzah*."

Under Salomon's prompting, Isaac asked the two brothers if Benjamin had indeed died over three months ago, if they had witnessed his death, and if they were his only brothers. After each answered in the affirmative, Isaac stated that he personally could attest that Miriam was more than twelve years old and that Benjamin had been older than thirteen.

Then he asked Ezra, "Do you wish *halitzah* or to take the widow in levirate marriage?"

When Ezra replied, "*Halitzah*," Joseph examined the brother's black leather shoe and then asked him to put it on.

This was the signal for Miriam to begin the legal dialogue from the twenty-fifth chapter of Deuteronomy. She spoke the Hebrew words as if in a daze.

"My husband's brother refuses to establish a name for his brother in Israel. He will not perform the *levir*'s duty."

Ezra stood up and reiterated, "I cannot marry her."

Now came the part Miriam dreaded. She crouched down and un-laced Ezra's shoe, being careful to use only her right hand. She tried with some difficulty to gather a mouthful of saliva for the next step, but her mouth was dry from fasting all morning because Jewish law required that her saliva be her own, not from any food she'd eaten.

Finally she managed to pull off Ezra's shoe, and once she'd done so, she spit on the ground in front of him and declared, "Thus shall be done to the man who refuses to build up his brother's house."

The men of the minyan proclaimed, "*Halutz annal*," three times and it was done. Benjamin's brothers had done their duty and freed his widow to remarry.

With *halitzah* behind her, Miriam's family began to lose patience with the thin, grey ghost who was liable to start crying at any moment. The rest of Troyes was celebrating, making it difficult to move between their mournful house and the joyous streets. For after seven barren years, Philippe's Queen Bertha had given birth to a baby girl. Regional pride was running high as the Champagnois gossiped about the virility, or rather the lack thereof, of the king, who was reputed to spend more time in his lover John's bed than in the queen's and who had barely managed to father a daughter in seven years of marriage.

In comparison, Count Thibault, who was twice the king's age, had sired three healthy boys in the same time. Troyes buzzed with happy speculation at whether Thibault would be able to arrange a match be-tween the new princess and one of his sons.

Conversation at Salomon's table also turned to the topic of matri-mony, adding to Miriam's distress.

"The man I marry isn't going to have any brothers." Rachel took a large bite of apple flummery. "Then I won't need to worry about *halitzah*."

"Or you could marry someone who already has children," Joheved said.

"Rachel, don't talk with your mouth full," Rivka said before turning to her sister. "It isn't such a terrible thing for a widow to marry her brother-in-law. Sarah, you did."

Sarah put down her wine cup and thought for a moment. "I suppose it was better than marrying a stranger. But even though it's traditional for a childless widow to marry again after three months, both of us were still too grieved to celebrate our wedding properly."

"Could we please discuss something else for a change?" Miriam asked, her eyes filling with tears.

But Rivka was not going to change the subject. "I was waiting at the bakery when Fleur asked me if we'd found a new husband for Miriam yet, it being three months since she had been widowed."

Conversation at the table halted as Rivka continued, "If we hadn't, Fleur hoped that we might consider her cousin, Leontin, whose year of mourning for his late wife is almost over."

Miriam gasped, and her pale visage grew almost white. Her father, on the other hand, began to redden perceptibly as he struggled to control his anger.

"How desperate does she think we are to imagine that I would accept such an *am haaretz* for a son-in-law?" Salomon stood up menacingly. "Leontin can barely read Torah and wouldn't know what to do with a tractate of Talmud if it fell in his lap. My daughter will not marry an ignorant boor, no matter how rich he is!" He slammed his fist down on the table.

Rivka stood up and put her hands on her hips. "I didn't say I thought Leontin would be a good match for Miriam, but I do say the best cure for her unhappiness would be to get her married as soon as possible." She stared defiantly at her husband. "At least I'm looking out for our daughter's interests, while you've got your nose buried in your books."

Meir could see the storm clouds gathering. He picked up little Isaac and asked Sarah if it was time to make sure all the chickens were safely in their coop. She quickly agreed, and as soon as he closed the door behind them, Salomon exploded.

"How dare you suggest I'm neglecting my daughter!"

"Oh *non*—you're such a doting father." Rivka's words dripped sarcasm. "You teach them Talmud and to pray with tefillin. Well, as soon as the Cold Fair starts, I want you to find Miriam a husband." Her voice brooked no argument.

"I will not be hurried about this." Salomon's voice was equally firm.

"You think a bridegroom will just come to us, like before," Rivka shot back. "But our daughter's a widow now; it won't be so easy."

Miriam had enough of everyone discussing her as if she weren't present. "That's right, Mama, I'm a widow now, not a child, so you and Papa can't marry me off if I don't want to." The rest of the family stared at her in astonishment. This was the most she'd spoken in weeks. "And right now, I don't want to, so you can stop fighting about it."

"Well," Rivka was almost speechless. She turned and pointed her finger at Salomon. "This is your fault. They're just like you. All book learning about petty legalities and no consideration for what's really important. I've had enough!" She stalked out the door, slamming it behind her.

Salomon stood up and yelled, "Don't you walk out on me." He lifted his wine cup, and his horrified daughters were sure he was going to throw it at the closed door. But after a visible struggle, he set down the cup and addressed them with a saying from chapter four of Pirke Avot.

"Ben Zoma says: Who is strong? One who conquers his *yetzer hara*.
Who is rich? One who is content with his portion.

Now the strong man isn't just someone who won't follow his *yetzer hara*, his inclination toward evil, but also the one who conquers his anger. The man who is enraged but restrains his angry words and doesn't answer quickly—this is true strength." With these words Salomon strode out into the salon.

"Papa may have conquered his *yetzer hara*, but I am definitely not content with my portion." Miriam headed for the door. "I'm going to bed."

Meir peeked in, and seeing all was calm, deposited their sleepy child in Joheved's lap. "Maybe this would be a good time for the rest of us to go to bed."

"What about Mama?" Rachel asked. "I don't want to go to bed until she comes back."

Meir looked at her with a puzzled expression. "I just saw her going upstairs, talking with your Aunt Sarah. Sarah was saying something about how she had to marry again three months after her husband died and she didn't recommend it."

The next morning at breakfast, neither Salomon nor Rivka showed any sign of poor temper. Rivka was humming a little tune as she served the stirabout, fruit, and cheese, and Salomon smiled as he asked everyone how they slept the previous night. He, himself, he informed them, had slept excellently well.

"By the way, Miriam, I had a long talk last night with your mother and aunt." He paused to slice himself some more cheese. "As you reminded us, you are indeed an adult now, but that doesn't end my obligation. The prophet Jeremiah tells us:

Take wives for your sons and give your daughters to husbands.

And in Tractate Kiddushin (marriage), we learn that to marry off his daughter,

A father should give her a dowry, clothe her, and adorn her, so that men will leap to marry her."

He smiled sympathetically at her. "So you see that finding you a husband is a mitzvah I cannot neglect."

"Salomon, I see that if you didn't have children you would probably teach Torah to the cats," Rivka gently interrupted him. "Please tell Miriam what you propose to do."

"*Ma fille*, Sarah reminded us that your grief is too fresh for you to think about a new husband," Salomon said. "We think it best to have your availability circulated at the Cold Fair, and then your suitors can present themselves at the Hot Fair, at which time you'll consider their offers."

Sarah gave Miriam's hand a squeeze. "I have no doubt that you will have many suitable matches to choose from, one of which will appeal to you." Sarah didn't mention how they had come to this conclusion, that the rigors of childbirth ensured that young widowers greatly outnumbered young widows.

"You will have our guidance to help you make your choice, but it will be your decision," Rivka concluded, refilling her grandson's bowl with Miriam's leftover stirabout. "Le Bon Dieu willing, you can be married next summer." She looked at Miriam hopefully.

"*Merci*, Papa. *Merci*, Mama," Miriam replied softly. Now she was safe for at least six months.

But if her family expected Miriam's disposition to improve now that the pressure to marry was gone, they were disappointed. When Samuel and Marona spent Shabbat in Troyes, Miriam's decline could not be ignored. Miriam's hair used to be the same lustrous chestnut color as Joheved's, but now it was as dull as weathered wood. Her grey eyes with their dark circles looked drab and colorless compared with Joheved's vivid blue or Rachel's dazzling green. And she was so thin.

"Salomon, please excuse our interference, but you are family and . . ." Samuel paused, unsure how to best broach the subject. "My wife and I couldn't help but notice how pale and gaunt Miriam has become. Perhaps Marona should make her a tonic? She knows some excellent remedies."

"If you have a tonic to heal a broken heart, I'd order a thousand of them," Salomon replied sadly. "She won't eat, she won't drink wine, she cries in her sleep. I have to keep her from sharpening the pruning knives for fear that she might injure herself." He shook his head and sighed, "Rachel tells me that Miriam is dreading Hanukkah, that she can't bear celebrating the new vintage that killed her Benjamin."

Samuel put his arm around Salomon's shoulders. "Let her spend Hanukkah with us. Marona will be glad to have a young face around." His voice softened. "She still mourns for our daughter, Hannah, and the two of them can comfort each other."

"I don't know," Salomon said. *Send Miriam away?*

"Nobody can match my wife's cooking for putting flesh on your bones, and if Miriam won't drink wine, Marona's ale is as heartening as you could want." Samuel's enthusiasm was growing. "One month with us and she'll be as good as new."

Rivka needed no convincing. "Perhaps the bad air in Troyes is upsetting Miriam. Some time in the country, breathing clean, sweet air, should be an excellent change for our daughter."

Sarah knew what Miriam really needed: someplace far away from Troyes, with new people to meet and different things to do; with nothing there to remind her of her loss.

three

Mayence, Allemagne
Fall 4839 (1078 CE)

udah ben Natan made a point of looking away as the plump young maidservant smiled seductively, then bent down and set a pitcher of ale on the table between him and his older brother. But his sibling gave her a wink, and when she returned with a steaming bowl of stirabout and a platter of smoked herring, he slipped her some coins. She paused halfway to the kitchen, counted her money, and blew her admirer a kiss.

Judah grimaced, then leaned across the table and complained to his brother, "Azariel, is your *yetzer hara* so strong that you find it necessary to bed the serving wench at every inn?"

Azariel chuckled and helped himself to the stirabout. "What's it to you who I bed? It takes the same amount of time to get from Paris to Mayence no matter how I spend my nights." The easy availability of women at most inns was a perquisite for the merchant who had to travel long distances.

What Azariel said was true, but Judah couldn't leave things be. "You just spent the last month home with your wife, too."

"Listen little brother, you've made your opinion clear." Azariel was starting to get annoyed. He and Judah made the round-trip between their home and the yeshiva twice a year, once for Passover and once for the Days of Awe, and they usually enjoyed each other's company.

Judah pulled his bowl away when Azariel tried to refill it. "I guess when the Creator handed out the *yetzers* in our family, you got the *yetzer hara* and I got the *yetzer tov*."

"I readily admit that you received the good looks, but no *yetzer hara*? That's impossible." Azariel smiled, refusing to be baited.

Both men, with their black hair, dark eyes, and finely chiseled features, were handsome, but Judah's nose was a bit straighter and his jaw more square. At least his jaw looked squarer; his brother's was hidden under a beard. Judah was just starting to grow a moustache.

"My passion is for Torah study, not seducing women," he announced virtuously.

Azariel eyed him skeptically over his cup of ale. "Don't tell me you're still a virgin?"

Judah's blushing silence was answer enough, and Azariel continued, "But you're almost twenty. You must have some *yetzer hara*, every man does. Don't tell me Lillit doesn't visit you?"

"Since you insist, I admit it." There was no point in denying it; Azariel could always tell when he was lying. In fact, the demon Lillit had visited Judah only the previous night. At first he had the horrible suspicion that Azariel had made this particular comment after noticing the stained sheets, but then he relaxed. The inn's sheets were so badly discolored that nobody could possibly tell a new stain from an old one.

Sure enough, his brother merely inquired salaciously, "And what form does she take when she visits?"

"None of your business!" In Mayence or Paris, Judah would immerse in the *mikvah* the morning after he dreamed of Lillit, but that was impossible now.

The dream was the one Judah usually had, where invisible hands began to caress his thighs and what lay between them. He'd try to push them away but be unable to move. Not daring to look, he'd feel the demon mount him from above, Lillit's favorite position. He'd try to escape, but the more vigorously he moved, the better Lillit liked it, until she finally forced him to spill his seed. He hated those vile dreams, he hated how remembering them gave him an erection, and right now he hated his brother for bringing up the subject.

Azariel folded his arms in front of him and leaned back in his chair. "You've been ill-tempered this whole trip. What's wrong?"

What is wrong with me? How could Judah tell Azariel that he missed Daniel, his old study partner? Slim with grey eyes and light brown hair, Daniel had come to study at the yeshiva two years ago. A serious student, only a year younger than Judah, they had become friends immediately.

Daniel didn't have Judah's breadth of Talmud knowledge, but once he took on a subject he was determined to mine its complete meaning. He and Judah questioned each other furiously until they were sure they understood every nuance, sometimes arguing late into the night. But now Daniel was gone. He'd returned to Cologne to get married and join his family's business.

Their last days together had been before Shavuot, when they had feverishly sought every opportunity to be together. As the time came to say good-bye, it was all Judah could do to keep from grabbing Daniel and begging him not to go. They embraced awkwardly and Daniel kissed his cheek. Alone in their room that night, Judah had cried himself to sleep.

Azariel saw that his brother's anger had turned to sadness. "Did you have a fight with your mother and Uncle Shimson before we left?" he asked gently.

Judah nodded, relieved that Azariel had given him something else to discuss. He and Azariel were actually half brothers. Azariel's mother had been their father, Natan's, first wife, but she had died in childbirth. Natan's brother Shimson soon found him a new wife, Alvina, his own wife's younger sister. Judah was still small when Natan had died, but Alvina didn't remarry. She devoted herself to increasing Natan's wealth for her son, the scholar. They continued to live with her sister and Shimson, one big happy family. Except recently they weren't so happy.

"Was it another argument about you getting married?" When Judah nodded again, Azariel lowered his voice conspiratorially. "What was the matter with the girl this time?" He stabbed a herring with his knife and waited.

"There wasn't any girl this time." Judah replied, his face bright with shame. "Uncle Shimson couldn't find anybody who'd risk being rejected like all the others."

"Nobody?" Azariel put down his fish and stared at his brother. Judah was rich, handsome, and a scholar. And nobody wanted their daughter to marry him?

"Nobody." Judah's humiliation was complete.

"What's the matter with you?" Why was his brother being so unco-operative? Surely any woman was better than Lillit. Besides, procreation was the first commandment and Judah was so pious.

"Nothing's the matter with me," Judah whispered fiercely. Others eating breakfast at the inn were staring at them. "I just didn't find any of them attractive enough to marry."

"What do you mean, not attractive?" Azariel had seen most of Ju-dah's prospective brides, and he would have gladly wed any of them— well almost any of them.

Judah looked for a relatively clean spot on the tablecloth to wipe his mouth. It had started the first time he came home from yeshiva. Each festival a strange girl and her parents would come to call. The girl was always buxom, pretty, and devoid of any shred of intelligence. She and her mother would look at him like he was a plate of pastries they couldn't wait to devour, while her father seemed to see a pile of gold. They filled him with terror, and he would refuse the match.

So it continued—another festival, another girl. Each girl plumper than the last, and the thought of touching all that jiggling flesh almost made him nauseous. The girls' parents started to look like vultures. Each girl he rejected protested to her friends, and soon Alvina began to complain that her stubborn son was making her an outcast in the community.

Azariel cleared his throat, and Judah realized he was waiting for an answer. "They were all too fat. When I see a woman, I don't like being reminded of a pig."

Azariel didn't know what to say. Most Frenchmen preferred volup-tuous women—whose ample breasts proved how well the next genera-tion would be nurtured, between whose generous thighs they would take their pleasure. Women, in turn, dressed to appear as plump and fruitful as possible. Some even wore neckbands that, when pulled tight, made their chins look doubled. What kind of man wouldn't want a full-figured wife?

"Perhaps he prefers boys," he muttered.

Azariel hadn't intended Judah to hear, but Judah had heard, and it was as if his brother had hit him.

Later, fuming over his brother's insinuations as they rode toward Mayence, Judah tried to recall the most complicated halachic (legal) discussion he could. He sent his mind back over Tractate Bava Metzia, an advanced text full of problems involving contracts and damages, but he kept returning to an aggadic (nonlegal) section at the beginning of the seventh chapter, one he had studied with Daniel a year ago. It began with a description of an exceptionally handsome rabbi:

> One who wishes to see the beauty of Rav Yohanan should bring a new silver cup and fill it with red pomegranate seeds, and place a garland of red roses around its rim, and set it where the sun meets the shade. That vision is the beauty of Rav Yohanan.

The text then proceeded to catalog the phenomenal beauty of several sages, eventually going back to the patriarch Jacob and the first man, Adam, but leaving out Rav Yohanan. Then the Gemara explained:

> The beauty of Rav Yohanan is not mentioned because Rav Yohanan did not have splendor of face (a beard). Rav Yohanan used to sit at the *mikvah*'s gate, and he said: "When the daughters of Israel come up from their immersion, let them meet me so that they will have sons as beautiful as me, learned in the Torah like me."

It was then that Daniel sighed and, not looking directly at Judah, said, "Rav Yohanan may have been more learned than you, but I doubt he was more beautiful than you. And you don't have a beard either."

Judah was too astonished to speak. Since childhood he was aware that others considered him attractive, but nobody ever called him beautiful.

Alvina, terrified of the Evil Eye, shushed anyone who mentioned her son's appearance.

"Rav Yohanan may have been proud of his beauty, but I find it a curse," Judah confided sadly. "In Paris the women give me covetous looks, while the men's eyes are like daggers. It's a relief to be back at the yeshiva."

Judah's reverie ended as they approached the city gates. The next morning, when Isaac ben Judah, the rosh yeshiva, sternly called Judah into his study, he found that returning to the yeshiva was anything but a relief. Leaning against the wall, his arms folded over his chest, Azariel looked like he didn't have a care in the world.

"What are you doing here?" Judah demanded. He had no idea why he was about to be disciplined, but he didn't need Azariel's presence to add to his dishonor.

Azariel shrugged his shoulders. "Uncle Shimson told me to deliver a letter to your *maître* and wait for your response."

The rosh yeshiva silenced them. "Judah, you are one of my finest students, so I'm grieved to hear your uncle call you a rebellious son. Is it true that despite his best efforts to find you a suitable bride, you have refused every match?"

Judah started to defend himself, but Isaac cut him off. "Your brother tells me that you have no injury or illness to explain transgressing our Creator's commandment to procreate."

Judah nodded and the old man continued, "You know the text from Tractate Kiddushin as well as I do:

> Until a man reaches the age of twenty, the Holy One sits and waits expectantly—When will the man take a wife? But when the young man reaches the age of twenty and has still not wed, He says . . ."

Judah realized he was expected to finish the verse.

"May the bones of this one be blasted."

"And what does Rav Huna say on this subject?"

"He who at the age of twenty is still not married will spend all his days in sinful thoughts."

Judah could no longer restrain himself. "But I spend all my days studying Torah, not thinking about sin."

"I know you fancy yourself another Ben Azzai, but even he married Rabbi Akiva's daughter." The rosh yeshiva held up his hand, forestalling any further argument. "I will not tolerate sin and disobedience among my students. If you are not married in a year, I will put you in *herem*."

Azariel squirmed as he shared the anguish of Judah's disgrace. But outside in the hall he saw an opportunity to return to his brother's good graces.

"You told me that our uncle brought you unattractive women." He tried to sound encouraging. "Tell me what you want, and I will find you a bride more to your liking."

Judah couldn't believe that he would actually be expelled from the yeshiva if he remained a bachelor. He paced the corridor, fists clenched, his shame turning to fury.

"I will not settle for less than Ben Azzai. I don't care what she looks like, but I want a scholar's daughter. And not only a scholar's daughter, but a learned woman herself." He threw the words at Azariel like a gauntlet. "Find me a woman who has studied about Ben Azzai, who knows the difference between Hillel and Shammai, and I swear I will marry her."

"And if I cannot find such a paragon?" Azariel was reluctant to leave Judah with such an oath on his lips.

"If you have not found her in a year, I will marry whomever you choose, no arguments."

Azariel grinned. "I will find you a bride beyond your expectations." He was an expert at locating unique and precious merchandise for his fastidious clients, and he would now put all his business skills at his brother's disposal. What a challenge!

The brothers said good-bye at Judah's lodgings, and once Azariel was out of sight, Judah gave in to despair. He greeted his landlord, an elderly silversmith busy at his workbench, then went upstairs and flopped down on his bed. He tried to distract himself with Talmud, only to be brought back to the story of beautiful Rav Yohanan.

> One day Rav Yohanan was swimming in the Jordan River. Reish Lakish (a gladiator, and some say an outlaw) saw him and (thinking he was a beautiful woman since he had no beard) jumped into the Jordan after him. Rav Yohanan said to him, "Your strength should be for Torah," and Lakish replied, "Your beauty belongs to women." Rav Yohanan said to him, "If you repent, I will give you my sister in marriage. She is even more beautiful than I." So Reish Lakish agreed . . . Rav Yohanan taught him Scripture and Mishnah, and made him into a great man.

Judah recalled how Daniel had sighed after they read that text. "If only we could marry each other's sisters? But then we're both already betrothed."

That was when Judah confessed that, despite his advanced age, he was not yet betrothed. At first Daniel was skeptical; people who remained single had something terribly wrong with them, like leprosy. Only Daniel's great affection for Judah swayed him toward sympathy.

"What difference does it make who you marry?" Daniel asked. "You're only going to see her twice a year for a couple of weeks. Most of the time, she'll be living in Paris, and you'll be studying here."

Azariel said the same thing. Yet each time Judah met a potential mate, it was like God hardening Pharaoh's heart in Egypt. Something in him would not let him acquiesce. Thinking about Daniel only made Judah feel worse, but he couldn't tear his thoughts away. The comparison to Rav Yohanan and Lakish didn't help any. Their story ended in tragedy.

"Judah, wake up." An insistent voice at the door interrupted his reminiscence. "It's time for evening prayers."

The voice belonged to Shmuel, better known as Shmuli, his roommate as well as the landlord's grandson. Shmuli was a chipper lad about fourteen years old, whose father insisted that his eldest son should study Talmud. Shmuli, on the other hand, would rather spend his time helping his grandfather work the precious metals. He cheerfully acknowledged his inability to remember much of what he heard in class. Not everyone could be a great scholar like his friend Judah.

When Judah learned that Shmuli would be his study partner, he had nearly packed his things and left the yeshiva. That he should be paired with its worst pupil was proof of his pariah status. But things had not turned out badly. Shmuli was as endearing as a frisky puppy and not nearly as stupid as Judah had been led to believe. The boy had no trouble understanding Gemara; he just had no interest in memorizing it.

Yet Judah longed for a study partner at his own level. Eventually he found the courage to approach one of the merchants who frequented the yeshiva, a mature man who confidently sat up front with the scholars. Unfortunately the fellow only stayed in Mayence a few weeks—his true destination was the Cold Fair in the French city of Troyes. But he was happy to study with Judah until his caravan left.

The next time, Judah had not yet made his selection when a dark, hawk-nosed merchant approached him. "Shalom aleichem. I believe we are both looking for study partners," he said with a curt bow. "Natan ben Abraham of Prague, at your service."

The man's voice was silky smooth and Judah looked at him closely. Natan had a young man's body, but his greying temples revealed him to be about twice Judah's age. On one hand he wore a large emerald set in a thick gold ring and on the other a ring with a black pearl. Judah introduced himself in return and waited. The older man intrigued him, yet he felt hesitant.

"Join me for supper and we'll discuss today's text." Natan sounded sure of himself. "The inn I'm staying at, Josef's Grotto, is a favorite with scholars; you'll find the atmosphere different from your usual tavern."

Swayed by the man's charisma, and curious about such a tavern, Judah agreed. Natan threw on his black, fur-lined cloak and they set off. Sure enough, the inn was entirely populated by men, either reading or engaged in quiet conversations. Natan showed Judah to a small table near the fire and explained that he expected to spend several months in town on business. He often arranged his affairs so as to winter in Mayence and continue his Talmud studies there.

Natan chatted about life in Prague and then extracted Judah's history, receiving the young man's gratitude by not commenting on Judah's bachelorhood. As they conversed, Judah found Natan both urbane and charming, and when the table was cleared and they began to study, he discovered that Natan was a proficient scholar as well.

And so the months passed. In the daytime Judah studied with Shmuli, but he spent his evenings at the scholars' inn with Natan. Sometimes Natan's associates joined them and Judah felt flattered to be accepted as an equal by the sophisticated older men. What did he care what they thought of him at the yeshiva?

One rainy evening in February, Judah and Natan were having their customary meal together. The sharp sounds of hail hitting the roof made Judah skittish and Natan seemed distracted as well. Suddenly there was a flash of lightning followed almost immediately by a crash of thunder. Judah jumped out of his seat, causing Natan to place his hand on Judah's arm in reassurance.

But instead of letting go once Judah had calmed, Natan smiled and whispered in his silky voice, "No need for you to go out in this foul weather. I have a comfortable room upstairs."

Judah was suddenly conscious of Natan's warm hand gripping his bare forearm. Natan was staring at him, waiting for his reply, and his penetrating gaze reminded Judah of the hungry expressions of his prospective brides and their mothers. To his horror, Judah felt his loins stir with arousal.

This was what the rosh yeshiva had warned him about, what would happen if he didn't marry by twenty. Judah didn't care if he was hit by lightning, he wasn't going to stay the night with Natan. He stuffed his books under his cloak and, making a feeble excuse about not feeling well, bolted out the door.

Sitting abandoned at their table, the merchant looked up as a younger man, perhaps about thirty, with sandy hair and a sympathetic smile, walked over and took the seat that Judah had so precipitously vacated.

"Shalom aleichem, Natan."

"Reuben, aleichem shalom." Natan's face lit up. "I was beginning to worry that you wouldn't be here this year."

"You don't look worried," Reuben said. "That was quite a beauty you were flirting with."

"I wasn't flirting with him. We were studying Talmud." When Reuben looked at him skeptically, Natan continued, "His name is Judah, and he's a new student at the yeshiva. Quite a good one in fact."

"Are you thinking of teaching him to play the game?"

"Not now that you've arrived." Natan smiled seductively. "But the idea is tempting."

"Try to restrain yourself. Otherwise you'll just upset the poor fellow and leave him frustrated."

"I'll try," Natan replied with a wink.

Reuben sighed. Natan would stop flirting with attractive men when the sky stopped being blue. "I'd like to unpack. What room are you in?"

"I'll show you." Natan picked up the dish containing the remains of Judah's meal. "You can finish this if you're hungry."

The next day after services, Natan inquired about Judah's health and then introduced Reuben, "Who has been my friend and study partner for many years. In fact I met him about ten years ago when he was studying at this very yeshiva. Maybe you'd like to study with us this evening."

Judah's jumble of feelings confused him. Last night he couldn't get away from Natan fast enough. Then he'd prayed desperately for the Merciful One to not blast his bones, to give him strength to conquer his *yetzer hara*. But today he watched with envy as Natan and Reuben argued with each other with an easy intimacy, and when they left together to share their midday meal, a stab of loneliness assailed him. After studying with Shmuli all afternoon, Judah knew he'd be back at Josef's Grotto that night, and on any other night Natan invited him.

In the weeks that followed, Judah's days fell into a pattern. Most nights the three men studied together, although sometimes Natan or Reuben spent the evening elsewhere. The first week in March, Natan announced that his business in Mayence was nearly finished. In that silky voice that seemed to penetrate to Judah's very core, he asked Judah to share a special farewell meal with him.

Judah gulped. "Will Reuben be there as well?"

"No," Natan replied softly, taking a step closer to Judah. The two of them were almost touching, and Judah could smell Natan's perfume. "I thought it would be pleasant to have only the two of us, like when we first met."

Judah again felt the blood rushing to his loins, but this time he didn't panic. He told himself that Natan wanted only what he said—a pleasant farewell dinner. Yet in his secret heart, he wondered if Natan was offering more than a meal, and that night he prayed once again for the Holy One to give him the strength to conquer his *yetzer hara*.

But the next afternoon, on his way to the bathhouse, he ran into Shmuli in one of Mayence's narrow alleys. The boy's clothes were torn and his nose was bleeding.

"What in heaven happened to you?!"

"Oh, Judah, I'm so glad to see you." The youth collapsed into Judah's arms and began to sob.

"Did the Edomites attack you?" These things tended to happen during the weeks before Easter.

"No, not the Edomites," Shmuli stammered.

"You mean another student did this?" Judah stared at him in shock. "Who would want to hurt you?"

"I won't tell you his name, but I had to fight him." Shmuli blew his nose on his sleeve. "He said bad things about me."

"Bad enough to warrant getting hurt and ruining your clothes?" Judah began to get a sinking feeling inside.

At first Shmuli whispered, but then his voice rose accusingly. "He said you're doing *mishkav zachur* and that I must be too since I sleep with you."

Judah could feel himself shaking. *Mon Dieu—someone has accused me of lying with men.* He forced himself to answer without screaming. "He just said that because I'm French."

The German students did hold a low opinion of the French ones, believing them too fond of rich food, good wine, and other sensual pleasures. Frenchmen considered Germans sanctimonious prigs, who would rather sit in a freezing house on Shabbat than have a servant relight a fire that had gone out.

"I suppose that just because your King Philippe took so long to have children doesn't mean that all Frenchmen are like that." Shmuli's eyes narrowed with suspicion. "But he said you spend all your time at that tavern where men go if they want to do *mishkav zachur.*"

"Josef's Grotto isn't . . . that kind of tavern." Judah couldn't bring himself to say the word. "Scholars go there to study in peace and quiet. Shmuli, you've been living with me all year. Do you think I'd frequent that kind of place?"

"I don't think that," Shmuli said loyally. "But he did. That's why I had to fight him."

"I was just on my way to the stews." Judah's heart swelled at his young defender's devotion. "Come with me and let's get you cleaned up."

As he sat in the warm water and listened to Shmuli proudly retell how he had fought the older boy, Judah knew he wouldn't be dining with Natan that night. And he would never go back to Josef's Grotto.

Judah faced Shmuli. "Listen. Just because two men are great friends and like to study together doesn't mean they're doing . . ."

"*Mishkav zachur,*" his young companion added.

"For example," Judah continued as if he hadn't heard Shmuli, "in the Bible, there were no truer friends than Jonathan and King David, and in the Talmud, there are many great companions: Rav Ami and Rav Assi, Rav Yohanan and Reish Lakish."

"Rav Yohanan, I just read about him in Berachot," Shmuli said excitedly. "Isn't he the one who was so beautiful that he used to sit by the *mikvah* so the women coming out would see him and have sons like him?" Shmuli proudly recited the passage, almost identical to the one in Bava Metzia.

"You remembered it perfectly." If the two of them hadn't been sitting naked together in a bath, Judah would have hugged him. "That same story is in another tractate of Talmud too. Here, let me teach it to you."

Judah recited the tale of Rav Yohanan and Reish Lakish up to the point when the two men first met in the river. Shmuli was impressed that a gladiator would want to become a rabbi.

"Unfortunately their story ends sadly," Judah said.

> "Rav Yohanan and Lakish were arguing in the study hall. A sword, a knife, and a dagger—from when can they receive ritual impurity? Rav Yohanan says: 'From the time they are tempered in the fire.' Reish Lakish says: 'From the time they are polished in water.' Rav Yohanan says: 'A brigand is an expert in brigandry.'"

Judah stopped to explain. "I'm sure Rav Yohanan didn't mean to insult his friend by calling him a brigand. He was only saying that he would defer to Reish Lakish's opinion because the gladiator's training had made him an expert on weapons."

Shmuli poured a bucket of hot water over his head to rinse the soap from his hair. "Of course not. It's forbidden to remind a repentant sinner of his previous deeds."

"In any case, Reish Lakish felt that Rav Yohanan had disparaged him, and Rav Yohanan saw Reish Lakish as belittling his teachings. It was a terrible misunderstanding.

> Rav Yohanan was offended and Reish Lakish became ill. Rav Yohanan's sister, she married Lakish, remember, came to him and cried, 'Pray for him for the sake of my children,' but he quoted Jeremiah to her: 'Leave your orphans, I will sustain them.' Reish Lakish died and Rav Yohanan mourned him so exceed-

ingly that the Sages asked, 'Who will go and comfort Rav Yohanan's heart?'

Let us send Rav Elazar ben Pedat, whose statements are brilliant. To everything Rav Yohanan said, Elazar ben Pedat would
say: 'There is a Baraita that supports you.' Rav Yohanan said: 'Are
you supposed to be like Lakish? He would pose twenty-four objections and I would give him twenty-four refutations, until the matter became clear. You can only say there is a Baraita that supports
me. Don't I already know that?' Yohanan went on rending his
clothes and crying, 'Where are you, Reish Lakish? Where are you?'
The Sages prayed for mercy for him and he died."

Judah and Shmuli sat in their bath, silently mourning the two sages
who had died of grief for each other hundreds of years ago. Judah remembered Daniel as well and wondered if he'd ever see his dear friend
again. But Shmuli's temperament was too sanguine to mourn very long
for people he didn't know.

"I just remembered something else I learned about Reish Lakish in
Berachot," he said proudly. "It's near the beginning.

Rav Levi bar Hama said in the name of Rav Simeon ben Lakish: A
man should always make his *yetzer tov* fight his *yetzer hara*. If he
triumphs, well and good—if not, he should study Torah. If he
triumphs, well and good—if not, he should recite the Shema. If
he now triumphs, well and good—if not, he should recall the day
of his death."

Then, despite the seriousness of the text he just recited, Shmuli
cheerfully declared, "I'm hungry. Can we go now?"

The next day at services Judah was both disappointed and relieved
to find that Natan, like many of the foreign merchants, had gone. Most
of the yeshiva students had also left to spend Passover with their families.
The only reason Judah was still in Mayence was that Azariel had writ-

ten that he didn't want to interrupt his search for Judah's bride to escort his brother home and back. Judah toyed with the idea of going to Cologne for Passover, of finding Daniel and spending the festival week with him, but he didn't have the nerve to show up uninvited.

March's grey and drizzly weather only added to Judah's despair. He'd see a man wearing a black cloak and remember Natan's silky voice, the smell of his perfume, and the feel of his hand on Judah's arm. But the excitement these memories generated sent him into a downward spiral of self-loathing. *How can I expect to deserve the learned bride I asked for while I harbor such sinful thoughts?*

Despite the Talmud's advice, studying Torah and saying the Shema were only temporarily successful at suppressing them, and Judah ended every day in desperate prayer. In a further attempt to control his unruly *yetzer hara*, Judah fasted on Mondays and Thursdays. But he was still growing, and by midafternoon he was so faint that the words on the Talmud page blurred before him.

One rainy morning in late April, Judah had to force himself to get out of bed. He hadn't heard from Azariel since before Passover and despaired of what had delayed him. Despite Judah's efforts to avoid sinful thoughts, Lillit had sent one of her incubi to torment him the previous night. Feeling unworthy of immersing his depraved body in the *mikvah*, he poured a bucket of cold water over his offending member, skipped breakfast, and went to services. Then, instead of eating his midday meal, he decided to take a walk in the freezing rain and ponder Reish Lakish's final piece of advice:

Recall the day of your death.

Refusing to be ousted by spring, winter had hurled one last storm at the Rhineland. Rain poured down in sheets, yet something drove Judah toward the Rhine River. The muddy brown water was raging below, as it tried furiously to pass through the narrow bridge he stood on.

Judah stared into the murky depths, fascinated as an occasional tree branch or other piece of debris rushed by. He bent over to get a better look, and the urge to lean just a little bit farther overtook him. The longing to let the power of the river carry him and his sinful nature away became a compulsion. In a few months he would be twenty, and the Holy One would blast his bones anyway. His tears merging with the rain on his face, Judah closed his eyes and waited for the next big gust of wind.

four

he day the Cold Fair opened was chilly and clear, and passing through the St. Jacques Gate, the city's easternmost entry, Miriam felt as if she were leaving a great burden behind. Riding through the forest that marked the beginning of Count André's lands, she looked in vain for something familiar about the road she and Benjamin had traversed only a few months before.

She rode out toward Troyes several times the following week, looking for that fateful clearing, but the skeletal silhouettes of the trees in winter looked nothing like the abundant foliage she remembered. Even the alkanet bushes were gone; felled by the cold, they would grow anew in the spring. One morning she crossed paths with a hunting party from the castle. They were startled to see a young woman riding alone in the forest, but when she introduced herself as a relation of Lord Samuel, everyone was quite cordial.

By the following Shabbat, Miriam felt as though she were living in a dream. Her old world, including everything that reminded her of Benjamin, had been replaced with a new one. In Ramerupt, mealtime was when Samuel, Marona, and Étienne, the steward, discussed the manor's business. There were no daily shopping trips; the estate provided almost everything its inhabitants required. Women rarely attended the small local synagogue, so Miriam and Marona prayed at home. Evenings were quiet, with everyone going to bed as soon as it was dark.

On the Sabbath, when business talk was forbidden, meals were more festive. The three of them didn't sing quite as enthusiastically as a table full of yeshiva students, but Miriam found in their subdued voices a comforting memory of her childhood, when it had only been herself singing with Joheved, Mama, and Grandmama Leah. Her hosts found Miriam's knowledge of scripture an unexpected delight. They didn't know which impressed them more, that Salomon had written a commentary on the Torah or that Miriam had memorized most of it and could share it with them.

One Shabbat afternoon Miriam was intrigued when Marona suggested a game of chess. Chess was considered more an intellectual pastime than a game of chance, notwithstanding the wagers placed whenever two experienced players matched their skill. She had played during festivals but never at home. Papa thought chess took time away from Torah study.

In Ramerupt there wasn't much else to do after the Sabbath midday meal, especially when the weather discouraged walking outdoors. So Marona unlocked a cabinet and brought out the most beautiful chess set Miriam had ever seen. Marona's father had brought it back from the Orient, and it became part of her dowry. The board, instead of the usual inlaid woods, was made of alternating squares of silver and gilt. The chessmen were silver or carved ivory. The king had his sword drawn, the knights sat on horseback, and since the Saracens had no bishops, there were small elephants instead. Miriam had heard of elephants, larger than the biggest bull, from Papa's foreign visitors, but she could never imagine what they looked like.

Perhaps Marona's skill was rusty from disuse or Miriam's mind had been honed by Torah study, but there was no great disparity between them. During a long turn Miriam struck a thoughtful pose, one that Marona's daughter, Hannah, had habitually adopted when they had played together. Suddenly Miriam's concentration was broken by her opponent's sobs.

"I'm sorry," Marona mumbled as she wept. "I haven't played chess since my daughter died, and I didn't realize how much you'd remind me of her."

Aware that even the hint of Benjamin's memory could send her into tears, Miriam was filled with such empathy that she got up and put her arms around the older woman. Soon both were crying and bemoaning their losses, questioning what they could have done to deserve such punishment from their Creator and doubting they could ever be happy again. Eventually the last tear was shed, and they were reduced to small sniffs and sighs.

Marona blew her nose. "I thank you, dear. I haven't had a good cry in quite some time."

"I know. Everyone at home gets so upset when I start bawling that I try to stop right away."

"Feel free to weep as much as you need to."

Miriam gave Marona a small smile. "*Merci.*"

"I believe it was your move before our little cloudburst," Marona said, smiling in turn. "Can you remember your strategy or should we start over?"

Miriam felt almost lighthearted. "Let's play on. I don't mind if I lose."

And so the courier found them, an hour later, when he came to announce Countess Alice's desire that Miriam should ride with her and her ladies on Monday. He arrived with trepidation, not sure what activities he would interrupt in a Jewish household on their Sabbath, and was reassured to find these ladies engaged in the same pastime those at court found so compelling.

Before Miriam could think of a polite way to refuse, Marona announced that of course her guest accepted the countess's hospitality. She then offered the man some bread, cheese, and ale, and while he ate, questioned him about what time Miriam should be at the castle and whether they were merely going riding or if there was a hunt. Only a simple morning ride was involved, with refreshments served afterward.

When the man left, Marona turned to her dismayed guest and declared, "Samuel is Count André's vassal, and if you don't ride with Countess Alice's ladies, it might be considered be an insult." She smiled and patted Miriam's hand. "The countess can't be older than twenty. It will be nice for you to spend time with people your own age."

"But what will I talk about with the Edomite ladies?" Miriam asked. "What could we possibly have in common?"

"Don't worry, dear. If you listen and ask questions, they're bound to think you're a brilliant conversationalist."

Marona was right. Countess Alice and her ladies-in-waiting weren't very different from the merchants' wives and daughters in Troyes. As they rode along the forest lanes, talk revolved around the latest court gossip—who was in favor and who was out, who had quarreled with whom and why, which knight was smitten with which lady and whether the feeling was requited.

But most of all the ladies couldn't resist talking about the countess's new son, Gautier, his father's heir, who had recently been christened. Miriam of course knew about babies; she was training to be a midwife. She easily held her own in the discussion, even sharing a few anecdotes about her young nephew.

The road came to a fallow field, and a redhead named Rosaline suggested a race to the far end and back. Before Miriam could decide to race, the others took off, Aunt Sarah's horse not far behind, and by the time their steeds had rounded the field, she was in the lead. Miriam worried briefly that she ought to let the countess win, but soon gave herself over to the pleasure of the race, the ground rushing beneath her and the wind in her face.

When Miriam's mount finally slowed to a walk, her heart was pounding. The others gathered around her, praising her horse, and the countess asked what price she would take for the animal.

"I cannot take any price," Miriam declared between gasps. "The mare doesn't belong to me, but to my aunt."

As to why her aunt needed such a fleet horse, Miriam replied as she had often heard Sarah respond. "She is a midwife who never knows when some mother's life may depend on her horse's swiftness."

Countess Alice was silent a moment and then said excitedly, "Your aunt must be the Jewish midwife who delivered little Hugues of Troyes. At Gautier's christening, Adelaide spoke with me at length of her ordeal. In comparison, my experience, which I thought I would barely survive, seems like a pleasant outing."

The excitement of winning the race loosened Miriam's tongue. She admitted that, as her aunt's apprentice, she had assisted during that very birth. Alice was most eager to hear the whole tale again, from the midwife's perspective, although her ladies were more interested in Miriam's description of Countess Adelaide's lavish bedroom. Before Miriam ran out of things to say, they arrived at a small meadow next to the Aube River where servants were laying out their repast.

Relieved to find no shortage of permitted foods, Miriam helped herself to smoked fish, pickled vegetables, bread and butter, and a large spoonful of strawberry preserves. She was trying to decide whether to take an apple or a pear when one of the younger ladies shyly approached her. Hair so blond it was almost white, pallid blue eyes, creamy skin— the ideal of womanhood that French noblewomen aspired to. Yet her mouth was too thin and her eyes too closely set to be considered beautiful. Miriam recalled that this girl had not seemed quite so comfortable on her horse.

"Besides a midwife, you're an accomplished rider," she complimented Miriam, who thanked her and motioned her to sit down nearby.

"Oh, pardon me. I've forgotten my manners again." The girl blushed. "I'm Emeline de Méry-sur-Seine and I've only just come to court." Her voice, not loud to begin with, dropped to a whisper. "I'd like to ask you a favor."

"I'd be happy to help you if I'm able," Miriam replied. What could this Edomite girl want from her? Hopefully not anything in her midwiving capacity.

"I was wondering if you might be so kind as to help me with my riding."

Miriam sighed with relief. "I'll be glad to ride with you tomorrow, if you like. I'm visiting Lord Samuel and Lady Marona for the winter. Their manor is just south of here, at Ramerupt-sur-Aube." She used the estate's full title, to distinguish it from the town that housed the count's castle.

The next morning Miriam was already outside when Emeline arrived at Samuel's gate. It had snowed lightly the night before and the world

looked freshly cleaned. At first they rode together in a companionable silence, Miriam appreciating the stillness of the monochromatic winter
scenery. Hopefully Emeline wasn't insulted by Miriam not talking to her.

"You have no idea how much I appreciate this peace and quiet," Emeline said softly. "The ladies at court never stop their silly chatter, while
I'm used to women who only speak when they have something necessary
to say."

"They must be very unusual women."

"I used to live in a convent." Emeline sighed. "I expected to spend my
whole life there in prayer and study."

"Why did you leave?" Miriam asked. Clearly this had not been
Emeline's choice.

"My brother was injured in a tournament, so badly that he'll be
lucky to survive, never mind marry and father the next baron of
Méry-sur-Seine. I pray for his health every day." Emeline's chin began
to quiver, and she paused to regain her composure. "My brother made
me his heir and began negotiations for me to marry Baron Hugh de
Plancy."

"I'm sorry about your brother," Miriam said. The poor girl, suddenly
thrust from a holy life into a secular one. "Perhaps Le Bon Dieu will hear
your prayers and heal him."

"His life is in Le Bon Dieu's hands now." A tear ran down Emeline's
cheek. Then she sat up straight, and her sad expression was replaced by
one of determination. "I'm sixteen years old and I don't know nearly
enough about managing an estate. I must learn everything I can from
Countess Alice before the wedding."

"Won't your husband be running things?"

"He's supposed to," Emeline said. "But men go off to war or to visit
their vassals or to tournaments." Her voice quavered at the mention of
tournaments and then became bitter. "I don't know why my brother
went to that tournament. He wasn't some poor landless *juvene* who
needed to fight for glory and booty. He had his own castle already."

Miriam felt a stab of pain as she remembered Benjamin and the foolish risks he took. "If silly ladies can learn these things, a serious student
like you should have no trouble."

During the next month the weather stayed mild, allowing Miriam to ride with Emeline nearly every day. Marona encouraged her to continue joining Countess Alice's ladies for chess as well as riding. Life seemed like a continual festival, and Miriam worried about the work she ought to be doing in Troyes.

But when Joheved and Meir brought little Isaac to Ramerupt to celebrate the last two nights of Hanukkah with his grandparents, Joheved wouldn't hear of Miriam leaving.

At Joheved's first glimpse of her sister, she stopped in her tracks, her face suffused with pleasure. "The air in Ramerupt must agree with you, Miriam. Your hair is shiny again and there's color in your cheeks." She gave her sister a fierce hug. "It feels like you've gained back some weight too."

"That's not the air." Meir kissed Marona's cheek. "You can thank my mother's cooking and ale."

"Whatever it is about Ramerupt, Miriam must stay for another month at least." Joheved took her sister's arm and walked toward the house.

"I agree," Marona said.

"But Joheved," Miriam said. "I can't leave all the chores at home to the rest of you."

"Of course you can. This is the slowest time of year in the vineyard."

"So how are Mama and Papa?" Miriam asked. "And Rachel?"

"They are well, may the Holy One protect them, but there's a new family in Troyes I want to tell you about," Joheved said. "Moses haCohen and his wife Francesca, from Rome—a doctor."

"He should be an improvement over our old doctor," Meir said, handing his son into Marona's outstretched arms. "Moses has studied at Salerno's school of medicine, as well as with Saracen physicians in Bavel."

Once they were seated in the salon, Marona motioned for a servant to pour everyone some ale. "Any doctor would be an improvement over your old one," she said, wrinkling her nose.

"One of the first things he did was call on Aunt Sarah," Joheved said.

"He was so polite, inquiring about the herb dealers and apothecaries she considered the most adept."

Marona raised her eyebrows, intrigued.

"She talked to him for quite a while about his medical studies, especially those under the Saracens." Meir paused to take a long drink, then turned to his mother. "Mama, nobody makes ale as good as yours."

Miriam leaned forward. "Did you hear what he told her?"

"I only heard her ask if it were true that they performed autopsies there," Meir said. "Then I had to go back to my students. But after he left, Sarah told us how pleased she was that a skilled physician was taking up residence in town."

"Francesca is younger than Moses, about our age," Joheved added. "She attends synagogue every day, but she rarely speaks to anyone except me."

"Do they have any children?" Miriam asked, her attention focused on Marona cuddling Isaac.

"Not yet, but Francesca is eager to meet you."

Joheved hoped to avoid any subject that might remind Miriam of Benjamin, but eventually she felt obliged to report how the recent vintage had turned out. And Miriam wanted them to share whatever Talmud the yeshiva students were studying. But all in all it was a good visit. Joheved was glad to see that, though her sister did get choked up occasionally, the only time Miriam actually cried was when Joheved bid her adieu.

Once Miriam realized she was going to remain in Ramerupt, she began to chafe at being so useless. "Surely you can find something for me to do besides spinning wool," she told Marona.

"This is a slow time for us too," Marona said. "But if you wait another few weeks, we will be busier here than you could possibly imagine."

"Busy with what?"

"Soon the ewes will begin dropping their lambs and some of them will need assistance. You're a midwife, you ought to be a great help."

"*Moi!* Be a midwife to sheep!" Miriam's mouth dropped. "But I don't know anything about sheep, except how to cook them."

Marona smiled at her consternation. "Don't worry, it's not much different from what you already know about women, except that the ewes usually bear twins."

"Twins?" The young midwife's voice was hesitant. The last woman she'd attended was Muriel, and that had been a disaster. If sheep weren't much different from women, staying here could become a nightmare.

"*Oui*. The first lambs usually come before the Edomite's New Year, and nearly all of them are born by Purim. For two months we eat and sleep on the run, hurrying between the sheepfold and the barn. Believe me, by the time Purim comes our idea of a celebration is ten hours' sleep in a row," Marona said. "But the baby lambs are so adorable, and when it's all over and you see them playing in the pasture . . ." Marona sighed with contentment.

Miriam gulped. *How will I manage two months of ewes giving birth every night?* But Marona and the shepherds would be there to help. Surely she'd be an expert midwife by springtime, even if the mothers were all sheep.

The next day, however, all thoughts of ewes and lambs were driven from Miriam's thoughts when the countess's courier brought her an invitation to a hunt.

"Let me see," Marona said as she propelled Miriam upstairs. "We've got to find you something suitable to wear." She began rummaging through a chest of clothes.

"What's wrong with what I've been wearing so far?"

"For the hunt you should wear something the ladies haven't seen before." Marona was talking to herself as much as to Miriam. "Something colorful and festive. My things are too large, but you could wear one of Hannah's outfits. Where is that *bliaut* that always made me think of autumn leaves?"

"Here we are." Marona held up a tawny gold tunic and matching deep yellow chemise. The orange and red embroidery at the neck and sleeves did give the impression of fall foliage.

"This is too beautiful to wear for riding a horse."

But Marona waved Miriam's objections aside. "It will reflect poorly on me and Samuel if you don't dress as well as the court ladies, especially since you don't have a hawk."

As Miriam could see when she joined the crowd waiting for the hunt to start, nearly every highborn woman had her own hunting hawk. Whether a noble falcon or a poor sparrow hawk, carrying the bird on her wrist was a way of saying, "I am of gentle birth and need not do any disagreeable work with my hands." Emeline was inordinately proud of her own small merlin and gladly let Miriam admire it up close.

Goshawks, gyrfalcons, lanners—more types of hunting birds than Miriam had ever imagined. With ladies along, only birds and hares would be the prey this fine morning, not large animals such as deer or boar. It was exhilarating to watch the knights and ladies on their horses, dressed in every color in the rainbow, each with a bird on their gauntlet. Dogs raced along to flush the game, horns blew, and then Count André gave the signal.

Away they ran—over fields and brooks, through thicket and countryside. When the quarry was sighted, a covey of partridges or a flock of ducks, then the hawks were all unhooded together. Immediately came shouts and wagers as the birds soared after their prey. Miriam was awed by the hawks' graceful beauty in flight and amazed that such wild creatures allowed themselves to be lured back to their owners' fists.

The banquet the servants laid out afterward was a lavish display of food. Much of it wasn't kosher, but there were more than enough fish and egg dishes, plus several kinds of bread and plenty of preserved fruit.

She had just filled her plate when she noticed several children approaching through the trees. As they drew closer, Miriam took a step back in dismay. Large, pleading eyes stared at her out of black-streaked faces. Even among the beggars in Troyes she had never seen children so thin or so filthy, their matted hair and torn clothes covered with soot.

Before she could decide whether to hand them some food or just toss it in their direction, one of the count's men raced past her, shouting, "Get away from here, you scum."

The children slowly backed away, and when he yelled at them again,

"If you're not gone by the time I count to ten, I'll set the dogs on you," they turned and ran into the forest.

Her appetite gone, Miriam made her way to where the ladies sat, giggling and exchanging flirtatious glances with the knights. At a lull between courses, Rosaline was bold enough to meet one of the young men behind the hedge. When she eventually rejoined the others, her hair and clothing were mussed.

"I don't know what to do." Rosaline sighed. "Faubert begs me to meet him tonight after everyone has gone to bed. He swears he cannot live without me." She continued breathlessly, "I want to be with him more than anything, but . . ."

"You don't want to end up enceinte," interrupted one of her friends. The others tittered behind their hands.

"But I thought there were certain herbs you could take, rue or pennyroyal," an older lady said. She turned to Miriam. "Isn't that true?"

Miriam was already wondering how soon she could leave, and the last thing she wanted to discuss with a group of frivolous unmarried ladies was how to avoid pregnancy. Yet she couldn't deny her knowledge. "There are, but unless you're an expert, you have no idea how fresh they are or if the dealer is even selling the correct stuff. After all, what is the defrauded woman to do nine months later? Ask for her money back?"

"So I should consult an expert like you?" Rosaline asked.

"What if there's no expert around?" a brunette interrupted. "Are there any herbs we can grow ourselves?"

The older woman lowered her voice and stared at Miriam. "I heard that Jewish women use something called a *mokh*."

Miriam shot Emeline a pleading look.

"Miriam," Emeline said. "I think I left my psalter at Ramerupt-sur-Aube. Could you ride back with me to get it?"

As they walked to where the horses were tethered, Miriam flinched when the servants tossed the leftover food to the dogs. Then, with great relief, she bid farewell to the countess and rode away with Emeline.

"*Merci beaucoup* for rescuing me."

Emeline wrinkled her nose in disgust. "I could see that you were as distressed by the conversation as I was."

Miriam was more distressed by the hungry children's rejection, but she replied, "Knights have a reputation for lechery, but I didn't realize the ladies at court were no better than the serving wenches at the Troyes fairs."

"That's one of the reasons I prefer your company," Emeline said. "I'd forgotten that you live in Troyes. What's it like in such a big city?"

How could she describe Troyes, its busy streets crowded with ten thousand inhabitants, to someone who was used to Ramerupt's two hundred residents? "Troyes is so big that it takes an entire day to walk around the outer walls. Inside, there are so many houses built so close together that you can't see the sun except at noontime. Everyone in Troyes is busy, either making, buying, or selling all sorts of goods, and sometimes it's so noisy you can't hear yourself think."

Emeline surveyed the serene forest. "It sounds dreadful. You must be glad to be staying here."

Miriam didn't know what to say. Ramerupt was more peaceful than Troyes and Benjamin's memory didn't haunt her so much, but it wasn't home.

That evening Miriam tried to remember the exhilaration of the hunt, but the pleasure of the morning's ride had been tainted by what followed. When she asked about the black-faced children, Marona explained that they were charcoal burners, runaway serfs living in the forest, whose trade was producing charcoal from burned wood. Despite the estate's self-sufficiency, she bought charcoal from them.

Lying in bed, keenly aware of the charcoal brazier heating her room, Miriam was haunted by those hungry children's eyes. If only she could escape from this world of idleness and immorality and return to her pious home. Unable to sleep, Miriam remembered the Hanukkah gift that Joheved had brought her. Papa had finished writing a draft of his commentary on Psalms, and he wanted her to make sure his explanations were understandable, yet concise. Just what she needed to clear her mind.

She removed the manuscript from the chest that held her belongings and opened it to Psalm 1.

> Happy is the man who has not walked in the counsel of the wicked
> Nor stood in the way of sinners, nor sat in the seat of the scornful
> Rather, the Torah of Adonai is his delight and in his Torah he meditates day and night . . .
> For Adonai knows the way of the righteous, and the way of the wicked will perish

Miriam read the verses again and again, letting the comforting words flow over her. The text was speaking directly to her heavy heart, urging her to forsake the sinners whose company she had been keeping and return to the paths of righteousness.

When she turned to her father's comments, she saw that first he explained how the psalmist praised the man who avoided the wicked. Because he did not even walk with sinners, he did not stand with them, and because he did not stand with sinners, he did not sit with them.

She'd begun by riding with the wicked, Miriam reminded herself, and sure enough, she'd ended up sitting with them and listening to their evil talk.

To bridge the first and second verse, Papa concluded, "Hence we learn that the company of scorners brings one to neglect the study of Torah." Then he pointed out that the pronoun "his" in the second verse meant the diligent student, not the Holy One. At first the Law is "the Torah of Adonai," but after the student strives to understand it, it becomes his own. Papa emphasized that the diligent student doesn't just utter words of Torah but meditates on them in his heart.

Miriam sighed. *How many days have passed since I've meditated on words of Torah? Too many.*

With the final verses, he concluded, "Because the Holy One knows the ways of the righteous, He finds the ways of the wicked so despicable that on the Day of Judgment, the wicked will not be written in the congregation of the righteous."

Miriam considered her father's words. Even if the yeshiva still held memories of Benjamin, she needed and missed the intellectual and spiritual activity. If she wasted more time in the company of the Ramerupt court, she would end up just as morally empty. Studying this psalm had made her realize that she must leave for Troyes as soon as possible.

But once back in bed, her firm resolution wavered. Was her grief healed enough that places and activities she associated with Benjamin wouldn't wound her anew? And what about her duty to those who had succored her? She'd promised Marona to help with the lambing. If she stayed, delivering all those lambs might be a way of atoning for Muriel's stillborn, as well as enabling her to avoid Muriel altogether for several more months.

Miriam's thoughts tumbled back and forth until she finally fell asleep, and she woke to find her decision made for her. Winter, which had teased the province all month with barely a hint of cold, had arrived with a vengeance. Hail was drumming on the roof, and by noon snow flurries were whipping through the courtyard.

She thanked the Almighty for the blizzard that solved her dilemma. Until spring, nobody would be riding for pleasure, saving her from further socializing with Count André's court. Now she wouldn't disappoint Marona by leaving early. Hopefully she wouldn't disappoint her later by failing to midwife her sheep properly.

five

Despite the bitter weather, Samuel's shepherds kept a vigil over the sheepfold, and as soon as a ewe showed signs of impending birth, they moved her into the barn. Miriam tried to remain an observer, but one day she was the only one idle as a ewe struggled in vain to deliver its twins.

Marona shouted encouragement. "Just do as I told you and you'll be fine."

Miriam remembered her instructions. First, if any legs are out, determine if it's a front leg or rear leg. Lambs are born either headfirst or back legs first. If a back leg was out but its mate was in, all she had to do was pull out the missing limb and the rest of the lamb would follow. If a foreleg came out, she'd have to push it back in and hope the proper leg appeared.

But there were no legs sticking out of this ewe.

Miriam slowly approached the miserable creature. She remembered Countess Adelaide's difficult labor, and while one of the shepherds held the struggling ewe, she slipped her hand into the sheep's womb. Groping through a tangle of limbs, she felt a wave of despair. *How can I possibly tell which leg belongs to which, let alone which ones are front or back?* In desperation she grabbed a leg and followed it to the body. Thank goodness, there was its rump, and, below it, the other hind leg. She managed to secure the two legs and began to pull, praying that the second lamb would stay out of its way. Luck was with her, for once she dragged out the first twin, the second one quickly emerged.

That first exhilarating week Miriam personally attended over a dozen ewes, and she lost count of how many deliveries she either helped with or watched. She almost cried with relief the first time she delivered a lamb whose cord was wrapped around its neck. When the lamb didn't exit despite being headfirst, she checked for and then untangled its cord. Once it was born, it took all her restraint not to hug the little fellow.

A month later, after lambing daily in freezing weather, Miriam's enthusiasm faded into steady persistence. She stayed up late into the night as long as there were laboring ewes to tend. Then she woke at dawn, had a quick breakfast of stirabout and warm ale, and returned to the barn. Still the lambs kept coming, and eventually Miriam found herself a proficient sheep midwife rather than merely a helper. She also found herself caring for a baby lamb whose mother refused to nurse it.

Marona had shrugged her shoulders and said, "I have no idea why it happens, but some ewes reject their offspring. A male becomes lamb stew, but a female is worth some effort to save."

When Miriam was confronted by a ewe that rebuffed every attempt of the newborn to nurse, she had one of the dairymaids teach her how to feed the lamb with her fingers and a container of milk. Yet once the small creature was drinking readily from a pail, it continued to suck on Miriam's fingers. The lamb never failed to greet her appearance with excitement, which only increased Miriam's affection for it.

The lambing season was still upon them at Purim, and thus the festival caused only a ripple in the manor's flow of work. The small Jewish community of Ramerupt read the Megillah and feasted, but the celebration was tame compared to Troyes, and Miriam only cried once at missing Benjamin. The week after Purim saw the first glimpse of warm weather, and the sheep eagerly returned to their pastures for the new grass that peeked through the melting snow.

Miriam expected to return home for Passover, but she saw that Marona again needed her help. Samuel was seriously ill. It started innocuously enough with a late winter cold. Despite consuming copious amounts of Marona's chicken broth, he developed both a fever and a hacking cough. A week later, when he began coughing up thick sputum flecked with blood and his breathing became so labored that he was forced to sleep sitting up, Marona began to fear for his life.

In desperation she sent off two letters, one to each of her sons. To Meshullam, she wrote that his father was ill and he should spend Passover at his parents' home. Meir's letter stated that Samuel was sick and asked him to please arrange for a visit by the new physician.

Meir consulted with Joheved, then saddled his horse and rode to Moses's home. Relieved to find the doctor at home, he showed him Marona's note. "My father must be ill indeed for my mother to seek a physician's presence."

Moses called for his horse to be readied and began to pack his medical kit. "Did your mother even hint at the nature of your father's illness? If I knew more about his ailment I could bring an appropriate medicine."

"I'm sorry, she wrote nothing more than what I told you," Meir replied. "I must warn you, my mother doesn't like doctors."

"That's a shame," Moses said. "People who don't like doctors usually don't send for one until it's too late, and then his failure only makes them dislike doctors even more."

An hour later they rode into the manor's courtyard. As two servants ran out to see to their horses, Moses said to Meir, "I'm sure you're eager to see your father. Let me relieve myself first, then I'll be right up."

Meir was indeed anxious to get upstairs and directed one of the servants to show Moses to the privy.

"Quickly man, what ails your master?" Moses questioned the man as they walked.

"They say that he has a bad fever and coughs so much he can scarcely breathe."

After relieving himself, Moses had only a few moments left before entering the house. "What has been done for him?"

"I believe her ladyship is giving him broth and some herbal infusions." The servant continued proudly, "Lady Marona is as good a healer as they come. She cured my wife of ague last winter and my cousin of the flux the year before."

Before he reached the door, Marona opened it herself and welcomed him. Moses cautioned her to say nothing until he had examined the patient. She knitted her brows but remained silent as they headed upstairs to the sickroom, Miriam following behind. At first appearance, the elderly man propped up in bed before them could have just fallen asleep. His light grey hair, while thin, still covered most of his head, and his beard, a darker shade of grey, was neatly trimmed.

On closer examination, Moses observed his patient's blue-tinged lips and unfocused eyes, and heard the labored gasps of someone who cannot quite catch his breath. He picked up Samuel's hand to take his pulse, then leaned over and listened to his chest. Marona had ordered the servants to save Samuel's latest urine for the doctor to examine, and Moses carefully pulled out a container from his bag and poured the liquid into it.

Marona, Miriam, and Meir stared at him in astonishment. The doctor's container was transparent, the yellow urine clearly visible through its walls. They watched, eyes wide, as Moses swirled the liquid in his flask, sniffed its odor, and then delicately inserted his small finger inside to take a taste.

Only then did he turn to Marona. "Please describe your husband's diet since he's been ill."

Marona was pleasantly surprised by Moses's polite professionalism. "He has eaten little besides chicken broth and a bit of bread these last ten days. I also made him a tisane of steeped sage and thyme." When Moses remained silent, she continued, "He has the soup twice a day and the tisane several times."

In Salerno Moses had been taught to deliver a discourse on his patient's disease before prescribing any treatment. "It appears that your husband has the sweating sickness complicated with catarrh of the lungs. Let me explain."

Miriam, standing in the doorway, stepped into the room as he continued, "A man's health is maintained by the proper equilibrium of the four humors in his body: blood, phlegm, yellow bile, and black bile. These correspond to the four elements: air, water, fire, and earth. Blood, being like air, is hot and moist; phlegm is cold and moist like water; yellow bile is hot and dry, similar to fire; and black bile is cold and dry, as is earth."

He made sure he had Marona's attention. "Old people become cold and dry as they age, so that if Lord Samuel were in perfect health I would recommend that his diet tend toward the warm and moist. Do you understand?"

Marona slowly nodded. "And since he probably has too much phlegm, should I correct his diet toward the hot and dry?"

"You are correct. Since both sage and thyme have this character, your soup and herbal infusions are a good start." Moses's face took on an optimistic expression. "With aggressive treatment and the Holy One's help, recovery should come soon."

Marona took hold of Meir's arm for support as tears of relief came to her eyes. "Thank Heaven that Troyes has a new doctor just when we need one."

Once downstairs, Moses adopted a graver tone. "I did not want to alarm the patient, but it was a lucky thing you called me in. I only hope it's not too late." His dour speech was interrupted as his stomach growled.

"I'm so sorry." Meir turned to his mother and explained, "I hurried the poor doctor here without *disner.*"

"By all means dine with us, Moses." Marona directed servants to prepare the table and asked Miriam show the doctor her medicinal herbs.

Miriam accompanied Moses to the cellar, where he inspected the many dried branches hanging from hooks. When they returned, Marona assured him that she collected sage and thyme before the plants flowered and that neither had been exposed to sunlight.

"That's well and good for treating a mild cold, but for your husband's illness we need herbs, thyme especially, which have been stored in an airtight vessel. I will direct the apothecary to prepare some for me to bring tomorrow."

"You need to return so soon?" Meir's trepidation was obvious as they took their places at the dining table. "But you can send it over in the morning with my wife."

"Joheved is coming here tomorrow?" Miriam smiled broadly.

"I must stay in Ramerupt and offer prayers until my father is well, and knowing how much my wife misses you, I suggested she join me here." Meir grinned shyly. He didn't need to say how lonely he would feel.

Miriam turned to the doctor. "Where did you get that transparent container you used upstairs?"

Moses handed her the vessel. "It's called glass, and it's made by heating sand so hot that it melts. Then the glassmaker molds the molten stuff into whatever shape he desires."

Miriam held the glass up to the light. "Amazing—you can see right through it. It must be very expensive."

"I bought it in Bavel when I went to medical school." Moses took another piece of meat. "It's not so expensive there—all the physicians have them."

"You studied in Bavel?" Meir's eyes opened wide. "Are the great yeshivot still training Talmud students there?"

"I'm sad to say that the Bavel yeshivot are no longer the great academies they once were." The doctor sighed. Then, so the family wouldn't think he'd forgotten his patient, he said to the nearest servant, "Excuse me, but could you go upstairs and see if your master has finished his tisane?"

When the servant returned to announce that Lord Samuel had emptied his cup, Moses addressed Marona. "Regarding foodstuffs, I want a special recipe prepared for your husband. I believe that a nice blancmange, made with shredded chicken breasts, rice flour, and almond milk, will warm and moisten him. He is not to eat fish or squashes, both being wet and cold in the second degree, and on no account should he consume mushrooms, which are wet and cold in the third degree."

Whenever Moses began to lecture about food and humors, most of his listeners quickly grew bored. Miriam and Marona, however, looked attentive, so Moses became more voluble. "When our patient, may the Almighty protect him, is a bit better, say next week or so, I'd like him to start eating roasted meat and drinking wine spiced with cinnamon and cloves, all of which are hot and dry to the first degree."

He tossed the two women a question. "Guess what food is both hot and dry to the third degree?"

"Ginger?" ventured Marona.

"Close." He smiled. "Ginger is hot to the third degree, but because it's a root, it's considered wet to the first degree. However, I am talking about a spice."

"It has to be pepper." Miriam couldn't think of any spice that was hotter.

"You're right." Moses beamed at her. "All seeds are dry to some degree, but pepper is the hottest."

He paused for a moment and suggested that Marona liberally add pepper to the next batch of Samuel's broth. Then, he stood to say adieu.

Marona walked him to the gate. "I'm surprised you didn't bleed my husband. That's all the other doctors want to do."

"My good lady." The physician sounded shocked. "It is dangerous to perform bloodletting during the month of Adar. When the month of Nissan arrives, we'll see if his condition warrants it. Even then, I would not bleed him except on the favorable days of Sunday or Wednesday."

The next day the doctor arrived accompanied by Joheved and little Isaac. Meir held his son while the sisters embraced.

"Miriam, look at you!" Joheved grinned at the improvement in her sister's appearance since their last meeting. Miriam's cheeks were now rosy and filled out. "I was right. Country living does agree with you."

"I don't know if I'm completely well," Miriam said. "But I believe I'm feeling better. Tell me, how are Mama and Papa?"

Joheved laughed. "Papa's frantically working on his pre-Pesach sermon, and Mama's desperate that she won't get the house cleaned in time for the festival."

"Papa always worries about his sermons." Miriam smiled in return. "Maybe if he preached more often than twice a year, he wouldn't get so nervous." Her expression turned serious. "Shouldn't I go home to help Mama now that you're here?"

"Not when I have my first chance to visit with you in months," Joheved said. "Let Rachel do some work around the house for a change. It won't hurt her to get dust on her hands." She leaned over and whispered, "I have something to tell you about Rachel when we're alone."

With the two young women engaged in conversation, Moses inquired about his patient and sighed with relief to hear that Samuel's condition was stable. In addition to a sealed jar of thyme, Moses brought with him a large bouquet of daisies. He presented both to Marona, who awkwardly thanked him for the lovely blossoms.

Moses chuckled. "But these are for your husband. If spring were full upon us I would have looked for cowslip or coughwort, but this early in the year daisies will have to do. Chop the entire plant up fine and mix it with curds. Daily use will purify his blood, an excellent thing since we cannot bleed him, and it will also help loosen his mucus."

"I have some cowslip root," Marona said. "We boil it in water to bathe wounds, but I don't know about coughwort."

Moses shook his head. "We need cowslip leaves and flowers to make an effective expectorant. As for coughwort, perhaps you know it by a different name. The plant sends up yellow flowers in early spring, and the leaves, which are shaped like an animal's hoof, come up after the flowers are gone."

"Do you mean coltsfoot?" Miriam asked. "It has yellow flowers that close up at night and when it's cloudy."

Moses nodded. "If it grows around here, we should make every effort to procure some."

"I'm sure I've seen it nearby," Marona said. "I think it blooms first on the south-facing slopes."

Once inside, Moses visited the sickroom and again checked his patient's pulse, breathing, and urine. He announced himself satisfied with Samuel's progress and suggested that the sickbed be moved to a room with a large south-facing window. Any *mazikim* still lurking about would be dispelled by the sunshine.

His duty done, Moses joined the household for their midday meal. Meir gave the doctor a chance to eat undisturbed by describing his own efforts on Samuel's behalf. "At night I sit by his bed and study Torah. To make my prayers more powerful, I begin and end each one by reciting from Numbers:

Moses cried to Adonai, saying, 'Oh God, pray heal her.'

And from Deuteronomy:

> Adonai will ward off from you all sickness; He will not bring upon
> you any of the dreaded diseases of Egypt."

The doctor nodded. "Very good. Those particular verses provide protection against most fevers."

"I have been reminded that 'Charity delivers from death.'" Meir smiled at Joheved. "So my mother, on my father's behalf, will provide, from our manor's mill, the flour required to make matzah for the needy families in Troyes and Ramerupt, as well as a lamb each from our flocks for their seders."

As dessert was served, Miriam was torn. Should she ask the physician to continue his fascinating lecture about food and the four humors, or should she do nothing to prolong the meal so she could visit with Joheved? Sure that Moses would be coming to Ramerupt regularly, she offered to take Joheved to look for coltsfoot.

Since their path lay through the pastures, Miriam brought a pail of milk for her adopted lamb. Her sister's eyes widened as the lamb eagerly ran to Miriam and began to suck on her fingers.

Warmed by the obvious affection between them, Joheved caught herself about to comment that Miriam had managed to get a baby without a husband. She said instead, "Motherhood agrees with you. I pray the Holy One soon provides you with a husband and children."

To Joheved's gratification, Miriam responded, "Amen."

This was the opening Joheved was waiting for. "You know, it's a rare woman who gets to choose her husband from as many suitors as you'll have," she began. "Especially when she's old enough to have an idea what she wants."

She watched Miriam's face for any sign of pain, but her sister's expression remained calm. "Not that I can complain about Meir, but I was lucky. He could have been terrible."

Miriam wasn't sure she was ready for this conversation. "I haven't given much thought to what I want."

"But you must—how else will you know who's the right one?" Joheved noticed a small field of daisies and they headed in that direction. If they couldn't find coltsfoot, at least they wouldn't come back empty-handed.

"He has to be a scholar," Miriam said. "Papa would never accept anything less." She saw Joheved's frown and quickly continued, "I know, Papa's not marrying him. Very well then, I want my husband to be as learned as I am, although I doubt that anyone except a scholar would offer to marry me."

"That's probably true. But your suitors will come from many places. How far away from Troyes are you willing to live?"

Miriam was startled to realize that her husband might want her to move. "I don't want to live away from Troyes at all. Who would be the Jewish community's midwife?"

"Aunt Sarah could train somebody else, and it's not like there wouldn't be Jewish women who need a midwife in your new home," Joheved replied. "The man's business might be located far away, and once you're married you can't very well refuse to live with him."

"If he does business at the Champagne fairs, we could live together in Troyes during those months, and he could travel the rest of the time," Miriam said with resolve. "Many women live like that."

Especially if they don't get along with their husbands, Joheved thought. "Then it's settled that your scholarly husband should live nearby. But what about his individual traits—what kind of person will he be?"

"He should be honest, kind, considerate, slow to anger, faithful . . ." Miriam faltered, uncomfortable with specifics.

"Is this a man you're describing or are you listing the Thirteen Divine Attributes?" Joheved teased her sister. "Don't you care what he looks like?"

"Not really. Just as long as he's not hideous or deformed."

Joheved thought back to that day in the wine cellar when Meir first arrived in Troyes. She could never decide whether her heart had recognized him or if she had truly responded to an attractive stranger. But she knew that his presence had unaccountably quickened her pulse and caused her to blush. Shouldn't Miriam look for a man who affected her similarly?

"Miriam, what about his . . . ?" She groped to find the right words. "I mean, don't you think that your husband should be a man who kindles some kind of fire in you?"

Joheved regretted her gaucherie as tears welled up in Miriam's eyes.

"*Non!* I had that with Benjamin and look where it got me. I never want to feel that way about anyone ever again. You can keep your passion and fire, I don't want it." Miriam turned her back on Joheved and headed to a distant clump of flowers.

Joheved knew she wasn't wrong to bring up the subject. Miriam needed to be prepared. Still, she was the one who had wounded her sister, so she ought to be the one to make amends.

"Miriam, I'm sorry . . ."

"You don't need to apologize, you were just trying to be helpful. I guess my healing still has a way to go." Miriam sniffed a few times and continued, "I can't carry any more of these flowers, let's go back. We'll have to look for coltsfoot another time."

They walked slowly, trying not to drop any daisies, and Miriam remembered her sister's earlier remark. "Joheved, what was it you wanted to tell me about Rachel?"

"You know how everyone thinks that Rachel is such a lovely child—" Joheved stopped. *How petty I sound.*

"She is, may the Holy One protect her."

"I know it sounds mean, but I always thought that once Rachel got older she'd get the same bad skin, unruly hair, and awkwardness the rest of us have." Joheved wanted Miriam to understand the awe she now felt. "But these last six months, seemingly overnight, Rachel has become even more beautiful." Joheved quickly added, "May the Almighty protect her."

"But she's barely ten years old."

"I know, yet she looks years older." Joheved sighed. "She's a terrible distraction for the poor yeshiva students."

"What are Mama and Papa doing about her?"

"Papa hasn't done anything. To him, she's still the little girl who used to sit on his lap as he wrote his *kuntres*. Mama, of course, wants to keep Rachel in the kitchen or out in the garden, away from the boys, but Rachel wants to learn Torah just like we did."

"Rachel learning Torah?" Miriam shook her head in amazement at what was happening at home.

Joheved giggled. "She's not entirely innocent of her effect on the boys. She seems determined to provoke Eliezer."

"Eliezer? Asher's little brother?" Miriam winced. Asher had been Benjamin's study partner and best friend.

"He's not so little anymore. He's almost as tall as Meir," Joheved said. "He's also Papa's best student. He studies a text only once or twice and he's memorized it. But Eliezer is vain about his intellect." She frowned slightly. "So Rachel is determined to demonstrate his ignorance."

"Surely Papa doesn't allow it."

"It might be good for Eliezer to be humbled by a girl," Joheved said. "Papa doesn't object because Rachel is studying like mad, trying to find the texts that Eliezer doesn't know."

"Our Rachel—a *talmid chacham*?"

Joheved beamed with approval. "*Oui*. Remember, she has Papa's commentaries to help her."

Miriam allowed just the hint of a smile to show. Life in Troyes must be very interesting. "I can't wait to see her again, and to study with her."

Owing to several cases of flux in Troyes, Moses couldn't return to Ramerupt until after the Sabbath, and when he arrived, the household was in an excellent mood. Marona had coaxed little Isaac to sleep with her, leaving Joheved and Meir a night of uninterrupted privacy. Samuel's fever had broken that night as well, and he had awoken clearheaded and demanding to see his grandson. Joheved introduced Miriam to Francesca, who had accompanied her husband, and while the doctor was checking on Samuel, Francesca happily whispered that she was almost sure she was pregnant.

Everyone gathered around the dining table, giddy with relief at Moses's pronouncement that Samuel was indeed on the mend and would probably be much improved by Passover.

"I would feel more confident if I could treat him with coltsfoot," the doctor said. "Without it, his cough could worsen and a new fever result."

Marona's face fell. What if Samuel had a relapse during Passover? "I don't suppose you'd consider . . . *Non*, it's too much to ask."

"Let me be the judge of that," Moses replied.

"Would you consider spending the Passover week here in Ramerupt?" she asked. "And your wife too, of course."

"Francesca and I would be honored."

Meir turned to his mother. "Since Moses and Meshullam are coming, maybe you could invite Salomon as well?"

Miriam leaned forward, her eyes bright with excitement. "Oh, Marona, could you? It would be wonderful to see my family. I'll do everything I can to help you." *Then Mama won't have to do all that work to get our house ready for the festival.*

Marona considered what effort the extra company would entail. Cleaning the house, replacing the rushes, and removing all leaven was the same no matter how many guests were coming. Making the dishes kosher for Passover required washing them with soap and water, then plunging them into boiling water, followed by rinsing in cold water and a final dip in boiling water. Most of the work went into preparing the pots of boiling water; once they were ready, koshering a few extra items would be simple. Koshering the iron hooks, tripods, and spits in the hearth was almost no effort at all—just pass them each through the fire. So why not invite more guests?

"An excellent idea, Meir. I don't know why I didn't think of it myself." She smiled at Miriam. "Now, we can both spend Passover with our families."

SÍX

With growing apprehension, Meshullam ben Samuel approached his parents' estate. As the servants hurried to greet him, he was relieved to see no signs of grief on their faces. Étienne, the manor's steward since Meshullam's childhood, ran with a young man's spryness to help the young lord dismount.

"How is he?" Meshullam braced himself for the answer.

"Your father has rallied recently, and the doctor believes he will, albeit slowly, recover."

"But my mother hates doctors."

"This one is different. Your brother brought him up from Troyes over a fortnight ago."

"Meir still lives in Troyes?" There was disapproval in Meshullam's voice.

Étienne frowned in return. "*Oui*, my lord, he does."

"I must have a chat with him." Meshullam strode past Étienne toward his father's room.

"Lord Samuel's bed has been moved to the salon," Étienne said. "I'll get your wife and children while you visit him."

Meshullam could hear his brother's voice, softly praying, interrupted by a hacking cough. He entered and halted in shock at his father's appearance. Samuel's hair, once full and grey, was now sparse and nearly white, and his skin seemed as fragile as old parchment. To Meshullam's dismay, another paroxysm of coughing shook Samuel. *Mon Dieu, he might die any moment.*

Apparently unfazed, Meir encouraged his father to drink the contents of a cup sitting nearby. Finding it empty he started toward the doorway, only to find his way barred.

"Papa, look who's here." Meir gave his brother a hug.

Samuel looked up, smiled, and held out his arms to his oldest son. "You're just in time for Passover."

Meir headed into the hall. "I'll get some more medicine."

"Where's Mama? Shouldn't she be tending to Papa's needs?"

"She's outside. People are here every day to buy lambs for the butchers in Troyes."

Meshullam's frustration grew. He'd spent several harrowing days trying to get here, expecting to find the worst, only to learn that his mother had neglected her husband's health to attend to manorial duties, duties that Meir should have assumed.

"Find a servant to give Papa his drink." He grabbed Meir's arm and hauled him into the courtyard. "You and I are going to have a long-overdue talk . . . in private."

Loath to argue in front of the household, Meir followed his brother outside the manor walls. High on a hill, overlooking the pastures of sheep, he would hear what the devil was troubling Meshullam. He had no idea that his wife was searching for herbs not far away.

"Aha—there you are." Joheved triumphantly climbed through the bushes toward the patch of coltsfoot.

After Miriam discovered a small clump yesterday, Joheved was determined to find the elusive herb as well. Just as she knelt to pick the small flowers, she heard men approaching. One voice belonged to her husband. She crouched down and forced herself to keep still.

Meir was indignant. "Why shouldn't I live in Troyes?"

"Everyone says you're a brilliant scholar, so you can't be as stupid as you sound." That must be Meshullam. He could only have just arrived, yet the brothers were already quarrelling.

"What are you talking about?" Joheved could imagine her husband's frustrated expression.

"I'll explain it to you." Meshullam's voice dripped with sarcasm. "And

I won't need Talmudic logic. You should be living here in Ramerupt, learning how to run the estate."

"Between Salomon's vineyard and yeshiva, I'm quite content in Troyes," Meir said. "You're the eldest, you run the estate."

"I've worked hard to establish myself among the cloth manufacturers in Flanders," Meshullam countered. "You have no profession to give up."

"So neither of us runs the estate."

"Then after Papa dies and Count André finds a new vassal, who's going to support you in your scholarly life of luxury?"

"I'm not living in luxury," Meir said. "I can earn my keep by helping Salomon in the vineyard."

Meshullam unleashed a stronger salvo. "Maybe so, but who's going to pay for your children's clothes and books, your daughters' dowries? Where's all the yeshiva's free parchment going to come from?"

Meir had no answer and Meshullam made his winning point. "And what happens to Mama if she can't continue to live here?"

"I don't know." Meir's voice was so soft Joheved could barely hear him. "But I don't want to leave the yeshiva and manage an estate." He sounded like Rachel did when Mama forced her to stop reading and do her chores.

"And I don't want to have a son who's a cripple, but I do."

Joheved saw to the crux of the matter. Meir had one healthy son and prospects for more, while Meshullam had none. The estate had to go to the son who could best provide future heirs. Poor Meir. He loved the scholar's life, and he excelled at it, but he would have to do as many Jewish men, including Papa, had sadly done before him—leave the yeshiva to support his family.

Meir must have realized this. "I'm sorry, Meshullam. I've been acting like a spoiled child." He sounded beaten and broken.

There was silence on the other side of the bushes, and Joheved held her breath for fear that they might discover her. Then she heard Meshullam's voice coming from down the hill.

"Let's keep this to ourselves. No point upsetting Mama and Papa with talk of what will happen after he's gone."

"Agreed." The last words Joheved could make out were those of her husband. "I also need time to break the news to my wife."

Oblivious to the coltsfoot beneath her, Joheved sank down on the ground. It was so unfair—Meir would be miserable in Ramerupt, buried in the countryside. Look at Papa. Even now, ten years later and head of his own small yeshiva, he still missed his old colleagues in the Rhineland and bitterly regretted that he'd been forced to leave them.

The coltsfoot. She jumped up and was relieved to see that the small plants were undamaged. She picked as many as she could carry, the jubilation she'd felt when she'd first found the elusive herb now gone. Somehow she'd have to hide her despair. Meir mustn't know she'd been listening.

Pushing her way through the bushes, Joheved stopped to look down at the bucolic scene. The gentle hills were green with new grass and dotted with sheep, whose soft bleating drifted up to her. Below, the manor stood serene and protected behind its grey stone walls, surrounded by fields of wheat. How peaceful and pleasant it looked. It didn't seem possible that anyone could be unhappy living here.

She was still admiring the view when a new thought startled her. *I will have to move to Ramerupt as well.* A stab of guilt assailed her; she'd probably be happier living here than her husband. Nobody in Ramerupt would know she'd been poor. Here she'd have more servants than she'd know what to do with, and they'd call her Lady Joheved. No one could make her spin and do embroidery if what she really wanted to do was study Torah, and she'd have Meir for her study partner. But her good life would be bought at the price of his misery.

Still trying to sort out her feelings, Joheved reached the manor gate. The doctor and Meshullam's family had arrived; the courtyard was a bustle of people. Francesca and Miriam were talking to a small, slender woman dressed in traveling clothes, whom Joheved assumed to be Meshullam's wife, Mathilde.

Marona was hugging two reticent little girls, while Moses was talking with an extremely thin boy. Joheved tried not to stare, but it was difficult, for there was obviously something wrong with his legs. He wore some kind of leather supports tied to them, and he leaned heavily on a pair of crutches. As Joheved surmised, the girls were introduced as Meshullam's daughters, Columbine and Iris, and the crippled boy was his son, Jacob.

After *souper* Joheved returned from the privy to find that the men had taken the children to search for *hametz* on this night before Passover began. Marona had secreted small crusts of bread in several rooms, and Joheved could hear the children's squeals of pleasure as they discovered them. Relieved at avoiding Meir, she sat down at the table with the women. Their conversation revolved around childbirth, and Joheved was glad to let her sister and Meshullam's wife supply the bulk of it.

"It was a miracle that I survived Jacob's birth," Mathilde said breathlessly, as if she had only given birth recently.

Miriam leaned over and whispered something in her ear, so that the two of them quickly glanced at Francesca before Mathilde continued, her demeanor subdued. Joheved listened with only half an ear as her sister-in-law first described the harrowing ordeal that had left her poor son so disabled, followed by her efforts to starve herself during subsequent pregnancies so as to produce babies small enough to fit through her narrow birth passage. It was only when Mathilde declared that she'd decided not to bear any more children that Joheved's attention returned.

Francesca's eyes were wide with surprise. "But won't your husband divorce you if you won't have relations with him?"

"Who said anything about not having relations with my husband?" Mathilde said. "All I do is apply some spearmint juice to a *mokh* before we use the bed, and drink a cup of wine mixed with a spoonful of wild carrot seeds the next morning, and, voilà, no more babies."

"Miriam, is that the same as Yehudit's sterilizing potion in Tractate Yevamot?" Joheved had forgotten her audience. When she saw the shock on Mathilde and Francesca's faces at her mention of studying Talmud, she blushed and hesitated, leaving Miriam to explain.

"In the Talmud, we learned about Rav Chiya's wife Yehudit, who bore two sets of twins and suffered so terribly during their births that she disguised herself and asked her husband if women, as well as men, were commanded to procreate."

Joheved could no longer remain silent. "He told her that women were not obligated to procreate, so she drank a sterilizing potion. When Rav Chiya found out, he was greatly grieved, but he couldn't challenge her decision."

"I don't think Yehudit used wild carrot seeds in wine." Miriam answered her sister's original question. "Her potion sounds permanent. Where did you get your recipe, Mathilde?"

"My midwife told me to use it."

"I know mint's a contraceptive, but I've never heard of using wild carrot seeds before," Miriam said. "I'll have to start growing them for my patients."

Salomon, Rivka, and Rachel arrived early the next morning, and as happy as they were to find Miriam in good health, she was happier to see them. Joheved had warned her about Rachel, but Miriam was awed by her not-so-little sister's beauty and a little sad to see the grey in Papa's beard when she hugged him. Of course he and Mama were getting older too. Still, it felt so good to have her family together again.

Surrounded by friends and family, grateful that her husband had escaped the Angel of Death, Marona hummed a happy tune as she laid out her best linens and dishes for the festive meal. Freed from the burden of preparing their own homes for the festival, Rivka and Mathilde cheerfully discussed which ritual food would be best placed on which platter as they set the table. Rivka was especially pleased at how well Miriam looked, not that she would tempt the Evil Eye by saying so.

Francesca insisted on helping Miriam make the *haroset,* the thick concoction of fruit, wine, nuts, and spices meant to recall the mortar from which the Israelite slaves built bricks for their Egyptian task masters.

"To think that I never believed the rumors about Rav Salomon teaching you and Joheved Talmud," Francesca said.

Miriam grinned. "Now you can tell everyone that they're true. And I hear that Rachel is studying Talmud as well." For months she'd had to sleep all alone, and now she would share a bed with her little sister again. If only Aunt Sarah could have come, but one midwife had to remain in Troyes.

Besides the usual apples and walnuts, Francesca added some chopped figs and dates that her mother had sent from Rome. Then, with an embarrassed smile, she said, "I've been meaning to ask you what a *mokh* is. I didn't want look stupid last night."

"A *mokh* is a small plug of wool that a woman places in her womb to prevent pregnancy," Miriam explained. "Most women don't know about them because they want to get pregnant."

The *haroset* was almost done. Miriam mixed in the cinnamon and ginger, used because they contain some stalks even when ground, thus resembling the straw that the Hebrew slaves kneaded into the clay. She sighed with pleasure as Rachel chose the most perfect circles of matzah from the batch her family had brought from Troyes and carefully stacked them on the table.

The delicious smells coming from the hearth had everyone's mouths watering when Salomon stuck his head in the kitchen and announced, "You women had better start getting dressed; we'll be starting the afternoon prayers soon."

"But Papa, we saved the garlic for you." Rachel held out a handful of the cloves.

"I'd better get to work then." He hurried to the pantry table. "Heaven forbid that I should be responsible for delaying the seder."

Miriam smiled as her father sat down. She could not remember a festival when Papa hadn't cut up the garlic. He had a special technique for chopping the cloves into tiny pieces without any sticking to the knife. He sprinkled a pinch of salt and a drop of olive oil over the garlic, then he began to dice it.

"You see," he explained to Mathilde's curious daughters, who were amazed to see the scholar working in the kitchen. "The salt acts as an abrasive, helping to cut the garlic, and the oil keeps the pieces from sticking to the knife's blade."

When Joheved and Miriam finished their prayers and came downstairs, Joheved dressed in her blue silk wedding dress and Miriam in the deep yellow outfit that Marona had given her, Rivka's face shone with pride. If Rivka noticed Rachel's look of envy, she gave no indication of it. As much as Rachel begged for a new dress for festivals, Rivka insisted on no new clothes until her daughter stopped growing. If the family's old wine-colored wool *bliauts* were good enough for her and her husband, they were good enough for her daughter.

Once everyone took their seats around the large table, Salomon began by breaking off a piece of matzah, holding it up and declaring, "This is the matzah, bread of affliction, which our fathers ate in the land of Egypt." Then, gazing fondly at his middle daughter, now healthy again, he asked, "Matzah is also called the bread of poverty. How do we remember this?"

Miriam, who had heard Papa explain the significance of matzah many times, was ready with the answer. She smiled at him and replied, "The rest of the year, we eat our bread with salt. But salt is too expensive for slaves, so tonight we eat our matzah, the bread of poverty, without salt." And indeed, there were no saltcellars on the table.

Now it was time for the youngest boy present to ask the four questions, whose answers were found in the Haggadah, the text that told the story of the Israelites' redemption from slavery in Egypt. Rachel always asked them at home, and she stared sullenly at her plate as Jacob struggled through the text.

"Why is this night different from all other nights?"

His words, which seemed to require a great deal of exertion, were garbled and strange, but it didn't matter. Everyone knew the questions; they were the same every year. Miriam felt a wave of sadness for the boy who spoke with such difficulty. But Meshullam and Mathilde beamed with pride.

As they continued with the seder, telling the story of the Israelites' delivery from slavery into freedom, then thanking and praising the Holy One for the miracles that brought this about, Meir grew increasingly morose. Here they were, singing about freedom, and he was as much a slave to this estate as the villeins were. And it would take a miracle to free him.

The next morning, when Miriam and Joheved were gathering more coltsfoot, Miriam confronted her sister. "Is something the matter between you and Meir? I haven't seen you both so miserable since the demon bound him."

Joheved explained what she had overheard, and it was as if a weight had been lifted from her even before her sister spoke.

"Poor Meir, no wonder he looks crushed." Miriam thought for a moment. "I don't understand why he can't let the steward run the estate for him. That's the fellow's job, after all."

Joheved didn't know what was the lord's responsibility and what was the steward's, and she said so.

"I spent a lot of time riding with the countess and her ladies this winter." Miriam's voice rose with excitement. "And I learned that lords rarely stay home and oversee one estate."

"They don't?"

"All noble ladies manage their husbands' estates when the men are off fighting or visiting other lords." Miriam grabbed Joheved's shoulders. "And you can too."

"*Moi?*" Joheved nearly dropped her armful of coltsfoot. "Run this estate by myself?"

"Not right away. At first you can just help Samuel and Marona," Miriam said. "You'll need a good steward, but that's easy. The squires here are training to become stewards, and when you get a good one, you keep him."

As they filled their bags, Joheved pondered her sister's proposal. Suddenly tears came to her eyes.

"What's the matter?" Miriam asked.

"I know your solution is a good one, but if Meir stays at the yeshiva in Troyes while I live in Ramerupt, I won't have anyone to study with." And she'd also be spending most of her nights alone in bed.

Miriam put her arm around Joheved's waist. Another loss. She and Joheved had grown up studying Torah together. "Troyes isn't that far away, surely you can spend Shabbat with us."

Miriam's feelings warred within her when Salomon suggested that the festival week would be a good time to review Tractate Pesachim.

She very much missed studying with her sisters, and if Joheved's scheme worked, this might be their last opportunity to study together. But how could she study Pesachim without thinking of Benjamin? That was the tractate they were studying when he asked to marry her.

Joheved longed to study with Miriam and their father. But Mama wouldn't want her openly learning Talmud with Meshullam and Samuel, and heaven knows what Marona and Mathilde would think.

Rachel had no such inhibitions. After the midday meal, when Salomon laid his *kuntres* on the cleared table, Rachel eagerly asked him what tractate they would be studying, smiled at his answer, and sat down next to him. Then she called to Miriam, "Come be my study partner."

Miriam quickly sat on Rachel's other side, and Joheved sighed as their mother's lips set into a tight, angry line. A moment later Rivka stalked out, muttering, "Excuse me. I need some fresh air." Marona and Francesca followed her.

Mathilde could see that her older daughter's interest was piqued, and she quickly ushered the two girls from the dining room. Columbine's plaintive, "Why can't I stay and study too? Jacob gets to," was followed by Mathilde's, "Because I said so."

In the end there were nine of them, four pairs and Salomon. Meshullam, the only one who could understand Jacob's speech, was the obvious partner for his son, and the doctor sat with Samuel. They started in the tenth and final chapter of Tractate Pesachim, with the Mishnah that began:

> On the eves of Pesach . . . even the poorest in Israel may not eat unless he reclines, and they may not give him less than four cups of wine.

Except for Jacob, they took turns reading the Gemara out loud. His eyes followed the reader, and when he wanted to ask a question, he spoke slowly to his father, who then repeated it for him. They had reached a debate in the text over when exactly during the seder one is required to recline.

Moses had just recited,

"Matzah requires reclining, but *maror* does not require reclining,"

when Jacob stopped him and asked, "Why?"

"A good question." Salomon nodded his approval. "Meir, I think you can give your nephew the answer."

"Matzah is to commemorate our freedom, so we recline like free men when we eat it." Meir tried to hide his resentment. "However, *maror* is a reminder of our slavery, so we don't recline at that time."

When Salomon asked Miriam to read the next section, she sat up straight and eagerly took the manuscript. She hadn't read Talmud in almost six months and didn't want to make a mistake in front of the others. So she began slowly,

"A woman is not required to recline in the presence of her husband."

Rachel's voice rose as she interrupted her sister. "Why should being married exempt a woman from this mitzvah?"

"Because she is subservient to her husband and therefore not free," Moses replied.

Meir admired the doctor's equanimity. If the man was surprised or disapproved of women studying Talmud, he hid it well. "The text I saw in Mayence didn't have the words, 'in the presence of her husband.' It said only,

A woman does not require reclining."

"Now all women are exempt from reclining?" Rachel's eyes were blazing. "Papa, is this so?"

"I was taught that women are exempt from reclining because they do not usually eat in this manner, not even free women." Salomon tried to mollify his daughter. "But don't be so hasty, read the next line." Which Rachel did.

"But if she is a prominent woman, she is required to recline."

"And we are all prominent women here," Miriam declared. Salomon smiled and directed her to the next paragraph.

> Rav Yehoshua ben Levi said: Women are obligated in the mitzvah of drinking the four cups, for they too were in the miracle.

Miriam saw that the following line offered no explanation for this, so she asked, "What does Rav Yehoshua mean, Papa?"

Salomon surveyed the group. "What do you think?"

Joheved replied, "The Israelites were redeemed from Egypt because of their righteous women. It says so in Tractate Sotah."

"Because all Israel, men and women, experienced the miracles that the Holy One performed in Egypt," Samuel said.

"Women are obligated to eat matzah at the seder, though they are usually exempt from positive time-bound mitzvot," Rachel said. "Therefore they should also be obligated to drink the four cups of wine. We don't need to mention a miracle."

"But Rav Yehoshua does mention it," Miriam said. "So we want to know why."

"I think what he means is that women were enslaved just as the men were, and therefore the miracles that redeemed the Israelites freed both men and women." Meir supported his father.

"Meir is correct," Salomon said, and pointed out a Baraita on the next page.

> All are obligated to drink the four cups—men, women, and even children.

"This shows us that the miracle of the Exodus was performed for every Israelite," he concluded, "which is why we all celebrate Passover together."

The next few mornings Miriam, Rachel, and Joheved picked colts-foot and daisies for Samuel's tisane, and in the afternoon they studied Talmud with their father and the other men. Miriam felt a wisp of regret when she saw Marona playing chess with Mathilde or Francesca, but she stayed with her sisters. Each morning she asked Joheved if Meir had said anything about not going back to Troyes, but her sister shook her head each time.

Passover was nearly over when Meir broached the subject.

"Joheved," he began hesitantly. "This month I've spent with my father has forced me to confront his future and mine."

"I've been thinking about that as well," she said.

"You have?" Meir stared at her.

"It's clear that Jacob can never be lord here, while Isaac, may the Holy One protect him, is perfectly healthy. And we may hope to be blessed with more sons."

"That's true," Meir said. "While my father has apparently regained his health, he is still an old man."

"Which means that it will eventually fall to our family to manage this estate." Joheved used the words "eventually" and "our family" to prepare Meir for her conclusion.

"Which means that it falls to me, now," he corrected her.

"You're not going back to the yeshiva?" She had to ask him even though she knew the answer.

"*Non.*" His voice was firm. "I must take on my obligations here. I'm sorry, but you'll have to leave Troyes too."

"I'm not sorry for me, I'm sorry for you." She reached out and took his arm to console him. "I'm content to live anywhere you live, if it's where you want to live."

He shook off her hand. "You know very well where I want to live. Don't make this worse with your pity."

"Then stay in Troyes and let the steward manage the manor," she begged him. "You can come back and check on things."

"Absolutely not." He cut her off when she tried to speak again. "I must fulfill my duty to my parents."

The next day Meir found himself alone with Samuel while putting away their tefillin after morning prayers.

"Meir," his father said. "You've been a devoted son these last months, but I think you've done your job. I'm well enough now that you can return to the yeshiva."

Meir took a deep breath. "I'm not going back to Troyes, Papa. I'm staying in Ramerupt and learning to run the estate."

"What!" Samuel's face darkened with fury. "After all I've done for you, this is how you treat me, this is the respect you give me. Marona! Marona, where are you?" He was immediately overcome with a coughing fit.

Marona and Joheved rushed in from the kitchen. Samuel pointed a shaking finger at his astonished son. "Your son, for if what he says is true, he's no son of mine, has the temerity to tell me that he's not going back to the yeshiva." He had barely gotten the words out when he began coughing again.

"Not going back to the yeshiva?" Marona gasped. "After your father and I have worked so hard . . . to send you to school . . . after all we've saved . . . and sacrificed . . . so we could have one son . . . a scholar." Her words were punctuated by sobs. "How can you be so ungrateful . . . and perverse?"

Samuel walked over and put his arm around his weeping wife. "Now look at what you've done," he accused Meir. "I want you to apologize to your mother at once, pack your things, and get ready to return to Troyes. I intend to die with a *talmid chacham* for a son, whether you like it or not."

"But Samuel." Marona wiped her eyes with her sleeve. "We can't make the boy study if he doesn't want to."

"I'm his father. If I say he studies Torah, he studies Torah."

Meir was paralyzed with shock at his parents' unexpected response, but finally he managed to speak. "I do want to study Torah, more than anything." He looked at Joheved. "But who's going to manage this manor if I don't learn to do it?"

"I'm not in the grave yet, and even if I were, your mother is a competent administrator." Samuel still sounded angry.

"Papa, be reasonable," Meir said. "You and Mama won't live forever. How will I support my family then?"

"Your mother and I will work out something. Your job is to study Torah and become a great scholar."

Joheved watched with amazement. She had never known how important Meir's being a scholar was to his parents, and apparently Meir hadn't known either. Now was the time to present her sister's solution.

"Miriam says that noble ladies administer their husbands' estates all the time," she said. "Could I learn how to do it?"

Marona looked at her with respect. "Of course you could, you're an intelligent girl." Marona gave her husband a hopeful smile. "Then Meir could study in Troyes while Joheved and the children lived here with us."

Samuel and Marona couldn't miss the stricken look that the young couple exchanged at this suggestion. Samuel's eyes were twinkling as he said, "Just because Meir studies in Troyes doesn't mean he has to live there. Look at the doctor. During Passover he stayed with us and still visited his patients in Troyes every day."

"I suppose it's not too far to ride," Meir said slowly. In just a few moments, his world had been turned over and righted again in a different spot.

"But Meir doesn't need to start riding so much yet." Marona was already being practical. "Let them both stay in Troyes and Joheved can ride out here a few times a week."

Meir stood up and faced his father. "I can't let Joheved shoulder my obligations. I must have some part in running this place if I am to be the lord here."

"All right, stubborn one." Samuel thought for a moment. "You can oversee the wheat harvest and the manorial court."

"And when the lamb buyers come in the spring," Meir added.

"Very well," Samuel said. "But when Salomon's family leaves, you're going with them."

Joheved let out her breath in a sigh of satisfaction. Miriam would be so happy to hear that they'd be returning to Troyes together.

seven

Mayence
Spring 4839 (1079 CE)

udah tried to dry his eyes, but his sleeve was soaking wet from the rain. *What is wrong with me?* This was the second time he'd cried in two months. As unpleasant as seders in Paris had been the last few years, Passover at Shmuli's family's was worse. Different food, different songs—everything that night conspired to make him cry with homesickness.

But he wasn't welcome at home anymore. Even his brother had apparently abandoned him. Judah gazed down at the turbulent river and, feeling utterly alone, leaned forward into the wind. Nobody would miss him if he were gone.

"Careful there," a familiar voice called out as a firm hand took hold of his arm. "The Rhine's strength and beauty are magnificent, but it's too slippery here at the edge."

"I saw you at services this morning," Reuben continued. "You were looking pretty glum and so I followed you."

Dazed, Judah allowed Reuben to lead him to Josef's Grotto, where the older man gently removed Judah's sodden cloak and hung it near the fire. Then he propelled Judah upstairs and into a room. Putting up no resistance, Judah sat on the bed, silent and trembling, as Reuben stripped him of his tunic, hose, and boots.

"I'll take these wet clothes downstairs to dry." Reuben rummaged around in his trunk, pulled out some garments, and tossed them to the stunned young man. "Come down as soon as you're dressed; I'll order you some nice hot soup."

Judah could barely dress himself, he was shaking so hard. Moments before he had been completely vulnerable, naked except for his chemise, on Reuben's bed. The next thing he knew, Reuben was sounding like his mother, upset at him coming home in wet clothes and worried about him catching cold. Sure enough, when Judah arrived at Reuben's table, his rescuer was clucking about how Judah's soup better be hearty enough and not just broth.

When he saw that Judah hadn't touched his bowl, Reuben leaned over and said softly, "Fasting won't weaken your *yetzer hara*. It will just make you light-headed and unable to study." He sadly surveyed the disheveled young man who could have been himself a decade ago. "Believe me, I should know."

Judah studied Reuben's concerned expression, then picked up a piece of bread and began eating the soup. It was delicious.

"They say the greater the man, the more powerful his *yetzer hara*. But that's no consolation if yours is too powerful to control." Reuben signaled to the serving girl, and she left the tureen on their table.

Judah grabbed Reuben's arm. "But how can I fight my *yetzer hara*? Tell me what to do!"

Reuben thought about his own youthful days, when he had first met Natan. His *yetzer* had been so powerful then—could anything have controlled it? "Where do you live? I mean where is your home town?"

"Paris. Why do you want to know?"

"I thought it might be someplace far away." He shook his head slowly. "The best thing for a young man like you is to study at a yeshiva close to home so you can live with your wife. Use your *yetzer hara* to father sons."

Judah, ashamed to admit that he didn't have a wife, nodded and returned to his soup.

Reuben hoped Judah would take his advice before it was too late, though it hadn't kept him from sinning. Relations with his wife was like eating warm stirabout on a cold morning—nice, wholesome, and bland. Unfortunately Natan's bed was a zesty stew in comparison, heavily spiced with garlic, saffron, and pepper. No matter how great his desire to repent each Yom Kippur, to be content with a diet of stirabout, Reuben's *yetzer hara* would not let him forget that there were more savory alternatives.

But Judah hadn't been with a man yet, hadn't started playing the game. Reuben began speaking about the reward of bedding women—his two young sons, how clever and adorable they were, how much he missed them when he was away on business. They talked until someone called out that it wasn't raining any more.

Judah suddenly noticed the setting sun. "Look how late it is. I promised Shmuli I'd help him with his lessons."

"Your clothes are dry." Reuben gathered Judah's garments and handed them to him. "I'll wait here while you change."

When Judah returned, Reuben walked him to the door and wished him good luck. Judah mumbled his thanks and began the muddy walk home. The sun was low on the horizon, and he marveled at the most glorious sunset he'd seen in a long time. Reuben had just saved his life; perhaps his advice would save him from sin.

But Judah had no wife, and his prospects of acquiring one were growing dimmer with every passing day. He sighed. Just when having his own family looked so attractive. The sun disappeared in a blaze of molten gold and Judah's spirits sank as well.

He arrived at the silversmith's in no mood for company. He told Shmuli he needed to rest and nobody should disturb him. He had just begun to doze when he heard Shmuli calling for him.

"Go away," he grumbled. "I told you to leave me alone."

Shmuli opened the door to make sure that Judah heard him. He was grinning with excitement. "Wake up. Your brother's here!"

Judah threw on his chemise and was struggling to pull up his hose when the bedroom door flew open.

His brother, Azariel, stood before him. "What are you doing in bed in the middle of the day? Are you ill?"

"Just a little tired."

Azariel surveyed his brother's thin frame. "You don't look well. You've lost weight."

"I've been fasting and staying up late studying," Judah said. "In hopes that the Merciful One would notice my piety and make your quest successful."

"Whatever you did, it worked." Azariel triumphantly clasped Judah around the shoulders. "I've found her."

Judah hugged his brother tightly. "Are you sure?"

Azariel nodded vigorously. "She's your *bashert*, all right. She's everything you wanted and more."

"I can't believe you're here. I'd nearly given up hope." Judah could feel the tears forming. "Tell me everything."

"Please tell him at the table," Shmuli said. "I want to hear everything too, but I'm hungry."

Azariel sniffed the air, redolent with the smells of home cooking. "Now that you mention it, I'm famished." He propelled Judah down the stairs. "Come. We'll have my tale over supper."

"Good." Shmuli grinned. "Grandmama will want to hear all about it."

Shmuli's grandparents, Yosef and Hilda, were already at the table. They waited patiently as Azariel satisfied his initial hunger with a bowl of stew and several pieces of bread.

"My first thought in searching for Judah's bride was that, as long as I was already in Mayence, I might as well look in Allemagne." Azariel paused until Yosef finished slicing everyone some braised beef. "I surveyed Mayence, Worms, Cologne, every other city with a decent number of Jews. Reasoning that I would be more likely to find a learned woman where there were learned men, I made a special effort in the yeshiva towns, but to no avail."

He helped himself to more stew. "So I decided that, since my goal was so elusive, I might as well be comfortable. I spent part of the winter in sunny Provence and the rest in Sepharad."

"Is it true that it never snows in Sepharad?" Hilda asked.

"It snows sometimes, but never as much as it does here," Azariel replied.

"Enough with the weather," Yosef said. "What happened in Sepharad?"

"I had no difficulty finding learned women," Azariel continued with a sigh. "But they were inevitably married, to rabbis. Undaunted, I returned to Paris for Passover."

Judah groaned. "Where I suppose you enlightened my mother and Uncle Shimson. As if I weren't low enough in their opinion."

"On the contrary, Alvina was thrilled," Azariel said.

Shmuli elbowed Judah. "Stop interrupting. We must be just about at the good part."

Azariel nodded, picked up his wine cup, and took a long drink. "From Paris, I headed north." He turned to Hilda and winked. "They say the spring flowers are especially beautiful in Flanders."

"You Frenchmen," she said with a blushing smile. "Go on with your story."

"I was staying in a small inn at the French-Flemish border, not expecting anything, but I told the story of my search anyway. Their reaction started out the same as everyplace else I had been." He turned to his brother and shrugged.

"Pardon me, Judah, but first they said you were crazy for wanting to marry such a woman, and then that I was crazy for wasting so much time looking for one." Azariel rolled his eyes at the insults he had suffered. "Finally they got around to deciding that my search was doomed, that no father would let his daughters study enough Talmud to know Hillel from Shammai, let alone who Ben Azzai was."

Azariel was grinning now. "I doubt most of those men knew who Ben Azzai was anyway. Then, to my surprise, a man sitting quietly by the fire interrupted them and said, 'Young women like that do exist, and I know because I just spent a week at Passover studying Gemara with three of them, daughters of a local rabbi. My brother is married to the eldest.'

"You could have knocked me over with a feather," Azariel said. "The fellow's name was Meshullam ben Samuel, and he told me that one of his sisters-in-law was a recent widow, and as far as he knew, not yet betrothed again. She'd been staying with his parents in Ramerupt-sur-Aube, and he suggested that, if I rode hard, I could reach their manor before the Sabbath."

Azariel pleasurably took in the rapt expressions of those sitting around the table. "I couldn't have ridden faster if Ashmodai, King of the Demons himself, was behind me, and may the Holy One forgive me, I reached Samuel's estate just after sunset." He turned to his hostess and asked for more beef. "This meat is delicious. Be sure and give my brother another piece."

Hilda immediately handed him the carving board. "And was she there?"

"Alas no, she had already left with her family. But I spent a delightful Shabbat with Meshullam's parents, who confirmed his information and couldn't say enough wonderful things about her."

So far Judah had eaten his food as in a trance, afraid that if he said anything he might wake up and find himself back upstairs alone in bed. Now he looked up and asked, "So who is she? Who is her father?"

"Her name is Miriam, and she's the middle daughter of Salomon ben Isaac, the rosh yeshiva of Troyes," Azariel said. "He has no sons, which is probably why his daughters are so educated."

Yosef slapped his thigh. "That explains it. A rosh yeshiva could teach his daughters Talmud and nobody would dare to criticize him."

"Miriam is around seventeen years old, a childless widow, and though she performed *halitzah* last fall after Sukkot, she has refused to consider another match." Azariel leaned back in his chair and crossed his arms.

The room was warm, but the hairs on Judah's arms stood up and he shivered. "She was performing *halitzah* at almost the same time I was challenging you to find her . . ." His voice trailed off.

Hilda's eyes widened. "She must truly be your *bashert*, Judah, the one fated for you."

"That's why you didn't want any of those other women," Shmuli said, smiling with excitement.

It is written in Tractate Sotah:

> On the night of a boy's conception a Heavenly voice proclaims,
> "He shall marry the daughter of 'A.'"

Yosef and Hilda sought out each other's gaze. While it was tacitly understood that all matches are decreed on high, with each soul descending to the world already linked with another, few were blessed to see the Creator's hand at work.

Even Azariel was not immune from the sense of being part of a larger plan. "So the following day I rode to Troyes, attended services, and stayed to study. I introduced myself to Salomon, a modest and kindly man, a good teacher. He invited me to dine with them, while warning me that he had promised Miriam that she could wait until summer before choosing a new husband."

Azariel grinned at Judah. "But then he smiled and told me that nothing would make him happier than to see his daughter wed as soon as possible, and even more so if her husband was a yeshiva student."

Without taking his eyes off his brother, Judah began eating another slice of beef.

"Walking into their courtyard, I knew I needed to make the biggest sale of my career," Azariel said. "But I felt confident. After all, I had excellent merchandise."

As a servant brought out dessert, stewed fruit and *grimseli*, strips of dough baked in honey, Azariel silently recalled the meal he'd shared with Miriam's family. Surrounded by students debating and asking questions about the morning's lesson, it had been a lively meal. He'd expected Salomon's daughters to join in, but it was still odd to hear women's voices discussing Torah in such a scholarly fashion. Through it all, Azariel felt himself being watched, wondered about.

He, in turn, surreptitiously inspected his host's three daughters. The youngest was an exquisite child, but she was too young. The eldest, with a squirming toddler in her lap, was obviously married to the fellow who was staring at Azariel with undisguised curiosity. That left the middle daughter, the object of his search.

"Her father merely introduced me as a stranger he'd met at services, leaving me to tell my tale over *disner*." Azariel dipped his second *grimseli* into a dish of preserves. "I had just begun when the older daughter's husband interrupted me and said, 'I've got it. You're Judah ben Natan's brother. I studied with him my last year in Worms. No wonder you look familiar.'"

Meir ben Samuel—it had to be him. Judah said the name aloud. "An excellent student and a pious one too."

"You're right." Azariel nodded, impressed with Judah's memory. "He said almost the exact same thing about you. I added that you didn't gamble, didn't drink excessively, and rarely lost your temper. When Meir's wife insisted that you must have some vice, I admitted that you were stubborn as a mule, which is why you were still unmarried at age nineteen."

"Never mind who said what," Shmuli said. "What did Miriam look like?"

"My brother once told me he didn't like plump women." Azariel chuckled. "Well, he won't have that problem with this one. She's almost as skinny as he is. She's neither a great beauty nor hideously ugly; her hair is a nondescript shade of light brown, she has a high forehead, grey eyes, a decent-looking nose, a wide mouth, and small chin. There— did I leave anything out?" He thought for a moment and then added, "She did have a pleasant voice."

Judah gulped. "What did she say? Did she ask any questions about me?"

"She didn't ask any questions. She listened attentively, which I considered a good sign. When I got to the part about you wanting a wife who was familiar with Ben Azzai, she smiled and said, 'Ben Azzai, how interesting. In the third Mishnah of Tractate Sotah, he states that a man is obligated to teach his daughter Torah so its merit will protect her, while Rav Eliezer disagrees and says that anyone who teaches his daughter Torah teaches her lewdness.'" Azariel paused at the memory. "I must admit that when she smiled, she was rather attractive."

"That's all she said?" Judah frowned. She hadn't asked what he looked like or how he intended to support her?

"She did say one more thing." Azariel grinned at his audience. "When her father asked her what she thought, she answered that she thought she would be interested in meeting a man who admired Ben Azzai so highly."

Judah pondered Miriam's response. Not that he disagreed with Ben Azzai's opinion on educating women, but he felt guilty for gaining Miriam's approval under false circumstances. But perhaps it was fate that caused them to both admire the same sage, albeit for different reasons.

Azariel's expression became serious. "Now, Judah, I am concerned about your appearance. You look like a peasant. Your clothes are covered with mud, and when was the last time you trimmed your beard?"

"What beard?" Judah had barely spoken when his brother reached over and tugged playfully on the tufts of hair growing from his chin.

Judah stroked the unfamiliar growth. "I had no idea."

Azariel started laughing. "Quick, get my brother a mirror."

Yosef rummaged through his workroom and came back with a large silver mirror. Judah took in his gaunt features and the dark circles under his eyes, but he could scarcely believe the scraggly beard sprouting on his cheeks and chin. "Tomorrow, without fail, I'll find a barber."

"You can wait and get barbered in Troyes," Azariel told him. "We're leaving at first light."

"But you just got here," Hilda objected.

"It's already taken me longer to get here than I expected," Azariel said. "We've got to get to Troyes before merchants start arriving for their Hot Fair, before one of them betroths your *bashert* first. Miriam said she wanted to meet you, but she didn't say she'd wait for you. We're leaving at dawn."

Judah jumped up. "I can't leave without saying good-bye to Rabbenu Isaac." Whether Miriam agreed to marry him or not, this would be his last night in Mayence.

"Well, don't take too long about it," Azariel said.

Judah raced to the yeshiva and heaved a sigh of relief to see a light in the rosh yeshiva's study window. A quiet knock on his teacher's door brought the old man himself to answer it.

"Judah, what brings you here at this hour?"

"I've come to say good-bye, Master. I'm leaving Mayence tomorrow morning."

Isaac's brow wrinkled in concern. "Judah, perhaps I was overzealous when I threatened you with *herem*."

"I'm not going because of the *herem*," Judah said. "My brother has returned and we have to leave immediately for Troyes so I can meet my *bashert.*" He smiled. "So I suppose, in a way, that I am leaving because of the *herem*. Thank you."

"Your *bashert* is in Troyes?"

"*Oui*. Her father is their rosh yeshiva, and my brother assures me that she knows Hillel, Shammai, and Ben Azzai."

"But Salomon's older daughters are already married. And Rachel can't be of marriageable age."

"The middle daughter was widowed last fall, Master." *My teacher knows these girls?*

"You're going to marry Miriam?"

"So far she's only agreed to meet me, but I'm sure my brother can negotiate a betrothal agreement." Judah squinted at Isaac. "But how do you know her?"

"Miriam is my niece. Her mother, Rivka, is my sister."

"Then I shall be your nephew!" Judah embraced his teacher and bounded for the door. "Everything turned out for the best."

"Wait," the rosh yeshiva called after him. "Let me write a few lines to my brother-in-law before you go."

As Isaac busied himself with quill and ink, Judah began looking forward to studying at a French yeshiva. That's why there were so few Frenchmen who studied here; the others must be going to Troyes now. And the fewer there were, the more the Germans felt safe in insulting them. But nobody would harass him in Troyes, not married to the rosh yeshiva's daughter.

The more Judah thought about it, the more he knew that Miriam was the one he'd been waiting for. He remembered the saying in Bereshit Rabbah, the Midrash on Genesis:

> Sometimes a man goes after his match and sometimes it comes to
> him. In the patriarch Isaac's case, Rivka came to him, as it is written:
> "Isaac went out to meditate . . . and he lifted his eyes, and behold,
> there were camels coming (with Rivka)." But our patriarch Jacob
> went after his match thus: "Jacob left Beersheva and went towards
> Haran (where Rachel lived)."

Therefore some men find an effortless match, like Isaac, who looked up to find his bride standing in front of him. But from others, and Judah knew he must be one of these, the Creator demands great effort, perhaps even suffering, before attaining the match prepared for him in Heaven. Jacob was exiled from his home and had to work years for his beloved Rachel.

Judah took his teacher's letter and hurried through the courtyard gate. Once he was married to Miriam he would no longer suffer sinful thoughts or be tempted by the likes of Natan. His *bashert* would save him.

Leaving Mayence, Judah and Azariel joined the springtime throng of merchants heading west to the province of Champagne. Judah gaped at the large number of people who apparently shared his destination, and whenever he saw a young man, he couldn't help but imagine a potential rival.

In Troyes, the last thing Miriam wanted to think about was Judah or his potential rivals. But Rachel, sure that Judah was the hero who would dry Miriam's tears, filled her ears with talk of *amour*. Every day Rachel asked Papa how long until Judah arrived.

"I don't know, *ma fille*," was his constant reply. "Azariel can't possibly get to Mayence and back in less than a month."

Miriam had a different question for him. "Papa, Judah ben Natan can't be my *bashert*. For how could Benjamin have wanted to marry me so much if he wasn't the right one?" *And how could I have wanted to marry him so much as well?*

Salomon turned to her and sighed. "In Tractate Moed Katan, we learn that a man may betroth a woman on the Ninth of Av, even on such a black fast day mourning for Jerusalem's destruction, lest another man precede him. Yet how can that be, the Gemara asks, if a couple is paired even in their mothers' wombs?"

He put his arm around her shoulders. "The answer is that, although a man is fated from Heaven to marry a certain woman, if another man prays for her fervently, the Holy One may listen to him." He continued sadly, "Even so, the original decree will ultimately be fulfilled. The man who prayed will die and her intended partner will then marry her. Perhaps the Merciful One took pity on Benjamin and allowed him to die rather than see you married to somebody else."

Tears rolled down her cheeks as Miriam remembered how happy Benjamin had been in his last days. Had the Holy One really answered Benjamin's prayer and let him die thinking that she would be his? But if so, what about her suffering? And why hadn't she died so that Benjamin could marry his *bashert*?

Salomon gave her a hug. "If the Holy One intended you for Judah, then somehow you will know."

Over the next few weeks, each time she thought of Benjamin, Miriam reminded herself of her father's words. Snatches of verses from Psalms tumbled through her thoughts.

> You are my God, my fate is in Your hand . . . Let me not be disappointed when I call You. Adonai, I set my hope on You; my God, in You I trust . . . Whoever has awe of Adonai shall be shown what path to choose. He shall live a happy life and his children shall inherit the land.

Would He indeed show her the path to choose? And would she recognize it? *Oui*—if the Holy One's path to a happy life and children were before her, she would see it.

Trusting in the future was more difficult when Miriam performed the springtime vineyard chores. Some of her best memories were of working with Benjamin, training the new shoots and trimming the canopy of leaves to achieve the best exposure of the grape bunches to sunlight, spending hours discussing the angles at which the various branches should be made to grow. It was as if they had been planning their future. Thank Heaven she'd be banished from the vineyard with everyone else when the grapevines flowered, and thus spared the memories the blossoms' scent would evoke.

Fortunately she was soon so occupied with midwifery that she had little time for reminiscing. Many merchants in Troyes traveled during the six months between the Cold and Hot fairs, and it seemed as if last summer each one had returned from his journey and almost immediately impregnated his wife.

"I've never seen so many babies born in the spring," Sarah complained as they walked home after their third birth that week. "I'm exhausted."

"I think I can handle the night births now," Miriam said. "I'll be sure to call for you if I need help." After spending the winter as midwife to hundreds of sheep, most pregnant with twins, assisting one woman, in labor with one child, was no longer an ordeal.

"All right. You can go out at night by yourself until the wedding." Sarah smiled and gave her a knowing look. "Then I'll take over so you can stay home at night with your new husband."

My new husband. Miriam gathered her courage. "What was it like to marry again so soon after your first husband died?"

Sarah stopped in her tracks, causing several nearby peddlers to approach and offer her their wares. Waving them off, she took Miriam's arm and pulled her close. "My marriage to Eleazar wasn't a love match like yours, but what little time we had together was pleasant enough. However, we were only married a month before he left for Constantinople. On the way home, his caravan was attacked by bandits and he was killed."

"How terrible for you."

Sarah paused. "Honestly, he had been gone so long I'd almost forgotten I was married."

"So you didn't grieve for him?"

"I was shocked when the news came, of course, and sad for his death, but his brother certainly grieved more than I did."

"You must have liked Eleazar's brother well enough," Miriam said. "Otherwise you could have asked for *halitzah*."

Sarah sighed. "It wasn't as simple as that. Eleazar's family didn't want to lose his *ketubah*, and most folks thought it wasn't fair for me to inherit all that property after such a short marriage. I didn't want trouble, so three months after Eleazar's death, I married his little brother, Levi."

"Was it difficult marrying someone who would always remind you of your first husband?"

Sarah shook her head. "Levi was fifteen years old, still a yeshiva student. Instead of a husband with a beard, I had one with pimples."

Miriam wanted to hear more about that second marriage, but when they arrived at the courtyard gate, Aunt Sarah said, "I'm tired. Maybe we can talk again after I take a nap."

Aunt Sarah was clearly not eager to discuss that second marriage. But as Joheved pointed out, Miriam had a choice. If Judah didn't appeal to her, she would wait and see if someone else at the Hot Fair did. She thought back to the babies she helped deliver recently, the yearning she felt as she washed, salted, and swaddled them. And the sense of loss when she handed them back to their mothers. How long would she have to wait for the day when the baby born would be hers?

Meir was also thinking about procreation, about the way Judah had debated him on the subject. Admittedly it had been over six years ago, and there is a great deal of difference between a thirteen-year-old boy and a man nearing twenty, but Judah was obviously still a great admirer of Ben Azzai, and Meir doubted it was because he approved of learned women. Several times Meir approached Salomon to discuss his concern about Judah, only to hesitate and allow another student to speak.

One morning Meir was helping little Isaac stack colored wooden blocks in the salon when Salomon sat down beside them.

"Can three people play?"

"Of course." Meir pushed some blocks toward Salomon.

Salomon picked up a yellow one and paused, as if deciding where to place it. "Meir, it seems that you have something on your mind."

"Judah ben Natan was in Worms at the same time as I was . . ." Meir's conscience told him to share his misgivings with Salomon, yet it seemed wrong to prejudice Miriam's family on the basis of a brief conversation so long ago.

Salomon slowly put his block on top of the pile. "And?"

"Rabbenu." Meir's voice held a warning. "Keep in mind that Judah was a boy when I knew him."

"I understand." Salomon congratulated himself on his perception.

Meir had been apprehensive. "Was Judah interested in Ben Azzai when you knew him?"

"*Oui*. He admired Ben Azzai very much."

Salomon stroked his beard. "I'd rather Miriam not wed a devotee of the hidden Torah." Ben Azzai, a mystic, died trying to understand the mysteries of the Torah. "It can be dangerous to study such things, and she's already been widowed once."

"Judah ben Natan was not interested in the arcane." Meir's tone was adamant. "I believe that he wanted to model himself after Ben Azzai's devotion to Torah over all else." Meir emphasized the words "all else."

Salomon frowned. "Do you mean that Judah shared Ben Azzai's view that devotion to Torah should be a man's only passion?"

Isaac added a red block to the pile, and Meir reached out to steady them. "When I became betrothed, Judah and I had a discussion, a debate actually, about marriage and procreation. For every text I quoted that praised them, he quoted one that disparaged them."

"Maybe he was arguing for Torah's sake?"

"I don't think so," Meir said. "Judah seemed dismissive of women, or maybe he was afraid of them. His final text was Ben Azzai's explanation of why he wouldn't procreate.

What can I do, my soul yearns for Torah. The world can increase through others."

Salomon shook his head. "There are many faults I can overlook in a Torah scholar, but I cannot allow my daughter to marry a man who believes his passion for Torah excuses him from fathering children."

With a scream of glee, Isaac chortled as his tower of blocks collapsed.

"But that was six years ago," Meir said, gathering up the fallen blocks. "A boy may think he'll be able to control his *yetzer hara,* while a man knows better."

"We shall see." Salomon sat stroking his beard, lost in thought while Meir and Isaac began building another tower.

—◠◠◠—

A month later the Mai Faire de Provins opened, filling both the Old Synagogue and the New Synagogue with an influx of merchants on Shabbat. While Miriam busied herself with delivering babies, Rachel scrutinized every stranger who bore even a superficial resemblance to Azariel ben Natan, but to no avail. She was frustrated that she could only attend the Old Synagogue, where her family prayed, rather than the New Synagogue, where most of the foreign merchants went.

It was also frustrating that Miriam was completely uninterested in her reports. "If I hear one more word about this fellow, I will scream," she warned Rachel. "We will hear from him when he arrives. That is, if he arrives."

The family had just sat down to *souper* when an attendant from the bathhouse delivered two letters. One was from Azariel, stating that he and Judah had arrived and were washing away the road's grime; the other was Uncle Isaac's, introducing his star pupil.

Upon hearing this news, Miriam lost her appetite so quickly that it was an effort to swallow the food in her mouth. Joheved took hold of her sister's hand and squeezed it reassuringly, while Rachel, after helping herself to Miriam's untouched dessert, begged to carry back the reply inviting the two men to *disner* the next day.

"Absolutely not!" Miriam nearly shouted. "Judah mustn't think I'm so eager to see him that I sent my sister as a spy."

The bathhouse attendant left with Salomon's invitation and soon returned with Azariel's response, suggesting that Salomon and Meir join them at services at the New Synagogue, so they could study together first.

Rachel smiled up at her father. "Papa, may I go to services with you and Meir? I won't bother you. I'll just sit and pray with the women, and come right home afterward."

"We'll see." Salomon stroked his beard for a while and then sent the messenger off with another invitation, this one to Isaac haParnas's family.

Rivka knew her husband hadn't invited the head of the Jewish community solely out of friendship. "Do you really think we'll start negotiations tomorrow?"

"It's possible. The moon will be waxing for a few more days, so the timing is auspicious," he replied. "In any case, he has contacts in Paris who may know Judah's family."

"What does Uncle Isaac say about Judah?" Joheved asked as Salomon scanned the letter from Mayence.

"Congratulations on the impending match—Judah is an excellent student, diligent and pious, and so on." Salomon shook his head. "If Judah has any shortcomings, his rosh yeshiva isn't about to tell me about them."

Miriam barely heard a word the others said. Her throat was too constricted to eat, and she concentrated on tearing her bread into small pieces. Until today Judah ben Natan had been merely a figment of her family's imagination. Now he was in Troyes, and tomorrow Isaac haParnas was invited to *disner*, just in case.

She sat up straight and surveyed her excited family. They might be planning a betrothal, but she wasn't—not yet. She didn't care if everyone in Troyes thought Judah was her *bashert*. She wasn't going to marry him unless she thought so too.

eight

That next morning Miriam could barely restrain her irritation as her mother and sisters chose what foods to serve. She didn't care what was on the menu; the finest dishes would taste like matzah.

"We'll begin with fish, followed by meat pies," Rivka said confidently. "Anna and I will see what looks best among the peddlers' offerings on Rue de l'Épicerie."

"You can stop in at the New Synagogue and see what looks best there, too," Rachel teased. Rue de l'Épicerie, the street of the grocers, was only one block from where Judah and his brother would be attending services.

Rivka ladled more of the stirabout from its pot in the hearth into serving bowls on the table. "I might just do that," she said. "If only to make sure that you are behaving yourself."

Joheved took a small spoonful of stirabout, blew on it, and fed it to Isaac. "Do you think we can have capon as well as chicken?" Capon was Meir's favorite, but traditionally chicken was served at a festive meal.

"I'll buy some of each," Rivka said. Heaven forbid she should present a less than ample table.

Of course there would also be stews and soups, egg pancakes, pickled vegetables, and fruit preserves.

"I'll have Claire bake an apple flummery. It's one of Miriam's favorites." Rivka sighed as she observed Miriam sitting there as if made of stone.

The menu settled, attention turned to her daughter's clothes.

107

"Miriam's pretty skinny. I bet she'd fit into the blue silk outfit that Johanna gave us. It's so beautiful." Rachel's voice was wistful. She would love to wear Isaac haParnas's wife's *bliaut* herself, but she was already too big for it.

Miriam had to say something; she would be wearing whatever they decided. "It's only a weekday. If I wear something that fancy, every woman at services will be suspicious." Besides, she didn't want to wear Joheved's betrothal clothes.

"Then wear your Shabbat wool," Joheved said.

Rivka surveyed Miriam from head to toe. "What about that gold silk *bliaut* that you wore at Pesach?"

"Please Mama, that's too elegant to wear, even on the Sabbath." Miriam twisted the tablecloth in her hands. Wearing that outfit would be tantamount to accepting Judah's offer.

"Don't you want Judah to see you looking your best?" Rachel asked. "Or do you want to test his devotion by meeting him in your old clothes?"

"Enough," Rivka said. "Miriam can wear whatever she likes to services and then change into the gold silk when she gets home." At the other end of the table, Salomon's students were hurrying to finish eating before he began the Grace After Meals.

Miriam closed her eyes, nodded, and joined the others in thanking the Holy One for the food they had just eaten. Let Mama dictate her dress. She would save her strength for fighting the match itself, if necessary.

At the inn where Judah and Azariel were staying, the two brothers were having a similar discussion. As far as Judah was concerned, his attractiveness was a burden, and he had no desire to draw attention to it. Then the barber did such an excellent job that Judah almost hadn't recognized himself in the mirror. Insisting that it would be a crime to disguise such a handsome jaw, the barber had removed the sparse tufts on Judah's cheeks and trimmed his beard so that it merely outlined his face. Then he'd tied Judah's hair behind like a horse's tail, further emphasizing his client's facial beauty.

Now Azariel wanted him to wear a red tunic.

"I hate wearing red," Judah grimaced. Alvina had made him wear it since childhood. "I'll never understand how such a conspicuous color can protect me from the Evil Eye."

"You could wear your purple silk *bliaut* over this blue chemise." Azariel rummaged around and produced a red ribbon. "At least tie your hair back with this. For your mother's sake."

He also made Judah eat a hearty breakfast. "I don't want your stomach growling during services, or worse, while you're being introduced to your *bashert* and her family."

They arrived at synagogue early and sat in the back. Judah expected that Salomon and his students, having already prayed at home, would show up later, and sure enough the large group shuffled in as he finished saying the morning blessings. He recognized Meir ben Samuel immediately; the young man had put on some weight but was otherwise unchanged.

Displaying more confidence than he felt, Judah strode forward to greet his old colleague. "Shalom aleichem, Meir. It's good to see you again. You're looking well."

"Judah, look how you've grown." Meir's gaze locked onto Judah's before reciting the blessing Jews make when seeing someone again after a lengthy absence. "*Baruch ata Adonai* . . . Who resurrects the dead."

The yeshiva students crowded around in curiosity, and Meir remembered his manners. He could see Rachel peeking over the balcony and said loudly, "Rabbenu Salomon ben Isaac, I'd like you to meet Judah ben Natan."

"What are you studying?" Judah asked Meir. "I hope it's something I'm familiar with."

"We're in the sixth chapter of Tractate Yevamot," Meir said nonchalantly. "I'm sure you're familiar with it."

Judah gulped hard and sat down. Obviously Meir had told Salomon about their final debate. One of the students, Judah thought his name was Eliezer, began chanting from the chapter's final Mishnah. They were only pages away from where Ben Azzai reveals that his great passion for

Torah prevents him from procreating. The text was burned in Judah's mind.

First Ben Azzai stated,

"Anyone who does not engage in procreation is a murderer,"

having arrived at this conclusion because in Genesis the verse "Be fruitful and multiply," is preceded by, "One who sheds a man's blood, by man shall his blood be shed." Then Rav Elazar, accusing Ben Azzai of hypocrisy, replied,

"Words are good when accompanied by practice. You interpret well, but you do not act well." And Ben Azzai said, "What shall I do? My soul desires Torah. The world can increase by the efforts of others."

Judah's gut tightened and, at the same time, his respect for Salomon rose as he recognized how the *talmid chacham* intended to test him. Eliezer was almost finished reciting the Mishnah.

"A man may not avoid procreation unless he has children. Shammai says two male children, and Hillel says a male and a female, as it is written—'Male and female He created them.'"

Salomon continued by quoting the Gemara,

"Shammai says: two males. What is the reason? They derive it from Moses, for it is written: The sons of Moses, Gershon and Eliezer."

Then he asked, "Who can explain this?"

Judah took a deep breath. Salomon wasn't looking in his direction, but the question was clearly directed at him. This was the battlefield on which he would win his *bashert*. He sat up straight and answered, "We know that after fathering only these two sons, Moses separated from his wife to remain pure whenever the Holy One wished to speak with him."

All eyes were upon him but none of the students looked confused, so Judah followed with more Gemara:

> "And Hillel (who requires both a son and a daughter)? They derive
> it from the creation of the world."

And explained this as well. "Because in the beginning, the Creator made exactly one male and one female." Judah's anxiety lessened as he took in all the heads nodding in agreement.

But then the room began filling with men from the Old Synagogue who usually stayed to study with Salomon and his students. They scrutinized the young scholar, and Judah spoke louder as he quoted the Gemara's next question.

> "And Shammai—why do they not agree with Hillel and derive
> from creation? Because we cannot derive the possible from what is
> impossible."

Sitting next to Shemayah, Meir could feel his study partner preparing to explain the Talmud's cryptic answer. He put a hand on Shemayah's arm. "Let's leave the stage to Judah."

Meir gave a sigh of relief as Shemayah relaxed back into his seat and whispered, "Very well. I am curious how he'll explain this section."

As Judah expected, his audience stared at him with puzzled expressions, so he continued, "Shammai disagrees with Hillel about deriving from creation because we cannot derive a case where alternatives exist from one where no alternative exists."

"Stand up," Meir called out, "so we can all hear you." Meir intended for everyone to see that Judah needed no book, that he was reciting completely from memory.

His chest tight and his heart pounding, Judah stood and addressed the larger group. "At creation, the Holy One had no choice but to create

Eve. How could humanity continue without one male and one female? But that is not the case now; if a man has two sons, there are many women they might marry."

No questions came, and Salomon's expression was inscrutable as he waved his hand for Judah to continue.

"And Hillel—why do they reject Shammai and not derive from Moses?"

Judah explained, "Hillel would say that Moses's situation was unique, that the prophet abstained from procreation because of his special relationship with the Holy One, not because he had fulfilled the mitzvah."

Judah smiled and added, "But we're not done with Shammai and Hillel." He must be doing well; nearly every face was smiling back at him. But not Salomon's.

"It is taught in a Baraita: Shammai says that two males and two females are required, but Hillel says a male and a female only. Rav Huna asks: What is the reason for this statement of Shammai?"

Judah paused to let his audience ponder Rav Huna's question. "Obviously we have two versions of Shammai's argument. We already know how Hillel proves his view, and here is the proof for Shammai's alternative statement, which also derives from creation.

After Eve gives birth to Cain, it is written: 'And she gave birth to his brother *et* Abel.'

The superfluous Hebrew word *et* refers to a twin sister. Thus Eve actually had two boys and two girls, Abel and his sister, plus Cain and his sister."

Judah could see the men grinning as they whispered to each other. How different it was from Mayence, where his words were often received with resentment. He had forgotten how good it felt to expound Torah in a yeshiva that appreciated him. Now if only Salomon would give some sign of approval. *What is the scholar waiting for?*

"But can't we object again that the situation at creation was unique, that today two males and two females are more than adequate?" an older man questioned Judah.

"Certainly," Judah replied, honored that the man had questioned him and not Salomon. "Yet we have still another Baraita, this one with a different version of Hillel's argument." He proceeded to recite it:

> "Shammai says one male and one female, but Hillel says either a male or a female. Rava asked: What is Hillel's reason? Because, as it is written: He did not create the world to be empty, He formed it for habitation."

Judah bowed slightly to the man who'd questioned him. "So according to this view, even a single child contributes to the world's habitation."

He turned to Salomon and met his pensive gaze. "However I must disagree with both Shammai and Hillel. I believe that a scholar should never consider himself as having fulfilled this mitzvah. He should father as many children as possible, for who knows what *talmid chacham* might issue from his wife's womb next?" This was what the rosh yeshiva wanted to hear; Judah was sure of it. Proof that, in one very important regard, Judah did not admire Ben Azzai.

Sure enough, Salomon's eyes twinkled back at Judah as the discussion continued with debates over whether a man is considered to have fulfilled the mitzvah of procreation if his children die in his lifetime (he has), or if he has only daughters but they give him grandsons, or vice versa?

"He also has," Judah pointed out. "According to a Baraita that states, 'Grandchildren are as children.'" He was ready to explain further but was silenced by the bells of Sext chiming noon.

Salomon held up his hand. "That's our lesson for today. After *disner* my students will learn this section of Talmud, while I attend to some important business."

"You expounded very well, Judah." Meir grinned and then whispered in his ear, "Now we'll see if your actions are as fine as your words."

Judah gulped out a thank-you. Expounding Torah was easy, but now he was about to meet a strange young woman and try to somehow convince her to marry him. His stomach twisted with anxiety. Please, he prayed, don't let her be like the others; don't let her look at me with hunger and greed.

Salomon's household was also tense. At least Rivka had a day's warning in order to prepare what she hoped would be a betrothal feast. She and Anna had scoured the markets for the finest meat and produce, while Johanna had ordered several kinds of fragrant breads. The rose petal bread was colored a delicate pink, other loaves were saffron yellow and parsley green, and a few were rich with raisins and candied fruit.

Rachel had come home, overflowing with tales of Judah's Talmudic prowess. But when it came to his appearance, she couldn't resist teasing Miriam. She had been so enthusiastic earlier that she knew no one would believe her if she said Judah was the handsomest man she'd ever seen. So she lied shamelessly.

"Now I know why he's remained unmarried so long." Rachel shook her head sadly. "Such a terrible disfigurement; he must have been injured as a child, but I suppose you won't notice it in the dark. Besides, it doesn't matter what he looks like, as long as he's a *talmid chacham*."

"And I suppose he's hunchbacked and covered with warts too." Joheved clearly didn't believe her little sister.

"*Mais oui.* How did you know?" Rachel tried not to giggle. "And he's bald as well, there's not a hair on his head."

Miriam didn't believe any of this either, but why would Rachel lie? What was she hiding? Could it be that Judah resembled Benjamin? Was he short with brown curly hair?

Miriam's throat tightened with fear, and she forced herself to swallow. "Please, Mon Dieu. If Judah ben Natan is my *bashert*, let him be as different from Benjamin as two men can be, so that I won't be haunted by memories of Benjamin when I see him."

Rivka handed her daughters the empty pitchers. "If you have nothing better to do than make jokes, you can go down to the cellar and fill the wine flasks."

"Miriam, don't go outside." She grabbed hold of her daughter's yellow silk sleeve and pulled her back. "It shouldn't look like you're so eager to meet our guests. Wait for them to come inside and then bring out the wine."

Suddenly there was the sound of men's voices at the gate. The party entered the house to the sight of a beautifully set table and the smells of a delicious meal. Rachel raced to greet Salomon, while Joheved welcomed her husband more sedately. Judah's eyes darted anxiously around the room, looking for the missing daughter, and then Miriam walked in from the kitchen, carrying a flask of wine.

Even a cursory glance at Judah was enough for Miriam to see that her little sister had been teasing her outrageously. She shot Rachel a look of disgust before turning back to Judah in relief. He was handsome, yes, but more important, he looked nothing like Benjamin. Judah was taller, slim and dark, with not so much as a wave to his hair, much less any curls. Benjamin's beard had been wild and bushy, while Judah barely had any facial hair at all. The Holy One had answered her prayer.

Miriam's expression filled Judah with a joyous relief of his own. Finally—a woman who looked at him without covetous eyes. And she was slender too, a far cry from the fleshy women his brother liked. It seemed to Judah that she looked familiar, and he decided it must be her resemblance to her uncle in Mayence. He said a silent prayer of thanks to the Almighty for leading him to his *bashert*, this woman who was everything he had asked for.

Brimming with confidence, Judah washed his hands and sat down at the long table. He scarcely noticed the excellent quality of the food and immediately joined in a discussion of whether it should be a mitzvah for women to procreate. Opinions fairly flew around the room.

"A Mishnah in the sixth chapter of Yevamot clearly states,

> The mitzvah of being fruitful and multiplying applies to men but not to women."

"But Torah addresses both men and women, as it is written:

> The Almighty blessed them and said to them: Be fruitful and multiply."

"Yet it is also written, 'Replenish the earth and conquer it.' Conquest is a male action, not a female action. Men conquer women, women do not conquer men."

"How can procreation be a mitzvah for the man and not for the woman? He can't be fruitful and multiply without her."

"The Tosefta on Yevamot teaches that men are forbidden to drink sterility potions, yet a women may do so."

"It's only right that women be exempt from procreation. The Merciful One would never issue a commandment whose performance regularly endangered a person's life."

They debated through dessert. Judah needed no further convincing, but he noted with pleasure that Miriam gave her views with as much assurance and knowledge as the male students. Anxiety replaced pleasure, however, when servants began clearing the table and the students got up to leave. Soon there were only the *parnas*, and his son and daughter-in-law, and Salomon's family left sitting with him and Azariel.

Azariel broke the silence. "Mistress Miriam, my brother has a present for you."

Isaac haParnas scowled at this breach of etiquette. Gifts were not exchanged until after an agreement had been reached, and as he understood it, while Judah had made his intentions known, Miriam had not yet accepted his offer. But his frown softened into a smile as Judah presented Miriam with a bag of strawberries.

"Strawberries." Miriam couldn't help but smile as she inhaled the ripe berries' sweet fragrance. She rarely got to eat them; they were too expensive to buy for the whole yeshiva. "How did you know? Did my father tell you?"

Judah felt a small stab of guilt for possibly misleading her. "I saw a peddler selling them on our way here, and since I'm fond of strawberries myself, I thought you might like some."

Salomon coughed to get everyone's attention. "Miriam, I know we conceded that you needn't choose a new husband until the Hot Fair, but perhaps you'd like to take a walk with Judah and see how you feel about him."

"All right. It should be pleasant along the Seine this time of year." Could she really decide to marry him after just a short walk? She turned to her mother. "If the leftover trenchers are ready, I can help Anna distribute them when we leave."

Judah's heart began to pound as his doubts assailed him. *What am I going to say to make her want to marry me?* Except for his mother, he'd never been alone with a woman or even had a conversation with one.

Still, he had no choice, and he paced the courtyard as Miriam put on her cloak and head covering. He was startled by the number of beggars who approached them at the gate, but Miriam and the maidservant calmly and efficiently got the meal-soaked serving breads into the many outstretched hands.

"They know our yeshiva is larger than the usual household, which guarantees more leftovers," she explained with a pang. One of the early bonds between her and Benjamin was the knowledge that each had grown up eating the bread trenchers, their families too poor to give them away.

Determined to concentrate on Judah, she tried to think of something noteworthy to say. At first it was easy. Sharing the strawberries while they walked, Miriam pointed out the various landmarks they passed as they made their way toward the river. It never occurred to her that Judah might be even more nervous than she was.

"This is the Old Synagogue, the one where my family usually goes." She slowed at the stone building. "It's cooler in the summer, but in the winter it's terribly drafty, and sometimes we pray in the New Synagogue if it's too cold out. Most Jews in Troyes attend one synagogue regularly, except when they're having a fight with someone, and then they go to the other one for a while."

Judah nodded and sighed. In Paris his mother seemed to be constantly changing synagogues, depending on which family he had most recently insulted by refusing to marry their daughter.

"Behind the synagogue, toward the castle," Miriam pointed northward, "is Rue de Vieille-Rome, where the *parnas* and the other rich families live." They walked silently past the giant cathedral, partially hidden behind scaffolds. "Grandmama said that some barbarians burned down the old cathedral about two hundred years ago, and the bishops have been trying to get a new one built ever since. You can barely see Bishop Hugues's palace behind it."

Scarcely aware of what she was saying, Miriam kept up her running commentary until they reached the St. Jacques Gate. Soon the city walls towered behind them, and they turned onto the towpath that paralleled the gentle Seine. All this time Judah, his throat nearly paralyzed with fear, had said nothing.

Her own anxiety growing, Miriam remembered that Judah had wanted a wife who knew the difference between Hillel and Shammai, and she searched her memory for some interesting debate between them. Of course—there was the story of how Hillel and Shammai dealt with converts in the second chapter of Tractate Shabbat.

She brought up the topic of the two sages and quickly quoted the Gemara.

> "Once a stranger came before Shammai and said to him, 'I will convert if you can teach me the whole Torah while I stand on one foot.' But Shammai indignantly pushed him away. The man then came to Hillel, who converted him, saying, 'That which is hateful to you, do not do to your fellow; this is the entire Torah, all the rest is commentary. Go and study it."

She continued with a few more stories about potential converts approaching the two sages, but Judah remained silent. *Why isn't Judah saying anything? Is he even listening to me? What is the matter with him?*

Judah was lost in his own thoughts. As they stood watching the river, he had been reminded of how he and Daniel had studied together at a grassy spot near the Rhine, and he recalled that Daniel had worn a cloak that was almost the same dark green as Miriam's. No wonder Miriam looked familiar. It wasn't her uncle she resembled; with her hair covered by the cloak's hood, she bore a remarkable likeness to his old friend.

Miriam couldn't stand his silence any longer. She faced him and began to cry. "Did I pass your test? They told me you were interested in Hillel and Shammai." She didn't try to wipe away the tears rolling down her cheeks. "Why don't you answer?"

Confronted with Miriam suddenly weeping on his account, her terrified suitor had no idea what to do. "Please don't cry. I was listening, honestly." In desperation Judah began repeating the Gemara she had just finished, but that didn't seem to help. Near tears himself, he stammered, "I'm sorry . . . I didn't mean to ignore you . . . It's just that I've never been this close to a woman before, except for my mother."

In a panic, he grabbed her hand and begged her, "Please don't be distressed. It's just that you look so much like my old study partner, I was enthralled just looking at you."

Then, like a drizzle turns into a squall, he unburdened himself to her. He told her not only about Daniel, but about how his mother and uncle had repeatedly tried and failed to get him married, and how the rosh yeshiva had threatened to put him in *herem*. When Azariel told the story, he made Judah sound heroic, bravely refusing to compromise what was right, but to hear Judah's side was to know his frustration and despair.

Miriam's tears dried as she filled with empathy for him. It was hard to lose someone you loved. "This last year has been terribly lonely for you, hasn't it?"

He nodded sadly. "Are you still upset with me?" When she smiled and shook her head, he said, "Forgive me if I said the wrong thing, but I really am inexperienced and shy when it comes to women."

She couldn't resist teasing him. "You can't be that shy with women; you're holding my hand and we've only just met."

As she expected, he dropped her hand immediately, his face as red as the beets they had eaten at *disner*. "You won't tell your father?" He looked around nervously.

"He won't mind," she said, amused at his consternation. "After all, he thinks we're going to be married."

"And are we?" Judah was suddenly serious.

"That depends," Miriam replied, equally serious at first. Then, with smiling eyes, she added, "I haven't shown you that I've studied Ben Azzai yet."

"You don't have to recite any more Talmud. I knew you were my *bashert* as soon as I saw you."

Miriam's heart began to pound. He sounded so confident. But she didn't have to make up her mind now; she could equivocate and see who else offered for her at the Hot Fair.

Judah saw the uncertainty on her face. "What about you? Have I passed your test?"

Miriam hesitated. *My test?* Judah was undeniably handsome, but he didn't make her heart race like Benjamin had. Perhaps that was for the best. Judah was a *talmid chacham*, he seemed eager to please her, and he was fond of strawberries. Maybe he was her *bashert*. But there was another thing she needed to know.

"I've been training to be a midwife," she said. "That means I have to stay here in Troyes. If you want to study in the Rhineland or return to Paris, I can't go with you."

Judah shuddered. He couldn't imagine which would be worse, returning to Mayence or living with his mother. "Of course I'll stay here. Why would I marry the daughter of the rosh yeshiva of Troyes and then go study somewhere else?"

Miriam watched as a heron gracefully flew down and landed in the water. So had he passed her test? She remembered her prayer before *disner* and sighed. Judah certainly looked as different from Benjamin as two men could be, and he was as at home in a yeshiva as Benjamin had been in a vineyard.

Her gaze lingered on the towpath continuing off into the distance. She had asked the Holy One to show her the path to choose and now she was standing on one with Judah. Hadn't she prayed for a sign and received one?

This time it was Miriam who shyly took his hand. Judah, overcome with elation, stood silently staring at the Seine. Suddenly the air was split with the sound of bells.

"Mon Dieu! They're chiming None already." Still holding Judah's hand, Miriam bolted back to the gate. "We've got to get back!"

The atmosphere around Salomon's dining table was heavy with impatience. With no negotiations yet, Azariel plied his hosts with questions about the Champagne fairs. "I hear they already attract more business than Cologne's."

Isaac saluted the scholar with his wine goblet. "Because of Salomon's yeshiva, now only the rare French youth still travels to Allemagne for Talmud study."

"I have no desire to compete with my masters in Mayence and Worms." Salomon held up his hand in protest. "Indeed it is impossible that I could. They are far beyond me in knowledge and wisdom, and I am merely grateful to be able to offer some Torah learning to those students who cannot travel such a distance, especially during wartime."

Mention of the civil war in Germany prompted the conversation to digress into politics. Rivka would rather have heard more about Judah's family, but she didn't want to offend Isaac and Azariel. And if all went well, the subject would come up eventually.

"I hear King Henry is holding his own against the usurper Rudolph." Isaac haParnas had contacts in the Rhineland, whose towns generally supported the king. "In fact, the counter-king is now so desperate for resources that he's begun appropriating Church lands."

"And this is the pope's man?" Salomon helped himself to more capon, shaking his head in disbelief.

Azariel took more chicken and topped his meat with a generous spoonful of quince preserves. "Luckily Henry keeps Pope Gregory too occupied to notice that our King Philippe has ignored the pontiff's demand that he deny Jews any position in his court."

"Count Thibault also has no intention of letting papal law dictate whom he may or may not trust in his court," Isaac said. "He continues to consult me as often as he ever has."

Azariel leaned forward in his chair. "Speaking of the nobility's foibles, probably half the women in the Parisian court have their jewels pawned to Judah's mother, Alvina."

With his audience's rapt attention, Azariel continued, "Judah, my uncle, and I are business partners, with Alvina putting up Judah's share of the capital. We're a very close family. Alvina is my uncle's sister-in-law."

"Your father and his brother married two sisters." Rivka sounded shocked. "That's very unlucky."

"I suppose you're right, because my father died shortly after Judah was born," Azariel said with a sigh. "But Alvina has invested her *ketubah* wisely, leaving Judah with the resources to study Torah as long as he likes."

"There's no need for us to pry into your financial affairs," Salomon said. "When my daughter has accepted your brother, then we can speak of money."

There was more discussion about business as Isaac and Joseph tried to determine which merchants they and Azariel had as common acquaintances. Meir shared the morning's Talmud lesson with Joheved, and students kept coming in to ask questions.

Finally Rachel offered to run down to the river. "I won't bother them. I'll just stand at a distance and watch."

"Very well," Salomon said, his frustration mounting.

True to her word, Rachel was back in no time. Grinning broadly, she announced, "You can start planning the wedding."

Rivka's eyes narrowed in suspicion. "You said you weren't going to interrupt them."

"I didn't. I came through the St. Jacques Gate and saw them standing on the towpath, and . . ." She paused dramatically. "He was holding her hand."

"He was *what*?" Azariel and Meir were equally incredulous.

Joheved remembered how Rachel had teased them about Judah's appearance. "You're not making this up? You actually saw them?"

"I'll take any oath you want—they *were* holding hands."

"There's no need for oaths," Salomon interrupted. "I believe you." Then he smiled. "Gentlemen, it's time to get down to business."

Isaac and Azariel stared at each other, eyes glittering at the thought of bargaining with such an expert opponent. But then Azariel's expression softened. "As much as I would enjoy spending days here negotiating a betrothal agreement, in all fairness I cannot. Alvina says that I am to accept any conditions you care to impose."

"Your family will pay all the wedding expenses." Isaac shrugged and smiled at Salomon. "I have to make some demands."

Azariel nodded. "Naturally."

"New clothes every year at Rosh Hashanah," Johanna said.

"And at Passover," Azariel added cheerfully.

"Judah will pay room and board for both himself and his wife," Joseph declared.

Salomon lifted his hands in protest. "My daughter is not going to pay to eat at my table. Miriam receives the same dowry as her older sister, one third of the vineyard at my death, plus room and board while her husband attends yeshiva here."

"If your home needs to be enlarged to house the newlyweds, we will pay that expense," Azariel offered.

"That will not be necessary," Rivka said. "My sister will share her house with Miriam. Both women are midwives, so their clients will only disturb one household at night."

"Then allow us to furnish the couple's room," Azariel said. "The bed, the linens, the chests, and chairs."

Nobody could think of anything else to ask for, so they settled back to wait, and wait. Impatience set in again, and Rachel was about to suggest that she go out to find them when the three o'clock bells began to toll. By the time each church in Troyes had had its say, Judah and Miriam were walking through the courtyard gate.

"There you are." Rachel brazenly called out to them, "What took you two so long?"

Judah could only blush, but Miriam smiled and replied, "It takes a long time to explain all the differences between Hillel and Shammai."

nine

he only thing remaining to discuss was the wedding date. "We must allow enough time to travel to Paris, make preparations, and then return," Azariel said.

"You have at least three weeks," Rivka said as they all walked together to morning services. "They should be married under a waxing moon, not a waning one."

Salomon stroked his beard for a moment and then added, "But we can't delay until the following month. Weddings are forbidden during the first nine days of Av."

"Wait—what is the best time of month for my sister?" Joheved had finally become *niddah* again, and was acutely aware that the wedding must be scheduled during Miriam's clean days.

Miriam blushed as the company turned to her. In the months since they'd returned from Ramerupt, Rachel had come to know her bedmate's rhythm, so she spoke for her embarrassed sister. "Miriam always has her flowers at the full moon."

"Her what?" Judah blurted out, and Miriam's blush deepened.

Salomon walked over and whispered to Judah, "A woman's 'flowers' are her 'monthly visitor.'" He used the Talmudic euphemism for a woman's menses. "Just as the grapevine flowers before it develops fruit, so too a woman must flower before she becomes pregnant."

At the same time, Rivka addressed Azariel. "We can have the wedding a week after the new moon, while it's still waxing."

"A Friday afternoon wedding would be auspicious." Meir grinned. "Then we'd have two days to celebrate."

Azariel considered the practical aspects. "That would give our people in Paris almost a week to get here. We wouldn't have to stop on the way to wait out the Sabbath."

"We are agreed then," Salomon declared. "The second Shabbat after the new moon next month . . . the eleventh of Tammuz."

Azariel shook his hand. "Excellent. Judah and I can leave for Paris tomorrow morning."

That evening Azariel presented Salomon's surprised family with a sturdy chest containing Judah's betrothal gifts. The women crowded around as he opened it, and Rachel sighed with awe. Inside, the box gleamed with precious metals, ropes of pearls, and jewelry set with gems of every color in the rainbow.

Azariel explained the abundance of jewelry. "To avoid shaming her clients by selling their forfeited baubles in Paris, Alvina has sent some pieces with me to offer at your fairs." He pulled out a man's ring with a large, blue stone and presented it to Salomon. "A sapphire, the stone of Issachar, is associated with understanding, especially of Torah."

Azariel and Judah exchanged pleased looks when Salomon tried the ring on several fingers before allowing it to remain on the third finger of his right hand. Most prominent men wore rings. Emeralds were merchants' favorite, since the gem of Zebulun was reputed to bring success in trade, while knights prized agates, the stone of Naphtali, for its ability to make a man secure on his mount.

Then Azariel turned to Miriam. "Knowing that you are a midwife, Alvina suggested something with rubies." He opened a small velvet pouch and removed a gold filigree necklace and matching earrings. The delicate pieces were set with a pattern of small rubies placed to form squares, with a larger ruby in each square's center.

Miriam held them up for her family to admire. The necklace came to a V between her breasts, and she felt a pang of inadequacy as she imagined the bountiful cleavage this necklace was designed to adorn. The earrings dangled almost to her shoulders. So this was how Judah had the means to study Talmud as long as he liked.

"They're beautiful," Miriam said, returning the jewels to their bag. "But I can't imagine wearing anything so elaborate."

"These are for your wedding day." Azariel coaxed her to take the pouch and then handed her a bolt of fabric.

Miriam tried not to grimace as she unwrapped the bright red brocade. And she was expected to wear the ostentatious jewelry as well. Judah hadn't seemed like the kind of man who expected his wife's appearance to proclaim his prosperity. Had she misjudged him?

Not knowing the woman's taste, Alvina had been reluctant to choose a gift for Rivka. Instead she had instructed Azariel to offer her counterpart a choice of several pieces. But Rivka just stared at the small mountain of pearls and gemstones.

"My good mistress, perhaps you would consider this pearl and amethyst set." He pointed out a modest brooch and earrings. "The amethyst is the stone of Gad, and one who wears it is protected from *mazikim* and not seized by the sudden faintness of heart that they cause."

"*Merci*, they are very nice." Rivka gave a sigh of relief and took the amethysts.

"The purple jewels will go well with your wine-colored *bliaut*," Salomon encouraged her.

Now only Rachel remained without a present, and she alternated between nervous excitement and fear that she would be left out of the gift giving.

"For my young mistress, surely we can improve on your red threads." Azariel searched the chest again and pulled out a necklace of what appeared to be small red beads. "This is coral found in the Red Sea," he informed them. "The red stones offer constant protection from the Evil Eye."

Rachel beamed as Rivka fastened on the necklace and cut the threads around her wrists. "*Merci, merci*. It's beautiful." She reluctantly tucked the coral beads under her chemise, where nobody would see her lovely jewels.

A week later Rachel was playing in the garden with the new kittens when she was supposed to be weeding. A woman she had never seen before entered the courtyard and knocked on the front door. But nobody answered; Salomon and Baruch were busy in the vineyard, trying to remove the shoots that sprouted everyplace other than on the dressed branches. Rivka and Miriam were in Provins shopping for her trousseau at the Mai Faire. Joheved was in Ramerupt.

The woman walked over to Rachel. "Perhaps you can help me. I'd like to buy some wine."

"It would be best if you came back later," Rachel said. Hopefully Papa or Miriam would be back by then.

The buyer crossed her arms over her ample bosom. "I either purchase my wine immediately or not at all." Her voice was stern. "My barge leaves for Paris this afternoon."

Rachel knew how to negotiate wine sales; she had seen her sisters do it plenty of times. So she led the woman into the cellar and poured out samples from the casks that had not been set aside for Miriam's wedding.

The woman was certainly in a hurry, for she scarcely bargained with the price that Rachel heard her sisters start at. The sale quickly made, the woman directed a carter to get her barrels and then removed an emerald ring from her middle finger. "Take this as security for the price of your wine. I'll redeem it when I return at the Hot Fair."

"*Merci*, Mistress. Drink it in good health." Proud of selling the wine at such a good price, Rachel tied the ring into the sleeve of her chemise and wrote the sale into the wine account book.

She meant to give the ring to Papa when he returned, but Mama and Miriam came back first, and in the excitement of seeing what they'd purchased, she forgot. Then, in the tumult that only multiplied as Miriam's wedding day drew closer, the woman wine buyer and her ring disappeared from Rachel's mind.

Suddenly the month of Tammuz was upon them, and every bed in the Jewish Quarter seemed filled with wedding guests from Paris. But with every woman who congratulated her for finding such a handsome, learned, and rich bridegroom, Miriam grew more morose. She hadn't cared how poor and unattractive Benjamin was, and she'd been so eager to go to the *mikvah* before their wedding day. Now she felt only anxiety as Mama and Joheved accompanied her to the synagogue's ritual bath.

Miriam had heard her clients complain about the *mikvah*, but she had never been down into it before. It lay deep below the building, behind a large wooden door. Mama lit the lamp hanging next to the key and unlocked the door.

Miriam stared into a dark corridor completely lined with stones and felt her stomach tighten. Mama started down the steps, beckoning her to follow. The stone stairs sloped precipitously, and when Miriam reached out to steady herself, the damp and slimy wall made her quickly pull back her hand. As she continued her descent, drops of condensation landed on her head and rolled down her face. Finally the steps ended at the entrance to a small room with a domed ceiling. That is, they appeared to end. When Miriam got closer, she could see that they continued down into a black pool of water.

Mama placed the lamp on its shelf on the wall, and the two women crowded into the small space. Trying not to worry about who had used the *mikvah* last and how rarely it was cleaned, Miriam undressed and hung her clothes on the pegs provided for this purpose. Spreading out her arms and fingers to make sure the water reached every part of her skin, she took a deep breath and slowly lowered herself into the murky ritual bath.

Apparently the temperature didn't vary much underground, for the water was neither warm nor cold. Miriam slipped beneath the surface, deep enough that her hair was completely covered, letting her body float so that none of her limbs touched the sides. She lay submerged, trying to relax and imagine herself a baby in its womb, until she was forced up to take a breath.

She sank into the tepid water twice more before rising to say the blessing: "*Baruch ata Adonai* . . . Who commanded us with immersion." The Talmud taught that this was the only blessing Jews say after performing the *mitzvah* instead of before.

The atmosphere was very close, and Miriam couldn't wait to get into the fresh air. At any moment the ceiling might collapse and she'd be buried alive. Even Mama and Joheved's welcoming embraces did nothing to allay her fears. How could Mama endure years of coming to this dank cave of a room alone at night? No wonder Joheved preferred to immerse in the Aube.

Anxiety about her wedding night now replaced anxiety about the *mikvah*, compelling Miriam to seek her mother's guidance. "Mama," she asked as Rivka brushed her hair, "what was it like when you and Papa, you know, first slept together?"

Rivka nearly dropped the brush. "That was a long time ago. I think Joheved is better qualified to advise you."

"But Papa was a stranger when you married him, not like Joheved and Meir."

Non, not like Joheved and Meir at all. They didn't realize that she knew, but from the upstairs windows Rivka had seen them hugging and kissing before the wedding. Once she even watched her husband quickly turn back when he came around a corner and saw them together. *Non*, it wasn't like that when she'd married. She sighed.

"Miriam, I can't help you. You're older than I was then, and you've found something appealing about Judah that made you accept his suit." Rivka couldn't bring herself to tell her daughter about the fear and pain she had endured. "Imagine the wonderful children you and Judah will have."

"*Merci*, Mama." Miriam reached out and took her mother's hand. Mama's entire life revolved around Papa and their children, but Miriam's would be different. She was a midwife and she studied Talmud. She would never be as cowed by her husband as her mother was.

"Here's one suggestion I can offer." Rivka kissed her daughter good night. "Drink a lot of wine at the wedding banquet, and try not to worry."

Convinced that her parents' wedding night had been a debacle, Miriam wondered what she could do to avoid a similar fate. Perhaps she should consult Aunt Sarah, who'd had two wedding nights. But Aunt Sarah was out with a woman in labor, and though Miriam was awake to hear the bells chiming both Matins at midnight and Lauds at three, she never saw her aunt return. Then it seemed as though she had just fallen asleep when the bells tolling Prime woke her at dawn, each one loudly proclaiming, "Today is Friday, your wedding day."

The rest of the day passed in a blur. Miriam barely looked in Joheved's mirror as she was sewn into the red silk *bliaut* and the violet chemise with matching red and gold embroidery, as her hair was loosened and she was adorned with her new jewelry. At the synagogue her mind played tricks on her, and she had to look at Judah several times to prove to herself that she wasn't marrying Benjamin after all.

As sunset approached to mark the beginning of Shabbat, Miriam felt like a lonely island in a sea of merriment. Had she made a mistake marrying Judah so quickly? Why hadn't she waited to see who else at the Hot Fair wanted to marry her? Following her mother's advice, she had emptied as many cups of wine as she could in between all the dancing, eating, and visiting. It seemed that every woman in Troyes wanted to chat with her, dance with her, or both, while the men kept Judah equally occupied. Neither of them made any effort to leave the party, but their guests finally forced the newlyweds out of the courtyard and into Aunt Sarah's house.

Upstairs Joheved helped Miriam out of her fancy clothes and jewelry, all the while providing an encouraging and detailed description of the pleasures that marriage would soon offer her. Too soon Miriam was left wearing only a chemise, and, forcing one foot in front of the other, she walked toward her new room, a room where Judah, and Heaven knows what experience, was waiting for her.

As she approached the door, she detected a familiar odor and stopped in dismay. Somebody, undoubtedly hoping the aphrodisiac fragrance would have the appropriate effect, had risked Salomon's wrath to trespass into the vineyard and gather some grape blossoms to decorate the wedding chamber.

Miriam's heart sank as she remembered how Benjamin had contrived for them to meet outside the vineyard during this season so many years before, a meeting that ended with a kiss and a proposal of marriage. The cloying scent of grape flowers brought that time back as if it were yesterday.

Fighting tears, she entered her new bedroom and faced her new husband. The sweet smell of grape flowers was even stronger inside, and, the wine having made her maudlin instead of relaxed, Miriam's grief welled up and threatened to choke her.

Judah, who had been pacing back and forth, heard the door finally open. Startled, he jerked around and watched his bride slowly enter the room. Earlier that evening his new mother-in-law had addressed him. In an urgent whisper she had begged him, "Be gentle," the only words she had thus far spoken to him. Now her plea haunted him, and he regretted how he had arrogantly rejected Azariel's offer of instructions, saying that he didn't need to learn how to seduce serving wenches.

Stop worrying, Judah told himself. Miriam was a widow; she'd know what to do. Rooted to the spot, he waited for his wife to approach him, but she took only enough steps to close the door behind her.

Somebody had left them a dish of strawberries, but Miriam's stomach was too jumpy to eat, even her favorite fruit. Sure that she'd burst into tears if she tried to say anything, she could only think of Benjamin and how this should have been their wedding chamber.

"What are you waiting for?" Judah asked helplessly.

Miriam was brought back to reality at the desperation in his voice. Without thinking, she replied, "I'm waiting for you. Who do you think I'm waiting for?"

"But I don't know what to do." He hesitated and, even in the darkened room, she could see him blush. "I thought you'd know . . . you being a widow after all."

As soon as the words were out of his mouth, Judah could have kicked himself. *How could I be so stupid as to mention my bride's deceased husband?* Miriam's face crumpled, and he watched with trepidation as she struggled to speak.

"But I was widowed from *erusin*, not *nisuin*. Didn't you listen when they read the *ketubah* amount for a virgin?" The mention of her widowhood was all Miriam needed to lose control. Her tears flowed slowly at first, but then she sank down on the bed and began to bawl like a child.

Twice his tactlessness had made Miriam cry, but Judah didn't know what to do except wait. He sat down on the bed and reminded himself that, like the patriarch Jacob, he too was destined to overcome many obstacles before obtaining his *bashert*.

When she finally quieted, he said softly, "I'm sorry for your loss. Would you like to tell me about him?" If her first husband stood between them, it was better to know now.

"His name was Benjamin ben Reuben, and he was one of my father's first students."

Judah groaned inwardly. She had spent years growing fond of the fellow. "And undoubtedly one of his best students too."

"*Non*, not anywhere near as good as you are," she said. "Benjamin was a better vintner than Talmud student." It was strange to be discussing her first husband with her second, but the need to unburden herself was too great, especially with Judah listening so sympathetically.

Judah didn't mind listening. His mind was whirling with the night's possible outcomes. One thing was becoming certain—despite years of trying to prevent erections and then feeling mortified when they appeared anyway, tonight even Lillit wouldn't be able to arouse him. That gave him an idea.

"Miriam," he gently interrupted her. "I see that Benjamin was very dear to you and . . ." He hesitated, grasping the enormity of what he was about to propose. "Perhaps it would be best if we wait awhile, until you feel ready, before we, uh, use the bed."

Miriam grabbed his hands and squeezed them. "You mean it?" Her voice was incredulous, but the way her face lit up convinced Judah that he had made the correct decision.

He pulled one of his hands away and patted hers soothingly. "Absolutely. It wouldn't be right if you were thinking about another man."

"But what about the bed? If it isn't bloodstained, they'll ask all sorts of embarrassing questions."

"That's easily solved." To his new wife's amazement, Judah pulled back the covers, took his knife and made a quick cut across his hand, after which he wiped the blood into the sheet.

Miriam thanked him profusely. She told him how difficult it was for her when Benjamin died, how impatient everyone was, and ended up explaining how painful it felt to smell the grape blossoms now when they only served to remind her of that grief.

"The scent is cloying." He flashed her a conspiratorial grin. "Why don't we just throw them out the window?"

With a sudden flurry of activity, the offending blossoms were gone, and Miriam was relieved to smell the herbs that were strewn among the rushes on the floor.

"So what shall we do now?" he asked. "We can't very well go down-stairs and rejoin the wedding banquet."

Despite her lack of rest, Miriam was too jittery to go to sleep. Then she remembered Marona and Samuel's wedding gift. "Would you like to play chess? Meir's parents gave us a set."

"I've never played chess." Tonight would be a night of many firsts, just not the one he'd anticipated.

"Then I'll teach you." She set up the board and chessmen before he could protest.

Judah learned the fundamentals quickly but played without enthusiasm. *At least there will be some mating going on in this room tonight,* he thought, no longer sure that delaying their coupling had been a good idea.

Miriam soon suspected that, unlike serious players, her husband would not object if they talked during their game. He was being so nice; she wanted to pay him a compliment.

"You look very handsome today." Did he actually frown when she said that? She started again. "I know red isn't one of my best colors, but the red silk brocade was becoming on you."

"Stop." He held up his hand to silence her. "There's something about me you need to understand. As far as I'm concerned, my appearance is a curse. And I hate the color red. Ever since I was little, my mother made me wear it."

"Shall we throw our wedding clothes out the window, too?" she asked with a smile.

He sighed. "As much as I'd like to, we'll probably have to wear them all this week, as well as when my mother decides to visit us for holidays.

She's done so much for me, I don't want to hurt her feelings over something so silly." He made a chess move that he immediately regretted.

She took the errant piece and they returned to the silent chess game. Until she remembered something she was curious about.

"You really don't know what to do with a woman?" When he nodded, she asked him, "Didn't you study the Arayot at your old yeshiva? Papa teaches them to his students before their weddings. He even taught some to me and Joheved, but mostly she learned them from Meir and I learned them from her."

Suddenly Judah understood about the private lessons that his companions had been privy to. "Nobody had a chance to teach me," he replied. "Remember, I wasn't betrothed yet. And then I left Mayence immediately after Azariel arrived."

She sighed. "I suppose that explains it."

"You've studied the Arayot. Perhaps you could teach me."

"Oh *non*, I couldn't." Miriam blushed. "I'd be too embarrassed, especially since we haven't . . . I mean since we hardly know each other."

"Maybe I should ask Meir to teach me then?" Judah hated to admit his inadequate learning, but this was Torah knowledge he needed to know.

"*Non*, you should have Papa teach you," Miriam said with steel in her voice. Heaven forbid that Meir, and then Joheved, should learn of her new husband's deficiencies.

"Very well," he said. "By the way, do you think your father would mind if I called him Papa? My father died so long ago that I don't even remember him."

"Oh Judah, that's a wonderful idea." Miriam felt a rush of affection for him. "Papa's always wanted a son."

They concentrated on the chess game until Miriam paused and looked up at him. "Because you were so interested in Ben Azzai, Papa gave me a list of places in the Talmud that mention him, and I've been studying them. But I don't understand the part in Tractate Chagigah, in the second chapter, where Ben Azzai saw the Divine Presence and died. Papa helped me a little, but he didn't have time to explain it fully. So I was thinking that maybe you could."

"I've never studied that section." Judah felt chagrined that his learned wife had asked him about two different areas of Talmud and he was ignorant of both of them. "You must be having doubts about my reputation for scholarship."

"Not at all," she said. "Papa doesn't teach that chapter of Chagigah either. He'd rather not encourage any esoteric studies like the Divine Chariot."

"He's right. That knowledge is dangerous." Judah shook his head quickly. "Besides, to use it properly you need to recite all sorts of secret Divine Names that nobody knows anymore."

"Papa says that Ben Azzai knew the secret names." Miriam recalled the text and a daring thought occurred to her. "I may not be able to teach you Arayot, but I can teach you from Chagigah. And then you can help me understand it."

"You would?" Judah jumped up to open the shutters and then halted. "But it's too dark to read, and Heaven knows what people would say if they saw light up here."

"I don't need to read it. I know it by heart."

Without hesitation, Judah sat down on the bed next to her. He wanted to make sure he heard every word over the noise below. "Can you start with the part about Ben Azzai?"

"I'll quote a little of the Mishnah first, so you'll know where we are." She took a deep breath and began.

> "Arayot may not be expounded before three, Creation before two, and the Divine Chariot before one alone, unless he is a sage who understands from his own knowledge."

Judah's mind began to focus as he remembered that Mishnah.

"Then," she continued, "in the Gemara where they discuss the Divine Chariot, there's a Baraita about Ben Azzai:

> Four entered the Orchard; Ben Azzai, Ben Zoma, Acher, and Rabbi Akiva. Rabbi Akiva said to them: When you come near the pure marble stones, do not say—water, water."

She paused and asked him, "Should I recite more or shall we try to figure out this part first?"

Judah scratched his head. "Let's finish the passage. The later texts may help us understand the beginning."

Miriam nodded. "After Rav Akiva's warning, the Gemara goes:

> Ben Azzai gazed and died. Of him it is written, 'Grievous in the eyes of Adonai' is the death of His pious ones. Ben Zoma gazed and was stricken . . . Acher cut down the plants. Rabbi Akiva departed in peace."

She turned to Judah. "I think this is a good place to stop for now. The next few pages are mainly about Acher and Rav Meir." She leaned back against the pillow, truly relaxed for the first time in days. "Who was Acher anyway?"

"His real name was Elisha ben Abuyah; he started out a great scholar, but he died as a heretic. The Mishnah uses his real name, but in the Gemara he's only called Acher, the Other."

"So 'cut down the plants' means he became an apostate?"

Judah nodded. "This is a bizarre text. Could you repeat the Gemara a few times with me until I know it, too? Then we can try to make sense out of it."

They recited the verses together until he had them memorized. "Well, I know what all the words mean, but that doesn't mean I understand the passage." Judah scratched his forehead. "What does your father, I mean Papa, say?"

"First, he told me that the 'Orchard' they entered was the Garden of Eden." Miriam strained to recall exactly how he'd explained it. "He said that the four men, the greatest sages of their generation, were studying the secrets of the Divine Chariot, and they used a Divine Name to ascend into Heaven."

She shook her head in amazement. Was the story of the four sages any more bizarre than her and Judah studying it on their wedding night instead of doing what newlyweds usually did? Yet she had to admit that she was enjoying herself, and it sounded like Judah was too.

"It seems that Rabbi Akiva had been there before, since he knew about the marble and warned the others," Judah said. "But why did the four enter Heaven to begin with?"

"I don't know. Wouldn't you want to see Heaven?" She'd take her chances visiting Heaven if only she could be with Benjamin again.

"Not if it were that dangerous," Judah said with a shiver. Had it only been a few months ago that he'd been ready to jump into the Rhine? And now he was married to a woman who knew more about Ben Azzai than he did. "Rabbi Akiva warned them not to say, 'water, water,' and they obeyed him, yet even so . . ." Judah scratched his forehead again.

"True, they didn't say anything about water," Miriam said. "But they gazed."

"Does your father say what they saw?" Judah asked eagerly.

"Papa told me that they looked directly at the Divine Presence, and that Ben Azzai's soul separated from his body and refused to return."

"Ben Azzai died young, before he was able to father any children," Judah said. "No wonder the Sages said his death was grievous to the Holy One."

"How sad."

"What about Rabbi Akiva? Why wasn't he harmed?"

"Papa says there are two possibilities. One is that Rabbi Akiva never gazed directly at the Divine Presence," she replied. "But Papa showed me where the Gemara asks what verse Akiva expounded to save himself from the others' fates, so maybe he did look."

Again Miriam marveled at her strange situation. Sitting in bed together in the dark, both of them talking about Papa, it was almost like studying Talmud with Joheved.

"So what did Rabbi Akiva say?"

Miriam quoted the Gemara's answer. "It's the passage about Elijah's vision in First Kings:

A great and mighty wind, splitting mountains and shattering rocks; but Adonai was not in the wind. After the wind came an earthquake; but Adonai was not in the earthquake. After the earthquake came a fire, but Adonai was not in the fire. And after the fire came a soft murmuring sound . . . and behold, Adonai was passing."

Before she'd said four words, Judah was reciting the text with her. She looked up at him and said quietly, "Papa explained that instead of trying to perceive what the Almighty is, Rabbi Akiva concentrated on what He is not."

The newlyweds sat silently on the bed, wondering about the men who had actually encountered the Divine Presence. Judah yawned and Miriam suddenly felt tired as well. The music downstairs wasn't so loud and they could hear the guests bidding each other *Bonne nuit* and Shabbat shalom.

"Shall we eat the strawberries now or wait until morning?" he asked her, hinting that it was bedtime.

"We'd better eat them now and not encourage any mice." Miriam, her appetite now returning, helped herself to several.

The fruit finished, there remained the tricky task of getting undressed and into bed together. Miriam removed her chemise under the covers, and then, unable to bring herself to stand there naked to hang it up, she tucked the garment under her pillow. Then she would be able to modestly put it on again in the morning without leaving the bed. Judah must have done the same, because he didn't hang up his chemise either.

Miriam held her breath. They were naked in bed together. Was her new husband really going to roll over and leave her in peace? Did she want him to?

"*Bonne nuit*, Miriam," Judah whispered. "Thank you for teaching me from Chagigah."

"*Bonne nuit*, Judah." She waited nervously for any hint of movement from his side of the bed, but there was none. She listened to his even breathing, and finally, exhausted from lack of sleep and days filled with anxiety, she drifted off to sleep as well.

ten

iriam's chest tightened as she prepared to take her new mother-in-law shopping at the Hot Fair. Her first impression of Alvina was of a *femme formidable,* and she had seen nothing yet to change that opinion. Alvina was not a tall woman, but her erect carriage belied that fact. Perfectly groomed and dressed in the latest Paris fashions, even Judah probably never saw her without her makeup.

Outside in Salomon's courtyard, as the family gathered prior to attending services on Sunday, Alvina had stared at her for a while before embracing her. Miriam could almost see the abacus in Alvina's mind, calculating her daughter-in-law's pluses and minuses.

Sure enough Alvina said, "You're nothing special to look at, but then my son has made it clear for years that he is not interested in outward appearances."

"*Oui*, Judah follows the advice in Pirke Avot, which says:

> Do not look at the vessel, but at its contents. A new flask may contain old wine and an old flask may not even contain new wine."

Miriam felt proud at not allowing her mother-in-law to intimidate her.

Alvina didn't exactly smile, but there was a gleam of satisfaction in her eyes.

The next day, as they stood at the entrance to the cloth sellers' tent, Alvina gazed around in awe. Miriam smiled to herself. It was good to see that even a sophisticated Parisian jewelry seller found the Troyes Hot Fair impressive.

Miriam began by taking them past the woolens, looking for Nissim. "I know you want to see the silks, but there's a wool merchant here who can tell us which ones we should check first."

"You're sure you don't want any silk for yourself?"

"*Merci, non.* I have my wedding outfit and the one Marona gave me," Miriam said. Two silk *bliauts* were plenty.

Many of the merchants they passed congratulated her on her recent nuptials and offered her special reduced prices on their wares. But Miriam didn't stop; today was for Alvina.

Nissim stood at his usual table, and he began waving when they were still a distance away. "Miriam, it's good to see you again. To what do I owe this pleasure?"

"This is my mother-in-law, Alvina. I hope you can recommend some silk dealers for her."

He and Alvina appraised each other shrewdly. "Would you prefer the finest quality, regardless of price or an excellent but slightly flawed piece of silk for a significant discount?" he asked her.

"That would depend on the price of each, and how slight the flaw was," Alvina replied cautiously.

Nissim nodded and recommended several merchants, pointing out their tables as he spoke. "Gamliel sells the best silk in Troyes, but he knows it and won't bargain much. The others occasionally match his quality and may give you a better price. Hanina is your man if you're willing to accept minor flaws."

"Have you seen Hiyya?" Miriam asked. "Alvina is in the jewelry business and I'd like them to meet."

"He was at services at the New Synagogue this morning. I'll tell him you're looking for him." Nissim leaned forward and lowered his voice. "By the way, I have a very unusual piece of wool, but I'm not sure what to do with it."

Alvina was intrigued. "Unusual, how so?"

Nissim looked around to make sure they weren't being observed, then pulled out a wrapped bolt from under the table. "The dyer who did this material must still be kicking himself." He shook his head. "The poor fellow didn't have quite enough indigo, so he tried to make up the difference with another dye."

Rubbing the material between her fingers, Alvina tsked in disgust. "He wasted all that indigo dye, not to mention this excellent wool."

"You'd expect the best wool if he were planning to dye it with indigo," Nissim said.

"So he takes a heavy loss," Alvina said. "Why the secrecy?"

"The wool guilds guard their reputations, and only the finest fabric from each city is allowed at the Troyes fairs."

"For those who value comfort and durability over appearance," Miriam said pointedly to Alvina, "this material should serve well. I personally find the different blues swirled together rather interesting." Perhaps Papa would like it since his wine-colored wool *bliaut* was ten years old. "How much wine do you think this cloth is worth?"

When Nissim named a price a fraction of what she would have paid for similar wool dyed properly, Miriam nodded.

"Now Alvina needs to see some silk," she said. "I'll come back later and let you know how many lengths we want." Judah preferred subdued colors; she might buy some for him too.

As they headed for the silk tables, Alvina took her arm. "Save your family's wine. If you're going to get this wool for your father, you may as well buy some for yourself and Judah from my account."

Ignoring the fact that he had been married almost a month and was still a virgin, Judah had never felt happier in his life. Even at the height of his friendship with Daniel, their joy had remained private. But in Troyes, the rosh yeshiva's son-in-law basked in public approval. Seated at Salomon's side, Judah spent his days, and most of his nights, learning Talmud with some of the most erudite men he had ever met.

In the Rhineland, Judah's first task had been to memorize the text and understand what each word meant, and if he were diligent he would eventually grasp the give-and-take of the arguments. But the men he sat with now were not only cognizant of each argument, each scholar brought his own unique wisdom. The merchant from Barcelona had learned how a particular Torah verse was used to support argument A, while one from Narbonne knew why a different verse had been rejected, and the scholar from Kairouan understood how a certain verse, which ought to have supported argument B, in fact supported argument C instead.

It was as if, after years of enjoying food with salt alone, Judah was suddenly offered pepper and saffron. Yet there was more. His mother was pleased with him. Instead of lodging at Sarah's, his mother had taken a room with Samuelis, the widow whose house shared Salomon's courtyard. Alvina so was busy getting acquainted with the jewelry merchants in town that he seldom saw her. She hadn't looked this happy in years.

But the best thing was discovering his father-in-law's *kuntres*, the commentary that Salomon was writing on the Talmud. Judah remembered the day well; he had been married almost two weeks at the time. The morning had not begun auspiciously. The night before, with the moon just past full, Miriam brought out her *sinar* and warned him that she was *niddah*. Judah, having overlooked the fact that his wife would naturally become *niddah* if they didn't have relations, froze.

All the whispered rumors about menstruating women came back to him: when a woman meets a snake on the road, it is enough for her to announce "I am *niddah*" for the reptile to hastily glide away; a scholar is forbidden to greet a *niddah* because the utterances of her mouth are unclean; one should not walk behind a *niddah* and tread upon her footsteps since even the dust beneath her feet causes impurity; her very gaze is injurious, causing drops of blood to form on her reflection in a mirror. Now Miriam was *niddah*.

He slowly backed away. "Perhaps it would be better if I slept downstairs?" he stammered.

Her eyes narrowed in anger. "If you want to sleep with the servants, I won't stop you," she replied. "Considering that you have no trouble restraining yourself while I'm permitted to you, I don't see why my being *niddah* should require more diligence."

But Judah remembered a story in Tractate Shabbat about a student who had died young because he slept in the same bed as his wife while she was *niddah*, even though he didn't so much as touch her little finger. So Judah set up a cot at the other end of the room from their marital bed.

When he woke up the next morning, Miriam was gone, and at breakfast he learned that she was attending the doctor's wife, Francesca. Miriam still had not returned at midday, and Judah began to realize that he had no idea what form his new wife's displeasure would take. He ate little for *disner*; his stomach was a bit queasy.

After the meal Salomon announced that he would be teaching Tractate Niddah that summer, giving Judah the uncomfortable suspicion that Miriam had communicated with her father.

Salomon began with a brief introduction. "Vessels the *niddah* touches today are clean, even for her husband. For we are already impure from graves, houses of dead people, and corpses; and we will remain impure until the days of the Messiah.

"However," he continued, seeming to stare straight at Judah. "Her husband restricts himself and does not eat from the same bowl as her, neither does he sit on her seat or receive anything directly from her hand. This custom is proper to prevent sin between them."

"So if a *niddah* wishes to give her husband something, say a book," Rachel said. "How does she do it?"

"She may hand it to another person, who in turn gives it to her husband," Salomon replied. "Or she may put it down and leave it for him to pick up."

"And in the synagogue?" asked Shemayah. "I heard that women are forbidden to enter while they're bleeding, while it is permitted during their 'white' days."

Salomon stroked his beard a moment. "Maybe some women do this because they think the synagogue is like the Holy Temple. But if this is the reason, then what about the rest of us who are impure from corpses? For we all attend synagogue.

"*Niddah* affects only a woman's relationship with her husband." Salomon emphasized the word "husband." "If she wishes, she attends services as usual, prays as usual, and if she is accustomed to study Torah, she studies as usual."

These were their teacher's final words. All but the youngest students followed Salomon and Joheved to the vineyard, where they would review that day's lesson while they helped with the season's outdoor chores. The youngest boys needed to spend every waking hour learning Talmud with Meir if they were to follow the advanced lessons once the Hot Fair opened.

Judah had no viticulture skills, but he still accompanied Miriam and the others to the vineyard. Today, reluctant to expose himself to further chastisement on the subject of *niddah*, he remained behind. In the salon he could hear Meir and the boys finishing the ninth chapter of Tractate Berachot. He stepped closer to listen.

> "Whoever is modest in the privy is safe from three things: from snakes, from scorpions and from demons."

Many of the boys were grinning, and as they continued discussing behavior in the privy, they read each line with increasing mirth.

Meir was sure he would burst out laughing when he noticed Judah listening. "You're just in time. There's a teaching from your old friend, Ben Azzai, in this section. If you can teach it, I'll go work in the vineyard."

Before Judah could object, Meir was halfway through the courtyard. Doubled over with laughter, Meir nearly collided with Miriam coming through the gate. Francesca had easily given birth to a small but healthy baby girl, so the young midwife was in an excellent mood. But as soon as she entered the salon, she knew something was amiss. The students were smirking and giggling behind their hands.

"Judah, why aren't you in the vineyard?"

"Meir asked me to take over for him," Judah said. "We're at the end of Tractate Berachot, that section about privies."

No wonder Meir was laughing. But she wasn't going to leave her husband in this embarrassing situation. "Wait a moment, I'll go find Papa's *kuntres* on Berachot."

Judah had no time to wonder what Miriam was talking about before she laid a small, well-worn volume on the table for him to pick up. "You may find this useful."

He thumbed through the thin manuscript quickly at first, then slowed abruptly and looked up at his wife in awe. "Mon Dieu! Papa has written a commentary on the whole tractate."

Miriam beamed with pride. "And not only this tractate, but most of the others too. He started writing them when he was a student, so he wouldn't forget his teachers' explanations."

Judah was so eager to read Salomon's *kuntres* that he almost asked Miriam to teach the class. But instead, he turned to the pamphlet's end and found the page they were on. He scanned Salomon's explanations and, full of confidence, stood up to teach a room full of rowdy thirteen-year-old boys what the Talmud said about defecation.

> "Isi bar Nassan taught: Behind a wall, one defecates only if his fellow cannot hear his lower sneeze, and in the open only if his fellow cannot see him."

Judah quoted the text and then gave Salomon's explanation. "This means that he may relieve himself if others are nearby, but only if they can neither see nor hear him; while in a field he must move out of sight."

"Is a lower sneeze what I think it is?" The other boys snickered as the questioner farted loudly.

"I have confidence that you can all ascertain what the Gemara means by a 'lower sneeze.' Any other questions?"

The students didn't know what to make of Judah, who neither cracked a smile nor grew angry at their silliness. In fact, Judah was so engrossed in Salomon's *kuntres* that nothing could disturb his equanimity.

"Now here's a saying of Ben Azzai's that concerns how one may use a piece of wood to relieve constipation."

Sure this next passage would have the class in stitches, Judah steeled himself to recite it with aplomb.

> "Manipulate and then sit, but do not sit and then manipulate; for one who does this, even spells performed in Sepharad will find him."

Judah sighed as the boys burst out laughing. There was no point asking for suggested meanings. But Salomon's commentary explained it. "This means that anyone so immodest as to expose himself first will bring down evil forces upon him, even from so far away as Sepharad."

Once the students made the connection between immodest behavior and evil spells, Judah was able to finish Ben Azzai's text without any of them giggling.

> "And if he forgets, but sits and then manipulates? What saves him? Let him say: Neither *Tachim* nor *Tachtim*, not spells of a sorcerer nor spells of a sorceress, upon me."

Judah nodded in approval as his students recited the protective words with great care. "Rabbenu Salomon writes that *Tachim* and *Tachtim* are two evil spells that sorcerers cast using excrement." He waited in vain for questions.

"Since you don't have any questions for me, I have one for you," he said. "What have you learned from this text?"

"How to cure constipation?" one boy suggested irreverently.

"An incantation to protect us in the privy," another promptly responded, scowling at his fellow's comment.

"Those are both good, practical answers. But what about our relationship with our Creator?" Judah took in the blank looks facing him and realized he'd have to explain it himself. "A man should behave modestly even when no one can see him. This is how the Holy One, blessed be He, judges us, on how we behave when we're alone, even during such mundane activities as using the privy."

Pleased with the lesson, Judah dispersed the boys to study the text with their partners, warning them to pronounce the words properly. With his father-in-law's commentaries, maybe teaching the boys wouldn't be difficult. He remembered how Salomon explained the beginning of chapter four of Pirke Avot.

"Ben Zoma says: Who is wise? One who learns from everyone.

This means learning from those who are lesser than him; both lesser in age and lesser in knowledge."

Judah was still immersed in Salomon's *kuntres* when a woman arrived and announced that she was prepared to pay for the wine she had bought earlier. He called for Miriam just as Salomon and the rest of the household came back from the vineyard.

"Here's the money I owe you." The woman laid a heavy purse in Salomon's hand. "Now I'd like my ring back."

He stared at her in confusion. "What ring?"

"The emerald ring that I left with your daughter as security for the transaction." She looked directly at Rachel.

Miriam watched with apprehension as Rachel grew pale with fright. Frantically checking her chemise sleeves and finding nothing, she dashed upstairs, Joheved and Miriam in her wake.

"Mon Dieu. Please let me find it." Rachel was crying now as she tore around the room, searching through the chests and then among the rushes on the floor. "That lady's ring. I tied it in my sleeve and now it's gone!"

The three of them continued to search the room until Rivka came upstairs. It was obvious by their mother's fury that she had been told the whole story, and the verbal assault she launched on Rachel made Miriam cringe.

"Now get downstairs, you irresponsible child." Rivka eventually finished her vituperation. "And help your father sort out this disaster."

If Rachel had hoped for private mortification, she was horrified to find that the entire student body was crowded into the salon, curious to see how their rosh yeshiva was going to handle the situation.

The lady merchant was still there, scowling fiercely. "You careless little idiot," she burst out when she saw Rachel on the stairs. "You lost my lucky emerald ring, the one my mother gave me when I got married. Why didn't you give it to an adult right away?" She continued muttering to herself, "Who would have guessed that this girl could look so mature and not even be twelve years old?"

Everyone staring at her, Rachel gulped out her tearful apology. "I'm sorry, Papa. I meant to give you the ring, but it was just before Miriam's wedding and with all the excitement . . . I forgot."

"There's no point looking for it any longer," Rivka conceded bitterly after the students spent a good hour sifting through the rushes downstairs. "That was over a month ago; it could have fallen out anyplace."

"The ring that this woman deposited with Rachel is obviously lost, without hope of recovery." Salomon spoke solemnly, as if he were a judge on the *beit din*. He motioned to Meir, Judah, and Shemayah to come closer, and they consulted briefly. "Legally, I am not responsible for any loss caused by my young daughter, who is still a minor."

The woman began to object, and Salomon silenced her by continuing loudly, "However, since you sustained a loss through a member of my household, I shall reimburse the market value of your ring, but not any additional value you may have attached to it for sentimental reasons."

"But will you accept my word as to the ring's value?" The woman's eyebrows rose skeptically.

"You and my daughter will accompany me to Avram the goldsmith, each describe the ring, and there we will establish its worth," Salomon said. And there he would pawn his sapphire ring to get the money to pay for it.

"Let my father go with you," Eliezer said unexpectedly. "He has several emeralds with him, and if one of them is about the same size as the one Rachel lost, it will be easier to determine its cost."

"Alvina should go as well," Miriam said. "She's in the jewelry business."

Alvina's presence had an unexpected effect; once at Avram's, Salomon was too ashamed to pawn Alvina's gift in front of her. Then Rachel surprised them by offering her coral beads to offset what her father would owe for a new emerald ring. Even with Rachel's necklace, Salomon still owed the goldsmith a good deal of money, but the woman was satisfied.

Yet compared to Rivka, Salomon didn't seem too upset. When anyone asked him about the loss, he quoted from Pirke Avot:

Who is rich? One who is content with his portion.

After nearly two months of marriage, the chief difference in Miriam's life was sharing a bed with Judah instead of with Rachel. She continued to attend laboring women with Aunt Sarah about once a week, alternate leading women's services with Joheved, and study Talmud with her sisters. Most of her days were still spent in her family's vineyard, where every task brought back memories of she and Benjamin doing them together.

Benjamin also intruded into Miriam's thoughts at night as she wistfully contemplated Judah's sleeping form beside her. The first time she visited the *mikvah* as a married woman she felt only relief at being allowed to honor Benjamin's memory. But a week ago, after her second visit to the *mikvah*, her emotions were tangled. Relief was still there, but rejection had crept in too.

How could Judah lie naked next to her in bed so peaceably every night? Did he find her unattractive, undesirable? Miriam thought of Ben Azzai and wondered if her husband had deliberately married a woman he didn't find appealing so he could study Torah without distraction.

But Judah was having difficulty restraining himself. At first he slept with his wife as unaffected as he had slept with Shmuli. But as he studied Arayot with Salomon and Tractate Niddah with the merchants, he realized that, with his twentieth birthday approaching, he was married in name only. Worse yet, he was becoming attracted to some of the visiting scholars.

When another evening study session drew to a close, he wondered if he would be breaking an oath to ask Miriam not to wait much longer. He had just packed up his manuscripts when Levi, one of the younger merchants, approached him. Judah recognized him as one of the more flirtatious of his fellows. A clever scholar with curling auburn locks and a ready grin, it was no wonder he was so popular.

"I appreciated how you explained that passage at the end of the third chapter." Levi threw his arm around Judah's shoulders and quoted the Gemara.

> "Why does a man seek a woman, but a woman does not seek a man? It is like one who loses a belonging; who searches for whom? The owner of the lost item searches for his belonging. Why does a man face down and a woman face up at the man? This one, the place where he was created, and that one, the place where she was created."

"As you enlightened us," Levi said, squeezing Judah tighter, "the unmarried man searches for a bride because the Holy One took a rib from the first man to create Eve, and thus men seek the rib that Adam lost so long ago. As for the second question, I did not understand until today that it refers to how a man lies with a woman. Thus a man faces down, toward the earth from which he was formed, while a woman, made from man's rib, faces him."

Levi's voice dropped and he whispered to Judah, "And thus two men both face downward when they lie together."

Judah was speechless, but his body betrayed him with a sudden tightening in his loins. Before he could think of a response, Levi, recognizing the answering warmth in Judah's face, added suggestively, "Perhaps you'd like to resume this discussion at my lodgings. There are some other passages we might explore together."

Judah's consternation must have been obvious, because another merchant burst out laughing. "You're wasting your time on this one, Levi. He can't play the game—he lives here in Troyes. He's the rosh yeshiva's new son-in-law."

Levi smiled ruefully and apologized. "A thousand pardons, *mon ami*. I've never seen you at the fair before and assumed you were a visitor as well. I don't suppose you have any opportunity to travel?" he asked hopefully.

Judah could only shake his head. Levi loosed his hold on Judah's shoulders and grinned. "Newly married, eh? You'd better be getting back to your wife's bed and let her appreciate your beauty."

Emotions in turmoil, Judah headed home. Miriam was surprised to see him so early—as the fair drew to a close Papa and Meir stayed up studying even later. She sensed that something was wrong, which her husband's words confirmed.

"Miriam, uh, I need to speak with you." Judah struggled to find the right words. "I know I promised to let you mourn as long as you wanted, but, uh . . . I'll be twenty soon, and . . . I don't want my bones blasted for remaining . . . celibate."

"You mean tonight?!" she blurted out, her fear still stronger than her need for affection.

Judah wondered for the first time if he should have married one of those women who had gazed at him so lustfully in Paris. "I suppose we can wait a few days more until the Sabbath," he said. "I expect that you remember the part in Tractate Ketubot, where Rav Yehudah says that a Torah scholar should be intimate with his wife weekly, from Erev Shabbat to Erev Shabbat."

Miriam let out a relieved sigh. "I have studied that text. Papa teaches that Sabbath eve is the appropriate night for enjoyment, relaxation, and physical pleasure. Besides, scholars usually study late on other nights."

If Judah wanted to use the bed once a week, it was fine with her. Yet she knew very well that Meir, who was just as pious a scholar, was intimate with Joheved far more often. It was no secret that Joheved was pregnant again, even before her son's third birthday. And if Miriam wanted children, there was no way around it.

They spent some time discussing that day's Talmud lesson before going to bed. Miriam, now discouraged that Judah hadn't offered to kiss her good night, scolded herself for vacillating between her deceased husband and her living one. It took her a while to fall asleep, and then something woke her.

Like other midwives, Miriam slept lightly, and she listened carefully for voices below. But the only thing she heard was Judah whispering the anti-demonic Ninety-first Psalm, and she concluded that he must have awakened from a nightmare. She was trying to relax back into slumber when she felt his hand on her naked shoulder. It was the first time he'd touched her since they were married.

"Miriam?" His voice, though soft, was ragged with emotion.

"What's wrong?"

"Lillit visited me tonight, just a little while ago."

"Oh *non*!" Miriam was frightened and mortified: frightened because any demon children Judah fathered with Lillit might claim a portion of their inheritance from his human heirs when he died and mortified because it was her delay that had left him vulnerable to Lillit's attack. "Did she . . . I mean, did you?"

"*Non*, I woke up just in time." Aroused almost to the brink of orgasm and suddenly aware of how soft his wife's bare skin felt, Judah wasn't sure how to communicate his need to her.

"Thank Heaven you were strong enough to resist her." Miriam was conscious of Judah's hand, slowly moving down her shoulder and across her back.

"Just barely." He silently caressed her back as he mustered his courage. "Miriam, I can't wait until Shabbat, not the way Lillit left me feeling." There, he'd said it.

"Of course not." Miriam took a deep breath. "I've been terribly selfish, thinking only of my needs and ignoring yours."

She turned around and kissed him. It wasn't as exciting as kissing Benjamin, but it was nice. Scolding herself for thinking of another man at such a time, she tried to respond more ardently to her husband's efforts.

Judah didn't need anything else to arouse his desire; the pressure of her warm flesh against his was more than enough. He sensed Miriam's enjoyment and, hoping to give his wife more pleasure, delayed his entry as long as he could. His *yetzer hara*, free from restraint for the first time in his life, reveled in the sensation of her naked belly pressed against the most sensitive portion of his anatomy. Without volition, his hands found her buttocks and pulled her tightly against him. It was impossible for Miriam to kiss him and remain immobile, and her slightest movement filled him with exquisite agitation.

Suddenly aware that he was approaching the verge, he managed to roll Miriam onto her back while they were kissing. Then he released her only long enough to gasp, "Please, I can't last any longer."

Miriam spread her legs and lifted her hips to make it easier for him. He fumbled a bit at the opening to her womb, but eventually she felt his erection between her lower lips. Recalling how Rivka had begged him to be gentle, Judah probed lightly and halted at her virginity's obstacle.

Miriam held her breath and braced herself for the pain that would come next. But there was none.

Judah was so aroused that just feeling the tip of his manhood enveloped by her warmth was enough to push him over the edge. Before he could decide how much force to exert, a spasm of unimaginable pleasure overcame him, and he spilled out his seed at the entrance of his wife's womb.

"*Merci*, that was wonderful," he whispered. He kissed her briefly and lay back beside her. "Now we are truly married."

Snuggled in her husband's arms, her mind racing, Miriam couldn't believe that it was over so soon. She had enjoyed the hugging and kissing, and was greatly relieved at her lack of pain, but from what her older sister had told her, the holy deed took longer than this. Judah probably finished so soon because Lillit had already aroused him, she told herself. Next time he'd take longer. *And next time it would hurt.*

eleven

Ramerupt
Winter 4840 (1079–80 CE)

ver the next six months, Judah and Miriam's marital relations continued to be almost identical to their first coupling. Kissing her until he was so aroused he couldn't stand it, Judah would enter only as far as her virginity allowed before the tightness of her nether lips brought him such rapture that he climaxed almost immediately. In his naïveté, Judah accepted his experience as normal.

Miriam wasn't so sure, and recalling a Talmud text that described how long a mar man must be alone with her lover to be suspected of adultery, she searched Tractate Sotah and found what she wanted on the fourth page.

> How long is their seclusion? The time it takes for cohabitation . . .
> the time it takes to circle a palm tree. Rav Yehoshua says: the time
> it takes to drink a cup. Ben Azzai says: the time it takes to roast an
> egg. Rav Akiva says: the time it takes to swallow an egg. Rav Ye-
> huda says: the time it takes to swallow three eggs.

Reassured that she and Judah took at least as long as Rav Yehoshua (Papa explained that each rabbi gave as example the amount of time he personally took with his wife), Miriam assumed that her hymen had been broken too gently to be painful.

Joheved stood outside the manor's kitchen door and scanned the cloudy February sky. "Do you think they'll come tonight, Marona? It's barely snowing now."

"It looks like the storm's over, but, remember, it's been snowing all week and we have no idea how high the drifts are." Marona observed her daughter-in-law's disappointment and added, "Still, the carts have likely worn a decent path between Ramerupt and Troyes today."

"We have at least an hour until sunset." Miriam hoped Judah would make the trip for Shabbat. Between the snow and being *niddah*, she hadn't seen him for almost three weeks.

"The shepherds and I can handle the few ewes that go into labor tonight," Marona said with an encouraging smile. "You two go upstairs and get ready for your husbands."

As they changed clothes and helped each other with their hair, Miriam wondered if their mother had forgiven Rachel yet for thrusting them back into poverty. After a disappointing Hanukkah, when the vintage proved to be merely adequate, the atmosphere at home had become so unpleasant that she and Joheved jumped to help with the lambing at Ramerupt. Miriam told Meir not to worry about Joheved's pregnancy. With her and Marona in attendance, Joheved would be surrounded by experienced midwives. Distracted, wondering when she would become pregnant herself, Miriam didn't recognize the men's voices downstairs until Joheved darted for the door.

Once seated around Marona's table, Joheved's concerns were focused on the vineyard's fruitfulness. "Is the pruning on schedule, Meir? Does Papa have enough workers who know what they're doing? Maybe I should go back and help."

"The pruning can manage without you," Miriam interrupted. "You shouldn't be walking back and forth to the vineyard in your condition, not in this cold weather."

"Don't worry," Meir said. "Both Baruch and Rachel spend nearly all day pruning the vines. Which means that Eliezer is putting in a fair amount of time there as well."

"Rachel spends all day in the vineyard?" Miriam asked.

"I suspect she is still trying to avoid your mother," Judah said. "Whatever the reason, Papa is delighted with her company."

Miriam glanced at Joheved, Meir's hand resting protectively on her bulging belly, and sighed.

"What's the matter, dear?" Marona asked.

Miriam quickly tried to think of something to say. "I was just thinking about poor Shemayah. Is he any better?"

"Shemayah?" asked Samuel. "Is he the student who pines for your little sister? I can't keep these boys' names straight."

"You're thinking of Eliezer, Papa; that's his father's name too," Meir replied. "This Shemayah is my study partner."

What could he say about Shemayah? Splendid company as long as the topic was Torah, the man was a complainer. Everything irritated him; students who forgot their lessons, pigs that overran the city streets, the tanneries' stench, his in-laws, and especially his wife, Brunetta.

When Shemayah first began criticizing her, Meir tried to offer helpful advice, but it soon became obvious that his friend was not going to change his ways or his attitude. When Meir grew so exasperated that he asked Shemayah why he didn't divorce Brunetta if she vexed him so, Shemayah replied bitterly that he was a poor man. Where would he find the assets to pay her *ketubah*? After that, Meir just tried to change the subject whenever the topic of Shemayah's unhappy marriage came up.

Meir sighed. "I thought that when his wife became pregnant, things were getting better at home, but then their baby boy died after being circumcised."

Samuel nodded. "Now I remember him."

Meir turned to Miriam. "I don't think he's any better at all. He can't make up his mind what to do, so he just sits around moping. If Judah hadn't coaxed him into helping with Salomon's *kuntres*, I doubt he'd get out of bed in the morning."

Joheved raised her eyebrows. "I used to think his constant complaining was annoying, but this melancholy is worse."

"He's not the only man to see his first child die." Miriam's sympathy was entirely with Brunetta. "There's no reason to blame his wife; she didn't know her family was cursed."

"Her father knew and he should have warned them." Meir explained further for his parents' benefit. "After the boy bled to death, it came out that both Shemayah's mother-in-law and her sister had baby boys die the same way after circumcision."

"But in the sixth chapter of Tractate Yevamot it says that even with two such deaths in a family we still circumcise a third time." Judah quoted the Gemara.

> "There were four sisters in Tzippori; the first had her son circumcised and he died, the second also and he died, and the third also and he died. The fourth sister came to Rabban Gamliel and he said to her: Do not circumcise."

Judah concluded, "Thus we learn that only after three such tragedies is the pattern clear."

"Shemayah is free to divorce Brunetta without paying her *ketubah*." Joheved's exasperation was clear. "After all his whining, you would think he'd be glad to be rid of her."

"Perhaps he's the kind of man who likes to complain, who thinks it keeps the Evil Eye away," Marona suggested.

"My mother taught me that a man who complains over trivial matters is asking the Accuser to give him something serious to complain about," Samuel said. "That's why I tried to raise my children with sanguine personalities."

Meir smiled at his father. "Shemayah married for money and there's no guarantee that he'll find another wealthy father-in-law to support him while he studies Torah."

"He hasn't seen Brunetta since the baby died." Miriam's voice began to rise. "He can't just leave her waiting like this. He needs to decide one way or another."

"It's been long enough that she could insist he divorce her," Joheved said. "So she's waiting too."

"She has to. Who else would marry her now that everyone knows about her family's curse?" Miriam shook her head sadly. "If Shemayah divorces her, she'll probably never marry again."

"There's nothing I can do to hurry him." Meir sighed. "He must decide if healthy sons or money is more important."

"I think he should stay with her," Samuel declared. "After all, most men lose children. Why should this Shemayah expect that he'd be any different?" Samuel spoke from sad experience; only two of his five children were still alive.

"Come, it's Shabbat," Marona said. "Let's not dwell on this unhappy topic. Meir, please lead us in some Sabbath songs."

The evening continued in a more pleasant fashion, with Joheved agreeing to stay in Ramerupt through Passover to observe the lamb buyers. In the meantime, she was learning so much about running the manor by watching Marona.

One of the first things Joheved learned, to her disappointment, was that the lady of the manor does not get to sleep late. In winter Marona woke before dawn, then quickly dressed and said her morning prayers before breakfast. She spent the rest of the morning with the steward hearing reports from the manor's staff and dealing with whichever of their problems required intervention. There were items needing repair, goods to be inspected, servants to be disciplined, and quarrels between villeins to be adjudicated. Samuel preferred to pray and study in the morning, receiving his summary of the proceedings later.

If there was time before the midday meal to visit the sick, Marona did so, but in the winter this task had to be postponed. Once home she went over the finances, with separate accounts for rents and income received from the villeins, sales of wool, sheep and wheat produced by the estate, household expenses, charitable donations, and all payments pertaining to Count André, including the knights and the squires they supported for him. There was also a personal treasury for purchasing things like her family's apparel and books. Joheved thanked Heaven that Grandmama Leah had taught her how to keep the wine accounts.

Every afternoon Marona left time to play with little Isaac, and if the weather permitted, to stroll or ride around the estate's grounds. If not, she'd enjoy a game of chess with Miriam. Before *souper* she supervised the cook's menus and tasted any cheese or ale produced that day. During the evening she saw that any visitors were suitably housed and entertained. Guests were rare this time of year, but during the fair seasons they often hosted merchants who couldn't reach Troyes before dark.

Joheved learned something new from her mother-in-law every day, yet she vacillated between returning to Troyes and staying in Ramerupt. Like Shemayah, it was easier to decide by not deciding. Which is exactly what Shemayah was doing, she realized with sudden insight. He had no intention of divorcing his wife; he was perfectly content to remain at the yeshiva in Troyes indefinitely while his wife continued to live in her father's house in Provins.

Snow was falling gently when Judah and Meir left on Sunday morning. It snowed for the rest of the week, preventing Miriam from returning to Troyes for Purim and her husband from visiting the next Shabbat. Finally an evening came when she could see the moon through the clouds. Maybe Judah would come before she was *niddah* again?

Miriam was ready for bed when Joheved clutched her belly and gasped. Miriam ran to her sister's side. "Is it the baby?"

Joheved took another sharp intake of breath. "How can it be? Aunt Sarah said I wasn't due until after Passover."

Marona turned to Miriam. "Let's find out."

Together they helped Joheved up the stairs, pausing several times for her to catch her breath. "But if the baby's coming now, it won't live. It's only been eight months."

Like days of the week, months of pregnancy came under the sovereignty of specific planets, with Saturn ruling the eighth and Jupiter the ninth. Between the malevolent influence of Saturn and the unlucky even number eight, the Talmud considered a child born in the eighth month to be nonviable. Some Sages said that such a child shouldn't be nursed except when it would be dangerous for the mother to retain her milk.

"Whether it's been eight months or nine, this baby is coming," Miriam said after examining her sister. "Your womb is fully open and I can feel the head."

Joheved moaned as another contraction shook her. "That one really hurt."

"Quickly now," Miriam said to Marona. "Find all our tefillin. We don't have time for chalk."

Marona headed for the door. "I'll send a servant with the birthing stool, and Samuel will start saying psalms."

"My birth amulet . . . it's is in the chest . . . near my bed." Joheved could barely get the words out. "Somebody . . . should go . . . get Meir."

By the time Marona returned, Joheved was on the birthing stool. "Try to relax between the pains," Miriam urged her.

"I can't . . . it hurts too much." Joheved squeezed Marona's hand. "Mon Dieu, I need to push."

Before Miriam could worry about possible problems and how she would deal with them without her midwife's kit, the baby's head was in her hands.

"Mazel tov!" Marona shouted as Miriam delivered the rest of him. "Another son for you."

When his in-laws came downstairs for breakfast, Meir was gone. Moments after his father's servant woke him to share the good news, Meir threw on his mantle and mounted his horse. The streets of Troyes were just coming alive. Trying to avoid the chamber pots being emptied from above, Meir rode past yawning maidservants drawing water at the wells and heavily dressed men with farm tools on their way to the fields. The sweet aroma of freshly baked bread caught his nose as he passed a bakery, a few patrons already lined up outside. He'd have plenty to eat in Ramerupt, he admonished his growling stomach.

Once outside the city walls, Meir admired the silent landscape that seemed to glide past him as he rode. The brown soil was a stark contrast to the snow-covered trees and bushes surrounding the fields, and Meir inhaled the earthy odor of freshly tilled loam. He easily found the manservant's trail through the forest and grinned as a startled doe with her twin fawns bolted from his path.

A boy, another boy—it's a miracle! And both Joheved and the baby were fine—another miracle. And it was all over before he even knew she was in labor—that was truly a miracle.

The gates at Ramerupt-sur-Aube were open, and as soon as he dismounted a servant handed him a warm drink. Miriam was all smiles as she assured him that all was well. A short stab of pain assailed him as he passed the door to his sister's old bedroom, and his already rapid stride quickened.

The door to his room was open and there was Joheved, sitting up in bed, three sets of tefillin still hanging at its head—his father's, hers, and Miriam's. Then he was at the bed's side, and it took every bit of restraint he could manage not to take his wife in his arms and hug her tightly. Childbirth had made her *niddah*, and it would be seven days before he could touch her again.

"He's so little," Meir said as he cradled the tiny infant. "Was Isaac ever this small?"

"Joheved was worried that he might be an eighth month baby," Miriam said. "But I don't think so. He has plenty of hair and all his nails are fully formed."

She fought back tears as Meir recited the blessing of thanksgiving, *"Baruch ata Adonai . . . Shehecheyanu . . .* Who has kept us alive, sustained us, and brought us to this season."

Miriam sighed. *How long will it be before I hear Judah saying those words, carrying our child in his arms?* The baby stirred, began to whimper, and Meir gave him back to Joheved, who put the baby to her breast. Watching the baby suck greedily, Miriam felt a pang of longing that was almost painful.

Before Miriam could get to bed, Judah and Salomon rode up, soon followed by carts carrying her family and the entire yeshiva's student body, all of whom would be staying until after the baby's circumcision. With the yeshiva students in residence, Joheved and her baby would be continually protected by their studies and prayers.

The day before the *brit milah* members of the Jewish community began to arrive from Troyes, including Avram the goldsmith and his son Obadiah. In addition to his metalwork, Avram was also the local mohel, and Obadiah was his apprentice in both trades. Obadiah had spent a couple of years at the yeshiva, during which Salomon had made sure to teach the sections in Tractate Shabbat that dealt with circumcision. Miriam remembered him as a mediocre student who preferred to be elsewhere.

Avram immediately joined the other men, leaving his son alone at the dining table to prepare the mohel's paraphernalia. Unsure whether her presence would be an intrusion or welcome company, Miriam stood at the door with her distaff and spindle.

"Do you mind if I join you?" she asked.

Obadiah didn't look up. "Suit yourself."

Not wanting to appear rude, Miriam sat down at the end of the table and began spinning wool. She watched silently as Obadiah cut and rolled the linen into several small bandages. His thumbnails were very long and cut to form a triangle with a sharp point. When he unpacked the mohel's knife and began sharpening it, first one side and then the other, she had to question him.

"I've never seen a knife with both sides sharp," she said. "Isn't it dangerous?"

"The *azmil* isn't a kitchen knife." He sounded annoyed. "When the mohel picks it up, he doesn't waste time checking for the sharp side."

"It would be more dangerous than other knives." Miriam recalled the accidents she'd seen pruning the vineyard.

Obadiah apparently took that as a compliment because he nodded and said, "*Oui.* We have to handle it very carefully."

Miriam was about to ask about his odd nails when Avram came in. "Finish your sharpening later, Obadiah. It's time for afternoon prayers."

Meir and Shemayah hurried by, and Miriam worried that the mohel's presence might throw Shemayah into deeper melancholy, but the next day he appeared more wistful than despondent.

Salomon had also been wondering about Shemayah, but he realized that he was too irritable to deal with his student properly. He disliked public speaking, and now he not only had to prepare his annual Passover sermon, but he was expected to give a *drash* at the baby's *brit* as well.

To make matters worse, he learned that Samuel had invited Count André and his court to the banquet—to do otherwise would be an insult to the sovereign. No matter that it was Lent and Notzrim were expected to fast until Easter. Étienne, the steward, assured Marona that the noble guests were only forbidden to eat meat and would gladly feast on fish and fowl.

Salomon was annoyed at having to teach Torah to non-Jews, but he felt guilty about the enormous amount of money fate had saved him by Joheved giving birth in Ramerupt, and thus emptying Samuel's coffers for the banquet instead of his own.

And what a banquet it was. He nodded his head in approval as he surveyed Samuel's main hall: Garlands of flowers hung from the rafters and around the three large, arched windows. The great room was further illuminated by the twin hearths burning brightly along with dozens of oil lamps. Tables were set up throughout the hall, all covered with clean white cloths and those near the main hearth set with silver plates and goblets.

It was a magnificent feast, even if the main dishes were restricted to fish and fowl. There were fishes of every variety, baked and boiled with pepper, garlic, and other savory spices, not to mention the fish soups; birds Salomon had never eaten before, like crane and stork, as well as a noble peacock served with its tail spread wide behind it. There was even a great molded lion, made of white chicken and pink jelly.

And piled high on their platters were the pastries, all kinds of fish tarts and pies containing small birds like quail, partridge, or pigeon. Each course was more succulent than the last, and each was followed by various amusements. Musicians, jugglers, acrobats, jongleurs, all the entertainers who had wintered with Count André were eager to gladden the hearts of Lord Samuel's guests.

Determined to give an impressive *drash*, one appropriate for Notzrim, Salomon decided to teach about Noah's Ark. Surely even the most ignorant of Count André's court would be familiar with that subject. Slowly he went through the text, focusing on some of the anomalies his daughters and students had noticed.

"Were all the people so wicked that they deserved to be destroyed, even the little children?" Surely his compassionate daughter, Miriam, had asked about this. "Whenever you find a society of lewdness, idolatry, robbery, and corruption, punishment of an indiscriminate nature comes, killing both the guilty and innocent." Salomon was gratified to see many members of the court nodding their heads sadly.

"There are many ways the Almighty could have saved Noah; why did He burden him with constructing an ark?" He recalled Joheved asking that question. "So the wicked men might see him building the ark and ask about it, and thus confronted with their impending destruction, perhaps they would repent."

Of course all the Jews were paying close attention, but now many of the Edomites had quieted to hear him better.

"It rained for forty days and forty nights, but how long did Noah and all the animals stay in the ark altogether?" A student who'd actually begun to think about the text usually asked about this. "The rain began to fall on the seventeenth day of the second month, and one solar year later, on the twenty-seventh day of the second month, the earth had dried sufficiently that the ark's inhabitants could leave."

"A whole year! How could they stay on the ark so long?" Count André burst out.

Salomon smiled at the sovereign. "An excellent question. Before the flood, the Almighty made a covenant with Noah and the animals such that fruit and grain to feed them would not spoil, the carnivorous animals would not eat their vegetarian fellows, and the wombs of the females were closed so no babies would be born on the ark."

Now Salomon had everyone's eyes on him. "And finally, the most difficult question. How could the Almighty repent that He had made man and have it grieve His heart? Didn't He know when He created Adam and Eve what would happen in the future?"

Salomon paused for a moment before concluding, "When a man fathers a son, he rejoices and makes others rejoice with him, even though he knows that his son will sin and some day his son will die. So too is the way of our Creator. Although it was clear to Him that in the end man would commit evil deeds and be destroyed, He still created humanity, for the sake of the righteous who were to issue from them."

With the room's applause in his ears, Salomon took a long drink of wine, bowed to Samuel and Count André, and with great relief, sat down to enjoy his meal.

Outside, the snow was melting and the meadows were green with new grass. Yeshiva students vied with the castle's squires at foot races, ball games, and throwing contests. Indoors, two distinguished men sat at Marona's chessboard, surrounded by an excited crowd whispering wagers. And there was dancing. Women and men dressed in their finest woolens and silks, their jewels catching the light, swayed and turned with the music.

The proud parents wore their blue wedding silks, with Meir laughingly admitting that his *bliaut* needed to be widened almost as much as Joheved's. With none of his relatives in attendance, Judah had no need to wear red, so he and Miriam wore their betrothal clothing—she in the gold silk outfit that Marona had given her, and he in purple. Moses, the doctor, was resplendent in dark blue, darting here and there, advising his many patients on what food they should consume or avoid according to their various diagnoses.

Rachel grudgingly wore the mottled blue wool that Miriam had bought everyone at the Hot Fair, but she still drew every male eye to her. Eliezer watched in anguished fury as man after man showered attention on her, and he swore that by summer's end she'd be legally his.

The next morning it was time for farewells. The yeshiva students would start heading home for Passover, with those who lived at a distance, like Eliezer, leaving immediately. Alvina, hoping that Miriam would be pregnant, had discouraged Judah from coming to Paris for the festival; she would visit them in the summer. With the lamb buyers arriving soon, Meir and Joheved were remaining in Ramerupt.

"Since we had such an excellent time last year," Marona gushed to Salomon and Moses. "You must all come and spend Passover with us again."

The only person not looking forward to the holiday was Shemayah. Every Jew who could possibly get home for Passover was endeavoring to do so, but he could not contemplate observing the holiday in either Troyes or Provins. Expecting his source of funds to be cut off, he was overcome with remorse when the moneylender who held his father-in-law's letter of credit paid out his stipend as usual.

Upon returning to Salomon's, he discovered his teacher filled with indignation, furiously waving a piece of parchment. Salomon's gaze never left his face as he ordered, "Judah, call in our remaining students. Shemayah, you especially should listen to this." He began to read the letter in his hand.

"A man's wife presses charges against him for driving her out of his house, and for not fulfilling his duties toward her. But the husband claims that he acted within the law because he married her under erroneous assumptions. He says that she has been afflicted with leprosy, the evidence clearly visible on her face. He further claims that even before the marriage she felt the presence of the disease, but when he married her, he was not aware of these secret defects. Thus the marriage is invalid and she is not entitled to her *ketubah*."

Salomon made sure he had everyone's attention. "The wife, however, claims that she was in perfect health at her marriage, that even now her body is clear of blemishes except for two warts that have grown on her face due to the aggravation she has suffered from her husband. Members of the community testify that they have known the husband for years and never heard him complain about his wife's skin disease before; also that the husband's claim that lepers are prepared to receive his wife is a brazen lie, a rumor that he himself has spread."

Salomon strode angrily around the room, muttering under his breath. Shemayah felt his throat tighten; these circumstances were too close for comfort. What would his teacher decide? Salomon began his reply without consulting his advanced students. "Since no signs of blemish were detected on the woman while she lived in her father's house, and only appeared after she entered her husband's home, he may not claim that she had hidden blemishes when he married her."

Salomon took a deep breath, and then shook his head in disgust. "Indeed the husband has proved himself guilty of evil practices. He has shown that he is not of the seed of Abraham our father, whose nature it was to have pity and love for his fellows, especially so for his own flesh with whom he entered the covenant of marriage. This man should have set his mind on bringing his wife closer to himself, instead of rejecting her."

His students shrank back at his vehemence, but once started on his tirade, Salomon was not going to stop until he'd said everything he needed to say. "Even among those who deny the existence of the Almighty, we find many who do not alienate their wives. Yet this man repudiated holy matrimony as evidenced by the abominable calumnies he raised against the wife of his youth. It is only just, and so the law requires, that he must divorce her and pay her *ketubah* in full."

Salomon's voiced softened, and Shemayah felt sure his teacher was speaking to him in particular. "But it would be much better if he would receive his wife back with affection and love; for then he might be privileged to receive Heavenly mercy and be redeemed, and have children by her."

"That's a strong answer, Papa," Judah said. "Perhaps you should wait and write your response when you feel calmer."

"I assure you that time will not cool my outrage," Salomon replied. "How dare he treat a daughter of Israel so callously?"

Salomon then beckoned Shemayah to follow him. "Judah, could you please help our remaining students with their lessons while I speak with Shemayah privately?"

After the room emptied, Shemayah's stomach clenched when Salomon picked up another piece of parchment.

"And how shall we solve this woman's problem?" Salomon began. "The wife claims that her husband, a *chacham* who studies at a yeshiva less than one day's ride from home, has not visited her or even contacted her since their son died some months ago. Witnesses testify that he is neither ill nor incapacitated, and that he continues to receive support from his father-in-law."

Shemayah was unable to speak, his throat tight with panic. Salomon continued, "The husband who behaves thus toward the wife of his youth does not deserve to be called a *chacham*, and his fellow students should be ashamed to associate with him. Like the evil man we just heard about, if this husband cannot receive his wife back with honor and affection, he should divorce her."

"My son, you're trembling." Salomon poured out a cup of wine. "Here, have a drink."

As Salomon waited for Shemayah to finish, he spoke in a conversational tone. "During the fifteen years I studied in the Rhineland, I always managed to get home for the three festivals. In fact, when someone there asked me a question about their holiday liturgy, I had to admit ignorance, for I never attended a festival service in either Mayence or Worms."

Just as casually, Salomon stroked his beard. "So Shemayah, what are your plans for Passover?"

"I don't know." His voice was shaking.

"Let me make two suggestions," Salomon said. "You can go back to Provins and celebrate Passover with your family, or . . ." He paused and placed the parchment on the table. It was blank. The two men locked eyes, and Salomon continued very softly, "Or I can call Judah back in here, and you can write your wife a *get* of divorce in front of us."

Shemayah suddenly felt as if he had dropped an enormous weight he'd been carrying. "I'm going to Provins, of course." Then his face clouded. "If they'll have me."

"I'm sure they'll be delighted to see you." Salomon patted his student's shoulder and added, "But just in case, I suggest you bring your wife a present, perhaps something from Avram."

twelve

Troyes
Summer 4840 (1080 CE)

Asher, I have nothing against your brother. Eliezer is one of my finest students. And your father's offer is tempting." Salomon was trying to be diplomatic. "But I cannot give Rachel in marriage to a man for whom she has such a manifest disaffection."

"There's nothing I can do to change your mind?"

Salomon shook his head and ushered the two young men out. Rivka would be furious to learn that he turned down this opportunity to pay off their debts. He sighed and returned to the text he was preparing.

As soon as the door closed, Eliezer burst out, "Belle Assez doesn't hate me. I know it." He still called her by the nickname his brother had given her years ago.

"Unfortunately her father disagrees," Asher said glumly. "We should have waited for Papa to get here; he never fails to close a deal."

"But who knows how long he'll have to wait for that ship to arrive from Bavel?" Eliezer needed to argue with somebody, and his brother was the only available target. "We had to talk with Rabbenu Salomon before anyone else approached him."

"We talked to him all right, for all the good it did you," Asher said. "Now I have business to attend to."

Reluctant to encounter anyone, Eliezer stomped off toward the privy. This had to be Belle Assez's doing. Probably in a fit of pique sometime, she'd told Salomon that she hated him. Well, he wasn't going to let the little witch torture him any longer. As soon as his father arrived, he'd have him arrange another match, to be consummated as soon as possible. He'd show her.

Eliezer had nearly turned the corner when he heard somebody coming out of the privy, so he ducked behind the cellar door. But the Creator must have a sense of humor, he thought in annoyance, because the last person he wanted to see was about to walk past him.

"Belle Assez, I have something important to say to you." He grabbed her arm and pulled her out of view behind the house.

"Let go of me."

He forced her to face him. "What the devil made you tell your father you disliked me?"

"What are you talking about? I've never said anything of the kind." *Mon Dieu, he's having delusions.* "In fact, I've never discussed you with my father at all."

Maybe he'd been out in the sun too long and gotten possessed by the heat demon, Keteb Meriri. Mama was always warning her to stay indoors in midafternoon, especially during the month of Tammuz when the demon was most active. "Eliezer, you're not well. Come into the cellar and cool off."

"There's nothing wrong with me—just answer my question."

"I already told you. I've never said anything bad about you to Papa. Never!"

He released his grip. "Then why would he tell me, not one hour ago, that he wouldn't consider a betrothal between us because of the manifest disaffection you feel for me?"

"You just asked to marry me and my father turned you down?" Rachel's voice rose in indignation. "Because I didn't like you?"

Eliezer was so shocked by her change of appearance that he could only nod. The two of them had sparred so many times that he thought he knew her anger, but now he saw that he had misjudged her. He took a step backward.

"How dare Papa discuss such an important matter without my presence? What does he think I am, a cask of wine to be sold to the highest bidder?" She stamped her foot so hard that a cloud of dust billowed around her. "He can't treat me like this."

Eliezer waited silently as she continued to furiously abuse her father and almost missed it when she railed, "And if Papa thinks I'm like my sisters, that I'll calmly accept for my husband any scholar he brings home to *disner*, he'd better think again. I'd sooner marry you than a stranger."

"So you will marry me," he said triumphantly.

"What?" Rachel had been too busy spilling her wrath to notice exactly what she'd said.

"You just said you'd sooner marry me than a stranger," he accused her. "I heard you quite clearly."

She looked up at him in alarm, a bird caught in a trap. He seemed taller than she recollected, and, close up, she could see that his brown eyes had small gold specks around the pupils. His eyebrows were definitely black, but in the bright sunshine the curls that had escaped his hat looked more brown than black. Rachel wondered what color his beard would turn out to be.

Somehow she had just agreed to marry this young man standing before her, and, surprisingly, the idea pleased her. Suddenly, before she could elude his grasp, he put his arms around her and kissed her. She struggled to escape, but his embrace was like iron and his mouth moved over hers with a fierce hunger, as if he intended to devour her that very moment. Her legs, however, were free.

An explosion of pain between his thighs sank Eliezer to the ground, clutching his groin.

"Eliezer, stop this nonsense and get up immediately."

But he couldn't stand up—he couldn't move. He could barely squeak out a reply. "I can't—it hurts too much."

Suspecting a trick, she cautiously knelt down beside him. Only when she saw the tears in his eyes did she realize he was injured. "How could this happen? I've seen boys fight, and they hit each other much harder than I did, yet nobody gets hurt."

"It's different . . . getting hit down there."

Her face flushed as understanding dawned on her. "Wait here. I'll be back right away with something for the pain."

She ducked into the cellar and quickly returned with a large cup in her hand. "Drink this. It's our strongest wine."

"What did you have to hit me like that for?" Eliezer found his voice again. "I wasn't hurting you."

"You startled me," she said. "I'm sorry, I didn't mean to hurt you." Why had she rebelled against his kisses? She began to feel sorry about that action as well.

"I didn't mean to frighten you," Eliezer said, wondering if he had been possessed by Keteb Meriri. "I hope this hasn't changed your mind."

"I guess I'll still marry you, but I want you to understand something," she said. "First of all, don't run back to Papa about this. You'll just make him mad. Let me talk to him."

"I'll wait until my father arrives for the Hot Fair then."

"Secondly, just because I've agreed to marry you doesn't mean you can kiss me anytime you feel like it." Rachel regretted her choice of words at once. She wanted him to kiss her again so she could appreciate it properly, but she didn't want him thinking he owned her.

"Don't worry about that," came his stinging reply. "After what I just went through, I'd rather kiss a rabid dog."

"Liar." Unable to resist his challenge, she leaned over and kissed him.

Stunned into acquiescence by her boldness, Eliezer sat back as her lips softly played on his, her fingers stroking the back of his neck. Then he pulled her into his lap, the ache in his loins soon replaced by an altogether different feeling. When he thought he was about to die of pleasure, she pulled away.

"We can't sit here all day like this," she rebuked him, as if it were his idea to start kissing again. "I have work to do in the vineyard and I'm sure you have studying to do." She shook out her skirts and began to walk away.

"*Non*, I don't." He caught up to her and pulled her toward him. "I've already memorized today's lesson."

"Then you can help in the vineyard," she said. "But no more kissing until our fathers have signed a betrothal agreement."

Eliezer allowed her to take his silence for assent. Walking beside her, he grinned as he imagined what Asher would say about the afternoon's amazing conclusion. Then a disturbing thought assailed him.

"Belle Assez, where did you learn to kiss like that?"

"Are you accusing me of kissing somebody else first?"

"Of course not," he said, recalling her earlier display of anger. But there was a calm expression on her face. "*Oui* actually," he admitted with a smile.

She smiled back at him. "I've learned a lot from spying on my sisters."

"Both your sisters?" Eliezer had heard rumors about Meir's virility, something to do with a magic mirror, and he'd seen Joheved and Meir embrace passionately on occasion. "I'd have called Miriam and Judah a couple of cold fish."

"I don't mean Miriam and Judah, I mean Miriam and Benjamin, the one she was betrothed to first."

"Oh." Eliezer sighed, sadly remembering his brother's best friend. But the afternoon's events had been too wonderful for him to think about death, and when his intended asked him what he thought of to-day's Talmud lesson, he deliberately gave an answer she'd be sure to contradict.

Sure that the footsteps coming up the steps belonged to her husband, Miriam rolled over so the light from the open door wouldn't wake her fully. She didn't mind him coming home so late. While she was *niddah* during the Hot Fair, Judah could stay up studying every night. But instead of opening, there was a soft knock on the door.

"Mistress Miriam," the maidservant Jeanne whispered. "Cresslin is here for you. His wife needs you tonight."

It was about time, Miriam thought, as she quickly dressed and headed downstairs. Muriel looked big enough to burst. "Is my aunt still asleep?" she asked Jeanne.

"*Oui*. Shall I wake her?"

"*Non*, let her sleep." Miriam took up her midwife's basket and headed for the door. "I'll send for her if I need her."

Cresslin was waiting outside with a lamp, not that they needed it. During the fair seasons Count Thibault kept torches burning throughout the city streets at night. They had only gone a block when she saw

Judah coming toward her, accompanied by Meir, Shemayah, and her father.

"I don't know what time I'll be back," she said.

"I understand," Judah replied. "If you're not back in the morning, I'll have breakfast with Papa and be extra quiet when I return from synagogue for *disner*."

She hurried off to Muriel's, her face burning as she heard Shemayah say, "Between her delivering babies all night and him staying out studying, those two will still be barren when the Hot Fair closes."

Muriel's front door opened as they approached, and one of the servants took Miriam's cloak. Climbing upstairs to the lying-in chamber, Miriam tried to shake off memories of the previous time she'd been there. There was a stack of ferns waiting outside the door, and Miriam saw that the room was already prepared. The walls were chalked against Lillit, and both Muriel's birth amulet and her husband's tefillin were hanging on the bedstead. A sweet smell came from the fennel scattered among the rushes.

"Her water broke just before Matins," Muriel's sister said.

Conscious of Muriel's female relatives watching her, Miriam slowly examined the pregnant woman. Were they even now wishing that Aunt Sarah had come?

"Her womb is not yet open," Miriam said. "But that usually happens quickly when a mother already has children."

Something tugged at her mind, and she again ran her hands over the huge belly, probing gently here and there. Miriam could feel her throat tighten as her excitement grew. Forcing herself to remain calm, she continued her examination until she was almost certain.

She stood up and addressed Muriel. "Cresslin needs to go out again and get my aunt." She quickly smiled at the worried women. "I believe there are two babies to be born tonight."

Miriam sent her mind back to the barn at Ramerupt, to the hundreds of twin lambs she'd delivered. As long as neither baby was sideways, she should be able to handle the birth. And it felt like at least one head was pointed down.

By the time Sarah arrived, a head was clearly visible whenever Muriel had a contraction. The experienced midwife congratulated Miriam on her acumen; Muriel was indeed having twins. "If you don't mind, Miriam, I'll let you continue from here." Sarah leaned back on the bench and closed her eyes.

By the time the bells tolled Prime, Muriel's womb was completely open and her pains were coming very fast. When Muriel cried out that she needed to push, Miriam threw some rosemary on the brazier to sweeten the air, and soon the first baby's head was in her hands.

"It's a daughter for you," she said, handing the small but well-formed child to Aunt Sarah to slap.

Miriam reached up to check its twin and feeling a foot, took a deep breath. If this had been a lamb, she would simply have grabbed the other foot and pulled. But with a woman maybe she should try to turn the baby around.

She looked questioningly at her aunt. "I have a leg."

"We have a little time," Sarah said. "Try to shove it back in; now that the first child is out, this one may have room to turn. But if the foot is still down when Muriel needs to push again, then take its fellow and draw the baby out."

Aunt Sarah didn't say it, but Miriam knew she had to be careful that turning the baby didn't crush or tangle its cord. However, luck was with them, and though the second baby refused to turn, Miriam was able to find both feet and guide him into the world.

For this one was a boy, and soon the room was filled with sounds of babies crying and women jabbering. Miriam sagged into Aunt Sarah's arms and sobbed with relief. She had asked for help, but she had delivered both babies herself.

When mother and infants were cleaned up and settled, Miriam finally came downstairs, where she was surprised to find Judah and a group of swarthy strangers in turbans among those praying for Muriel and the twins.

"When Cresslin came to get Sarah and I heard there were twins, I thought they would need more prayers than usual," Judah said. "So I brought along the Eastern merchants I study with in the morning. They all get up early anyway."

"*Merci*, Judah. That was very diligent of you." Miriam knew he would appreciate the comparison to Ben Azzai, whom the Talmud considered the exemplar of diligence.

Salomon suspected nothing unusual when his wife announced a month later that she needed to speak to him. Trying to decide if they could afford new garments for Rosh Hashanah, he set aside several responsa inquiries when Rivka walked into the salon. But when Rachel, Joheved, and Miriam followed her, it became clear that new clothing was not her objective.

"Isn't it strange that nobody has approached you about marrying Rachel?" Rivka's eyes narrowed with suspicion. "After all, Joheved was younger at her betrothal, and that was before you became rosh yeshiva."

"With Joheved we had to act promptly. For who knew if Meir's family would wait or if another such offer would appear. But with Rachel there's no need for haste."

The truth, Salomon suddenly realized, was that he wanted to delay for his own sake. He couldn't abide the thought of anyone taking her away from him. The longer Salomon waited, the longer Rachel would stay his little girl.

Rachel stepped forward. "But surely some men at the Hot Fair have asked for me, Papa?"

"*Oui.*" Unwilling to meet her gaze, he began to sort through the letters before him. "Several approached me last summer, but I refused to betroth one daughter at the same time I was marrying off another."

"That was wise of you." Rivka surprised him with her support, until she continued, "But you should have told me."

"So what about this year?" Miriam asked.

"Rachel is still young." Why was he feeling uncomfortable, the way a deer must feel as hunters stalk it?

"What about Eliezer ben Shemiah?" Joheved tried to sound nonchalant. "Meir tells me that he was among the first to ask for her last year."

"Oy, Eliezer." Salomon sighed. "His brother did approach me, but surely you can't expect Rachel to marry him. Look at the way they fight all the time."

"But I like fighting with him, Papa." Rachel's voice was as sweet as honey. "And I think I'd like to marry him, too."

It was as though she had stabbed him in the heart. Meir and Judah studied Torah because they loved it, but not Eliezer. He studied because he couldn't abide somebody knowing things he did not. And Salomon was sure that he wanted to marry Rachel from the same competitive motive. Not because he cared for her. "But Rachel, dearest Rachel, don't you see that he only wants to marry you because you're beautiful and because your father is the rosh yeshiva?"

"I think you're wrong, Papa," Miriam said. "Maybe you can't see it because you're her father, but the way his eyes follow her, the way his face lights up when she enters the room . . ."

"The way he offered his father's help so promptly when she lost that ring last summer," Rivka added.

"All right." He threw up his hands in defeat. "She can marry him. But no legal betrothal, just an engagement, and that's only after I've reached an agreement with Shemiah. After what happened to Miriam, I will follow the Italian tradition—*erusin* and *nisuin* performed together, at the wedding."

"*Merci*, Papa." Rachel threw her arms around him. "I don't care whether it's an engagement or a betrothal, as long as we have a feast to celebrate and I get a new silk *bliaut*."

Joheved smiled with excitement. "We could have the banquet on the Fifteenth of Av."

"Wouldn't it be better if we had it earlier, while the moon is still waxing?" Rivka asked. Due to the lunar calendar, the moon was always full on the fifteenth day of a Jewish month.

"But the fifteenth day of Av is when all the maidens of Jerusalem went out dressed in white to dance in the vineyards, inviting the young men to court them," Joheved explained.

"To lift up their eyes and see who they would choose for themselves. Rabban Gamaliel said: 'There were never greater days of joy in Israel than the Fifteenth of Av.'

It says so in Tractate Taanit."

"But why the Fifteenth of Av, Papa?" Rachel asked. She hadn't studied Tractate Taanit yet.

"While the Israelites wandered in the desert, waiting for the generation of Egypt to die out so they could enter the Promised Land, people didn't get sick and die throughout the year like they do now," Salomon said. "Once a year, on the Ninth of Av, everyone dug a grave and slept in it. The next day they'd discover that one fortieth of them had died during the night."

"No wonder the Ninth of Av is a day of mourning," Rachel said, her eyes wide. "But what about the fifteenth?"

"After forty years of wandering, the Israelites dug graves like usual on the Ninth of Av. But everyone was still alive in the morning. Thinking they had miscalculated the calendar, they slept in their graves the next night and again nobody died," he said. "They did the same thing each night until the fifteenth. With the moon full, they realized that the evil ninth day had passed and they were finally worthy to enter the Land. So they declared the fifteenth a festival."

Salomon turned to his wife. "At least the full moon is not a waning moon, and Shemiah will surely have arrived by the Fifteenth of Av."

It was strange preparing for an unofficial betrothal feast, especially one so unofficial that the groom's father hadn't agreed to it yet. But Asher had Shemiah's letters of credit, and he set to work making the arrangements, including a visit to Avram to retire Salomon's debt and one to the cloth fair to purchase a suitable length of emerald green silk brocade, the same shade as Rachel's eyes.

Miriam tried to share the enthusiasm of her mother and sisters, but Rachel's love match only brought back more memories of Benjamin. *How could it be seven years since our betrothal?* If that wasn't enough to dampen her spirits, she was surrounded by babies. Each birth she attended was a stabbing reminder that she and Judah had been intimate for almost a year and she still wasn't pregnant.

At home, watching Joheved nurse little Samuel or Anna hold her baby daughter, Miriam was filled with a bitterness she couldn't dispel, as though she had swallowed something rotten. Even the animals seemed determine to taunt her, as litters of kittens roamed the courtyard.

Miriam was not the only one dismayed by her barrenness. When Alvina arrived in Troyes, she was pleased that Miriam would stay up until Judah and the other men returned from the study hall. To make the wait less lonely, Alvina would join her in a game of chess.

But as the Hot Fair waned, Judah began coming home later and later, and eventually the two women found themselves giving up and going to bed. Even worse, Miriam was called to check her patients at least weekly, often not coming home until morning.

Alvina said nothing untoward, but her frustration grew. Finally, one night when the Matins bells chimed and Miriam leaned over to blow out the lamp, her mother-in-law stopped her and, in a firm voice, declared that she would wait until her son returned, even if she had to stay awake until the sun rose.

It was shortly after Lauds when an exhausted but exhilarated Judah bid Salomon good night and quietly let himself into his house, only to find his mother waiting up for him. Miriam groggily heard the men's voices outside and awoke completely as soon as she heard Alvina speak.

"What do you mean by letting your wife go to bed by herself when she's not *niddah*?" Alvina was trying to whisper, but her voice was loud enough for Miriam to hear. "I've been waiting over a year for a grandchild, and I don't want to wait forever."

Miriam couldn't make out Judah's reply, but Alvina's next words were quite clear. "At first I thought it was your flat-chested wife's fault, that you should have married someone more womanly, but now I see that the fault is yours." Before her son could say anything, she continued, "If you cannot bring yourself to sleep with your wife, you should divorce her and marry one you find more attractive."

This demand brought an audible response. "I find my wife very attractive; in fact, we are perfectly compatible. But I am a scholar and during the Hot Fair . . ." His voice lowered and Miriam lost the rest of his defense. She strained to hear them both, unsure of whose side she supported.

Whatever Judah said apparently did not mollify his mother. "Meir and Shemayah can stay up as late as they like; Meir has a newborn and Shemayah's wife is pregnant."

Again the conversation became too quiet to hear, but eventually Alvina gave her son an ultimatum. "All right then, wait until the Hot Fair is finished and you feel rested. But I still want you to consult with Azariel. He's had no trouble getting his wife with child."

Judah was halfway up the stairs at this point, so Miriam clearly heard his irate reply. "Since you insist, I'll speak to him. Now *bonne nuite*, Mama!"

Miriam could feel him trembling once he got into bed, although she didn't know if it was with anger or humiliation. Embarrassed by the ribald songs and stories that most Frenchmen enjoyed, he would surely find discussing his own marital intimacies mortifying, even with his brother.

But if he was going to consult Azariel, perhaps she ought to consult Aunt Sarah. After all, who knew more about pregnancy? But in the morning Miriam decided to wait a few days until she was due to flower. She might already be pregnant, and why trouble her aunt for nothing?

Judah, on the other hand, cornered his brother immediately after *disner*. The sooner their loathsome conversation was finished, the sooner his mother would be satisfied and he could return to his studies.

Azariel, not eager to give advice to a man so obviously reluctant to hear it, kept their discussion short. "How often do you use the bed?"

Judah expected that question. "On Friday nights and after Miriam comes back from the *mikvah*, as the Talmud recommends."

Azariel sighed. "Once a week for scholars is the minimum. And if you want to have sons, the Sages advocate twice a night."

"I guess we can use the bed more often," Judah said. That should be easy enough.

But later, he wasn't so sure. Now he didn't have to do anything special to seduce Miriam; she expected them to be intimate on Erev Shabbat.

More frequent relations would require him to take the initiative. And there was another potential problem. His wife was a demure and pious woman; what if she didn't want to use the bed more often?

Judah decided that it might be better if he waited, not only for the Hot Fair to finish, but until the end of Elul as well. He could scarcely expect to have the strength to lie with his wife twice a night while he was also getting up at midnight and before dawn for penitential prayers, not to mention spending his days treading grapes to help Salomon make wine. It would be best to wait until after Yom Kippur.

When Miriam flowered on the twelfth of Av, she too chose to delay matters. She'd wait until Elul to talk to Aunt Sarah, especially since her family was so busy arranging for Rachel's engagement feast.

thirteen

liezer was furious to learn that he and Rachel would merely be engaged, not betrothed. He wanted a union that couldn't be broken if his fiancée had a fit of pique. But then his father, Shemiah, arrived, and with him a gift for Salomon that guaranteed their contract would not be breached. The students milled around excitedly as Shemiah untied ropes, unfastened locks, and finally opened the first chest. There had been a few discreet wagers placed on what treasure they contained, but nobody was prepared for what they saw.

The chest was full of books, covers embossed with Hebrew letters. Salomon picked one up, gently peeked inside, and exhaled in awe. It was a tractate of Talmud, written by a master scribe, and the other boxes surely contained the tractates that completed the set. These chests could not have been more valuable if they had been filled with gold, or with pepper.

"They're from Bavel," Shemiah said, beaming with pride as Meir and Judah stepped forward to examine them.

Joheved watched her father's eyes glitter with desire. "I think Papa feels the same about those books as Eliezer feels about our sister," she whispered to Miriam.

Miriam nodded in agreement. "Papa will never let Rachel change her mind. He'd have to give them back."

Rachel's feelings warred within her. How could she not feel flattered at such a valuable betrothal gift? Then she noticed the smug look on Eliezer's face, and the trapped feeling she'd felt when he first kissed her welled up in her. She knew what he was thinking—he owned her now; her father had just sold her for the price of a set of Talmud.

Eliezer saw the scowl on her face and read her thoughts as easily as she read his. With a grin, he pulled a small bag from his sleeve and offered it to her. Rachel wanted to throw it back in his insufferable face, but she smiled graciously and reached inside. Her smile took on real warmth as she pulled out the red coral necklace she'd been forced to surrender last summer.

"Allow me." He fastened it around her neck, at the same time caressing her skin in a way that sent shivers down her back. Then, just before she put the bag away, he asked her, "Are you sure it's empty?"

Indeed, there was something at the bottom, something that turned out to be an exquisite emerald and diamond brooch. "For you to wear at our engagement banquet, along with these." He produced another bag that held the matching earrings.

Jewels! He gave me jewels.

Reluctant to publicly kiss his palm in gratitude, she stood in flustered silence until Rivka whispered, "Rachel, where are your manners?"

"Oh *non*, it is I who should be thanking her," Eliezer replied, as charming as only he could be.

He bent down to kiss her hand, and again Rachel felt shivers at his touch. I will not give in to him, she told herself. We will see who ends up owning whom.

When Miriam found herself *niddah* again, she consulted Aunt Sarah and was quickly informed of the difficulty.

"I'm still intact?" Miriam sputtered. "How can that be? Judah and I use the bed every week when I'm clean."

"There's no doubt, dear. In spite of whatever you and Judah are doing, you are still a virgin." Sarah smiled at her niece's innocence. "Don't worry, I can cure you with a sharp knife."

Miriam couldn't look Aunt Sarah in the eye, she was so embarrassed. "I feel so stupid."

"You're not the first woman I've seen with this problem. Pious yeshiva students seem to think that everything they need to know is in the

Talmud." Sarah waited for Miriam to look at her. "Do you regret marrying Judah? If so, you shouldn't have any trouble getting a divorce."

Miriam gulped. Ask Judah for a divorce? "He's not Benjamin, but I'm not sorry I married him."

"Yet." Sarah hesitated and then added, "It took three years before I regretted marrying Levi."

"What was the matter with him?" Maybe it had taken Aunt Sarah even longer to get pregnant.

"Levi would stay out late gambling, and losing, whenever he got the chance." Sarah grimaced at the memory. "If I hadn't been such a popular midwife, we would have starved."

"Judah stays out late, but he's studying," Miriam said. According to the family accounts, he rarely spent any money.

"Whatever Judah is doing at night, it's not what he needs to do to get you pregnant."

"So, what should I do?"

"When a woman complains to me that her husband's ardor has flagged, I recommend a potion to strengthen his *yetzer hara.*"

"Really? What's in it?"

"It's called cantharides. It's made from a beetle that lives near the Mediterranean Sea, and its effect is equally powerful for men and women," Sarah explained. "The wife puts a small amount in a cup of wine—too much is dangerous—and the husband drinks it at bedtime."

"And then?" Miriam asked, her eyes wide.

"He is soon seized with insatiable desire, and his wife will find him eager to perform the holy deed many times." Sarah smiled benignly at Miriam. Her niece would not remain barren for lack of trying. "Under its influence, even the greatest scholar will be quite unable to subdue his *yetzer.*"

Miriam couldn't imagine Judah in such a state. Or herself, for that matter. "Does the wife drink some as well, so her passion matches his?"

"Perhaps a small amount," Sarah warned her.

Miriam swallowed hard. "Supposing, just supposing, that I agree to this treatment. When would be the best time?" Maybe she should just have Sarah open her and that would be enough.

"The best time to open you would be when you have your flowers. You wouldn't notice the extra blood, and it would give you time to heal," Sarah said. "As for the potion, I'd advise using it when you return from the *mikvah*."

"I'm *niddah* now." Miriam paused to calculate when she'd be clean again. "So I'll be going to the *mikvah* again just before Selichot. But I don't want to do this while we're preparing for the Days of Awe."

Selichot—the word itself means prayer of repentance—was the highlight of the penitential month of Elul. All month the pious rose at midnight and again before dawn to confess their sins and plead for the Almighty's forgiveness. Ordinary Jews were satisfied with the Selichot service that took place at midnight on the Saturday preceding Rosh Hashanah.

Only a few women left their homes in the middle of the night for the service at the synagogue. Joheved had gone a few times after she married, but once little Isaac was born she began staying home, and Miriam would join her in the penitential prayers in the salon. But now Miriam was married, so she decided to accompany Judah for Selichot. She would reap one benefit of not having children.

Wrapped in a heavy cloak, Miriam waited quietly between her father and husband as Meir lit the torch. When Judah closed the courtyard gate, several neighbors approached to join them. They slowly walked through the silent streets, meeting other torch-lit groups making their somber way toward the old stone synagogue. Wisps of fog floated by, and Miriam could almost imagine the *mazikim* heading back to Gehenna after their Shabbat respite. No wonder Mama wouldn't let Rachel go.

Inside, the synagogue lacked the usual cheerful hubbub of voices. Lit only by the torches below, the women's gallery was dark and shadowy, and without a word of discussion Miriam and the other women returned downstairs to take up places along the side. When the Matins bells finished chiming, Papa mounted the raised bima in the center and the service began, as it says in Psalms,

"At midnight I will rise to give thanks unto You."

At other times prominent men bid for the privilege of being the synagogue's reader, but tonight the community turned to its most pious and learned member to plead their case. He began by quoting from Mishnah Tractate Taanit, a litany in which the important men of scripture, from Abraham through Ezra, were listed as examples of the Holy One's mercy.

> "He who answered Abraham on Mount Moriah, may He answer us and hearken to our cries this day . . . He who answered Joseph in the dungeon, may He answer us . . . He who answered Moses at the Red Sea, may He answer us . . ."

Miriam reflected on her own predicament. Should she only have her hymen cut or give Judah the potion as well? And if the latter, should she drink some herself? Such a powerful potion would be dangerous. What if it affected her but not him?

She forced her thoughts back to Selichot as the congregation responded by reciting the Thirteen Divine Attributes revealed to Moses after the Israelites sinned with the golden calf. When Moses prayed on their behalf, "Show me Your glory," the Almighty forgave them and proclaimed,

> Adonai, Adonai, a God compassionate and gracious, slow to anger, abounding in mercy and faithfulness, extending kindness to the thousandth generation, forgiving iniquity, transgression and sin and acquitting . . .

Miriam smiled to herself as she remembered how she and Joheved had argued about what the attributes actually were and how to get thirteen of them from this list.

Papa reminded the congregation, "The reason we recite the Thirteen Divine Attributes so often during our *selichot* prayers is because in Tractate Rosh Hashanah,

Rav Yohanan said: The Holy One, Blessed be He, told Moses, 'Any time that Israel sins, let them say this prayer before Me and I will forgive them.'

Thus we repeat this supplication of Moses, hoping that our prayers will prove equally efficacious."

But penitential prayers recited without remorse are worthless, so the congregation followed the Thirteen Divine Attributes with a confession of sins. In previous years Miriam barely paid attention to the words as she beat her breast when each sin was admitted, but this time she felt increasingly troubled as she declared, "We have acted perversely . . . we have been presumptuous . . . we have led others astray,"

Wouldn't she be committing these sins if she gave the potion to Judah without telling him? But being fruitful and multiplying was the first commandment the Holy One gave man after creating him; surely her actions would not be sinful if that was the intended result. And shouldn't she use every means available to get pregnant? Yet what about the danger? As the service drew to a close, she made her decision. They would both drink the potion; may the Holy One grant her mercy and forgiveness.

By Yom Kippur, Miriam had asked for and received Judah's forgiveness for any injury she caused or might cause him, and he had done the same with her. He even asked her to forgive him for not fulfilling his marital duties more diligently and practically begged her to let him increase their frequency.

Without a hint of what lay in store for her husband, she agreed that after her next visit to the *mikvah*, they could perform the holy deed on Tuesday night as well as on Erev Shabbat. That was a propitious time, since it was only after the Holy One finished with creation on Tuesday that He said "it was good" twice. Besides, everyone knew that a child conceived on Sunday or Monday would be born on Shabbat, which would surely entail desecrating the holy day.

Miriam's flowers began the day after Yom Kippur, and that night she yelped briefly as Aunt Sarah took her sharpest knife and cut out the recalcitrant membrane. But three days later, on the eve of Sukkot, came news that threatened to scuttle their plan. The women were nearly finished with preparations for the evening meal in the sukkah, when Meir burst through the gate, picked up little Isaac, and began swinging him around.

"Guess who's going to be Bridegroom of the Law and Bridegroom of the Beginning at Simchat Torah?" he shouted. When his son happily replied, "Who?" Meir proudly answered, "Your Uncle Judah and I."

"What's a Bridegroom of the Law?" the little boy asked.

Meir tried to explain it simply. "Simchat Torah, which means 'rejoicing in the law,' is when we read the last verse of Deuteronomy. But instead of ending there, we show that Torah study never ends by immediately continuing with the first chapter of Genesis."

"But what does it have to do with weddings?"

"There isn't a real wedding." Meir smiled at his son's confusion. "On Simchat Torah we honor two men by choosing one to bless the reading at the end of the Torah and the other to bless the beginning. The one who has the end is the Bridegroom of the Law and the one who has the beginning is?"

"The Bridegroom of the Beginning!" Isaac yelled back.

Meir swung Isaac around again. "And we have a big party for them and their wives, almost as much fun as a real wedding."

Joheved's forehead creased in worry. "Can we afford it?" Though men no longer bid for Simchat Torah honors, those chosen were expected to make a substantial contribution to the charity fund. She suspected this was the reason that Salomon's name had never been picked.

"With our fine wheat harvest, the manor's revenue should be sufficient." He smiled at Miriam and added, "And if it's not, I'm sure Judah can make up the difference."

"Probably," she replied, trying to hide her dismay. "Alvina did a good deal of business at the Hot Fair after they granted her residency. So she didn't have to split her profits with a local middleman."

Meir's grin widened. "I wouldn't be surprised if they chose Judah for that very reason, to get some of that money back."

The Jewish community of Troyes was very particular about whom they considered a resident. No one could just move into the city and begin doing business there; even when an outsider married into a local Jewish family, he might wait years before being considered a resident. Out of respect for Salomon, Meir had become one upon his marriage to Joheved, but then his family's business at the fairs was limited, just occasional trading in the livestock market.

Judah received the same benefit, but when Alvina insisted that this advantage also accrued to her, many protested that they were Parisians, not true citizens of Troyes. In the end, a compromise was reached where she was permitted to do business as a resident, provided that her fair profits remained in Troyes in the form of a letter of credit for her son and Miriam.

"What am I going to do?" Miriam ran in desperation to Aunt Sarah when she heard the news. "Simchat Torah is the night I'll be ready to visit the *mikvah*. How will I manage if Judah's going to be Bridegroom of the Law?"

"Then he'll be in a festive mood," Sarah said. "You're lucky he's the Bridegroom of the Law. Most of his reading will be done by the time you go to bed, and he'll only have to chant a little in the morning before Meir takes over."

"If there's any difficulty that night, I won't give him the potion."

"Don't be pessimistic." Sarah gave her niece a quick hug. "Remember what an honor it is to be Bride of the Law."

Miriam smiled. *It will be like getting married again—only this time Judah and I will have a real wedding night.*

As the festival of Sukkot drew to a close, with Simchat Torah as its climax, Miriam was drawn into the exciting preparations. Rivka could scarcely contain her pride as she helped her two oldest daughters into their wedding clothes. To Miriam's relief, Judah assumed his role as bridegroom and wore his red silk *bliaut* without complaint. He even managed a smile when she whispered that she had visited the *mikvah* while he and Meir were at the bathhouse.

When the sky darkened, Judah and Meir's attendants arrived at the courtyard. Eight men, bearing banners and torches, would escort the bridegrooms to and from the synagogue. There were four ladies each to escort Joheved and Miriam as well. After several toasts of Salomon's best wine, the party enthusiastically set off.

For Miriam, the evening was a startling reminder of her wedding. Again Judah was the hero. Special hymns greeted his arrival at the synagogue; sweets and scented sprays showered down at him as he headed to the seat of honor, where he was given the Torah scroll to hold. When it came time for his recitation, Miriam could see that he made an effort to actually read the holy text even though he knew it by heart.

> "So Moses the servant of the Eternal died there in Moab, according to the word of the Eternal. He buried him in the valley in the land of Moab, near Beth-peor; and no man knows his burial place to this day . . ."

Miriam smiled as she remembered how Papa's commentary on these verses anticipated a student's question. "How is it possible that Moses died, and then (afterward) wrote, 'So Moses died there'? Some say that Joshua wrote from here onward, but our text says that Moses died according to the word of the Eternal, which teaches us that the Holy One, blessed be He, dictated this passage to Moses, who then wrote it in tears."

When Judah finished the blessings following the Torah reading, pandemonium broke out. Lusty songs split the air as a crowd of dancing men, dressed in their finest, surrounded him and Meir. One by one, each danced with a Torah scroll while the rest of the men kept the two bridegrooms at the center of the swirling mass. Upstairs in their gallery, the women sang and danced around Miriam and Joheved.

Eventually Meir finished his portion, and the celebration spilled into the synagogue courtyard. Banners and torches waving, the crowd soon filled the street outside. Musicians appeared out of nowhere, and the singing grew louder as men and women mingled.

Back home the festive meal awaited them. Miriam had no need to ply Judah with wine; men continually brought him up to dance, and each time he sat down another cup was thrust at him. Miriam had her share of dances, and as she drank more wine she began to appreciate how very attractive Judah was. She saw that she was but one of many females whose gaze followed his dancing form, his dark hair loose around his shoulders and his red silk tunic shining in the torchlight. She also noticed that Judah was growing unsteady on his feet and remembered that she still had a long night ahead of her.

"Judah, it's getting late." She separated him from the men he was dancing with and, hoping she sounded seductive, said, "Have a cup of wine with me upstairs before we go to bed."

Judah's companions sent him off with jokes and suggestive remarks concerning his bridegroom status, and as Miriam pulled him toward the house, they serenaded the couple.

> Rejoice O Bridegroom with the wife of your youth
> Let your heart be merry now and when you grow old
> Sons to your sons shall you see, your old age's crown . . .

Judah was drunker than she had anticipated, making it a struggle to get him up the stairs. He tried to sing the rest of the verses, only to stop and go back to the beginning again.

By the time Miriam managed to get him into their bedroom, he had only reached the third line: "Sons to your sons shall you see, your old age's crown."

With trembling hands Miriam picked up the waiting wine goblet. "I saved a cup of Papa's finest vintage for us to share tonight." She boldly took a long swallow, and then waited anxiously for Judah to finish it.

He sat down heavily on the bed and tugged at his boots. "Could you help me get these off, I'm exhausted." He leaned back and put his feet up for her to reach.

The first boot required some effort, and by the time Miriam had worked the second one off and collapsed on the bed herself, Judah was snoring next to her. *Mon Dieu, what am I going to do now?*

It took awhile to remove all her finery, and when she finally stood to hang up her *bliaut*, she began to notice an itching, tingling sensation in that hidden place between her legs. As it grew more insistent, Miriam approached her husband's prostrate form and began to strip off his clothes. He moaned as she pulled down his *braises*, and she extinguished the lamp.

Not that dream again, not tonight. Judah could feel the hands undressing him, caressing him intimately, yet, try as he might to stay unaffected, he was soon burning with desire. He opened his eyes, or he dreamed that he opened his eyes, because it was too dark to see more than a long-haired female form above him. He knew he should fight the demon and prevent her from mounting him, but his aching loins betrayed him and he was helpless to stop his hips from rising in cooperation as her damp warmth enveloped him. She had bewitched him somehow, and all he could do was writhe in this sweet agony until she at last forced his seed from him.

Still breathing heavily, Miriam fell back on the bed. But their coupling had only sated her temporarily. The heat was returning to her veins, stronger this time. Unable to resist, she turned toward Judah. But he was faster. Before she could kiss him, he was on top of her, furiously driving into her. Sensations she had never imagined possible spread from her womb throughout her body. She moaned, she screamed—a fiery passion was consuming her from the inside. And as the ultimate pleasure began to swell within her, she knew that Judah's frenzied motions would both fuel and quench that blaze.

"Who are you, demon?" Judah demanded afterward, when he was finally able to catch his breath. "What is your name?"

"I'm Miriam, your wife." *How can he not know who I am?*

"That's impossible." In the year he had been intimate with Miriam, it had never been like this. Never! He could feel desire pulsating through him again. "What have you done to me, demon? I can't get enough of you!"

The best response to his questions was to seal his lips with hers. Her breasts and womb were throbbing, and she didn't have to wait long. With each coupling, it took her less time to climax while Judah took longer. All her faculties were focused on the waves of passion sweeping over her, and she was only dimly aware of the Matins bells ringing.

Hours later, as Judah continued to pummel her swollen flesh, all Miriam could do was pray for an end to this pleasure/torment. Had she given Judah too much of the potion? What if he was still affected when it came time for morning services? But this had been her doing, and she was obligated to continue as long as he needed her.

Soon his appetite began to flag. After what seemed like an endless series of thrusts, he let out a strangled cry and crumpled atop her. Her limbs almost too weak to move, Miriam somehow found the strength to roll his limp body off of hers. Succumbing to exhaustion, her final awareness was of church bells chiming Lauds.

fourteen

Ramerupt
Winter 4841 (1081 CE)

Miriam, please consider Samuel and Marona's invitation." Judah spoke softly, trying not to disturb her. "The good air in Ramerupt may help you feel better."

Miriam slowly turned toward him, trying to minimize the wave of nausea that came whenever she lifted her head from the pillow. Why couldn't she have a normal pregnancy? Other women threw up in the morning and felt better immediately, or they felt nauseous for a short time in the afternoon. But she, the midwife, had to be different. She vomited upon waking and her stomach remained queasy the entire day. Only in the evening did she have a few hours of relative comfort. By then, she was too tired to eat.

Neither dill nor lemon balm infusions seemed to help, although Miriam dutifully drank both. Her consolation was Aunt Sarah's assurance that the more nauseous a pregnant woman felt, the less likely she was to miscarry. At least the dill and lemon balm infusions tasted good.

"I suppose I wouldn't feel any worse." Miriam answered with a sigh. "But I'm going to ride there myself." Just the thought of traveling in a jostling cart upset her stomach.

"We can ride there together when it stops raining," Judah said.

It took several days for the weather to clear, and once in Ramerupt, Miriam felt no better, although she had to admit that the clean country air was an improvement over smoky, smelly Troyes. Marona insisted Miriam walk outside at least once a day, even if it was only a few turns around the courtyard. The chilly air seared her lungs, but it also cleared her head.

Eventually she was well enough to walk further and watch the villeins plowing the fields. A young peasant couple was maneuvering the heavy plough down the lengthy furrow, heaping the overturned earth into a ridge in the middle. No wonder the fields were so long and narrow, Miriam thought, as the woman struggled to turn the four oxen pulling the plough around at the furrow's end. Seeing her in profile, Miriam realized that the villein was pregnant. A surge of empathy filled her, and she hurried toward the village.

Ramerupt-sur-Aube was nearly devoid of life. The communal oven sat unattended, and the stocks on the village green held no wrongdoers. The only people she saw were several men working to repair a cotter's roof before the next storm and a few others milling around the alehouse. The pungent odor of fermenting barley compelled Miriam to return to the manor, where she learned that company had arrived.

Miriam was expecting Joheved, who was bringing her sons to spend the winter away from Troyes, where the pox was rampant. But here was Emeline as well. How different she looked. Dressed in an elegant pink *bliaut* that made her skin look fair instead of sallow, Emeline's light blue eyes sparkled with pleasure.

"You've changed since I saw you last," Miriam said.

Emeline smiled broadly. "I was going to say the same thing to you. According to Lady Marona, you've married the handsomest man in France and you're expecting a baby before the Hot Fair."

Miriam smiled too. It was so nice to see her friend again. "What are you doing in Ramerupt? I thought you'd be married by now." Miriam was afraid to ask about Emeline's brother.

"My wedding to Hugh de Plancy is set for May Day." Her voice held no enthusiasm. "After my brother died, Count Thibault became my guardian and took months to approve the arrangements."

"I'm so sorry," Miriam murmured. "I asked about you at court last winter, and they said you'd gone home."

Joheved and Marona offered more expressions of sympathy.

"Thank you, it's been almost six months now." Emeline paused and looked out the window. "There's so much that's happened to me since we last spoke."

"Then you must stay and tell us everything," Marona said.

"Whatever you're cooking smells tempting," Emeline replied.

Miriam noticed that something did smell tempting. Her stomach growled in response and Marona chuckled. "I see your walk outdoors has revived your appetite." She turned to Emeline and said, "Even with this one eating for two, we have more than enough for guests."

Samuel and his steward, Étienne, listened politely as Emeline explained about her brother's injury and how he had removed her from a convent to make her heiress of Méry-sur-Seine.

"Hugh seems an excellent match." Samuel nodded with approval. "The Plancys are also of the old aristocracy, and with the two fiefs so close together, it should be simple to manage them both."

When the servants brought out dessert and Joheved took little Samuel onto her lap to nurse him, Emeline stared at her in astonishment. "You're nursing your own child? But only villeins do that, not noble ladies." She put her hand over her mouth and quickly added, "I didn't mean to insult you."

Joheved smiled at the infant in her arms. "I choose to suckle my son myself. I want him nourished from my own substance, not an ignorant peasant's."

After having longingly watched so many mothers nurse their newborns, Miriam wasn't going to let another women nurse her child either. She felt a fluttering in her belly, one that definitely wasn't coming from her stomach, and gave a small gasp.

"Is anything the matter?" Marona asked.

"I think I just felt the baby move." Miriam concentrated on her midsection. "*Oui*, there it goes again."

Reluctant to alert the Evil Eye, no one at the table offered Miriam congratulations. But all three women smiled.

Miriam felt no more movement until she got into bed that night, and when she did, it reminded her of the villager she'd seen earlier. "Don't you have other people who can plow for you instead of pregnant women?" she asked Joheved.

"I don't see why you should care about them so much. After all, it is Le Bon Dieu's will whether one is born noble or villein." Joheved knew her voice sounded sharp, but once she nursed little Samuel, tucked Isaac in, finished her prayers, and got into bed, she just wanted to go to sleep. "Besides, she must have been working her own family's lands. We won't start plowing the demesne until next week."

"Her own family's lands?" Miriam asked in confusion. "I thought all the manor's land belong to Samuel."

"It's not so simple," Joheved said. "All land in Champagne belongs to Count Thibault, who grants fiefs to his vassals, like Count André, who divide it further among their own lords. So too is this manor split up. The demesne is Samuel's piece, and then there are smaller plots that he grants to his villeins."

"But if it means more work and paying higher rent, why would any villein want more land?" Miriam asked.

Joheved tried to suppress a yawn. "He might have more than one son and want each one to inherit enough to support a family. Also, an industrious villein can earn a good profit from his additional land, more than enough to hire men to do the extra work for him."

"What if he doesn't have any sons?"

"His land returns to the demesne, and Samuel can keep it or rent it out to a new man," Joheved replied. "Just as this estate would revert to Count André if Samuel didn't leave any heirs."

"I see." From now on, when Miriam said her morning blessings she'd pray the third one, "Blessed are you, Adonai our God, King of the world, for not making me a slave," with extra diligence.

During the next two months, Miriam's nausea diminished so that she was able help with the lambing, and to her surprise, Joheved spent every night with the laboring ewes. When she teased her older sister about how squeamish she used to be, Joheved replied that birthing lambs was nothing after changing dirty baby swaddling every day for nearly four years.

Emeline visited several times a week, and between her and Marona, Joheved's education progressed rapidly. Marona had great depth of experience, but she had spent her entire adult life in Ramerupt. In a small span of years, Emeline had seen many estates, both well and poorly managed, and acknowledged that she had learned far more from the latter. Miriam wasn't particularly interested in their discussions, but the company was better than sitting alone.

"You must be wary of corruption among those who serve you," Emeline warned Joheved as the four women walked about the estate one afternoon. "You can tolerate the miller who siphons off a bit of grain for his own use or the fisherman who underreports his catch from your streams, provided their thefts aren't egregious. But the steward who fills his own purse at your expense or the warden who takes bribes to allow poachers in your forest, these must be replaced immediately with honest fellows."

"Joheved won't find problems like that on our small fief," Marona said.

"How many officials do you have?" Emeline asked.

"First there's our steward, Étienne." Joheved began slowly, trying to remember the different duties the lesser officials performed. "Beneath him is Jean Paul, the reeve, who makes sure the villagers report for work promptly and don't slip off without finding a substitute. He also collects the villeins' rents, as well as any fines imposed on them."

Joheved had confided in Miriam her surprise at learning how much money the semiannual manorial court generated. There were fines for neglecting labor work, for allowing livestock to stray into the demesne, for permitting a cottage to fall into disrepair, as well as for such altercations between villeins as cursing, theft, and assault. A man and woman paid a fine for marrying without Lord Samuel's permission, as did adulterers and those who conceived a child out of wedlock. But the most common fine was for brewing violations, levied when an alewife's ale was too weak or who sold it before Marona's official tasting.

"The beadle, the reeve's deputy, his name is Pierre," Joheved continued. "He's responsible for saving seed from last year's crop and for seeing that the demesne is plowed properly. In late summer Pierre has two reap reeves as well, to supervise the harvest. Marona tastes the ale."

"You don't have a bailiff?" Emeline looked surprised.

"*Non*," Marona answered when a baffled Joheved turned to her. "We're too small to need a bailiff and a steward."

"Who takes care of the vineyard?" Emeline asked. "I heard that your family makes wonderful wine."

Miriam finally got a chance to say something. "It's our father who has the vineyard, back in Troyes."

Joheved gave Marona a shy glance. "Although it would be nice to plant one in Ramerupt eventually."

Upon hearing this, Emeline marched them around until Joheved and Miriam agreed on the best south-facing slope. "Your villeins should begin clear-cutting it at once," Emeline said.

"But it's February," Joheved objected. "We need everyone for spring plowing."

"Don't worry about overburdening the villeins," Emeline said. "In return for protection, it's their obligation to perform any labor their lord requires. And compared to what I've seen elsewhere, your villagers have it easy."

"Really?" Miriam found that difficult to believe.

"Definitely. Most peasants get requisitioned for castle upkeep, repairing roads and bridges, digging canals. I met one baron who made his villeins beat the water of his castle's moat to stop the frogs' croaking when he had a hangover."

Emeline smiled up at Marona. "But the greatest boon for your villagers is that Samuel is such a homebody. They never have to contribute for him to go on a pilgrimage, hold a tournament, or, most expensive, ransom him after he's been captured in battle."

Miriam held her tongue. Though villeins were made in the Creator's image, just like all men, it was apparent that Emeline, and Joheved for that matter, saw them as only slightly higher in creation than the oxen or horses they plowed with.

Emeline and Joheved were also interested in news from the outside, and when Judah and Meir came to visit, they questioned the men eagerly. Judah had no curiosity about subjects that took time away from Torah, but Meir was used to bringing such information to Joheved.

Once the Cold Fair ended, and both their sons survived the pox, news consisted mainly of how other children were battling the disease. Luckily the epidemic had been mild, although it hadn't seemed that way in Salomon's household when Baruch's little girl died.

This week, Emeline's last before returning home for Easter, Meir was bursting with news at *disner*. "The Parisian and German wine dealers are here to buy their Passover wine."

Miriam sighed and asked Judah about Papa's *kuntres*. Events outside of Troyes didn't interest her either.

Samuel, however, leaned forward eagerly. "What's the word from Allemagne?"

"It's no rumor. The pope's King Rudolf was mortally wounded last fall," Meir answered. "So King Henry, unopposed at home, has ordained his own pope, Clement, and gathered an army to march on Rome."

"As I anticipated." Samuel turned to Joheved. "That's why I ordered the spring fields planted in oats, to feed warhorses."

"If the war between king and pope worsens," Marona said, "wheat will be even more profitable in the fall."

"Oh dear." Emeline sighed. "What do the Parisians say about Archbishop Manasses? Is there any hope of reconciliation between him and Pope Gregory?"

In 1077 the archbishop of Rheims used the pretext that he feared being ambushed by enemies to refuse the papal legate's summons. In turn the outraged papal legate excommunicated him. For years letters went back and forth from Rheims to Rome concerning how to restore Manasses to his office.

"Evidently the pope imposed too many conditions for the archbishop to accept," Meir told her, shaking his head.

"What a terrible blow to King Philippe," Emeline said. "Do you think this was really about insulting the papal legate, or did Pope Gregory mean to remove one of the king's most faithful vassals and replace him with one more loyal to the Holy See?"

"I don't know," Meir answered. "But all is not black for King Philippe. Reliable sources in Paris tell us that Queen Bertha is enceinte again, that the child is due in midsummer." The reliable source was Judah's mother,

Alvina, who had heard the news from one of the queen's ladies-in-waiting.

"At least our king doesn't spend all his nights in John's bed," Samuel said.

Miriam and Judah exchanged glances and then excused themselves from the table. Let the others gossip; their Talmud discussion would continue in private.

"Papa asked me to help revise his commentary on Tractate Niddah," Judah said once they were alone in their room. "Well, I, uh, found the part about pregnancy in the third chapter, uh, particularly interesting."

"How so?" she asked. *Why does he sound so nervous?*

Once Miriam's pregnancy incapacitated her, marital relations between her and Judah ceased. His return to celibacy meant an agonizing struggle with his *yetzer hara*, especially during the intense Cold Fair study sessions when several of the younger merchants seemed far more attractive than they had in the summer. Judah was increasingly drawn to Levi, the vivacious redhead, so much so that it was almost a relief when the fair ended. Judah kept reminding himself that most scholars avoided cohabitation during early pregnancy, especially since the Sages stated that it was detrimental to the woman and to the fetus. But later on, the holy deed was recommended.

Not sure how well his wife was feeling, Judah had not approached her the previous night, despite it being Shabbat. But today Miriam seemed perfectly healthy. Hopefully, after they studied this section of Tractate Niddah, she would suggest they resume performing the holy act, if only for the baby's sake. Annoyed at his anxiety and cowardice, he brought out the text.

Trying not to be obvious, he began reciting just before the section on marital relations during pregnancy.

> "The Rabbis taught: The first three months, the child occupies the
> womb's lowest chamber; the middle three months, the middle
> chamber; the last three months, the upper chamber. When it is

time to leave, the child turns over and comes out, and this is what causes a woman's pain. It is also taught: the pangs of a female birth are harder than those of a male birth . . . why is this? This one emerges according to her position during cohabitation, and that one emerges according to his position during cohabitation. Thus this one needs to turn herself over, but that one does not turn himself."

Judah, observing his wife's puzzled expression and blushing, gave her Salomon's explanation. "Papa says that just as a man faces down during marital relations and a woman faces up, so too in birth do they assume the same positions—a boy emerges facing down and a girl facing up."

"But even if that were so," Miriam's voice made her skepticism clear. "Isn't there a contradiction between the first Baraita, which states that all babies turn over first, and the second, which says that only females do?"

"In the first one, they mean that the child turns over from head to foot." Judah thought it odd to be explaining this to a midwife. "That is, during pregnancy the baby's head is pointing up until just before birth, at which time he inverts so that his head will exit first."

"That much is true. But even in the short time I've been a midwife, it's apparent that gender has nothing to do with whether a baby is born facing up or facing down. In fact, nearly all children are born facing down."

Judah did not want to get into an argument with her, not now. "Maybe the Sages mean that males and females only face in different directions in the womb, and that is why females have to turn more to get out, thus causing more pain."

Miriam couldn't help but wonder where the Rabbis had gotten such information. "I can tell you that the amount of pain a woman feels in childbirth is completely unrelated to whether it's a boy or a girl. I've seen women delivering boys in terrible agony and women having girls in mild discomfort, as well as vice versa."

"Perhaps you should speak to Papa about it when your family comes up for Passover," Judah said, quick to mollify his wife. "In the meantime, why don't we continue?

> The Rabbis taught: The first three months, cohabitation is harmful to the woman and harmful to the child; the middle three months, it is harmful to the woman and beneficial for the child; the last three months, it is beneficial for the woman and beneficial for the child—since it results in the child being well-formed and strong."

"What does Papa say about this text?" Miriam remembered Joheved teaching her about this passage, and that the Sages had not offered any explanation for their opinions.

"He says that in early pregnancy, when the child is in the lower chamber, the pressure of cohabitation feels painful, but he doesn't know why it should be bad for the mother."

"I suppose the woman might also feel pain then, if she is being pressed by both the child and her husband." Yet Miriam couldn't recall any women complaining about such pain.

"By the middle months, when the child has moved up enough to be unaffected, the mother may still feel the extra pressure," Judah said. When would his wife realize that this discussion wasn't hypothetical?

"And during the final months, the baby is finally high enough that neither it nor the mother feels pressure," Miriam concluded, and then gave a small frown. "But lack of pain is not the same as beneficial. How does Papa explain that?"

"He states that the semen acts to purify the fluid that surrounds the child," Judah replied. "But don't ask me how he knows it. He doesn't say what is beneficial for the woman."

"I'm sure he learned it from his teachers in Allemagne." Miriam thought for a moment. "If a woman's child is strong and vigorous, her labor will likely be shorter and easier. Perhaps that is why it's beneficial for her."

"I'm sure you're right." Judah sat down next to her, hoping she would draw a similar conclusion about their situation.

But she continued with the text. "The next Baraita is nice.

> The Rabbis taught: There are three partners in creating a child—
> The Holy One, Blessed be He, the father and the mother. The fa-

ther's white seed forms the bones, sinews, nails, brain and white of his eye; the mother's red seed forms the skin, flesh, hair, blood and black of his eye; and the Holy One, Blessed be He, gives him breath and soul, his facial features, and eyesight, hearing, speech, and understanding. When his time comes to depart this world, the Holy One, Blessed be He, takes away His part and leaves the father and mother's parts."

Judah leaned closer to share Salomon's *kuntres* with her. "Papa points out that the literal meaning is: 'the seeing of the eye, the hearing of the ear, the speech of the mouth.' Eyes, ears, and mouth come from the parents, but the ability to see, hear, and speak with them are a gift from the Creator. For though a corpse still has these, he can no longer see, hear, or speak because the Holy One has taken back His contribution."

Judah remained silent and Miriam realized that her husband intended a subtle message for her. Feeling well for the first time in months, and amused at his shyness on the subject of marital relations, Miriam began to tease him.

"Judah," she said softly as she took his hand in hers. "I'm in my sixth month now? Aren't you worried that our child may not be as strong and as well-formed as he should be?"

As she anticipated, his face reddened when he understood the implications of her question. "I was more worried about you," he gulped in reply. "You were so ill before."

"I'm not ill now."

"It's not as though I haven't been thinking about it," he replied. Yet he found himself moving away from her.

Miriam forced herself not to smile as her husband tried to elude her. "Doesn't Ben Azzai say one should run to perform a mitzvah?" She leaned toward him. "How about now while it's still the Sabbath?"

"What? In the middle of the day? While it's still light?"

"Well, if you don't want to . . ."

"*Non*, it's not that." What was he doing, trying to avoid relations with her? The very opposite of what he'd planned.

"Do I need to come over there and help you undress?"

"Just let me close the shutters."

She practically did have to undress him. Judah kept his eyes closed until nearly the last moment, but when she rolled away from him as he prepared to enter, he had to look to see where she'd gone. Miriam was kneeling on her hands and knees, her backside facing him, and it was obvious what she intended him to do. He forced himself to think of the child, his child, who needed his semen, and this calmed him enough to enter her. But once inside, nothing could calm him.

A little while later, Miriam listened to Judah's steady breathing at her ear and wondered how soon she should get up. When they used the bed at night, they just fell asleep afterward and then woke the next morning. Still, it was pleasant, snuggled in her husband's arms like two spoons. In fact, it was more pleasant than the act that preceded it.

She thought back to Simchat Torah, when lust had burned through her veins and her womb had ached with desire. Had the brief burst of final pleasure been worth the torment preceding it? If that was what Joheved felt, Miriam was willing to forgo it. Let other women suffer Eve's curse,

Your desire shall be for your husband . . .

A man had enough power over his wife as it was. She was content with kissing before and snuggling after. She affectionately squeezed Judah's arm, draped over her belly.

The child gave a kick, and Judah pulled his hand away with a gasp. "Mon Dieu! Was that the baby?"

Miriam stifled a giggle. "That was him all right."

"Him? You think it's a boy?"

"If repeating the holy act ensures a male child," Miriam said, "then what we did on Simchat Torah should guarantee one."

"Oh." Hoping to feel his child move again, Judah replaced his arm.

He had been thinking about Simchat Torah for months, but, despite his usually excellent memory, he had no recollection of anything after services. Even Sarah's servants knew more about what happened that night than he did. Shortly after Miriam's pregnancy became known, he'd heard them gossiping.

The cook had commented lewdly that it was no surprise to her that the young mistress was enceinte, not after the way she and the master were going at it the night of their festival. Nearly all night, the maidservant Jeanne complained, judging by how long their cries, worse than cats in heat, had continued. The cook then muttered that she wouldn't have thought the master as lustful as that, him being so religious and all, after which Jeanne solemnly declared that strong drink helps the devil overcome even the most pious man.

That night was a mystery, but Judah remembered very well the rest of the week, and the week after. Even now he cringed at how naïve he'd been. For it was obvious that Miriam's door (the Talmudic euphemism for virginity) had been closed before Simchat Torah and was wide open afterward. Which meant that she was probably bleeding from when he'd opened her, yet they'd used the bed several more times that night.

Had his child been conceived in sin, while Miriam was *niddah*? His wife would think him a fool, but he had to ask.

"About that night on Simchat Torah?"

Miriam froze. "What about it?"

"It's pretty much a blank for me, but I'm sorry if I hurt you." He took a deep breath. "Did you bleed very much?"

"You didn't hurt me," she said. "And I didn't bleed." *Thank Heaven he has no memory of what happened.*

"You didn't? How is that possible?" The relief in Judah's voice was obvious, but there was doubt too.

It took Miriam a moment to realize that Judah's concern about Simchat Torah was whether they'd used the bed while she was bleeding. She patted his arm reassuringly. "I didn't bleed because two weeks earlier, while I was *niddah*, Aunt Sarah opened me with a sharp knife. I was completely healed by Simchat Torah. Don't worry, our child was conceived in purity."

At first Judah was too ashamed to mention his previous ineptitude.

But Miriam had gone to her aunt for help, so she'd obviously recognized it. He had to say something. "I'm sorry I was so incompetent. I can't imagine what you must think of me."

"Don't disparage yourself." She squeezed his hand. "Since my door was so tightly closed that it took a knife to open it, I'm grateful that you didn't use too much force and injure me." If anyone had been incompetent it had been herself. What kind of midwife could be unaware that she'd remained a virgin despite a whole year of marriage?

Not all Judah's anxieties were resolved either. One festival with too much drinking and his *yetzer hara* had completely escaped his control. This time he was lucky and the consequence was his wife's pregnancy, but next time . . . ? *Non*, he told himself firmly, there would be no next time.

fifteen

Troyes
Late Spring 4841 (1081 CE)

or the third time since she'd sat down to breakfast, Miriam adjusted her position on the bench. If she tried to eat over her dish on the table, her belly got in the way, and if she tried to bring a spoonful of stuff to her mouth, she risked spilling it. She shifted her weight again, and then, defeated, picked up her bowl of stirabout and drank it like a cup of soup.

Yet if trying to eat was bothersome, trying to sleep was worse. No sooner did she lie down than the baby began kicking her. The previous night had been particularly trying; at one point she'd awakened in pain with one of the child's limbs stuck under her ribcage.

When will this child be born? But she wasn't close to her time; the baby was still high in her womb. Lost in thought, she scarcely noticed when the courtyard geese began to squawk in alarm. Suddenly Joseph, the *parnas*'s son, was in the dining room.

"Joseph, to what do we owe this pleasure . . ." Salomon stood to greet his friend, and then, observing the consternation on the man's face, continued, "Whatever is the matter?"

Rivka brought a goblet of wine to their distraught guest, but Joseph waved it aside to address Miriam and Sarah. "You've got to come back with me. Johanna needs you."

Sarah's brows rose in surprise. "Johanna? Are you sure?"

"She's been feeling poorly since Passover but refused to consult the doctor," Joseph began. "Last night her belly ached so much that neither of us slept, and she was in such agony this morning that I ran to Moses's house and had him come immediately. He was only with Johanna a few

208

moments before he came out with this stupid grin on his face and told me, 'Your wife doesn't need a doctor, she needs a midwife!'"

"She's having a baby?" Miriam couldn't have understood him properly. "But your sons are—"

"Twenty, and already fathers themselves," he replied, shaking his head. "I can't believe it either. We assumed that she'd been through the change when her flowers stopped."

Sarah motioned Miriam to get their midwife supplies, scattering Samuelis's poultry as they hurried toward the gate. Salomon, Judah, and the yeshiva students followed in their wake. The blue door of the richest house on Rue de Vieille-Rome opened at their approach, and the two midwives rushed upstairs. Johanna was sitting in bed, sweat streaming down her face, while Moses stood besides her, taking her pulse.

"You're just in time," he greeted them as Johanna abruptly grimaced in pain. "I'll wait downstairs." He headed below, where the men had begun praying for Johanna and the baby's health, and called out, "Has anyone found a cradle yet?"

Sarah lifted her patient's chemise and began to palpate the woman's massive abdomen. Miriam then gently pushed her hand between the pair of corpulent thighs and reached into the birth passage to assess how far the womb had opened. A contraction came during this examination, and Miriam felt the baby's head bulge forward against her fingers.

It took two servants and both midwives to help the heavy woman onto the birthing stool. Miriam had never attended anyone so fat before—no wonder nobody suspected she was pregnant. And despite the folds of flesh that Miriam worried might impede the child's exit, Johanna eventually pushed out the largest baby Miriam had ever seen.

"Mazel tov! You have a son," she declared loudly. "And what a son—look at the size of him! He's a giant." Miriam gave the baby a measured swat and was rewarded with a resounding yowl.

As astonished servants cleaned the baby and the even more astonished mother, Miriam got an opportunity to observe her surroundings. She tried to hide her awe as she surreptitiously surveyed the intricately carved bed frame, the elaborate inlaid chests, the brightly patterned wall hangings, the soft furs that served as blankets. Instead of rushes on the floor, there was a heavy woven tapestry. Judah had provided some fine furnishings for their wedding chamber, but Johanna's bedroom was nearly as opulent as Countess Adelaide's.

Reluctant to leave such a beautiful room, Miriam stayed until Joseph's appearance made her presence intrusive. She came downstairs to find Isaac haParnas pouring wine for Salomon, Shemayah, and Meir. Judah was sitting at the dining table, engrossed, as usual, in some manuscript. Across the room, Sarah was deep in conversation with the doctor.

"Miriam." Sarah motioned for her to join them.

"Have a taste of this." Instead of a goblet of wine, Moses held out his clear glass urine container, which contained a pale yellow liquid, undoubtedly Johanna's.

Miriam looked at him in alarm. "Why?"

"You don't have to gulp it down," Sarah said with a smile. "Just dip your little finger in and put some on your tongue."

Not sure what she ought to discern, Miriam followed her aunt's instructions. "It tastes sweet, almost like honey." She tasted another drop to make sure.

Before she could say anything more, the doctor began to whisper, "Johanna has diabetes, that's what makes her urine sweet. It's not surprising, considering her size." He shook his head sadly. "I can advise her to change her diet so she'll lose weight, but otherwise there's little I can do for her."

Sarah frowned. "Don't be so pessimistic. It's not unusual for an older woman, especially a large one like Johanna, to develop diabetes during pregnancy, only to have it disappear after she gives birth. If I had known she was pregnant, and I could kick myself for not noticing, I would have checked her for the condition earlier."

She turned to Miriam. "Often the first sign of diabetes in a woman is the birth of an exceptionally large baby. Whenever you deliver one, you should taste the mother's urine. If it tastes sweet like this, inform the doctor."

Miriam had never heard of diabetes. "Can you treat it?"

"The disease clearly comes from the patient consuming too much sweet food," Moses said. "Until such time as her urine no longer tastes sweet, she should avoid desserts such as pastries, cakes, and pies, as well as fruit tarts and preserves."

Riding back to Ramerupt that afternoon, Meir eagerly anticipated sharing the day's surprising events with Joheved. His wife never complained about her isolation at his family's rural estate, but surely she felt lonely away from her family and friends. He brought her news every day, something from the morning Talmud lesson, as well as a story involving her parents or sisters. It was rarely exciting stuff, and Meir smiled as he imagined Joheved's reaction upon hearing about Johanna's unexpected pregnancy and its successful conclusion.

Meir was mistaken about Joheved missing Troyes' urban life. She had never been a social creature and was content with her small circle in Ramerupt. What she missed in Troyes was its yeshiva, the arguments and discussions that were as much a part of mealtime as the food, the lessons she overheard while working in the vineyard, the atmosphere of erudition that permeated the Jewish Quarter along with the tannery smell.

But Joheved was not exiled from her city of birth. She spent nearly every Shabbat in Troyes, and she would be returning for a lengthy stay at the beginning of the Hot Fair. Then she and Meir, and their sons, would take up residence in their old room on the second floor of her father's house until the vintage and Sukkot were finished. Many summer days would still be spent in Ramerupt, especially during the harvest. And something wonderful she had discovered today was likely to keep her even busier at the estate this summer, something she couldn't wait to tell her husband.

This morning an elderly housemaid who supervised the laundry had approached Joheved. "Is it true that brush is being cut back to make space for a vineyard?"

"*Oui,*" Joheved replied.

The woman broke into a toothless grin. "When I was a little girl," she whispered, as if imparting some great secret, "my brother and I used to play in the bushes on the slope above the far sheep meadow. If we crawled down low, it was like there were tunnels in them, our own secret passages."

Joheved couldn't imagine why this old servant thought she would be interested in these childhood memories. Hoping the woman wasn't senile, Joheved forced herself to listen patiently.

"We never told anyone about them, just me and my brother knew. They were such fun to hide in; nobody could ever find us. The best part was in the fall, when we could eat as much fruit as we wanted. I never tasted anything so sweet in all my life."

It took Joheved a little while to put everything together. "You mean there already is a vineyard on our land and you used to play in it?"

"*Oui*," the laundress said. "I can take you there now while the linens are soaking."

As they reached the last of the sheep meadows, Joheved looked anxiously at the southern slope rising above it. While it was true that no trees grew there, the hillside was so overgrown that it was impossible to distinguish any grapevines among the other shrubbery. Only when she began to push through the vegetation did she recognize the familiar leaves and curling stems. Then she rushed back to the manor, too impatient to return at the old servant's pace.

"Even if the other plants are removed," Joheved told her in-laws, "I have no idea if these ancient vines will yield worthwhile fruit."

"Certainly we must clear out the slope," Samuel said. He shook his head in amazement. "Who would have imagined a vineyard on the estate all these years?"

"How do we know if the grapes are any good?" Marona asked.

"I've been thinking about that." Joheved had been thinking of little else. "We could remove the other plants in a small area of the vineyard, then trim back and train the grapevines there, taking proper care of them all summer. In the fall my father and I will taste the ripe grapes."

Marona sighed with disappointment. "I hoped that we could begin removing the other bushes now, before the villeins are busy with the harvest." She shrugged in resignation. "But that would be a tremendous waste if it turned out that the grapes weren't worth the effort."

"This old vineyard has probably waited a hundred years to be put into production." Samuel patted his wife's hand. "If there's wine to be wrung from her, she can wait a few more."

But does Samuel have a few more years? Joheved tried to put the sad thought out of her head. Perhaps the desire to drink wine from his own vineyard would keep Meir's father, may the Holy One protect him, alive until then. Soon Joheved's enthusiasm dispelled her concern over Samuel's poor health.

"Just think of the surprise we'll have for Meir when he comes home," she said.

For an excuse to be outside, Joheved occupied herself with weeding the herb garden. Emeline would have disapproved, but the sun was pleasantly warm, and the soft, damp earth felt good in Joheved's hands. She was enjoying a sense of accomplishment at the large pile of exhumed weeds, when she heard the manor's gate opening. She jumped up to welcome her husband, only to realize that her hands were covered with dirt. Thus Meir was the one to greet her, as she bent over the well washing her hands.

His eyes were wide with excitement. "The most amazing thing happened today. I could hardly believe the news."

"Isn't it wonderful?" she agreed, wondering who had informed him of the secret vineyard first. "Who'd imagine that such a thing could remain hidden so long?"

Sure that somebody from Troyes had already told her about Johanna's baby, Meir tried to hide his disappointment. "I was so surprised when I arrived at the yeshiva only to learn that everyone had rushed off to the *parnas*'s house."

She stared at him in bewilderment. "Why are you talking about the *parnas?*" *What could he have to do with the new vineyard?*

"I'm talking about what happened at the *parnas*'s house." He couldn't understand her confusion, until he came to the obvious conclusion. "What did you think I was talking about?"

"Something wonderful and amazing happened here," she announced. "Here, on your own estate."

"That may be, but I'll wager it wasn't as wonderful and amazing as what happened in Troyes."

Joheved beamed with confidence. "I'll take your wager."

"Very well. Now tell about the wonderful and amazing thing I missed here."

As she informed him of the morning's discovery, his eyes widened and he nodded appreciatively, but he declared with a grin that he was still going to win.

"Mon Dieu, Mon Dieu," Joheved kept repeating as Meir shared the details. Uncovering a hundred-year-old abandoned vineyard in Ramerupt was certainly unexpected, but what happened to Johanna in Troyes was a miracle.

"I admit it, your story wins." She was still shaking her head in disbelief. She looked up with a seductive smile, "So what prize do I owe you?"

He laughed and gave her a quick kiss. "How about a cask of wine from our own vineyard?"

Before she could retort, they were interrupted by their eldest son yelling, "Papa, Papa," as he ran toward them. Not to be outdone, young Samuel's howls of hunger from the house sent Joheved hurrying inside. Ah, the joys of family life, Meir thought in amusement, as he imagined Joseph and Johanna, already grandparents, starting over with a newborn.

It was less than a month later, on a warm late Friday afternoon, that Meir was pacing Salomon's courtyard, waiting for his wife and sons' arrival for the Sabbath. As the sun sank lower in the sky, he was nearly ready to ride out and meet them when he heard Joheved outside the gate, wishing a good Sabbath to the merchant who had accompanied her. To his surprise, he could hear his parents adding their adieus.

"I'm sorry if we worried you." Trying to hide her exasperation, Joheved handed Meir their sleeping infant son. She waited until her in-laws were out of hearing and added, "At the last moment your father decided that he wanted to celebrate Shavuot in Troyes, and your mother couldn't dissuade him."

Meir sighed. "So of course, you and the boys waited for them." He was helping Samuel dismount when Salomon burst out the door and made a beeline for them.

"Isaac, you're just in time." With no apparent effort, Salomon hoisted his grandson onto his shoulders. "You can come with me to the stews, and then we'll go to synagogue."

"Do we still have time to stop at the bakery on the way, Grandpapa?" Despite Isaac's attempt at secrecy, his whisper was quite audible. "Or did we get here too late?"

"Shh," Salomon hushed him, as Meir and Joheved pretended to ignore their exchange.

Once the men left for services, Joheved got her chance to comment on Miriam's pregnancy. "The baby has definitely dropped since last week. You look like you're due any day."

"Don't say that. Judah would be terribly upset if his child's birth caused the Sabbath to be desecrated."

At least Miriam lived with the midwife, so nobody would be carrying anything outside on the Sabbath. Still, some forbidden work would be necessary if a baby was delivered that day. And of course, a boy born on Saturday would have to be circumcised the following Sabbath, necessitating more normally prohibited activity. But underlying these concerns was the fact that Jews believed just as firmly as their Notzrim neighbors that a child born under the influence of Saturn was particularly likely to suffer poverty, wounds, illness, or an untimely death.

"You're wearing a knife on your belt," Marona pointed out. During the days just prior to delivery, pregnant women were advised to keep a knife with them whenever they were alone, as protection against *mazikim*.

"It's easier to wear one all the time than to keep taking it off and putting it back on," Miriam said with a sigh.

"It's also easier than having Mama remind you about it constantly," Joheved said.

Suddenly Miriam clutched her belly.

Marona took her arm. "Is it the baby?"

"It's only my stomach," she reassured them. "All of a sudden I really need to use the privy." She hurried in that direction, muttering, "I must have eaten too much strawberry preserves today."

"Miriam—eating too much preserves." Joheved scoffed, hoping that the baby was on its way. "Not very likely."

When Miriam refused to attend the second day of Shavuot services because she was still experiencing bouts of diarrhea, Joheved reluctantly accepted that her sister was suffering from indigestion. But when they arrived home to set up the festival's feast and learned that Miriam's cramps were so severe that she couldn't leave her room, Aunt Sarah decided to investigate.

Closely followed by Rivka, Marona, and Joheved, the midwife hurried to Miriam's closed door. "How often have you been using the chamber pot?"

"I had to get up every few hours during the night. This morning it's been more frequent."

"Are you passing any blood?"

"*Non.* I'm not passing much of anything anymore. It's mostly just cramps now." Hearing the women whispering among themselves outside her door, Miriam gasped and asked the question whose answer was suddenly obvious, "Do you think the baby is coming?"

"I'd say it's a strong possibility," Aunt Sarah replied with a smile. "I'd like to examine you to make sure."

"But I'm hardly in any pain," Miriam protested when her labor was confirmed.

"Shh." Rivka looked around nervously. "Don't tempt the Evil Eye."

Aunt Sarah sprang into action. "Rivka, first go downstairs and get two pots of water boiling. I'll want to make an artemisia tisane in one, and we'll keep the other in reserve in case she needs an infusion of ragwort and columbine seeds to speed the birth. Then you can bring back Salomon's tefillin."

"I'll find the birth amulet that Judah got me at the Cold Fair," Miriam said. Rivka had been upset that they'd bought one so early in pregnancy, but Judah insisted that the best scribes were in Troyes only during the fairs. Waiting for the Hot Fair would obviously be too late.

"Can I run and get Judah?" Rachel was getting excited. She had immediately followed the other women upstairs.

"You get the chalk I keep in the pantry and start protecting this room. Do you remember what to do?"

"*Oui*, Aunt Sarah." Though it was almost four years since she chalked Joheved's room for Isaac's birth, Rachel remembered clearly. "First I draw a circle around the bed, and then I write 'Sanvi, Sansanvi, and Semanelaf, Adam and Eve, barring Lillit' on the door." She eyed the expensive wall hangings hesitantly before asking, "Should I chalk the walls as well?"

"Just do the one near the window," Miriam said, also reluctant to mar the fine fabric.

"May I get my tefillin too?" Rachel asked. She was proud of the black ritual boxes and straps that her father had bought her shortly after her twelfth birthday. "I'm not sure Mama will think to get them."

"Why don't you finish with the chalk first?" Sarah replied. When Rachel was gone, she addressed Miriam and Joheved, "I may not be as critical as my sister, but I don't condone you girls using tefillin either. Still, I admit it doesn't seem to have done you any harm and all three of you have managed to contract excellent marriages."

Sarah put her arm around Joheved's shoulders and walked her toward the stairs. "You can go to the synagogue and get the men. Have one of them bring back a Torah scroll." Sarah paused, unsure what to do with Meir's mother. "Marona, you can start loosening Miriam's hair—make sure she's not alone for a moment. I'll get my midwife supplies."

"Miriam," she called back from the landing. "You might as well put on some of Judah's clothes now."

Miriam hopped out of bed and rummaged through the bedside chest. "Shall we play chess?" She pulled out a man's chemise, then two sets of tefillin, before finally unearthing a chessboard. "Here's part of the wedding present you gave me. Now, where are all the pieces?"

"You're not in much pain, are you?"

"Actually not." Miriam shook her head in disbelief. "It's just that every so often I feel like I really, really need to go to the privy. But nothing comes out. It's so strange."

Miriam played chess with Marona while Rachel carefully applied the chalk. It wasn't long before the courtyard below was filled with loud, excited voices. To Miriam's frustration, Rivka refused to let her unshutter the window and look.

"Over a dozen men from the congregation came back with Judah," Joheved reported. "It started when a couple of students insisted on supporting him, so then their fathers felt obligated to join them, and their uncles as well. The next thing you know, their wives, not about to let the holiday feasts they'd prepared go to waste, announced that they were coming and that there had better be tables ready to hold all the food they were bringing."

Over the next hour, an increasing number of women dropped off dishes in Sarah's kitchen and then made their way upstairs to visit with Miriam, reassuring themselves that the new midwife was doing well. From the salon, an anxious Judah watched the steady stream of women callers with envy until Rachel took pity on him and brought him up to see her. But the sight of his wife, hair undone and wearing only one of his old chemises, calmly playing chess amidst a roomful of chattering companions, sent him backing out of the door immediately.

"Judah, it's all right," Miriam called out. "You can come in." Her guests quickly found excuses to withdraw, leaving only Joheved and Rachel in the room with him and Miriam.

"Where's Sarah?" Judah's voice rose in agitation. "And shouldn't your mother be here?" *How can these women just sit here and chitchat while my wife is in danger?*

"Judah, I'm perfectly fine." Miriam walked over and took his hand. "Mama and Aunt Sarah are in the courtyard making sure the meal is set up properly. Don't worry. They'll be back when they're needed."

This might have reassured Judah, except that while she was still holding his hand, Miriam suddenly felt the phantom urge to defecate, and she couldn't help but grasp him strongly until the feeling passed. Judah blanched and leaned against the bed.

"Rachel, could you go down to the kitchen and bring Judah a big cup of artemisia tisane?" Miriam helped her unsteady husband sit down. "His nerves need calming more than mine do."

sixteen

s the afternoon progressed, Miriam's spasms came steadily closer together, and with each one her need to defecate grew stronger. The crowd in the courtyard was growing larger and more festive. A trio of itinerant musicians, stopping in Troyes on their way to the Mai Faire de Provins, had learned of the gathering and offered their services in return for lodging.

Judah's students wavered between concern and amusement as their pious teacher's concentration failed again and again. At first he helped them review the Talmud tractate the scholars would be studying when the Hot Fair started, only to lapse into frequent silences once Sarah disappeared upstairs.

Finally, when Rivka rushed into the kitchen and began yelling for the servants to hurry and prepare the herbal infusions that Sarah wanted, he began reciting the biblical passage from the sixth chapter of Exodus that Jews pray when faced with danger.

> "Say therefore to the people of Israel; I am Adonai. I will free you from the labors of Egypt and deliver you from bondage. I will redeem you with an outstretched arm and through extraordinary chastisements. I will take you to be my people, and I will be your God."

These verses contained four of the Holy One's magical names, the Hebrew words for "I will free you," "I will deliver you," "I will redeem you," and "I will take you." The text was considered one of the most powerful protective incantations.

Upstairs, after Miriam's water broke and her need to push grew unbearable, Sarah tried to reassure her. "I know you think you're going to mess yourself. But believe me, you are going to push out a baby, not some giant piece of merde." As Sarah anticipated, the crude word drew giggles from her patient and lowered the tension in the room.

Once settled on the birthing stool, Miriam found that, though unable to dispel the feeling that she was indeed going to move her bowels, her need to push was too compelling to resist.

When Joheved saw the intense concentration on her sister's face, she began her first recitation of Psalm 20. Miriam gave a brief smile of appreciation, a smile that quickly turned into a grimace. Since Talmudic times, a difficult confinement had been eased by nine recitations of this prayer. And because the laboring woman had to be able to hear the verses, they were said by another of her gender standing close by.

"May Adonai answer you in time of trouble, the name of Jacob's
God keep you safe.
May He send you help from the sanctuary, and sustain you from
Zion . . .
May we shout for joy in your victory . . . rally and gather strength.
Adonai, grant victory, answer when we call."

By her sister's fifth recitation, Miriam was grunting heavily and quite red in the face. She desperately wanted to rest, but her body refused to let her. Yet, terrible as the compulsion was to continuously push with all her might, she knew that she was not suffering the kind of agony she had so often seen as a midwife.

Finally during the eighth recitation, as Joheved was saying, "Rally and gather strength," Miriam felt as though she was indeed passing the most giant piece of merde imaginable. She closed her eyes, giving herself over to forcing the huge thing out of her, until suddenly she realized that Joheved had stopped praying and a baby was crying.

"It's a boy!" female voices cried out. "Mazel tov!"

Rivka and Sarah were hugging each other, a small bundle clasped between them, as were Joheved and Marona. Rachel dashed out the door, eager to share the news with the anxious men downstairs. Miriam saw all this dimly, so overwhelming was the feeling of weariness, the relief at the cessation of her body's demand to keep pushing. She allowed herself to be cleansed and carried back to bed, where her son, washed and swaddled, was placed in her arms.

Exultant at the absence of any need to use the privy, she made the traditional parent's blessing at the birth of a son, "*Baruch ata Adonai* . . . Who is good and does good." The musicians below broke into raucous song, and then the door opened.

"What a *yom tov* this has been." Salomon was beaming with pleasure as he led his reluctant son-in-law into the lying-in chamber. He'd expected Meir to give him grandsons, but it surprised him that Judah, who seemed far more inhibited, had managed to father a son as well.

"Is Shavuot over?" Miriam asked as she held the baby up for the men to admire. "Was he born before sunset?"

Though Monday was an unpropitious day for beginning a new enterprise, children born that day, under the influence of the moon, would have a balanced disposition. Thank Heaven she'd given birth before Tuesday, when the baleful influence of Mars portended a life filled with war, enmity, envy, and destruction.

"I believe so." Salomon peeked through the shutters. "The sun is just setting now." He thumped Judah on the shoulders. "So what do you think of your new son? Isn't he handsome?"

Judah, who made it a point to focus his attention elsewhere during a circumcision, had never seen a newborn close-up before. Frankly, he did not think the red-faced child with its oddly shaped head was the least bit handsome. He was saved from having to answer his father-in-law by Jewish tradition, which dictated the first words a father says upon seeing his new child.

"*Barach ata Adonai* . . . Who has kept us alive, sustained us, and brought us to this season." Judah's voice shook, and, feeling a bit faint, he sank down onto a bench next to the bed. How well Miriam looked; he'd expected that she would be in pain or ill or, worse yet, angry with him for having caused her suffering.

"Judah, when was the last time you ate?" Miriam's sympathetic nature, buoyed by maternal instinct, exerted itself, and her husband admitted that he had eaten nothing after news of her condition had interrupted breakfast.

"Papa, could you see if there's some of today's feast left for me and Judah?" Miriam realized that she was hungry as well.

"Are you really all right?" Judah's skepticism made Miriam smile, and he couldn't help but smile in return.

She laughed, glad it was over and she was safe. "I've rarely felt better. Have you thought of a name for him?"

"I would have wanted to name a girl Alvina."

"So you want to name him after your father?" Was Judah being subtle about not mentioning the chosen name?

"*Non*, not Natan." Judah cringed at memories of the merchant from Prague, but when he saw her alarm, he calmed himself and added, "My brother's oldest son is already named for him."

"We could name him after my father." And use the name Salomon before Joheved did.

"It would hurt my mother's feelings if we ignored my father in favor of yours." Were they approaching an impasse? Should he suggest the name Benjamin or would she find that too painful?

"Oh, here's Mama and Papa coming, and look at all the food they've brought." Miriam grabbed a handful of strawberries, and the new parents set aside their discussion.

The next morning Miriam's family crowded around Sarah's dining table for breakfast. No matter how pleasant the late May weather, Miriam and the baby were confined to Sarah's house until he was safely circumcised. Samuel and Marona had left for Ramerupt, but Joheved didn't see much point in going back only to return a few days later for Shabbat and her nephew's *brit*. Besides, Miriam might need her.

Salomon beamed as his gaze took in his three grandsons. Isaac sat at his left and little Samuel sat further down on Joheved's lap. At the end of the table, Rivka held their latest in her arms.

"What a little *yom tov* baby you are," she cooed. "In one month you'll have had four feasts in your honor."

Isaac looked up at her, a questioning expression on his face, and Rivka counted them off on her fingers. "One feast yesterday for his birthday, two for his *brit milah,* one the night before and the other after the ceremony, another for his *pidyon ha-ben* next month."

"But Grandmama, yesterday's feast was for Shavuot, not his birthday."

Salomon tousled the boy's hair affectionately. "Ah, but we wouldn't have had the *yom tov* feast here if it hadn't been his birthday. So it was in his honor."

Isaac was only silent a moment. "What's a *pidyon ha-ben*?"

Everyone at the table knew the answer, but they waited for Salomon to explain it. "In the Torah we are taught that every firstborn male, both man and beast, belongs to the Holy One. When the Holy Temple stood, the firstborn sons worked for the priests, who ate the firstborn animals. If a father wanted to keep his son, he redeemed him by giving money to the priests instead. That's what *pidyon ha-ben* means, 'redeeming the son.' Today when we redeem him, we give the money to charity."

Isaac stared smugly at his little brother. "Only the firstborn son gets a *pidyon ha-ben*? Like me and this *yom tov* baby," he said proudly.

Salomon, Meir, and Joheved exchanged worried looks. Because of Joheved's earlier miscarriage, Isaac was not considered her firstborn, the first issue of her womb. Should they try to explain such distinctions to a four-year-old?

Meir put his arm around his son's shoulder. "Your mama had another baby before you, but it died," he said softly.

Isaac was silent for a moment. "So what if baby Yom Tov has the first *pidyon ha-ben,* I had the first *brit milah.*"

"The baby's name isn't Yom Tov," Joheved warned him. "We won't know what his name is until his *brit.*"

"But we can call still him baby Yom Tov," Rachel said. "The wrong name will confuse the *mazikim* more than no name."

"But they might name him Yom Tov." Meir winked at Isaac.

Miriam could barely keep her eyes open, but Meir's comment jerked her wide-awake. *Name him Yom Tov? Why not?*

She glanced at Judah, who was looking at her questioningly, and they exchanged nearly imperceptible nods. So Yom Tov it would be. She smiled at the knowledge that her son had not only been born on a festival, he'd been conceived on one as well.

"Let's just call him 'the baby' for now," she said.

Before she knew it, a week had passed and Miriam was trying to decide what to wear to her son's *brit milah* that morning.

"We don't have to wear red," she told Judah.

He deserved a reward. Except to use the privy, he'd never left her and the baby's side. Together they had studied various sections of Talmud concerning the laws of *brit milah*, and Miriam had to admit that he was a good teacher. He was becoming a devoted father too, holding the boy while they studied and bringing him to her at night so she needn't get out of bed.

"I don't mind wearing our wedding clothes," he replied. "It's traditional. Besides, didn't your mother make a red baby outfit to match?"

"*Oui.*"

"Then he'll have additional protection today."

Miriam wanted to nurse her new son before they left for the synagogue. She settled the baby at her breast and felt a flood of affection as he began to suck. Nursing was an unexpected delight of new motherhood. The physical release that came when her milk was suckled was one of the most pleasurable feelings she'd ever experienced, radiating from her breasts through her whole body. No wonder Joheved preferred to nurse her children herself.

After arriving in synagogue and hearing the other women describe how they shut their eyes during their sons' circumcisions, Miriam decided to watch the procedure. She was a midwife; blood and babies crying were nothing new to her. And if her other children were girls, she would never have another chance to see it.

Like at Samuel's *brit*, Obadiah carried in the mohel's supplies. He handed his father the *azmil* and gave Miriam the wine-soaked cloth for her baby to suck. She noticed that both men had the same odd pointed thumbnails, except Avram's were thick and yellow while Obadiah's were pale and thin like his other nails. A moment later she saw why they were cut that way.

In one smooth movement, Avram put his thumbnail under her son's foreskin, pulled it taut, and sliced off the extra skin. Then he used his sharp nails to push down the membrane underneath, exposing the corona. Miriam could feel Judah lean heavily on her shoulder when their child cried out, and for a moment she worried that he was going to faint. But then he steadied himself with his other hand and the weight lifted.

Out of the corner of her eye, Miriam saw Papa ascending the bima, and she stopped watching the mohel to take the cup of wine Papa offered her and join in the blessings for her health and that of her son. Papa's eyes twinkled when Judah whispered the chosen name in his ear, and smiling broadly he recited the blessing that announced Yom Tov's name to the congregation. When Miriam looked down again, Obadiah had finished the bandage, and with her son clutched to her bosom, she sat contentedly while the men congratulated Judah.

Only Obadiah hung back, petulantly asking his father, "When are you going to let me do the cutting, Papa? I'm ready."

Avram lowered his voice. "You don't expect me to let you do your first *milah* on the *parnas*'s grandson, or the rosh yeshiva's either? And the others were girls."

"So when? There's not another baby due for a month."

"You'll be ready when you're ready, not a day sooner." Then Avram noticed Miriam watching and led his son out of earshot.

Alvina arrived in Troyes two weeks later, annoyed that she'd missed both Yom Tov's birth and *brit milah*. That he wasn't named for her late husband only made matters worse.

Assuming she had an equally aggrieved ear in Salomon, she poured out her frustration to him on the way to synagogue. "Why did they have to name the baby after a holiday? It's not as if they didn't have perfectly good family names to use."

Judah shook his head in exasperation. "Mama, we've been over this. My son's name is Yom Tov and nothing is going to change it."

"Perhaps our children couldn't agree on a family name," Salomon said in a soothing tone. "Perhaps they didn't want to favor one grandfather over another."

Miriam abruptly stopped in the road. "Excuse me, Alvina, I think there's a rock in my shoe. Would you please hold Yom Tov while I shake it out?" As she anticipated, the new grandmother eagerly took the child and began to coo at him.

Salomon smiled at his daughter's subterfuge. "When I was born, my parents couldn't agree on a name for me. In fact they still hadn't chosen my name on the day of my *brit*."

"What happened?" Rachel asked eagerly. His voice sounded like he was about to tell a story.

"My father, may his merit protect us, refused to name me Isaac after my mother's father because that was his name, and my mother, may she rest in peace, wouldn't name me Jacob after his father because that was the name of her first husband."

Rachel heard a window opening above and jumped away from the street. "So did they each have a relative named Salomon?"

He chuckled. "*Non*, I'm not named for anyone in my family."

Apparently the building's occupant was only interested in fresh air, for nothing rained down on them. Rachel stepped back and took her father's arm. "Papa, stop teasing and tell us who you're named for."

"I'm named for King Salomon."

"*Non*, really."

Miriam and Judah turned to hear his reply. "Really, I was." He held up his hand to shush Rachel. "I was born on the last Shabbat of Shevat, so the haftarah portion read on my *brit milah* was from First Kings."

He waited to see which of them would figure it out first. Rachel, Miriam, and Judah quoted the text almost simultaneously,

"And Adonai gave Salomon wisdom, as He promised him."

Then they each added their own thought.

"You were named for the day you got circumcised," Miriam said with a sigh of relief. Yom Tov wasn't the only one in their family not named after a relative.

"You were born on the Sabbath?" Judah asked in disbelief.

"Your father thought of your name at the last moment, when he heard the haftarah chanted?" Rachel's eyes were wide with amazement. "Grandmama Leah didn't know what her own son's name was going to be?"

"*Oui* to all your questions," he said when they arrived at the synagogue.

"Your mother must have been very angry," Alvina said.

As the women headed for the stairs, Salomon turned to her. "Mama wasn't angry at all. She knew I'd be a scholar, so she was quite pleased with Papa for thinking of it."

Miriam leaned over to whisper to him, "That doesn't sound like the Grandmama Leah I used to know."

"That's the story my father told me." He shrugged his shoulders. "I have no recollection of the day myself."

Alvina's anger melted as she spent more time with her new grandson. She was also happily occupied with Rivka in arranging a sumptuous banquet in honor of his *pidyon ha-ben* on Midsummer Day, the first day of the Troyes Hot Fair.

Miriam's only request was for Moses haCohen to officiate. There were other Cohens in Troyes during the Hot Fair, older and more learned descendants of the ancient priestly tribe, but the doctor was her and Judah's friend. Miriam, often the guest of grateful parents whose firstborn sons she'd safely delivered, was familiar with the *pidyon ha-ben* ritual. The role of redeeming priest was merely ceremonial; any male Cohen might perform it.

When the longest day of the year arrived, Miriam and Judah agreed to appease his mother by dressing in their wedding finery. His red silk *bliaut* protected by a small cloth, Judah held Yom Tov at his shoulder and welcomed the last-minute arrivals. Miriam saw him greet Johanna and her heart sank.

Johanna walked slowly through the courtyard, leaning heavily on Joseph's arm. She looked like she'd aged ten years in the last few months. Rumors circulated about her declining health, with Shavuot being the only time she'd attended synagogue since the *brit* of her son Samson, an appropriate moniker considering his size. Miriam sighed sadly; Johanna had been a great friend to her family and it hurt to see her so ill.

"Is it true about Obadiah?" Johanna asked the women. Avram the mohel was there, but not his son.

Francesca motioned them to come closer. "Moses told me that he burned himself very badly," she whispered. "He may lose his hand."

"What happened?" Joheved asked.

The circle of women looked at each other, each waiting for someone who knew more to speak. Finally Francesca answered, "I'm not sure of the details, but I heard there was an accident at the shop . . . some molten metal spilled on him."

Their conversation stilled as the crowd divided to make space in front of Miriam for Judah to join her. When he handed Yom Tov to Moses haCohen and began explaining that this was his son, the firstborn of his mother's womb, Miriam couldn't help but think about how her life had changed. Of course motherhood changed every woman's life, but this was different.

When Benjamin died, Miriam was convinced that her ability to love again had died with him. Judah was a fine husband, and she felt a good deal of affection toward him, but it wasn't the passion she'd had for Benjamin. Yet in only a month, Yom Tov had kindled a love in her that frightened her with its intensity.

Judah was counting out five deniers. "I claim my firstborn son; here are your five silver shekels," Judah said as he gave the coins to Moses. Then he handed Yom Tov to Miriam.

It was her turn to speak. "This is my firstborn son, for the Holy One, Blessed be He, opened the doors of my womb with him." Miriam continued, with Judah joining her, "Just as our firstborn merited redemption, so may he merit Torah, marriage, and good deeds. *Baruch ata Adonai* . . . Who sanctifies the firstborn of Israel in their redemptions."

Miriam sighed with relief once Yom Tov was back in her arms, and she thought of the biblical Hannah. The prophet Samuel was Hannah's firstborn, and she had given him to the priests when he was weaned. *How could Hannah do it?* Miriam would die rather than let anyone take Yom Tov from her. Moreover, she knew she would fight, even kill if necessary, to protect him from harm.

By late afternoon most of the guests, including Alvina, had gone to the fair. Papa and Avram were deep in conversation under the apple tree, surrounded by Papa's students. Miriam began to help her mother and sisters clean up, but Aunt Sarah shooed her toward the house.

"You've had a long day," Sarah told her. "You should take a nap before *souper*."

Mama and Joheved agreed, but no sooner had Miriam reached Sarah's door than Papa waved her to join him.

"We have an important matter to discuss," he said. "And I want to hear from our midwives."

The men made room for her to sit down, and then looked at Avram expectantly.

"As many of you know," Avram's voice trembled with emotion, "Obadiah was seriously injured recently. Moses says my son will probably not lose his hand, but . . ." Avram paused to wipe away a tear. "But the hot metal burned him in such a way that . . ."

When Salomon saw that Avram was too overcome to speak, he continued, "Obadiah may be able to work as a goldsmith when he recovers his health, but he will never function as a mohel."

"So I must train a new apprentice," Avram said.

Miriam stifled a yawn. Why did they need her presence? Obviously one of Papa's students must take Obadiah's place.

"But who?" Salomon asked. "The mohel must be someone who is here in Troyes all the year, which excludes most merchants."

"He must be pious and learned in Jewish Law," Judah added. "Especially the laws dealing with circumcision."

"And he must be young," Joheved said. "Otherwise Papa would make an excellent mohel, he's so good with knives."

"That excludes me," Meir said with a sigh. "Even with more than ten years of practice, I can barely slaughter lambs or prune grapevines without injuring myself."

"True, those things are important." Avram's voice regained its strength. "But it is imperative that my new apprentice appreciate the gravity and delicacy of the *milah* procedure. He will be performing a vital mitzvah, one that cannot be delayed or interrupted."

"Can you do it, Judah?" Miriam asked.

"Just the thought of cutting down there upsets me." He shuddered. "I almost fainted during Yom Tov's *brit milah*."

Avram shook his head. "If a man cannot manage the necessary *kavanah*, he should not accept the position."

Miriam caught a glimpse of Shemayah, who looked like he was about to cry. Of course nobody suggested him as a candidate, a man whose son had bled to death after the *brit*, whose future sons could never be circumcised.

"What about one of our younger students, perhaps Eliezer?" Rivka asked.

"I've already talked to his father, as well as several others," Avram said. "They all say they may need their sons to help them with their business one day."

"But we must have a mohel in Troyes," Meir said, his voice rising with each word. "We won't be able to circumcise on the eighth day if we have to send to Paris for one."

Sarah and Salomon were exchanging meaningful glances, and Sarah coughed gently to get everyone's attention. "So far you've all been talking about a 'he.' But in Mayence there was a woman who did circumcisions, a midwife colleague of mine."

Everyone turned to stare at Miriam. As she gazed from one face to another, her heart began to pound and she swallowed nervously.

"Of course." Joheved broke into a smile. "Miriam would be perfect. She meets every condition."

"Not every condition," Avram said with a scowl. "She is a woman, which means that she is exempt from the mitzvah of *milah* and therefore cannot perform it on behalf of someone who is obligated."

"The Mishnah in Kiddushin does exempt mothers from those mitzvot that fathers are obligated to perform for their sons, such as *brit milah* and *pidyon ha-ben*," Joheved responded. "Yet when a father appoints an agent to do the circumcision for him, he is considered to have performed the mitzvah of *milah* himself. Thus it shouldn't matter who the agent is."

Miriam couldn't remain silent. "In Tractate Avoda Zarah, we have a Baraita that says:

> In a town with no Israelite doctor, but there is an idolater doctor, the idolater should do the circumcision."

Joheved further supported Miriam. "In the same tractate, Rav Yohanan and Rav disagree about women doing *milah*:

> Rav objects that a woman is not fit to circumcise since she is not subject to circumcision. But according to Rav Yohanan, she is fit, since a woman is considered as though she is circumcised."

Miriam smiled triumphantly at Joheved and continued, "And their debate ends when the Gemara asks:

> Can there be anyone who says that a woman is not fit to circumcise? Why it is written (in Exodus): So Zipporah took a flint and cut off her son's foreskin."

Meir and Judah sat quietly while their wives refuted Avram's objection, but their eyes betrayed their pride and pleasure. Salomon seemed to be enjoying himself as well, because he waited until his daughters finished before turning to Avram.

"The law is clear that when no competent man is available, a woman is fit to circumcise, in accordance with Rav Yohanan."

Shemayah coughed softly. "Just because Jewish Law holds Miriam fit, it doesn't mean that men in Troyes will allow her to circumcise their sons. I'm afraid some of them will be quite angry. Do you want to antagonize the community over this?"

"If the men of Troyes get so upset, then let one of them send his son to be Avram's apprentice," Judah said. It was clear how unlikely he considered this possibility.

"Since there is no alternative, I will train her." Avram looked like he had tasted something rotten and wanted to spit it out. "At least until I can find a male apprentice."

Salomon turned to Miriam. "We know that you are permitted to circumcise, and that Avram is willing to teach you, but we don't know if you want to be a *mohelet*." He smiled gently as he used the feminine form of the word.

Did she want to? It would be difficult with such a reluctant teacher. And what about Obadiah, who would surely resent her taking his place? Shemayah had a point; many in the community, both men and women, would object to a woman doing circumcisions. How would she endure their disapproval?

But *milah* was a vital mitzvah and no male was available. If she didn't agree then one day there would be no mohel in Troyes. Who would circumcise her sons, her nephews? *Mon Dieu, I would have to circumcise my own sons.*

Judah observed her hesitation. "You shouldn't do it unless you know you'll have the proper *kavanah*," he said. "But you don't have to decide now. Consider it for a while."

"Judah is right," Salomon said. "Don't decide today. But I think you'd make an excellent *mohelet*. You're the only mother I've ever seen who didn't close her eyes at her son's *brit*. You were watching the whole time."

And if she became Avram's apprentice, Miriam realized, everyone in town would be watching her. It would be very different from studying Talmud or wearing tefillin.

Part Two

seventeen

Troyes
Spring 4844 (1084 CE)

M iriam smiled down on the baby at her breast. It would be dawn soon—her favorite time of day. Everything was quiet and peaceful, Judah curled up in bed next to her and Yom Tov, may the Holy One protect him, asleep like a little angel in his trundle bed. How silly she'd been to worry about loving Yom Tov so much that there wouldn't be enough left for his baby brother.

This birth had been even easier than Yom Tov's. She recognized the phantom urge to defecate, and her new son was born before the bells of Troyes had a chance to toll twice. But the pregnancy was harder, with nausea lasting for months. She had been too ill to attend Johanna's funeral.

She still felt guilty about that. Could she or Aunt Sarah have helped Johanna if they'd known about her pregnancy earlier? Moses haCohen insisted that diabetes was nearly impossible to cure and that Miriam should worry about her own condition. Thank Heaven her health finally improved in midwinter, enabling her to continue her *mohelet* training.

Miriam sighed. Avram was a diligent teacher, and she was learning a great deal from him, but at every *brit* he announced that he was looking for an apprentice, should anyone know a capable boy who might be interested. For the first year she too hoped that he would find a replacement. Watching circumcisions up close was fascinating, but she couldn't ignore the shocked and angry expressions on people's faces when she followed after Avram carrying the mohel's supplies.

He admitted that she knew sufficient Talmud and that they would concentrate on the practical aspects of *milah*. The first thing he showed

235

her was how to sew the special linen bandage, the *haluk*. It was shaped like a finger with both ends open, and once the seam was tied off, the *haluk* was turned inside out so its smooth side would face the baby's skin. No loose threads were permitted; even a tiny thread might stick to the wound. Thanks to years of embroidery done under Mama's exacting standards, she was off to an auspicious start.

Sharpening the two-sided *azmil* was similar to preparing the knife she used to cut the baby's cord. Crushing cumin and mixing it with olive oil was simple for a midwife who used the same healing salve to seal the cord. But none of these, while essential to a safe *milah*, involved touching the baby, which Miriam increasingly wanted to do.

It was two years before she reached that goal. Two years of scrutinizing every *milah* Avram did, two years of making his *haluks* and salves, two years of checking on the babies three days later. It was also two years of knowing that her community was bitterly divided because of her. No one said anything to her, but she could see the faces at every *brit*, a few beaming in approval, but many more scowling with undisguised hostility. Maybe that's why Avram waited so long before he allowed her to actually participate in the ritual.

Last spring, after asking her dozens of times how to apply the *haluk* and salve, he suddenly turned to her after a *brit* and told her to bandage the child. Apparently she did this to his satisfaction, not that he ever complimented her, because he left her to bandage all the babies after that.

He also assigned her the odious task of circumcising the male stillborns and those who died before their *brit*.

"I must warn you that this is nothing like *milah* on a living baby," Avram told her the first time they joined those doing *tahara*, preparing an uncircumcised baby boy for burial.

"How so?" she asked.

"The dead one's skin is thick and rigid, and of course he will not jump or bleed when you make the cut."

Miriam nodded. "But why circumcise a dead child? Mitzvot are for the living."

"Father Abraham was the first to be circumcised," Avram said. "And so he stands at the entrance to Gan Eden, where he admits only those who are also circumcised."

"Do I have to wait for *tahara* or can I circumcise a stillborn immediately?" That would be one advantage of the midwife being a *mohelet*.

Avram shrugged. "Whenever you like. This is a custom, not a commandment."

Just thinking of those dead babies made Miriam shudder, and she shifted her son to the other breast. He seemed healthy enough, and tomorrow, after his *brit milah*, he would be out of danger from Lillit and her demons. She smiled with anticipation. Maybe tomorrow, with her own son's *milah*, Avram would let her do more than put on the bandage.

Across the courtyard, alone in her bed, Rachel wasn't sleeping either. Her breasts were too swollen and sore to lie on her belly, which meant that her flowers would start any day now. Then she'd suffer a week of cramps and back pain. Miriam mixed potions of wild celery and fenugreek for her, and hot baths helped too, but Miriam made it clear that when this problem afflicts a virgin of marriageable age, it's because there's too much corrupt seed in her, seed meant to be drawn out by a male during marital relations.

It wasn't fair. When women expelled their excess seed it hurt, but when men expelled theirs in nocturnal emissions, it felt good. A man could also relieve his needs with a harlot, while all she could do was wait until she was married. Rachel sighed. Only three months left.

Now she would only have to endure a few more months of flowers before pregnancy and nursing would make them merely an occasional annoyance. Look at Joheved, who only flowered once after she got pregnant with Isaac, and that was eight years and three children ago.

Rachel rolled onto her side, but that was equally uncomfortable. After beginning her flowers last year, she'd assumed that she and Eliezer would marry that summer. But Papa neglected to inform Eliezer's family in Provence, thus ensuring that they arrived at the Hot Fair unprepared to host a wedding. It still made her angry to think about it.

By then the Jewish community was occupied with the upcoming nuptials of the *parnas*'s son, Joseph, to a woman young enough to be his daughter, while all of Troyes was celebrating the marriage of Count Thibault's oldest son, Étienne-Henri, to Adèle de Angleterre, the bastard King Guillaume's only daughter. Both Thibault's cellarer and Isaac haParnas requisitioned Papa's best wine for their banquets, along with every other luxury victual in the city. Eliezer had begged his father not to delay, but Shemiah agreed with Papa that they should wait until more provisions were available.

Eliezer—she had such strange feelings about him. He could infuriate her like no one else, except maybe Papa. Yet she wanted to be with him every moment, and if they were apart, she often found herself wondering what he was doing.

Last summer wasn't so bad. Eliezer was occupied studying Talmud and getting to know Shemiah's clients, while she'd been busy helping Alvina with the jewelry business. Funny how she ended up working with Judah's mother. Jewels fascinated her, and the summer after Miriam's wedding she tried to surreptitiously watch whenever Alvina met with a customer. The following year Alvina permitted her open presence, and then Alvina took her on as an apprentice. No longer the careless child who lost the lady merchant's emerald ring, she now kept Alvina's accounts.

Then the Hot Fair ended, Eliezer went home for the Days of Awe, and she couldn't stop worrying about him. There were so many dangers on the road—storms, highwaymen, unstable bridges, dishonest innkeepers in league with thieves. What if he were injured, or worse, had an accident? Look what had happened to Miriam's fiancé. She was panic-stricken when the Cold Fair opened and Eliezer's family hadn't returned.

But they arrived before the week was out, and the look in Eliezer's eyes when he saw her was almost worth the separation. She so much wanted to be alone with him, but they could never steal more than a few moments together before Papa or Mama interrupted them. Not until Meir came to their rescue.

He approached Papa over *disner*, his face creased with worry. "Salomon, I must beg a favor from you."

Papa looked at him with concern and nodded.

"My mother is ill with the flux, and many on the estate, including the steward and the man we hired to prune the new vineyard, are stricken too," Meir explained. "With my poor father gone, may his merit protect us, Joheved is trying to run the manor, care for the sick, and nurse little Hannah too. We would be grateful if you could send Eliezer and Rachel over to prune our vines. The new vineyard is small; it will only take them a few weeks."

Papa stroked his beard. It was already mid-February and pruning needed to be finished before the end of March. Rachel and Eliezer held their breaths, not daring to look at each other. She hadn't prayed for anything so hard since he returned safely to Troyes. But Meir left Papa no choice. Joheved needed help, more help than one person could provide. Miriam couldn't go, not in her condition, and none of the other students had Eliezer's pruning skills.

Meir must have realized what was holding Papa back because he said, "I assure you that they will be carefully chaperoned."

"Very well," Papa finally said. "But only until your hired man is healthy again."

It took the fellow two weeks to regain his health, and then a snowstorm kept Rachel and Eliezer in Ramerupt even longer. It was wonderful. As long as they got the pruning done, they could sneak behind the bushes to steal kisses whenever they wanted. In the evening, Meir shared the day's Talmud lesson with them and Joheved. Poor Joheved—there was such a look of longing on her face when they studied Talmud together.

Rachel sighed in sympathy at the memory, then got up to use the chamber pot. No blood yet, but there would be any day.

When Hannah began to whimper, Meir woke just enough to see that it was still dark before pulling the covers over his head. Joheved said the baby's molars were coming in, but it was always something. The child had yet to give them a full night's sleep. A few moments later, Joheved brought Hannah back into bed with them. Meir groaned inwardly, as any chance of using the bed that morning evaporated. Not that they'd been able to do it in the morning for some time.

He tried to relax and ignore the small movements next to him, but sleep eluded him. When was he going to find the right moment to tell Joheved what he'd decided to do about Zipporah, Shemayah's daughter?

Last year, when Shemayah's wife gave birth to another boy, Avram refused to circumcise him. But the child bled to death from a small cut before he was six months old, and Shemayah was beside himself with grief. And not just because he'd lost another son.

"I don't know what to do about Zipporah," he confided to Meir. "Who will I find to marry her? With this death, there's no doubt that the women in my wife's family are cursed."

"With your scholarship and your father-in-law's wealth, someone will offer for her."

"Who?" The word was thrown down like a gauntlet. "Not anyone I would want as a son-in-law."

Shemayah looked so despondent that Meir spoke without thinking. "Don't worry. She can marry Isaac."

The effect this had on his study partner was extraordinary. Shemayah's face lit up and he threw his arms around Meir. "You would do that for me?" He hugged Meir tightly.

"Of course." Meir embraced Shemayah in return. "And once Isaac marries Zipporah, you'll have no trouble finding suitable husbands for any sisters she may have."

Afterward, Meir realized the problem he had created for himself. Knowing Joheved would be furious, he prevailed on Shemayah to keep his offer secret until he'd informed her.

But then his father died, and it seemed best to wait until they stopped mourning. Next Hannah was born, and he didn't want to disturb Joheved's good mood. And later, between pruning the new vineyard, helping Mama run the manor and keep its accounts, teaching Isaac and Samuel to read—she was so busy that he didn't want to spoil the rare time they spent together with news that was sure to provoke a quarrel.

Hannah was quiet now, and Joheved squeezed up next to him. Automatically he pulled her closer. Her back was warm alongside his chest, and her derriere pressed pleasurably against his thighs. A wave of tenderness coursed through him. If it weren't for Joheved, he'd be stuck in Ramerupt instead of teaching Talmud in Troyes' yeshiva.

Tomorrow was the *brit milah* for Miriam and Judah's new son. Maybe Joheved would be in a good enough mood that he could tell her then. Relieved with his decision, Meir drifted off, waking some time later to the sounds of his mother trying to hush his sons' boisterous start to the day. Joheved and Hannah were still asleep, and he dressed as quietly as he could. It was best not to wake such heavy sleepers. Their souls might have difficulty returning to their bodies.

When her daughter's whimpers finally woke her, Joheved could tell by the sunlight streaming through the shutters that it was well past dawn. She stretched and got up to change Hannah's swaddling. She hadn't felt truly rested since Meir's father died. She had so much to do afterward that the usual tiredness of early pregnancy never lifted.

Once they discovered that the old vineyard bore decent fruit, she'd felt compelled to uncover all the vines, prune them properly, and keep them in production. Never mind that she would have to do this in addition to all her normal duties. Thank Heaven that Meir recruited one of Papa's employees, a married man with two strapping adolescent sons, to move to Ramerupt and help work the new vineyard.

Hannah attended to, Joheved dressed and came downstairs to find the manor's account books laid out for her on the dining table, along with some bread, cheese, and fruit. The others had long since eaten breakfast. It looked to be a beautiful spring day, so Meir was probably going over their sons' lessons with them in the courtyard.

Sadness welled up in her. Before Hannah came along, when she started teaching Isaac to write the Hebrew letters and read from the Torah, little Samuel would sit on her lap or play nearby. But it wasn't long before he said something, or maybe asked a question, that proved he'd been learning right along with his brother. She'd been so proud, so eager to tell Meir about their clever young son. Now she scarcely saw them.

She was shocked when Meir decided that the boys should study with him and Papa. She was just as capable of teaching them Torah as her father was, but she had too many other demands on her time, Hannah chief among them. She admitted that Isaac was ready, but little Samuel was too young to leave her.

She cried as she watched them ride away that first day, Samuel seated in front of Meir on the tall grey horse, Isaac on his own dappled pony. It wasn't only that her babies were growing up and leaving her. They were going off to study Torah and she wasn't. Just thinking of that day brought her to tears. She blinked and settled Hannah down on the floor with a string of colored beads. As soon as she finished the manor's finances, her family could leave for Troyes.

At least she'd given up the yeshiva willingly, for Meir's sake. Not like poor Emeline, who'd been forced out of her convent and into a life she hated. After meeting in Ramerupt, the two of them had corresponded sporadically, using the Jewish merchant who did business with Plancy as a courier. Emeline had given Hugh de Plancy an heir, Hugh the Younger, but she wrote nothing of her personal life.

It was at the christening of Count André's latest child, almost two years ago, that she'd learned why not. Joheved hadn't wanted to attend the christening, but it was too soon after Samuel's death for Meir or Marona to socialize.

Emeline had seen her first and rushed to embrace her. "I prayed that you or Miriam would be here. You look wonderful; that blue silk is so becoming on you."

"*Merci*, it's good to see you, too." Joheved took Emeline's arm and whispered, "I wasn't sure I'd fit into it. I'm enceinte again."

"I am too," Emeline said in an even softer voice.

"We must find a place to sit down." No wonder Emeline looked so pale.

"Nobody at Plancy knows. They wouldn't have let me come if they did." Emeline's chin began to quiver. "I had to get away."

Emeline's tears were falling in earnest now, and Joheved propelled her toward a bench behind a hedge. "Who wouldn't have let you come? Your husband?"

Emeline could only shake her head. Finally her sobs weakened and she took a deep breath. "His mother, Gila . . . may God grant she be consumed in hellfire. She wouldn't even let me attend the christening of Prince Louis last year."

"You were invited to honor King Philippe's new son and your mother-in-law didn't let you go!" Joheved's voice rose with indignation. "What power can this woman have over you? You are the baroness of Plancy now. You've born a healthy heir."

"Oh, Joheved, my life is filled with such misery." Emeline sat up, blew her nose on her sleeve, and told her story. "Gila says she's the baroness of Plancy. She keeps the keys and runs the estate just like before, and rather badly from what I've seen. You wouldn't believe the laziness and corruption she tolerates. Everything I learned here in Ramerupt, including how to ride, has been completely wasted."

Emeline's voice hardened as she described her tormenter. "She has taken away my books and writing implements, saying that because Eve's words persuaded Adam to eat the apple, thus causing the woes of the world, women should speak as little as possible, and not read or write at all. You have no idea how difficult it was to get a letter to you. I waste my days in idleness, spinning or embroidering, my sole comfort the few hours I spend with my little Hugh. At night my husband has his way with me and then goes to cavort with his mistress."

Joheved's mouth dropped open. "His mistress?"

"*Oui*, she's been living there for years. They even have a son together."

Joheved didn't know what to say. No sooner had they finished sitting shiva for Lord Samuel than Marona had presented her with the manor's keys and account books. Joheved had tried to give them back, but Marona insisted. Meir was lord of the estate now, and that meant his wife was its lady.

Emeline began to weep again. "Death alone will free me."

"This melancholy isn't good for you or the baby. You should eat more pepper and roasted meats, and other foods that are warm and dry. No more fresh fruit for you." Joheved put back a pear from Emeline's plate. "You're already too damp and cold."

Emeline promised that she would try to eat better, and at the end of the day they parted. But Joheved heard nothing from Plancy until the following summer, when their merchant stopped by on his way to the Hot Fair. He reported that Emeline's child had been stillborn, and that she'd been too distraught to write.

Joheved sighed and forced her attention back to her ledgers. Lamb sales had been very good, and with the war still raging between King Henry and Pope Gregory, she followed Samuel's example and planted the spring fields in oats again. The first year after he died, several of the butchers and grain merchants tried to take advantage of her. They didn't realize she'd been negotiating wine deals for years, and she watched with pride as the merchants' shrewd expressions were replaced with grudging respect. But there were two monetary tasks she did not assume. Twice a year Meir presided over the manorial court, and his brother Meshullam continued to sell their wool.

Joheved checked the steward's numbers, and, satisfied they were accurate, closed the ledger. Now she only needed to pack the outfits her family would wear tomorrow for the *brit*.

Judah put down his goose quill pen and peered into the cow's inkhorn. It was nearly empty. The pot of ink on the table proved empty as well. Not wanting to disturb Miriam and the new baby, who were napping upstairs, he tiptoed to the cabinet that held his writing supplies. There were several inkpots, none of which contained any ink.

Just what he needed—out of ink with the Hot Fair still two months away. Maybe Eliezer could get one of his merchant friends to bring some back from the Mai Faire de Provins. It was Salomon who suggested that the two of them study together, and, despite their disparate styles, the match was a good one. Judah wanted to understand everything, and Eliezer wanted to know everything.

If it weren't for Eliezer, Judah would remain perpetually on the same passage, plumbing its depths, while if it weren't for Judah, Eliezer would rush through a chapter, content with memorizing only its most superficial meaning. One trait they had in common was impatience with anyone less intelligent. Thus the match spared them both a good deal of aggravation, as well as sparing other less clever students their disdain.

Unlike most study partners, they shared little of their private lives. Judah had refused to teach him the Arayot, insisting that Meir was more qualified. Marital relations was the last subject he wanted to discuss with his students.

But fate conspired against him. In honor of his youngest daughter's nuptials, Salomon had been prevailed upon to teach Tractate Kiddushin. Thus Judah found himself confronted with the verse,

> Rav Hisda said: I am superior to my colleagues because I married
> at sixteen. If I had married at fourteen, I would have said to Satan,
> "Arrows in your eyes."

Salomon had written that Rav Hisda, had he married even earlier, could have goaded his *yetzer hara* and still not been tempted to sin. Though Judah was almost certain that Rav Hisda was a superior scholar because sinful thoughts did not interfere with his study of Torah, he made a note that Salomon should explain the first line as well as the second one.

Judah considered his own situation. Fate had delayed his wedding until he was almost twenty, giving his *yetzer hara* years to plague him when his only companions were other yeshiva students. Even now intense study with certain men, thank Heaven not Eliezer, could excite him physically as well as mentally. Would males hold such an attraction for him if he had tasted women earlier?

Last summer, after an animated Talmud discussion with Levi during the Hot Fair, it happened again. He'd tried to hide his condition from Miriam when he got into bed, but as soon as he turned away from her, she questioned him.

"Judah, are you upset with me?"

"*Non*, of course not. I'm sorry if I woke you."

"It's all right, a midwife has to be a light sleeper." A long pause and then she said, "Do you find me unappealing then?"

"Certainly not. Why do you ask?"

"Judah, we've shared a bed for five years. Do you think I can't tell when you're aroused?"

"I didn't want to disturb you so late. I can wait until Erev Shabbat."

"Rava says that scholars who study in their own town and live at home should lie with their wives every day," she said.

It didn't seem right to use the bed if he'd been aroused by someone else, and certainly not every night. "Ben Azzai teaches that scholars shouldn't be on their wives like roosters."

Miriam knew the text, too. "And some say that Ben Azzai was concerned instead that scholars might neglect the mitzvah of procreation. Besides, once a day isn't much. Roosters mate a lot more often than that."

"They do?" How was he to know how often roosters did it?

Miriam's voice dropped seductively. "Yom Tov is two years old. I want to have another baby."

There was no argument he could make to that.

By the end of the Hot Fair she was pregnant, and by the beginning of the Cold Fair she was so ill that using the bed was impossible. Then his *yetzer hara* made his life truly miserable. Other scholars had never looked so attractive, and even some of his students began to stir him. Thank Heaven for cold water; the time-honored remedy was especially efficacious in the winter, even if it sent him to bed with teeth chattering.

Perhaps he should have hired a common woman; that's what Eliezer was doing before the wedding. But harlots lay with who knows how many men without washing and didn't care if they were *niddah*. The thought of touching one of them nearly made him gag.

His reminiscing was interrupted when Miriam came down, carrying the baby.

"Where's Yom Tov? And where is everyone else?" The day before a boy's *brit* was the most dangerous of all. Most students hadn't returned after Passover, but there should have been more men studying here than just Judah.

"Eliezer and the others are at your mother's, hoping to beg some of what she's cooking for tonight's feast," he said. "Papa just took Yom Tov to the privy."

She sat down next to him, but far enough away that there was no danger of them touching. "I'm sure you're pious enough to keep the demons away until they all come back."

"Do you know anyone going to Provins this week? We're almost out of ink."

Miriam rummaged through the cupboards. "Don't worry, there's plenty at Papa's. I didn't realize you've been using so much lately. I'll refill our ink pots tomorrow after the *brit*."

"Speaking of the *brit*..." Judah looked outside to make sure no one was approaching. "Do you think Avram will let you do any more of it?"

"I'm hoping he'll let me do the *priah*." She held up her thumbs, displaying their pointed nails. "If I can peel a grape with these, without any juice escaping, then I should be ready."

Priah was the thin membrane between the foreskin and the baby's penis. Immediately after the foreskin was removed, the mohel used those sharp thumbnails to slit the *priah* and fold it down over the base of the penis, exposing the crown.

"Learning that skill must be more difficult for apprentices who aren't vintners," Judah said.

She looked at him pleadingly. "Judah, what can I do so the men will be more accepting?"

He doubted there was anything she could do. She could wait twenty years and perform a thousand circumcisions, but some men would still grumble. "Forget about the men's approval. Work on winning over their wives. If the mothers see how conscientious you are with their sons, they will support you. Their husbands will come around eventually."

"I suppose you're right," Miriam said slowly. "But sometimes women are more traditional than men. Look how upset Mama was about me and Joheved learning Talmud."

"But you're their midwife. You already have their trust."

Their conversation ended when the front door opened and Yom Tov ran in, Salomon in his wake.

"Mama, Mama." Yom Tov lifted up his arms, eager to be picked up.

Seemingly without effort, Miriam shifted the baby to one hip and lifted Yom Tov up on the other. Judah couldn't help but smile. Such an excellent wife he had—and two fine sons. His *bashert* was worth waiting for, even if his *yetzer hara* had all those extra years to harass him. In five weeks they would be permitted to use the bed again, and though he would probably not want to tell Satan "arrows in your eye" when the Hot Fair opened, Judah felt reasonably confident that the merchants would not seem as attractive as during the Cold Fair.

eighteen

iriam's hand trembled as she sewed Judah into his wedding chemise. "I'm so nervous. What if Avram makes me do the whole *milah* today?"

"He won't if he sees your hand shaking like that."

"Judah." Her voice was a plea.

"Wouldn't Avram have warned you if he expected you to do the actual cutting?" he said.

"*Non.* The most expert mohel present performs the circumcision—which means an apprentice usually does it for the first time unexpectedly, because the mohel is ill or incapacitated."

Judah looked up with sudden comprehension. "Or says he is."

"*Oui.*" She nodded. "That way no one feels resentful that their son was selected for the apprentice's first attempt."

"You haven't done *priah* yet," Judah said. "Won't Avram have you do one step at a time?"

"Maybe he'll think it would be a privilege to circumcise my own child. It's not that Avram hasn't trained me in the rest of it. He asks questions constantly, about every detail."

"Miriam, if Avram should take sick today, I would be honored if you would circumcise my son on my behalf."

There was a soft knock and then Salomon appeared in the doorway. "Judah, are you ready? We need to leave for services."

"*Oui*, Papa." Judah slipped on his red brocade *bliaut* and tied his hair back. Then he was gone.

Miriam settled back to feed the baby, grateful that nursing him would calm her.

Later that morning, as the time for his *brit milah* approached, her anxiety returned. Avram seemed perfectly well, she told herself. If he were going to leave the cutting to her, he would have said something by now. It was only when he recited the mohel's blessing for circumcision that she relaxed.

But not for long. No sooner did Avram finish the cut, than he handed her the small flask of wine and said, "You can do *motzitzin* and *priah* today."

Miriam gulped. She had been prepared for *priah*, but, though she'd been practicing for months, she was not expecting to do *motzitzin*, drawing the blood, until later. Luckily Shimson, for that was the name they'd chosen for him, was occupied sucking the wine-soaked cloth she'd given him; he barely flinched as she grasped his penis in one hand and simultaneously slit the membrane with the other. Folding down her son's *priah* was actually easier than peeling a ripe grape, thank Heaven. Maybe *motzitzin* would also be easier in reality.

As she'd been taught, she first took a mouthful of Papa's strongest wine. Now came the tricky part. Even with her mouth filled with wine, she leaned over and sucked the blood from her son's wound, simultaneously swirling the wine around it. How many times had Avram watched as she took a mouthful of wine, and then admonished her not to swallow even a drop as she sucked up more and again some more. If the *brit* had been outdoors, she would have spit the wine-blood mixture into the ground, but inside the synagogue a pail of dirt was provided for this purpose.

When Avram first described *motzitzin* to her, Miriam had to fight to hide her disgust. Ingesting blood was forbidden by Jewish Law. Yet it was written in Tractate Shabbat,

> Rav Papa says: the mohel who does not draw blood is a danger and we dismiss him . . . Drawing blood is the same as bandaging with cumin. Just as it places the baby in danger if he does not bandage

with cumin, here too it is dangerous if he does not do it (*motz-itzin*).

Now that she'd actually done it, she realized that it was much the same as sucking on one's finger after accidentally cutting it. With her own son, it was almost a kiss. Certainly she'd kissed his little fingers and toes, and his brother's, many times. And it would probably be the same with other babies.

Later that week, the subject of blood came up again in the Talmud; in the Arayot, which Rachel was studying with her sisters.

She stared down at the text in dismay. "Please Joheved, tell me that Tractate Niddah doesn't say what I think it says about what is permitted on my wedding night."

Joheved patted her arm sympathetically. The Mishnah said:

> If a virgin has begun her flow while still in her father's house, Shammai says: She is allowed only the first marital intercourse. Hillel says: The whole night.

"I know the law is usually like Hillel, but here it is like Shammai: the bridegroom performs the initial penetration and then withdraws," Joheved said. "If it's any consolation, Meir says that Eliezer was upset when he read this section, too."

"But the blood of virginity is pure, not like *niddah*. How can we celebrate our wedding for seven days if we have to wait seven clean days before we can touch each other, sit on the same bench, eat from the same bowl?" Rachel's voice rose with frustration. "By that time I *will* be *niddah*."

"The Sages worry that there could be menstrual blood mixed in with that of your virginity," Miriam explained.

Joheved smiled at her little sister's disappointment. "But Papa isn't that strict. He agrees that the blood of virginity is not like *niddah*. He says that while using the bed is forbidden after the first time, you can still touch each other, eat from the same dish, even sleep together."

"At night, it can be nice doing everything except the holy deed," Miriam said. "And it gives you a week to heal."

A shadow of fear clouded Rachel's face. "Is the first time really so painful that I'll need a week to heal?"

"I have no idea." Joheved smiled at the memory. "Thanks to some vigorous horseback riding, my door was already open. So I didn't bleed at all on my wedding night."

"That's not fair, you were lucky." Rachel turned to Miriam. "What about you?"

"My experience won't help either." Miriam quickly tried to think of an explanation that wasn't too embarrassing. "My door was so tightly closed that Judah couldn't open it."

Joheved skeptically raised an eyebrow. "But there were bloodstains on the sheets."

"Judah made those by cutting his hand. He didn't want to injure me with too much force. Aunt Sarah cut my hymen later."

"So neither of you had any pain," Rachel accused her.

"True, but Mama did. She wouldn't say anything before my wedding; she probably didn't want to scare me. But I got her to tell me about it later." Miriam's voice dropped to a whisper, and her sisters leaned closer. "She said her door was tightly closed, too, and when Papa finally opened her, it was the most pain she'd ever felt, until childbirth, that is."

The three sat mutely in the bedroom that they had once shared. Finally Rachel broke the silence. "Do you think Aunt Sarah would open my door too?"

Miriam threw her arm around her younger sister's shoulders. "At your next flowers, I'll cut your hymen myself. Then you won't have to worry about blood or pain on your wedding night."

"And neither will Eliezer," Joheved added with a smile.

Rachel's good mood lasted slightly less than a week. The following Thursday afternoon she stormed out of the kitchen, slamming the door behind her. Her hands shaking with anger, she grabbed the nearest hoe and began hacking away at the weeds in Mama's vegetable garden.

Papa had no consideration for her happiness. In three days Eliezer would be going home for Shavuot. They'd had no time alone together since he returned after Passover, and it was clear that they would have none before he left again either. She slashed at another weed, uprooting both it and a lettuce growing nearby.

"Ahem." A feminine voice behind her coughed.

Rachel spun around, ready to confront her angry mother, but it was the widow Samuelis, whose house shared their courtyard.

"Shalom aleichem, Samuelis." Rachel hid her surprise.

Other than an occasional *bonjour*, Samuelis kept to herself, tending to her poultry and the women who bought them from her. She didn't chitchat with Mama or Aunt Sarah, or with other women at synagogue either. She lived alone, except during the Hot Fair when her son, and now Alvina, stayed with her.

"Aleichem shalom," Samuelis returned her greeting. "I would like you and Eliezer to join me for *souper* tonight."

"*Merci.*" Rachel smiled. She and Eliezer would finally share a meal away from Papa's stern visage.

"*Bien,* I'll expect you when the bells chime Vespers."

Rachel watched Samuelis limp across the courtyard, then hastily replanted the lettuce and continued her weeding more judiciously. *What could the old woman possibly want with us?*

Two hours later, she and Eliezer were sitting at Samuelis's small dining table, finishing their chicken stew. It was finally time for dessert, and when Samuelis returned from the kitchen with a platter of spiced almond cookies, she handed Rachel a rolled up scroll.

Samuelis smiled at her. "I can't abandon my poor clients."

What was the woman talking about? Rachel wondered as she began to scan the Hebrew document. Her jaw dropped, and she stared up at Eliezer, her eyes wide and questioning. It was a deed, conveying Samuelis's house and furnishings to her, Rachel bat Salomon, providing that she agree to carry on Samuelis's business.

Eliezer grinned at her astonishment. "It's my wedding present to you. I wanted you to get it before I left, so you'd have time to decorate."

"But . . . but," she stammered. *My own house, my very own house.* She turned to Samuelis. "Where are you going to live?"

"My son has finally convinced me to come live with him in Cologne," she said. "I thought you'd prefer a house near your family so I approached your fiancé about buying it."

"Oh, I do. But why do I have to keep raising chickens? There are plenty of poulterers in Troyes."

Samuelis chuckled. "Hasn't Alvina told you that my real business is lending money to women?" When Rachel shook her head, Samuelis continued, "The chickens are only so my clients can visit without suspicion, although it is nice that the baker brings me all sorts of tasty goods in exchange for my eggs."

Rachel looked at Samuelis with new respect. "All these years, I had no idea."

"Your grandmother knew, and your mother too." She handed Rachel a bird-shaped cookie. "Not that I've had to lend her money since your engagement."

Rachel grimaced. Of course, that was back when she'd lost the emerald ring. She stood up and kissed Samuelis's palm. "I'm honored that you trust me with your business."

"I've noticed that you don't gossip with the other girls, and from what Alvina tells me, you're well on your way to learning the trade." She called for her servant to clear the table. Then she picked up the lamp and led Rachel and Eliezer toward the stairs. "Eliezer, could you show your bride the upstairs rooms? Climbing stairs pains my knees."

Rachel tried not to hurry, but as soon as they came to a door, Eliezer pulled her inside. Except for a folded-up bedstead, the small room was empty. He took her in his arms.

"Oh, Eliezer. *Merci, merci beaucoup*," she whispered between kisses. "My own house, I can't believe it."

"I was hoping you'd like it." He pulled her closer.

Eventually she pulled away. "Shouldn't we see what's in the other rooms?"

The next room was as empty as the first, and again they reveled in the privacy it provided. When they entered the final room, Rachel let out a soft, "Oh."

The bed that took up most of the floor space had four tall corner posts, which supported a canopy and curtains that sloped down to protect the bed's occupants from flying insects. They stared at the huge bed, then at each other, then back at the bed, their thoughts nearly identical. Their own house—now they wouldn't be sleeping in a room next to her parents (except that Eliezer wasn't thinking of the word *sleeping*).

"I have a present for you, too, Eliezer." Rachel smiled shyly and then looked down at the floor. She wanted to tell him, but it was too embarrassing. "While you're gone, Miriam is going to cut . . ." She stopped, blushing. "Miriam is going to open my door, with a knife."

Eliezer's expression went from disbelief to relief to near rapture. He picked her up and hugged her so that she could hardly breathe. Fervent kisses followed, and it was only when Samuelis called out, asking if they were all right, that they broke off their embrace. It was just in time. They had no sooner reached the first floor than Salomon was knocking at the door, announcing that it was time for his daughter to come home.

Eliezer left early Sunday morning, joining a large group traveling south. Rachel couldn't hide her anxiety as she urged him to return safely, but Eliezer wasn't worried. Sunday was a good day to begin a journey, almost as lucky as Thursday. Coming home for Shavuot was the easiest of his three yearly trips to Arles. Fair weather guaranteed a fresh batch of petitioners and pilgrims heading for Rome, and his route coincided with the first leg of their journey.

But this year was different. In March, King Henry had entered Rome and sacked the city, forcing Pope Gregory to flee to Sicily. Now Henry's newly appointed pope, Clement, ruled in Rome, while Gregory plotted his revenge in Salerno. Eliezer tried to be optimistic. The war between Henry and Gregory was over, and no matter which of the two popes a man wanted to see, he still had to travel through Arles.

Along with other Jews, Rachel continued to count the Omer, the days between Passover and the Giving of the Law on Shavuot, and as she did, she wondered where Eliezer was each night. On the Friday before the festival, Joheved's family would arrive in Troyes. Rachel couldn't wait, for Joheved had promised to study the Arayot with her every day.

It wasn't that Miriam didn't know the Arayot, but she seemed to have absorbed Judah's piety and viewed marital relations as "the holy deed" rather than a source of pleasure. Also, between her midwife duties, mohel training, and new baby, she often kept Rachel waiting or postponed their studies until later. Sure enough, it looked like their first session would be just Rachel and Joheved, when Miriam hurried in to Samuelis's salon, baby Shimson in her arms.

She sat down and adjusted her chemise so Shimson could find her breast. "I'm sorry I'm late. What tractate are you on?"

"I thought we'd go over that Baraita at the end of chapter two of Nedarim, the one about the ministering angels," Joheved replied. "Papa hasn't written any commentary on it, so it should be interesting for the three of us to work on it."

She handed the manuscript to Rachel and pointed out where to start reading.

> "Rav Yohanan ben Dahavai said: Ministering angels told me four things. Why are there lame ones? Because they turn over the table. Why are there mute ones? Because they kiss 'that place.' Why are there deaf ones? Because they converse at the time of marital relations. Why are there blind ones? Because they look at 'that place.'"

Rachel put down the page and addressed her sisters, "Lame ones, mute ones? What is he talking about?"

Miriam was about to answer when Rachel continued, "I can see the text concerns using the bed, but does he mean that the parents become lame or their children are born lame? And what is 'turning over the table?'"

Miriam remembered how she'd seduced Judah on Simchat Torah. "Maybe it's when the woman is on top." She paused for a moment. "But that can't be right. Couples sometimes do that when the woman is pregnant, and they don't become lame. Their children aren't born lame either."

Rachel recalled hearing how Joheved captured the image of sheep mating to cure Meir of impotency. "Maybe it's like animals do, from behind. Then the woman would be turned over."

"But that's another position women use during pregnancy," Miriam said, shaking her head.

"Meir says that 'turning over the table' refers to *biah shelo kedarkah*—like men do with each other," Joheved said.

"But you can't get pregnant that way," Miriam objected.

"And you can't get pregnant by kissing 'that place' either," Joheved shot back. Then she relaxed and turned to Rachel. "Speaking of that place, how did your surgery go?"

"It hurt terribly when Miriam cut me, so I shudder to think how my wedding night would have been otherwise. But my flowers ended like usual after five days, and I'm nearly done with my clean days, thank Heaven."

She reached over and squeezed Miriam's hand. "You have such a gentle touch that when my first son is born, I want you to do his *brit milah*."

"Even if it's my first one?"

"Especially if it's your first one," Rachel replied.

"Who better to honor with your first *milah* than your own family?" Joheved said.

"I never liked the idea of a man doing all those things with the baby right in my lap," Rachel said. "It's immodest."

Joheved winced. "Don't say that. That's the excuse people use to argue that circumcision shouldn't be done in the mother's lap."

"Of course a mother should hold her son at such a time; he needs her comfort," Rachel said. "My argument is for women to do the circumcising."

"The mohel is completely focused on the baby," Miriam said. "I'm sure I wouldn't notice who was holding him."

"I certainly wouldn't have trusted Obadiah to do my son's *milah* in my lap," Rachel said. "Considering how he leered at me when he was a student."

"Let's not speak unkindly of Obadiah," Miriam said. "Not after what happened to him."

Rachel and Joheved both grimaced. Obadiah didn't wear a bandage anymore, but his deformed right hand, its burned fingers stuck together like a fish's fin, was a constant reminder of the vagaries of life.

Joheved held up the manuscript. "Let's get back to our text."

"How can conversing at the time of relations be bad?" Rachel asked. She couldn't imagine using the bed without some talking first.

"Apparently the Gemara wonders about that too," Joheved replied. "Listen to what it says next:

> We challenge that tradition. They asked Ima Shalom why her children were exceptionally beautiful. She said to them: He converses with me, not at the beginning of the night or at the end of the night, but at midnight.

Ima Shalom was Rav Eliezer's wife, by the way," she added. "Ah ha, here's your answer. There is no contradiction. Ima Shalom's conversation refers to words about marital relations, while Yohanan ben Dahavai means speaking about other matters."

Miriam put Shimson to her shoulder and patted him until he burped. "Now we know that Yohanan ben Dahavai was talking about the couple's children being affected by their behavior, not the couple themselves."

"Wait." Rachel read ahead in the text. "Listen to this.

> The Sages say *halakhah* is not like Yohanan ben Dahavai. Rather, all a man desires to do with his wife, he may do; like meat from a butcher's. If he wants to eat it with salt, he does so; roasted, he does so; boiled, he does so."

She looked up at Joheved questioningly, "So all the acts Yohanan ben Dahavai objects to are permitted?"

"If a husband and wife do them." Joheved nodded and pointed to the next passage.

> A woman came before Rabbi and said to him: I set a table for my husband and he turned it over. Rabbi said to her: My daughter, Torah permits you to him.

She turned to Rachel. "So even turning over the table is allowed, provided the woman is willing."

"The text continues with how children are damaged if the woman is not willing." Miriam leaned over to consult the page.

> The rebellious and faithless ones—these are the children of fear, children of rape, children of hatred, . . . children of anger, children of drunkenness, children of brazenness.

She sat up straight and smiled. "Look, Joheved, here's that saying of yours by Rav Shmuel.

> Brazenness—is this so? Rav Shmuel said in the name of Rabbi Yohanan: Any man whose wife solicits him for the holy deed will have children such as were unknown even in Moses's generation."

Joheved sat down next to Miriam and between giggles they finished the passage together.

> "For regarding Moses's generation it says, 'Get yourself intelligent, wise, and renowned men.' Then it is written, 'And I took as tribal heads, renowned and intelligent men.' He could not find 'wise men.' But regarding Leah it is written: Leah went out to him (her husband Jacob) and said, 'You shall sleep with me tonight, for I have hired you'; and then it says, 'The children of Issachar (the son conceived by that union) were acquainted with wisdom.'"

"What's so funny?" Rachel demanded.

Joheved and Miriam exchanged looks, each wondering how much she should tell their little sister. Then Joheved reached over and closed the book. "This text is also in Tractate Eruvin. It was the first Arayot Miriam and I studied together, while I was pregnant with Isaac. In fact, you could say that my Isaac is a child of brazenness." Joheved held up her hand to stop further questions. "I'll tell you about it when we study Eruvin."

Though on many days it seemed to Rachel that the sun would never set, the month did pass. Eliezer and his family arrived in the second week of June and took up lodgings in Samuelis's empty rooms. As protection against demons, his nephews shared his bed and his nieces roomed with Rachel.

After some discussion, Meir and Joheved agreed that he would let Eliezer transcribe his father's copy of Tractate Kallah while she loaned his copy to Rachel. After all, why shouldn't Rachel learn what was about to happen?

But Eliezer's initial response was rejection. "You don't need to teach me that Arayot, I've already seen it."

Meir smiled. "You're thinking of Yehuda Gaon's Tractate Kallah. You'll find this one quite different." He opened the manuscript to one of the more salacious passages. "I really think you should look it over, even if you don't want your own copy. Especially since Joheved has loaned one to your bride."

His face reddening, Eliezer added the book to the carryall he was packing. At the sound of women's voices outside, he hurried to the window and peeked out. "They're going to the stews now." He remained at the window until the voices faded away. "They won't be back from the *mikvah* for a while, but I'd better get over to my brother's."

"I'll walk with you." Meir threw his arm around Eliezer's shoulder. "Even in the daytime you shouldn't be alone."

Rachel had seen the slight movement behind Samuelis's window and she knew Eliezer was watching. She blew him a kiss and then, surrounded by her sisters, his sisters, and both their mothers, she made her way through the Broce aux Juifs' alleys to the bathhouse on the Rû Cordé Canal. There they unpacked a small feast and prepared for an evening celebrating the bride's first immersion. Rachel took her time undressing before climbing into the large bathtub, making sure that Eliezer's female relatives had ample time to inspect her body for flaws.

Of course there were none, and Rachel basked in the looks of awe her naked form induced. She leaned back to let Joheved wash and comb her curly hair, while Mama pared her nails. She had to be perfectly clean before she entered the *mikvah*. Wine goblets and meat pies were passed around the steaming room, and the women relaxed into telling stories about their own weddings, each one funnier than the last. Finally the fruit and cakes were consumed, and as dusk fell, the party left for the synagogue.

After immersing, Rachel hurried up the stairs as fast as she could without slipping. In the antechamber, her family members were chatting with Joseph's new wife, Fleur, who was waiting to use the *mikvah*. It had been scandalous enough that the *parnas*'s son decided to remarry immediately after the minimum three festivals had passed since Johanna's death. That he chose to marry a virgin only made people talk more. Papa had urged him to marry a woman closer to his own age, but to no avail.

The young woman had obviously not expected company, and Miriam was trying to put her at ease, but there was no hiding the fact that Fleur had been married almost a year and still wasn't pregnant. Rachel was unsympathetic—the girl's family had schemed for months, even before Johanna died, for her to marry Joseph and get their hands on the *parnas*'s wealth. It would serve them right if Fleur remained barren.

Rachel imagined herself married to such an old man and shuddered. Thank Heaven for Eliezer. He'd get her pregnant right away, she just knew it, and she wouldn't have to visit the *mikvah* again for a long time.

nineteen

achel woke to Samuelis's roosters crowing. Tomorrow morning she would wake up in a different bed, in a different house, and the noisy roosters would be her roosters. Tomorrow morning it would be Eliezer lying next to her, not his two nieces. Her stomach tightened, and she took a deep breath to calm herself. Careful not to disturb the girls, she slipped out of bed to use the chamber pot. Through the shutters she could see the predawn sky, streaked with greyish pink clouds.

She climbed back into bed, but sleep was impossible. *Why couldn't I have gotten married during the Cold Fair, when the nights are long, rather than today, the longest day of the year?* The *erusin* ceremony would take place at midday, followed by a betrothal banquet. Then, before sunset, they would read and witness her *ketubah*, and chant the seven wedding blessings, so that she and Eliezer would welcome the Sabbath as husband and wife.

Rachel could hear people moving downstairs. *Splash*—somebody was drawing water from the well. She reached under the mattress and pulled out her copy of Tractate Kallah. She'd finished page one when an alarming thought assailed her.

Did Eliezer know she'd read this? He knew she studied Arayot, but this was far more explicit. Should she pretend to be innocent and let him seduce her? Or should she be brazen like Leah with Jacob?

She skimmed the parts about love charms and special foods to increase desire, focusing her attention on the book's description of caresses recommended to arouse a virgin bride. When she'd memorized them, she slipped Tractate Kallah back under the mattress and pretended to let the girls wake her.

The morning passed even more slowly than she'd anticipated. She was never left alone, not even when she used the chamber pot. Heaven forbid she should venture outside and use the demon-infested privy. Five different people offered to brush her hair, each one finding new knots that the demon Feltrech had tied in her curls the night before.

When Mama finally declared that it was time to dress, Eliezer's nieces begged to stay behind and help. They smiled with delight as Mama laid out her bridal outfit.

"Look how the gold threads shine in the light." The younger girl couldn't resist reaching out to touch the emerald green brocade. "It's going to sparkle when you dance."

"The embroidery is real gold," her sister said.

Rivka held up the pale green chemise for Rachel to slip over her head. "The *bliaut* is fine silk," she said, pulling the sleeves down to her daughter's wrists. "But this chemise is extraordinary. The fabric is soft and subtle, yet it's not silk. And it takes color so well."

"It's called cotton and it comes all the way from Egypt," the older girl said. "Papa only started getting it last year." She lowered her voice in awe. "It's very expensive."

Rachel held still as her mother sewed up the chemise's sleeves. The cotton material felt incredibly smooth against her bare skin. What a change from the linen underclothes she usually wore, material she would not have called rough before.

Rivka helped her daughter into the green silk *bliaut*, then stood back to survey the result, her face beaming with pride. "May the Holy One protect you, Rachel, you do look lovely."

"You look very nice, too, Mama." After refusing to get a new *bliaut* for either Joheved or Miriam's wedding, Rivka had finally given in. Together they bought her a length of mauve silk to match her amethyst jewelry.

The younger girl stared at Rachel. "Your eyes are the same color as your *bliaut*."

"Quiet," the older niece interrupted her. "I think I hear the musicians."

In the silence that followed, faint strains of music could be heard in the distance.

Rivka handed Rachel the emerald brooch and earrings that Eliezer had given her at their engagement. "Quickly now, put these on. We'll arrange your veil downstairs."

In the courtyard Rachel mounted the waiting white horse, then, surrounded by musicians and her family holding torches—*Why do they need torches in the middle of the day?*—she was led to the synagogue. After a brief stint in the women's gallery to receive her wedding girdle and headpiece—gold and emeralds again, but somehow she wasn't as thrilled as with her engagement presents—Joheved anointed her with perfume. *How do they make this? It smells just like roses.*

Now, downstairs into the courtyard, all the people were staring at her, whispering how beautiful she was. Suddenly Eliezer ducked under her veil with her. He looked so serious, not excited or eager. What was he thinking?

They blessed the cup of wine for *erusin*, and he put the ring on her finger, reciting the ancient Hebrew words that legally bound them: "Behold, you are consecrated to me with this ring, according to the Law of Moses and Israel." His voice was a whisper and he wouldn't look her in the eye. *Is something wrong?*

Before Rachel could squeeze his hand reassuringly, wheat was flying at them from all directions and everyone was yelling, "Be fruitful and multiply." The musicians burst into song, and immediately Eliezer was dragged away by a line of dancing men while she was surrounded by a circle of women.

The dancers led them into the street, where tables, benches, and stalls laden with food filled the road now closed to traffic. In the center, under a canopy to shade them from the sun, stood a table with the two carved chairs usually used at a *brit milah*. She took her seat at Eliezer's right, where a tray with bread, salt, two boiled eggs, and a cooked chicken waited for them. Their parents sat down on either side of them, Eliezer made the blessing over the bread, and the feast began.

All sorts of succulent dishes were brought to them. Rachel downed her food eagerly, but Eliezer was barely touching his. *Is he that nervous about tonight? Maybe I shouldn't act so brazenly?*

In no time the sun was low in the sky, and people began walking back to the synagogue courtyard. A pathway in the crowd opened for Mama and Papa to lead Rachel to the raised platform in its center. She heard sniffles behind her, but to her surprise it was Papa crying, not Mama. She reached over to take his hand, and he held it tight until she reached the steps. Then he leaned over and gave her a kiss before relinquishing her to Eliezer.

Soon she and Eliezer would be alone. Her heart began to beat faster. *Maybe I shouldn't have eaten so much.* Rachel knew she should listen carefully as her *ketubah* was read, but she couldn't concentrate on the Aramaic words. Papa would make sure her *ketubah* was correct. The hazzan was chanting the seven wedding blessings, after which Eliezer would break the wine cup and . . . *I mustn't give in to panic.* But it was the sixth blessing already.

"Oh give abundant joy to these loving companions, even as You did gladden your creation in the Garden of Eden. *Baruch ata Adonai*, Who gives joy to groom and bride."

Mon Dieu, help me tonight. Please make everything go well. Don't let me do something wrong and be ashamed. She was dimly aware of the final blessing, the sound of the wine cup crashing against the synagogue wall, and cheers as she was picked up and carried through the streets, into her father's courtyard, past the front door of her new house, and finally into Samuelis's old bedroom, where Joheved was waiting for her.

The room smelled of roses, and sure enough garlands of them hung from the bedstead. Joheved helped her out of her wedding *bliaut*, then took out a small needle and began removing the stitches on the chemise's sleeves. "How are you feeling? Any final questions?"

"Oh, Joheved, I'm so afraid."

"But your door is open now. It won't hurt."

"I'm not afraid of that. I'm afraid of . . . I don't know." Rachel was shaking.

Joheved pulled out the last stitches and gave her little sister a hug. "I know it's scary, not knowing what's going to happen, and I wish I could describe it so you wouldn't worry. But trust me. It will be wonderful, you'll see. Now put on some more perfume and try to relax."

Rachel forced herself to take several deep breaths. She slipped on an old linen chemise, leaving its laces undone, then kissed her sister good night and ushered her out of the room.

Before she could turn around, a short knock at the door was followed almost immediately by Eliezer's appearance. He too was dressed only in a chemise, and she found herself staring at his bare feet. The skin there was so pale compared to his hands.

He hung up his new clothes, and she waited for him to embrace her. But he just stood there, on the other side of the bed, staring at her. *Well, if I am going to be brazen, this is the time.* She inhaled deeply and slipped the chemise's neckline down over her shoulders, allowing her only garment to fall to the floor.

Hours later, when she opened her eyes, it was pitch dark and church bells were chiming. She was lying on her side, Eliezer's arm around her. *Is it midnight already? Or even later?* She gasped and turned to face him.

"What's the matter, Belle Assez?" he whispered, calling her the nickname that his brother had teased her with long ago.

"What time is it? How long have I been asleep?"

He could hear the urgency in her voice. "You've just dozed a little while. It's only Compline."

In the hall outside their room, low voices bid each other "*bonne nuit*" and "Shabbat shalom."

"See," he said. "My parents and sisters are just going to bed now." He could feel her relaxing back into his arms. "Why does it matter what time it is?"

"Remember the Arayot in the tenth chapter of Eruvin, where Rava says that if you want to have male children you should perform the holy deed and then repeat it?"

Of course he remembered it. "What about it?"

"Does Rava say how much time may elapse between the first time and the second, in order that the second act count as a repetition and not as a new act?"

He smiled and pulled her closer. "*Non*, he doesn't. Neither do his colleagues." The smell of her body, mixed with the roses' perfume, permeated his senses, and he was acutely aware of her bare breasts pressing against his chest.

"Then we don't know if it's too late now or not." Her voice was a mixture of anxiety and disappointment.

"I don't think it's been that long since our first time," Eliezer whispered between kisses. "But just in case, we can use the bed now and then again right afterward. Would that make you feel better, Belle Assez?"

She wanted to tell him not to call her Belle Assez, that it might provoke the Evil Eye. But her resolve faded as his kisses became more insistent, and as his hands began moving over her body, she abandoned herself to his sweet caresses.

The next evening Miriam tried in vain to locate Judah and Yom Tov in the crush of people. They'd been standing next to her during Havdalah, the ceremony that marked the end of the Sabbath, but as soon as the braided candle was doused in the cup of wine, the musicians began playing a lively wedding song, and everyone not dancing bolted for the tables laden with food.

What if Yom Tov had gotten separated from Judah? What if he was crying, alone and lost, too small to see over the adults' heads? She took a deep breath and fought down her panic. Yom Tov wouldn't leave their courtyard, and if anyone saw him crying they'd bring him to the table reserved for the bride's family. She shifted Shimson to her hip and headed in that direction.

Rachel and Eliezer were already seated, smiling coyly as they ate together, feeding each other from their shared dishes. At one point, when the fruit preserves on Rachel's bread began dripping, Eliezer brought her sticky hand to his mouth and licked her fingers clean, his eyes never leaving hers.

Miriam reached up to brush away a tear. Five years ago she and Judah could only pretend to have shared the intimacies that Rachel and Eliezer had obviously enjoyed. Miriam dabbed away another tear. If only she'd been able to enjoy those intimacies with Benjamin.

"It's hard to watch them dance without crying too." Joheved, her attention focused on the center of the courtyard, sat down in the empty chair next to her sister.

Miriam turned to look in that direction, where Mama and Eliezer's mother were dancing together to a slow, poignant tune about marrying off one's youngest child. Tears shone on both women's cheeks, and on others' in the audience as well. Again Miriam's thoughts turned to the past; Benjamin had been his mother's youngest child. Miriam wept openly now, her old wound unexpectedly tender.

As if intuiting her emotions, Shimson began to fuss in her arms, and Miriam was forced to put her sadness away and attend to her baby. She finally managed to coax a burp out of him when Joheved leaned over and whispered, "Miriam, I need your advice."

Miriam looked up in surprise. Had her older sister ever asked her for advice? "Shall we go inside and talk privately?"

"No one will hear us over this din." Joheved sighed. "It's about an argument I had with Meir. I don't know what to do, and you're the only one I can talk to about it."

Miriam couldn't hide her apprehension. "What's the matter?"

"Meir is worried that Shemayah's daughter Zipporah, despite his scholarship and the family's wealth, will not be able to find a worthy husband."

"He's right to worry," Miriam said. "The poor girl's family is cursed, and I can't imagine what man would want to see his sons die so young."

Joheved's eyes narrowed in anger. "My husband has decided to solve Shemayah's problem by having Isaac marry her."

"He made the arrangement with Shemayah without consulting you?" Though Miriam knew how close the bond between study partners could be, she was still shocked.

"Meir told me that, as a father, arranging Isaac's marriage is his obligation. He reminded me that Papa agreed to our betrothal without consulting Mama, just as he did with you and Judah," Joheved said. "I tell you, his voice was like ice."

"What did you say?"

"Of course I tried to change his mind. I reminded him that Isaac is heir to our estate. If Isaac can't have sons, the land will revert to Count André."

"But that's not true, Joheved. If Isaac doesn't have any sons, then one of Samuel's sons will inherit, or maybe another of your grandsons." Miriam began to feel sorry for Shemayah and Meir. "Besides, we don't know that Zipporah herself is cursed, and, even if she is, the curse doesn't strike every baby boy."

Joheved clenched her fists. "How can he do this to Isaac, and to us? Make us suffer through every pregnancy, worrying if it will be a boy, and then if it is, forcing us to watch the poor child bleed to death?" She was almost crying. "And not just Isaac's sons, but his daughter's sons too."

"Did you ask him that?"

"*Oui*, and he told me that Shemayah is dearer to him than any brother, that he cannot bear to see his friend grieve over this unmarriageable daughter when he can prevent it."

Miriam didn't know what to say. She could sympathize with Joheved as well.

"He honors Shemayah above his own family," Joheved hissed.

"I know you're not fond of Shemayah, but are you sure you're not condemning him and his little girl because of something he said years ago while intoxicated?"

"I forgave him when he apologized." *But would I have been more charitable if I hadn't disliked the man?* "It is ironic that Shemayah, who thinks teaching daughters Torah is like teaching them lechery, will likely end up with only daughters to teach himself, daughters who would also never have sons. I wonder what Papa will think of his first grandson marrying such a girl?"

"Have you told Marona?"

"Meir told me not to. He doesn't intend to make it public for some time. Besides, if I can't convince him to see reason, then his mother probably wouldn't be able to either, and telling her will only make matters worse." Joheved wasn't sure if Meir would actually beat her for disobedience or just make life miserable for her in other ways.

"Maybe you don't have to change his mind," Miriam said. "If Meir hasn't made any announcement yet, why not wait until Zipporah is older and see what happens when she cuts herself?"

Joheved looked at her sister with admiration. "You're right. The girl is little more than a baby. Who knows if she'll survive childhood, let alone live to a marriageable age?"

"The pox will return before then too," Miriam said.

Joheved smiled. "I won't say anything more about it to Meir. But one thing I'll make sure of—Isaac isn't going to marry Shemayah's daughter until the girl has safely flowered."

Miriam was about to ask Joheved if she worried about her children for no reason, when Yom Tov ran up. "Mama, Mama, look at the food we've brought you." And there was Judah, followed by Alvina, each carrying a tray piled high with delicacies.

"Papa brought you a bowl of strawberries," Yom Tov added proudly, throwing himself into her embrace.

"*Merci*, Judah." Miriam smiled up at him. Then, with one arm clasping baby Shimson to her bosom and the other securely gripping Yom Tov's shoulder, she sniffed back her tears and silently thanked Heaven for the love she had been given. *For shame—mourning at my sister's wedding.*

When Sarah joined them, it was clear from her expression that something was amiss. "My son writes that there was a terrible fire in Mayence, that it started in the Jewish Quarter." Her brows creased with worry. "Only a few people were injured, but the quarter was destroyed, and much of the rest of the city burned as well."

"That's awful." Miriam shuddered and clutched Shimson a little tighter. With all the thatched-roof houses so close together, fire was an ever-present danger. Usually they were extinguished quickly with buckets of sand and water, limiting the damage to a few houses or a single block. But if the weather was dry and windy, the best people could do was pray.

"Was it an accident?" Alvina asked. "Or did the Edomites set it deliberately?"

"An accident, my son thinks. But many Jews are afraid that the burghers will blame them for the damage."

Joheved scowled. "They expect Jews to pay to reconstruct the city? They think the Jews have more money than the bishop?"

"Eleazar says that things in Mayence are so bad that Bishop Rudiger of Speyer has invited the Jews to settle in his city," Sarah continued.

"Rudiger's ministers promise safety for those who settle there, with all rights necessary to earn their livelihood and practice their religion."

"Surely the Bishop of Mayence will rebuild," Judah said. It was horrible to imagine the entire Jewish Quarter, its homes, shops, taverns, and the yeshiva, in ashes.

Sarah sighed heavily. "I expect he will. But if Eleazar wants to move his family to Speyer, he has my blessing."

Anna, carrying a tray of dirty dishes, paused on her way to the kitchen. "Baruch got a letter from my uncle. He says the new baby is doing well, and they intend to remain in Mayence."

Salomon's household rarely mentioned Catharina by name. A convert to Judaism, Catharina was considered a heretic by the Church. For her safety and that of the Troyes Jewish community, she'd fled her native city when she married Anna's uncle Samson.

"I wouldn't leave if the Old City burned down," Miriam said. "Not as long as our vineyard was still standing."

Joheved nodded in agreement. "Our burghers wouldn't get so angry; they know how much business the Jews bring to Troyes."

"And who's to say that things will be better in Speyer than in Mayence?" Alvina asked. "The bishop just wants the trade the Jews will create."

"Maybe Speyer will be better and maybe not," Sarah replied. "But if my son has to build a new house, he'd rather build in a new city. If demons have cursed the Jewish Quarter of Mayence, Eleazar will be safer in Speyer."

The following five nights found Salomon's family at five more feasts in honor of his daughter's nuptials, each provided by a different host. With foreign merchants still arriving in town, it was a simple matter to find a guest who had not attended one of the earlier meals, which allowed the seven wedding blessings to be recited again for his benefit.

The banquets were noisy affairs. Besides discussing their business, the merchants argued about that day's Talmud lesson, whether it was more prudent for the Jews of Mayence to rebuild or move to Speyer, and which pope they preferred, King Henry's Clement or the exiled Gregory.

But it seemed to Miriam that their loudest arguments were over women doing circumcisions.

Since Shimson's birth, four more Jewish boys had been born in Troyes, and for each one Miriam had done either *priah* or *motzitzin* in addition to bandaging the wound. The most recent *brit* was the day before the Hot Fair opened, and thus many foreign merchants were present. She could still hear the collective intake of breath that greeted her appearance, followed by whispers throughout the congregation. It wasn't until she'd put on the *haluk* that she realized that for the first time Avram had not asked if anyone knew of a boy who wanted to be the mohel's apprentice.

The debate began immediately. Many of the foreign merchants were outraged, arguing like Rav that women are not fit to perform *milah*. When confronted with Rav Yohanan's opinion that women are fit, and with the Talmudic rule that in disputes between Rav and Rav Yohanan, *halakhah* agrees with the latter, they declared that in this case Rav's view was the correct one.

By the time Rachel had been married a week, even those merchants who had never visited Troyes before knew that the *mohelet*-in-training was the rosh yeshiva's daughter, forcing those who studied with Salomon to modify their tactics. These men challenged the local community: how could it be that in Troyes, with over a hundred Jewish families and its own yeshiva, the mohel could not find a single male apprentice?

Judah in particular became an object of criticism. Meir's clumsiness was an insurmountable obstacle, but a scholar as pious as Judah should overcome his squeamishness rather than let his wife shame the town by proving that not a man among them was willing to undertake this essential mitzvah. Jewish law may allow a woman to perform *milah* when no man is available, but tradition demands that circumcision be a man's duty.

Three weeks later, Rachel further flouted tradition by announcing to her family how pleased she was that her flowers had not returned to trouble her. At Rosh Hashanah, she made sure that the entire women's gallery, and especially Fleur, heard her complain how nauseous she felt every afternoon.

Miriam gave silent thanks that her little sister hadn't provoked the Evil Eye by announcing that, should the child be a boy, she would be doing the circumcision.

twenty

Ramerupt
Early Spring 4845 (1085 CE)

 oheved leaned back into a pile of straw and pushed the hair from her eyes. "I appreciate your missing Purim in Troyes to help us with the lambing, Miriam. Each year it gets more difficult for Marona."

"I don't mind. Judah doesn't like Purim much after all."

Miriam gazed around the barn, crowded with sheep and newborn lambs, and smiled with satisfaction. There were only a few pregnant ewes left, and at the moment none of them needed attention. Joheved signaled to one of the milkmaids, who brought over a plate of bread and cheese, and a flask of ale.

She drank deeply and yawned. "I don't understand why I'm so tired." She stifled another yawn. "It's only an hour past sunset, and, thanks to you, I got plenty of sleep last night."

"Maybe you're enceinte again."

"How could I be?" Joheved stared up at her sister in disbelief. "Hannah is still nursing and my flowers haven't come back yet."

"If you think you're pregnant again too soon, I can give you some herbs to bring on your flowers."

Miriam ruefully recalled the lady-in-waiting from Ramerupt who had come to her for that very thing during the Cold Fair. She had wanted to warn Rosaline that it might be too late for the herbs to work, but the next step would have been a pessary, and no price would be worth the risk of inducing an abortion in such a prominent Edomite.

Joheved paused to consider her situation. "*Non*, I can manage two babies so close in age," she said with a small smile. "Speaking of pregnancy, Rachel looks due any day now."

Miriam shook her head. "More like next month, I think."

Joheved helped herself to some bread. "Just as long as she doesn't give birth the week before Passover."

"You mean just as long as she doesn't have a boy the week before Passover," Miriam corrected her. Nobody wanted a *brit milah* feast when bread and cakes were forbidden.

Both women were silent, trying to recall if they'd ever attended such a banquet during Passover.

"Are you really going to do the circumcision if she has a boy?" Joheved asked. "Rachel certainly thinks so, and Eliezer hasn't contradicted her."

Miriam took a deep breath. "I'm not sure I'm ready."

"But I saw you at the grape harvest. You could cut off a grape's skin without spilling any juice at all," Joheved said. "And you always slaughter a chicken with one quick cut, like you're supposed to."

"I need to practice cutting off the shreds first."

"The shreds?"

"If you were to watch a *milah* closely, which most people don't," Miriam said with a grin, "you'd see that the mohel doesn't always remove the entire foreskin with one cut. Sometimes there are shreds of skin left that have to be cut off later."

"Another task for the apprentice?" Joheved asked.

Miriam nodded. "One I haven't done yet. Only a couple of boys were born after the Hot Fair ended, and there weren't enough shreds left on them."

"Avram probably didn't want you doing your first real cutting during the Cold Fair either."

"Which was fine with me." Miriam nibbled on some cheese. "When you and I were starting to study Talmud, we could keep it a secret. Even now most people don't know how learned we are, or that we wear tefillin. But being a *mohelet* is different. *Milah* is done in public; even the training is public."

"You must have been disappointed when so many of the people who supported you during the fairs changed their tune," Joheved said. "I certainly was."

"Maybe a little, but not surprised," Miriam replied. "We may quarrel amongst ourselves over my fitness to do *milah*, but let the foreign merchants condemn me and the Jews of Troyes will rally to my defense."

Joheved pursed her lips. "Only to return to their previous opinions as soon as the merchants leave."

"Hopefully I kept a few supporters."

Again conversation lapsed as each sister wondered how long it would take the Jews of Troyes to accept a woman mohel, if ever.

"Speaking of the Cold Fair, did you see Rachel's fancy birth amulet?" Joheved asked. "She told me a new scribe named Mordecai made it for her."

"*Oui*. I was with her when he wrote it," Miriam replied. "The man seemed knowledgeable. He insisted that we come back later when the stars were propitious, that there were only a few hours during the week when amulets may be written."

Besides quoting Psalm 126, the amulet called upon the great, mighty, and awesome God, Adonai Zevaot is His Name, and the three angels, Sanvi, Sansanvi, and Semangelaf, in the name of Shaddai, Creator of heaven and earth, to protect Rachel daughter of Rivka in all of her 248 organs, to help, deliver, save, and rescue her from evil spirits; that all who seek her harm be humbled, destroyed, afflicted, and overthrown. The back of the parchment was decorated with pentagrams, hexagrams, and various other geometric forms.

Joheved poured them another cup of ale. "I wonder where you learn how to make amulets."

"It's probably like becoming a mohel," Miriam said. "You train with an expert."

"Do you think they let women do it?"

"If it's anything like writing a mezuzah or a Torah scroll, probably not." Miriam took a long drink of ale and handed the cup to Joheved. "I've never seen a woman write one."

Joheved had no sooner finished her drink than there was a commotion at the door and Meir burst in, his gaze darting around the room.

Relief lessened his expression of anxiety when he saw Joheved and Miriam. "Thank Heaven you're both here," he said between gasps. His face was shining and his chemise was damp with sweat. "You've got to come back to Troyes right away."

Miriam stood up. "What's the matter? Is it Rachel?"

"It's not her baby coming, if that's what you mean." He hurried them out into the courtyard where two horses were being saddled. "Anna's Uncle Samson arrived late this afternoon, so exhausted he could barely stand. He stayed awake just long enough to hand Eliezer a letter and tell him he was terribly sorry to bring him such bad news."

Meir paused to control his emotions. "The letter, from the *parnas* of Prague, said that during unusually heavy rains, a barge ferrying Shemiah and Asher capsized south of the city, drowning both of them. The Jews of Prague managed to recover their bodies and much of their merchandise. *Oui*," he answered the unspoken question. "Both men were positively identified before they were buried."

In unison Joheved and Miriam recited, "*Baruch Dayan Emet.*"

"Eliezer must be devastated," Miriam added.

Joheved held up her hand to halt the servant who was eager to help her onto her horse. "I don't want to sound callous, but Eliezer's father and brother must have died over a month ago." She looked up at Meir, already astride his mount. "Why can't we wait until morning?"

"Because that idiot Eliezer insists on leaving for Prague first thing in the morning, and your stubborn sister is just as adamant that he wait until after the baby comes. She swore that if he leaves, she's going with him!"

"Oy." Joheved rolled her eyes and let the servant assist her.

"There's more," Meir said as the manor gate was closed behind them. "Your father forbid Rachel from leaving, your mother blamed him for spoiling her so she won't listen to him or her husband, and soon the four of them were nearly hysterical. Judah and I tried to calm them, but . . ." he trailed off helplessly.

"Rachel cannot travel to Prague in her condition." Miriam's voice was firm. "Don't worry, we'll find some way to make her and Eliezer see reason."

Miriam entered her home to find Rachel and Eliezer, each red-eyed and sniffing back tears, staring sullenly at each other across her dining table. Judah sat forlornly between them, and he looked up hopefully as she entered.

"Thank Heaven you're back. Maybe you can talk some sense . . ."

Eliezer interrupted before Judah could finish. His voice was hoarse. "*Oui*, maybe you can talk some sense into my crazy wife, who wants to go gallivanting through France and Allemagne when she's due to give birth at any moment."

"It's you who wants to go gallivanting through France and Allemagne, no matter how foul the weather or how dangerous the roads," Rachel shot back before dissolving into more tears.

"My father and brother are dead," Eliezer shouted at her. "I can't sit here waiting for a sunny day. I have to find out what happened. I have to bring their things back to my mother." He was crying again before he'd finished saying, "my mother."

Meir turned to Miriam and sighed. "See what I mean."

"I've been trying to reason with them since Meir left," Judah added. "Your parents gave up and went to bed hours ago."

Eliezer put his hands on his hips. "I suggest you use your sisterly persuasion on my wife, because *I* am leaving for Prague at dawn."

Rachel glared at him. "And I will be right behind you."

"You will stay at home! I command it!"

Before Rachel could reply, there was a knock at the door. She quickly sat down and tried to look calm, while Eliezer seated himself next to Judah and opened the manuscript in front of them. Heaven forbid that whoever needed the midwife should see them fighting. Both of them looked pointedly away from the other as Miriam hurried to greet the late-night visitor.

But it was Samson who stood towering over them, his eyes swollen from lack of sleep. "I couldn't help but hear that Eliezer wants to leave for Prague in the morning." He turned to face the mourner. "I'm sorry, but that is impossible."

"You don't need to accompany me," Eliezer said. "I'll find someone else or I'll go alone."

"Going to Prague tomorrow *is* impossible!" Samson walked over to Eliezer and took him by the shoulders. "It was a miracle I was able to get here. Bridges are washed away, roads are too muddy for carts, and those on foot never know when their path will turn into quicksand."

Samson faced the rest of them. "I was crossing a river by holding a rope tied between two trees on opposite banks, when all of a sudden the water level began to rise. It had reached my chin, and I was starting to say my final Shema, when the water stopped rising. A smaller man would have drowned."

Rachel let out a moan. Eliezer was at least a cubit shorter than Samson.

"I'll pay you whatever you want," Eliezer began.

"No amount of money is worth my life," Samson replied. "Nothing will make me leave for Mayence until I'm sure the rivers have receded. And that won't be for at least a month, maybe longer."

Eliezer's face crumpled, and Samson put his arm around him. "But after that I'll take you all the way to Prague, no payment necessary."

Everyone stared at Eliezer. Would he agree?

Judah walked over and patted Eliezer's shoulder. "My study partner may be impetuous and stubborn, but he is not a fool. And it would be beyond foolish for someone so inexperienced to travel alone to Prague before the weather improves."

Miriam coughed delicately. "Eliezer, I hate to tempt the Evil Eye, but what if there's a problem with Rachel or the baby, and you aren't here?"

Both Eliezer and Rachel paled as these words sunk in. Eliezer hesitated, torn between his obligations to the living and the dead. Then he let out his breath. "I suppose I can wait until the baby comes."

A few days later Miriam was asking her mother to watch her children while she took a nap, when her maidservant, Jeanne, interrupted them.

"Excuse me, Mistress, there's a client at the door who's asking for you specifically."

Miriam was exhausted after spending most of the last few days, and nights, assuring Rachel that the pains she felt, no matter how uncomfortable, were false labor. Each time Rachel sent for her, convinced it was the real thing this time, Miriam found her little sister's womb still closed.

"That's odd," Miriam said. "None of our other patients are due to deliver." Who would ask for her and not Aunt Sarah?

"Don't worry about the children," Rivka said. "I'll look after them until you come home and have gotten some rest."

Miriam hugged her mother good-bye and followed the unknown woman to an inn near the count's palace. The woman knew nothing of the patient's condition, only that she had been sent to fetch the young Jewish midwife for a lady named Rosaline.

Miriam knew something was wrong as soon as she opened the door. Trying not to gag on the stench, she made her way to the window and forced open the shutters. Rosaline groaned weakly and turned her face away from the sudden light, but not before Miriam had gotten a good look at her. If Miriam hadn't remembered the name and red hair, she never would have recognized the lady-in-waiting from Ramerupt. Rosaline's body was shrunken, her skin sallow, her eyes listless and unfocused.

With a horrible feeling that she knew what was wrong, Miriam bent down and whispered, "Rosaline, what happened?"

"Your herbs didn't work, so I went to a woman the others use to rid themselves of pregnancy," Rosaline said, her body shaking. "At first everything was fine, but I kept bleeding and then my belly began to hurt. Each day I felt worse."

Miriam reached out to stroke Rosaline's forehead and felt the burning confirmation. Childbed fever!

Tears came to her eyes. There was little hope for a woman when the demons made her feverish after an abortion or giving birth. Usually, it was only a week before the woman was dead, another of Lillit's many victims.

On a chest nearby stood a towel and a basin of water, as well as a half-empty bowl of broth. At least somebody was caring for Rosaline. Miriam wet the towel and wrung it out. "Let me wash your face and hands. Then maybe you'll feel like having some more soup."

Rosaline let Miriam wipe away her sweat but refused the broth. "It's no use eating," she whispered. "I can tell by your expression that I'm going to die."

"You don't know that." Miriam was mortified that her fear was so obvious.

"It's God's punishment for my sin."

"And what is God's punishment for Faubert, or whoever the father is?" Before Rosaline could reply she apologized. "Pardon me, it's not my business."

But Rosaline didn't share Miriam's anger. "It was my sin to get rid of the baby."

Miriam wiped Rosaline's sweaty face again. "You should have some soup. If you keep your strength up, you may still recover."

Rosaline closed her eyes and turned her back to Miriam. Before Miriam could decide what to do, there was a knock on the door and a feminine voice called out, "Rosaline, are you there?"

The door rattled but Miriam had locked the latch behind her. "Rosaline, it's Beatrice." The voice outside became louder and more anxious. "Open the door."

Rosaline turned back and whispered to Miriam, "Let her in, she's my sister, but don't tell her what I did."

To Miriam's surprise, a nun rushed into the room.

"When your message arrived, I came as soon as I could—" Beatrice stopped and stared at Miriam.

"I'm Miriam, a *femme sage.*" She had to think of some reason for being there. "Your sister didn't want a doctor."

Beatrice sat down on the bed and took Rosaline's hand. "You're coming with me to Notre-Dame-aux-Nonnains so our infirmarian can care for you." She clearly expected to be obeyed. "All our nuns will pray for you."

Miriam could see that her presence was intrusive. "If you like I'll arrange for a litter when I leave."

"*Merci*, that would be helpful," Beatrice said. Then she closed her eyes and began reciting words in Latin.

Miriam closed the door behind her and, praying for Rosaline's health, slowly walked home. Brooding over whether she could have done something to help the young woman, she entered the courtyard without noticing that Aunt Sarah was heading right for her.

"Rachel was making such a fuss that Rivka insisted I examine her." Sarah's tone made it clear that they were no longer dealing with false labor.

Miriam headed to the well to wash; Rosaline's room was filthy with demons. "And?" she asked, lathering her arms up to her elbows.

"Her womb is beginning to open, but her water hasn't broken yet," came Aunt Sarah's authoritative reply.

"Should we break it for her? That would speed things."

"Let's give her a while first." Aunt Sarah didn't need to remind her niece that it was dangerous for a woman to labor too long after her water broke.

A bloodcurdling screech issued from Rachel's bedroom window just as Eliezer bolted into the courtyard. "Salomon and the others are on their way from the synagogue," he said, gazing up at the chamber with trepidation.

Miriam dried her hands, then followed Aunt Sarah upstairs to where Rivka was waiting for them. "I hope her baby is born quickly," Rivka whispered as Rachel let out another shriek.

But it was not to be the case. By the time Miriam and Rivka had chalked the room against Lillit, hung up Rachel's birth amulet, and tied the family's various tefillin on the bedstead, Salomon and Judah had arrived with a Torah scroll. A few hours later Meir returned from Ramerupt with Joheved, who immediately joined her female relatives. *Souper* was an ordeal, punctuated with cries from above, and each report was the same.

Despite unending cups of ragwort and columbine seed tisane, Rachel's progress was excruciatingly slow.

Her screams prevented everyone from sleeping that night, yet in the morning her womb had only opened two finger-widths. After much discussion, Miriam and Aunt Sarah agreed to break her water, after which Miriam went home to rest. She had a feeling it was going to be a long day . . . and a longer night.

By sunset, Aunt Sarah could get four fingers into Rachel's womb, and Miriam took over while her family had something to eat. It was fully dark when Joheved and Mama returned.

"Here, Miriam." Rivka placed several steaming bowls and a plate overflowing with food on the chest next to the bed. "I don't want you to go hungry tonight."

Rachel groaned as Miriam tore off a piece of bread and eagerly dunked it into a bowl of stew. "Can I have something to eat? I'm starving."

"Nothing for you except liquids until the baby's born," Miriam said. *Why are things going so slowly?* Infusions of ragwort and columbine seed usually speeded the birth process considerably. "Maybe you should have some artemisia tisane to help you relax."

"That ragwort drink tastes awful, and I bet the artemisia tastes worse." Rachel started to stick her tongue out at her sisters, but then her expression froze. She grabbed hold of Joheved and Rivka's hands, squeezed them tight, and screamed. Then, the contraction over, she fell back against the pillow, gasping for breath.

Miriam stood up and stretched. "Mama, you might as well go to bed. I don't think this baby is coming anytime soon. And when you're downstairs could you add a handful of artemisia leaves to a pot of water on the hearth?"

Rivka kissed her daughter's brow. "Rachel, it would go easier for you if you could relax when you're not in pain."

"How can I relax when I know it's going to hurt again in a moment?" Rachel muttered once her mother was out the door. Then she turned to Joheved. "I don't understand it. You and Miriam have had five babies between you, yet you hardly made a peep during labor. How could you bear the pain?"

Joheved and Miriam exchanged glances, waiting to see who would answer first. Then Joheved sighed. "It's difficult to recall the pain once it's over. I know that Isaac's birth hurt more than the others, but I forced myself not to scream because I didn't want to upset Meir. Remember, his sister had just died in childbirth."

"I don't mind upsetting Eliezer. It's time he worried about somebody besides himself," Rachel retorted. Then her expression softened. "How about you, Miriam? Even with Yom Tov you didn't cry out. And you told Joheved that you planned to yell your head off during labor, that it was the only time a woman got to scream and nobody thought she was crazy."

"You eavesdropped on us that night?" Joheved accused her.

Rachel grinned. "Of course I did—and on other nights too. You have no idea how much I learned by spying on you two."

"Getting back to your question." Miriam interrupted before her red-faced older sister could vent her outrage. "I didn't scream because I didn't need to. It wasn't that painful." Her tone became more professional. "I've attended lots of women in childbirth; some scream a lot, some a little, and some not at all. Yet I don't think the ones who scream are necessarily in more pain than those who merely groan."

"Maybe it's like in Tractate Bava Kamma," Joheved said. "You know, where the Mishnah starts:

> One who injures another is liable for five things—damage, pain, healing, loss of time and disgrace.

Then the Sages debate how to assess pain."

"That's right. I remember the text." Miriam nodded, her expression thoughtful. "Papa taught that payment for pain depends on how delicate a person is. In the Gemara it asks:

> Perhaps you have a sensitive person; he has more pain. Or you have a person who is not sensitive; he has no pain."

Joheved noticed Rachel's puzzled expression, and added, "These are different people with identical injuries."

"I've never studied Bava Kamma," Rachel admitted.

Joheved looked surprised. "You'd think that Papa would teach this section more often. It's interesting how the Rabbis take the Torah verse,

'Eye for eye, tooth for tooth,' and interpret it so that the assailant pays monetary damages."

"How can they do that?" Rachel asked. "The Torah is explicit.

> If anyone maims his fellow, as he did shall be done to him: break
> for break, eye for eye, tooth for tooth.

It says so twice." She began to grimace and breathe faster as another contraction came and went, but she didn't cry out.

"It's a complicated discussion," Miriam said. "I don't think this is the time to study it."

"Why not?" Rachel pushed herself up on her elbow. "Mama's gone to bed, and it's not like we have anything else to do."

"I think it's an excellent idea," Joheved said. It was certainly better than sitting there listening to her little sister scream. "Here's what the Mishnah says about pain:

> Even if he is burned, or injured on his fingernail, where it makes
> no wound, we consider how much (money) a similar man would
> take to suffer such pain.

Think about it while I go get your tisane and Papa's *kuntres*."

They spent the next several hours in study, and as Joheved hoped, Rachel was so distracted that she rarely did more than groan when her contractions came.

"I know Papa says that 'similar' refers to how sensitive a person is to pain, but maybe it means similar in wealth," Miriam suggested. "After all, wouldn't a rich man pay more to avoid pain than a poor man?"

Rachel clenched her sisters' hands as another contraction shook her. "I'd gladly pay a hundred dinars to avoid this pain."

"You have one hundred dinars?" Joheved looked at her in surprise.

"Of course I don't. But if I did, I'd pay that much."

"That's why I think Miriam's idea is wrong," Joheved said. "How much someone would pay to avoid pain depends on how bad the pain is, not on how rich he is."

"But can anyone possibly know how much another person suffers, even someone with the same injury?" Miriam asked.

"It's like the Gemara says; some people are very sensitive to pain and others are not." Rachel clutched Miriam's hand and groaned loudly. "Of course I had to be a sensitive one."

Miriam nodded. "I suppose so. Remember how much you suffered each month with your flowers?"

Joheved had suspected that Rachel's menstrual complaints were to gain Papa and Eliezer's attention, but she said nothing. Maybe Rachel really was more sensitive, and, in any case, a woman in labor should be judged favorably. Her thoughts were interrupted when Rachel squeezed her hand again.

"Mon Dieu! I think the pain is getting worse."

"Your contractions are getting closer together." Miriam washed her hands at the basin near the bed. "Let me check."

The examination was brief, but before it was over Rachel was screaming again. Before Miriam could reveal her sister's condition, there was an urgent knocking at the door. Joheved opened it just wide enough to identify her father and, behind him, Eliezer.

"Is everything all right?" Salomon asked. "Things were so quiet for so long that we dozed off."

"After all, we've been awake for almost two days now," Eliezer said, rubbing his eyes.

Joheved wouldn't have thought it possible for anyone to be heard over Rachel's shrieks, but they all understood when Miriam said, "Her womb is completely open now. One of you should get Mama and Aunt Sarah."

This proved unnecessary. Rachel's renewed cries had woken the entire neighborhood, and the two older women were at that moment entering the front door, followed by Meir and several students. Somehow everyone recognized the difference in Rachel's screams, and an anxious hubbub filled the salon.

"Do you think we should get the cowslip and pepper ready?" Miriam asked as Aunt Sarah conducted her own examination.

"The baby's head is in position, and your sister still seems quite strong. I think we can wait." Pepper was very expensive, and there was no need to make Rachel sneeze the baby out yet. Pepper could also be dangerous, especially at a first birth. If a woman pushed too vigorously, her flesh might tear. "But Joheved can start reciting from Exodus now."

As long as anyone could remember, when a Jewish woman was in hard labor, another woman, preferably one already a mother, whispered the eighth verse from chapter 11 in her ear as she prepared to push.

"Get you out and the people that follow you. After that I will go out, and he went out."

Now Rachel's cries were punctuated with gasps of "Mon Dieu, I can't stand it," until suddenly, "I need to push!"

They helped her onto the birthing stool, Joheved whispering the verse from Exodus with each contraction, and things moved swiftly to their conclusion.

"It's a boy!" Miriam announced to the suddenly silent room.

She held the baby up, expertly slapped his derriere, and as her newest nephew began to howl, she turned to Rachel and smiled. "Mazel tov, you have a son."

As the new mother began the prayer a parent says after the birth of a son, Miriam left her in Aunt Sarah's capable hands and slipped into the hall.

The men looked up at her eagerly, and she shared the happy news. Next Joheved came down the stairs, yawning and leaning heavily on the railing. Their arms supporting each other, the sisters slowly crossed the courtyard. The morning star had risen, and by the time they put on tefillin and prayed their morning prayers it would be nearly dawn.

There were still nine days before Passover began, leaving Rivka and Salomon one day to host their newest grandson's *brit milah* banquet before all leavened foodstuffs would be removed from their house for the festival. But all Miriam could think of was whether she would or wouldn't be performing her first circumcision on that day.

twenty-one

Troyes
Spring 4846 (1086 CE)

iriam put down the ledger and rubbed her eyes. Once this page was finished, Papa's wine accounts would be caught up through Passover. That left only Rachel and Alvina's, but she had until the Hot Fair to do them—that is, unless her sister returned early.

Last year, when Rachel, Eliezer, and their infant son left for Prague, Miriam had volunteered to take care of the "chicken" business for her sister for two months. It wasn't difficult, and it gave her an excuse to stay home and avoid the vineyard with its springtime memories of Benjamin.

Although Avram decided that Miriam was not sufficiently trained to circumcise Rachel's son, he allowed her to cut the remaining shreds. Judah knew she was relieved, but for everyone else, Miriam feigned disappointment. Since then she continued doing everything except removing the foreskin. Not that Avram had her do all the parts each time. He needed to keep in practice too.

When Rachel and Eliezer returned to Troyes there was a letter from Eliezer's mother, instructing him to sell Shemiah's goods at the Hot Fair, buy new merchandise, and transport it home to Arles. Of course Rachel would not be left behind, so when Alvina returned to Paris in August, Miriam kept servicing their clients. The Cold Fair brought a message that Rachel and Eliezer would spend the winter sailing the Mediterranean and gaining the trust of Shemiah's old business partners. They'd be back for the Hot Fair.

Miriam had fumed at Rachel's assumption that she would continue to manage the "chicken" business, but she couldn't abandon the poor women who needed loans. Especially with so many people desperate for money this winter.

Count Thibault's oldest son, Étienne-Henri, had stupidly attacked King Philippe and, even more stupidly, gotten himself captured, forcing Thibault to pay an enormous ransom to free him. Taxes reached new heights, yet most households wouldn't see the bulk of their income until summer.

Miriam looked back at her ledgers and gave a quick prayer of thanksgiving. Luckily Papa had sold his wine at higher prices than this year's quality deserved. Ever since Moses haCohen cured some rich Norman's intestinal illness with regular doses of Jewish wine, it seemed as if every nobleman in France wanted some. Still, she enjoyed staying home to deal with her various clients; it gave her the opportunity to teach Yom Tov Torah.

Thinking of him immediately brightened her mood. Yom Tov, her little scholar, was so happy to study with his cousin Shmuel and Isaac haParnas's grandson, Samson. Shmuel, who preferred the Hebrew version of his name to the French, had protested at being separated from his brother Isaac, who was learning Mishnah from Meir with the older boys.

So Miriam decided to teach the boys Mishnah herself. Written in Hebrew, Mishnah shouldn't be any harder to read than scripture. That was last autumn, and now the three boys, less than a year apart in age, were inseparable. Teaching them was a labor of love, and sometimes, when Yom Tov easily read a new text, she almost wept with pride.

But she missed not being able to study with her sisters. Rachel was far away, and Joheved was too busy caring for Leah, her newborn daughter. Judah offered to study Talmud with her, but they rarely had time except on Shabbat. Right now Judah sat opposite her at the dining table, quill pen suspended above the *kuntres* in front of him. With Eliezer away, he had decided to turn his attention to Papa's commentaries rather than look for a new study partner.

"What tractate are you working on?" she asked.

Judah blinked a couple of times and looked up at her. He smiled sheepishly. "Pardon me."

Miriam smiled back and repeated her question.

"Bava Kamma. Papa plans to teach it this summer."

Miriam was about to ask Judah to share the section he was preparing, when there was a knock on the door, followed by her father's voice.

"I saw by the light that you were still awake." Salomon walked in and pulled out a piece of parchment. "I'd like your opinions about this."

Judah took the letter and Salomon added, "Don't tell me what you think until Miriam has read it too."

Judah's initial expression was one of mild curiosity. But as he read further, his face reddened and he began to scowl. After reading it twice more, he handed Miriam the letter as if it were a rodent carcass.

Odd, there was no addressee, and a quick glance at the letter's end showed no author's signature either. The words looked like Hebrew, but after a confusing couple of lines, Miriam realized she was reading Aramaic. Whoever had written this letter had been very careful.

"My dear brother," the letter began. "I ask you to offer hospitality to a former pupil who will soon be arriving in Troyes. E is an excellent student and his father is a prominent merchant in Worms, but E is unable to continue his studies here. Apparently his relationship with his study partner became carnal in nature. Upon questioning, the study partner repented of his sin and claimed responsibility, admitting that he, the elder, had led his young friend astray. He agreed to leave the yeshiva but begged that E not be expelled on his account. Unfortunately the scandal prevents E from attending another yeshiva in Ashkenaz, but there should be no such difficulty in Troyes. I therefore urge you to take this youth, who speaks no French, under your wing."

The writer concluded, "Give my regards to my sister and nieces, as well as to your sons, two of my finest students, whom I remember fondly to this day."

Judah looked like he'd just met a demon. "Rav Isaac is sending us a student who lies with other men! And we are expected to accept him because of his rich father."

Salomon sighed heavily. "The letter is indeed written by my wife's brother, but I'm not sure your other conclusion is warranted. We don't know what sin the boy has committed."

"But it's obvious."

"*Non*, it's not!" Miriam surprised them with her vehemence. "If there had been witnesses, Uncle Isaac would have said so. The only obvious thing is that E's study partner cared for him so much that he was willing to accept the entire blame in order to protect him. That doesn't mean they were . . ." She couldn't speak the final words.

Miriam met her husband's eyes, now filled with pain, and silently appealed to him. *Has he forgotten about Daniel and the suffering he'd endured on account of their close friendship?*

Apparently not, because he turned to Salomon and said, "I spoke too quickly. We must assume that a scholar acted properly, no matter how sinful his behavior appeared."

"If E is such a good student, perhaps the others were jealous and accused him falsely," Miriam said.

Salomon stroked his beard as he looked back and forth between them. "We can probably assume that E and his study partner grew fond of each other, and that someone heard or saw something that appeared to be inappropriate."

"But to be shamed publicly like that—it's outrageous," Judah protested. "Study partners are supposed to be fond of each other, and plenty of them snuggle together under the covers at night if it's cold."

"Judah, I'm not saying the boy did anything wrong," Salomon replied soothingly. "But Isaac didn't send me that letter just to gossip. It's a warning."

"Against what?" Judah asked bitterly. "Are we supposed to keep him away from the other boys, make him sleep separately?"

"If E and his study partner were so close, he's probably feeling bereft at their separation. Not to mention the shame he's had to endure," Miriam said. "We must reach out to him with kindness."

"The boy's unhappiness will be compounded by his being away from home and unable to speak our language." Salomon's voice was somber. "We must prevent him from becoming too melancholy."

Judah nodded, recalling his own despair on the bridge above the Rhine that rainy night long ago.

"He could board with us," Miriam said. "It would give me more opportunity to practice the German Mama taught us when we were little."

Judah didn't look happy about her offer, but he agreed. "We could both keep a close watch over him."

"An excellent idea." Salomon clasped Judah's shoulder. "He can study with you until we find him an appropriate study partner."

Judah's stomach lurched as his *yetzer tov* sensed the approaching danger, but it was too late. He was committed to helping the boy.

"But we mustn't separate him from the other students." Miriam shook her head.

Salomon stroked his beard again. "I suggest that a few of the older boys move in with you as well. Then they can stay up late studying during the Hot Fair without risking a fire in the attic or disturbing the others."

"Don't worry, Papa," Miriam said. "We'll take good care of our first student from Allemagne."

Judah forced himself to relax. If his *yetzer hara* grew too unruly, Miriam would save him—again.

Much to Miriam's relief, Rachel and Eliezer arrived in Troyes the same week as the mysterious E and his rich father. Miriam gratefully gave up the "chicken" business and turned her attention to the task of making her new boarder comfortable.

E, that is Elisha, was small for his age, with a baby face and large brown eyes that looked like they might fill with tears at any moment. It was difficult to gauge his intellect because he cringed and fell silent as soon as his father even glanced in his direction.

Papa must have noticed this, because after a few days he took the man aside. "I appreciate you honoring my table, but I realize that you are here in Troyes for business, much of which is conducted when merchants dine together, and I'd hate for you to neglect your livelihood on my account. I'd be pleased, however, if you could join us on Shabbat."

"Papa was so diplomatic," Judah said later that night. "Now maybe we can hear more of what the boy has to say."

"What do you think of Elisha? Is he really that good a student or was Uncle Isaac just trying to get rid of him?"

"He seems to follow the discussions, and the few questions he's asked have been intelligent."

Miriam sighed. "He's not what I expected. He seems fragile somehow."

"Don't worry." Judah patted her hand. "We won't let anything happen to him."

"We will make him such a great scholar that people in Mayence will feel ashamed for treating him so badly."

Judah warmed at the determination in his wife's voice. Eight years ago he'd left Mayence in disgrace, and then the Holy One had blessed him. Now he would show his gratitude by seeing that Elisha prospered in Troyes, just as he had.

"*Bonne nuit.*" He leaned over and kissed her. "Starting tomorrow morning I'll be getting up early to study with the scholars from Byzantium."

Miriam nudged his shoulder. "Why don't you take Elisha with you? The servants say that he's usually up before dawn."

"Good idea." Judah wasn't sure if that was his *yetzer tov* or his *yetzer hara* talking. "And over breakfast afterward, we'll tell you what we learned."

Two months later, with the Hot Fair drawing to a close, Miriam had trained herself to get up when Judah did. She said her *selichot* prayers and then took Shimson into bed with her to nurse. Once he woke, her son was impatient to start the day, but before dawn, when he was still drowsy, she could coax him into a morning feeding in addition to one at bedtime.

As usual, the sun was rising over the courtyard walls when she heard Judah and Elisha coming through the gate, and she held Shimson up to the window to wave at them. The two were deep in conversation, Judah's arm around Elisha's shoulder and their heads inclined together as they walked.

Brimming with satisfaction, Miriam changed her son's swaddling and went downstairs to greet them. But Elisha was uncharacteristically silent at breakfast, allowing Judah to explain what they had learned that morning. And he was so subdued when they walked to synagogue that Miriam had to ask what was bothering him.

"I hope you're not coming down with something," she said with a frown.

"I'm fine," he said in German. "Perfectly fine."

Now Miriam was sure something was wrong. Elisha usually preferred French, only resorting to German when he was tired or frustrated.

"Judah, all this studying is keeping Elisha from getting enough sleep." She was half-teasing and half-serious. "It's a good thing he's going home where he can get some rest."

"Don't blame Judah—I wish I could study even more." Elisha sounded close to tears.

Miriam stopped and faced the youth. "What's the matter, Elisha? You can tell me."

Judah gently put his arm around Elisha. "Our new pupil isn't very happy about going home."

Of course not, Miriam thought. Not back to all that gossip and slander. "But surely you want to see your mother and sisters again."

"I do, but . . . not all the others."

"Elisha, you mustn't let their evil words bother you." Her voice rose with indignation. "Anyone who continues to tell lies about you so close to Yom Kippur should be ashamed of himself."

Behind Elisha's back, Judah put his finger to his lips and Miriam forced herself to keep still. *How could I be so tactless as to mention Elisha's troubles in front of him? Now I have one more sin to repent for.*

After services Elisha walked so slowly that Judah was sure they'd be late to *disner*. When they reached Salomon's street, Elisha halted.

"Judah, I have to talk with you before I leave," he said, staring down at the cobblestones.

"If it's about what Miriam said . . ."

Elisha interrupted before Judah could apologize. "I saw the letter that Rabbenu Isaac wrote about me."

Judah pulled Elisha into an alcove. "Don't worry about that letter; Papa, Miriam, and I were the only ones to read it."

"Judah, I have to tell you the truth before Yom Kippur."

"You don't need to confess to me. You haven't injured me."

"But I can't have you thinking I'm innocent when I'm not."

Judah's throat tightened. "What do you mean?"

Elisha was silent for so long that Judah wondered if he should start walking again. But when Elisha did speak, Judah's heart sank.

"It wasn't just a rumor. My study partner and I . . ." Elisha paused, seemingly unable to find the right words. "Our friendship was carnal." He quickly continued, "Not that we lay together, but we kissed and touched . . ."

"I don't want to hear what you did with your study partner." Judah tried to keep his voice down. "Repent your sins to the Merciful One, not to me."

"Now you're angry." Elisha's chin began to quiver. "I shouldn't have said anything."

Judah took a deep breath and tried to calm himself. "I'm not angry with you, Elisha. Relationships between study partners ought to be close ones, and sometimes a man's *yetzer* is too strong to control."

Now Judah was silent. Should he tell Elisha about Daniel? Would he have sinned if circumstances had been different, if Daniel had been older and more aggressive? And what about Natan? That reminded him of the advice Reuben had given him years ago.

"Elisha, do you have a fiancée back home?"

"I'm not sure. My father was negotiating with a girl's family, one of his cousins, but everything stopped when," Elisha hesitated, "when the rumors started. Why do you ask?"

"I think it would be good for you to get married as soon as possible, to start using your *yetzer hara* to make sons." Judah tried to sound encouraging. "I'm sure that when your cousin hears you teach all the Torah you've studied this summer, he'll be eager for you to marry his daughter."

"You think so?"

"Certainly," Judah replied. "I'll write a letter to take back to Worms, saying what a fine student you are, an asset to our yeshiva. Even better, I'll ask Papa to write the letter. That should get the girl's father to accept you."

Elisha's big brown eyes looked up at him hopefully. "You would do that for me?"

"Of course I would. You are a fine student and an asset to our yeshiva. Don't think we haven't noticed how you've argued on Miriam's behalf with all the merchants who think she shouldn't do circumcisions."

"If Troyes is happy with a *mohelet* instead of a mohel, then the foreigners' opinions shouldn't matter."

"I wouldn't say that Troyes is happy about it," Judah with a rueful smile. "But most have come to accept the situation."

"Supporting Miriam's position is the least I can do after all you two have done for me."

Before he could reply, Judah was crushed by Elisha's embrace. Judah allowed himself to return the hug before patting the boy's shoulder a few times and slowly pulling away.

"I'll miss you—both of you," Elisha added quickly as they started walking again.

"We'll miss you too." Judah was careful to say "we" instead of "I."

Miriam had no sooner said adieu to Elisha the next morning than Rachel raced in and dumped her ledgers on the table.

"I thought I'd never get these finished in time, but here they are—all my and Alvina's accounts for the Hot Fair." She unpinned the brooch holding her keys and handed them to Miriam. "Even with Thibault's extra taxes, you and Judah should have plenty to live on until next summer."

"Don't tell me you're leaving too." Miriam grabbed her younger sister's hand. "What about the Days of Awe and helping with the vintage?"

"If we leave right away, Eliezer and I can get to Arles in time for Rosh Hashanah with his mother," Rachel replied, her speech as hurried as the rest of her. "As for the wine, Papa will have plenty of help from all those Eastern merchants who are spending the holidays in Troyes."

Miriam could feel a lump forming in her throat. She'd squandered their summer together, sure that they'd have plenty of time to talk and study after Elisha and Eliezer were gone.

"Papa won't be happy about it."

"I know." Rachel's expression softened. "And I'll miss him, but I can't stay here. Eliezer would rather be discussing Jewish laws of commerce than actually engaging in it. Just between us, I've been handling most of the business. It's a good thing I've learned so much from Alvina."

"You sound like you enjoy it."

"I do. I love meeting new people, visiting new places, seeing new sights." Rachel's eyes were shining. "We've traveled down rivers so swift and wide that they made our Seine look like a puddle, and we've crossed snow-covered mountains so tall they seemed to touch the sky. You can't imagine what it's like to be on a ship in the middle of the sea: water as far as you can see in every direction, and at night there are so many stars."

Both women sighed. Miriam stood up and gave Rachel a long hug. "I'll pray that you have a safe and successful trip."

"Don't worry, we won't be gone so long this time. I want to be home for Passover." Rachel squeezed Miriam tightly in return. "I bet you do your first *brit milah* in the spring, and I want to be here to see it."

When the Cold Fair ended, Miriam felt that she had mastered *priah*, *motzitzin*, *haluk*, and cutting the shreds. But there were only two women due to deliver before Passover, and Avram would surely want to do at least one *milah* every four months. So Rachel had probably been right about spring. Miriam tucked Shimson into his cradle, then quickly got under the covers and snuggled against her husband's warm body. Even with a brazier burning since *souper*, the room was cold.

"Miriam," he whispered. "I'll be at the *parnas*'s for *disner* tomorrow with Papa, Shemayah, and Meir."

"I thought Joseph was ill."

"*Oui*, but Papa specifically asked me to go with him."

Miriam rolled over to face Judah. *So Papa wants to have a beit din there.* "I've heard rumors that Joseph wants to dispose of his property before he dies, that he intends to cheat Fleur out of her *ketubah*."

"I'm just going to have a meal there and listen to what Joseph has to say, if anything." Judah was still whispering, but his voice was louder.

"I wish we didn't have to get embroiled in this. People are already upset enough with me training as a *mohelet.*"

"Miriam, if Papa wants me to witness something, I'm not going to refuse."

"I know." Her sigh turned into a yawn. "Maybe I'm worrying over nothing."

"I hope so." He gave her a hug.

Miriam lay motionless in Judah's arms, waiting to see what he'd do next. At times Judah's excitement with studying Talmud had spilled over into their marital bed, although, until recently, he usually limited himself to twice a week. But once he started teaching Arayot to Elisha, he'd needed to use the bed nearly every night.

Maybe today's lesson wasn't that exciting, or maybe he was distracted by tomorrow's potential problems, but, whatever the reason, Judah slowly released her and settled down to sleep. Relieved rather than disappointed, Miriam tried to relax and not worry about Joseph and Fleur's predicament.

Too nervous to appreciate the fine meal Isaac haParnas's servants placed before him, Judah realized that Miriam was probably right. Joseph was too ill to come downstairs, and Fleur was conveniently away visiting friends. Besides Salomon, Meir, and Shemayah, the doctor, Moses haCohen, was also dining with them, making a beit din of five judges if necessary.

The conversation at the table wasn't illuminating. Apparently the pope had recently died, and even Papa seemed eager to discuss the significance of this.

"So despite all his efforts to claim authority over King Henry, Gregory dies in exile while Henry's Pope Clement rules Rome." Isaac haParnas nodded with satisfaction.

"Not that there's much left in Rome to rule," the doctor said sadly. "Not after the Saracens sacked the city."

"The Saracens?" Meir was too startled to care about appearing ignorant. "I thought the Norman army set fire to Rome."

"The Normans started the fires," Salomon said. "And then they and
the Saracens looted Rome together."

"Gregory was lucky to escape with his life," Moses added.

Judah listened only out of politeness. Naturally Isaac and Moses
were knowledgeable about politics. The doctor was now the court physician for the Count of Ramerupt, and one expected the *parnas* to have
the latest news. But Papa?

Moses was almost finished with his tale of Gregory's downfall.
"Henry declared Gregory guilty of high treason and appointed the Archbishop of Ravenna in his place."

Isaac haParnas chuckled. "And then there were two popes, Gregory
and Clement, each seeking support from the French bishops and nobles."

"Two popes?" Judah blurted out. "How could they have two popes?
It would be like having two kings."

"*Oui*," Salomon said gently. "And for a while there were two kings in
Allemagne, Henry and Rudolph, Pope Gregory's man."

That's right—there were. Judah felt like a fool for forgetting that
piece of information, and he resolved to keep his mouth closed until the
topic changed to Torah.

Meir lifted his wine cup in his host's direction. "So, Isaac, now that
Gregory's dead, what do you make of his reforms? Will the liege lords
give up their rights to appoint bishops?"

"And even less likely," Moses said with a grin, "will the clergy give up
their wives and mistresses?"

Isaac shrugged. "From what I've heard, both King Philippe and King
Guillaume have officially accepted the pope's authority, yet they continue to choose their own bishops and abbots."

"The pope is wise not to challenge them," Meir said. "Since it is the
sovereign who orders the Church's lands and income released to the new
bishop."

"But the clergy cannot serve two masters," Moses said. "They either
owe allegiance to the pope or to their lord."

"And if they owe allegiance only to the pope . . ." Salomon paused and stroked his beard. "Then it follows that they should renounce their feudal lands, return their offices to the lord who granted them, and live on tithes from the faithful."

Isaac shook his head. "That the clergy will never do."

Judah had enough of politics. They had long ago finished eating. He thought of Elisha and his other students at home speaking words of Torah while he was wasting time here. "Can any of you tell me why any of this matters to the Jews?" he demanded suddenly.

There was silence until Isaac stood up and asked them to visit his son for a little while.

As they walked upstairs, Salomon put his arm around Judah's shoulder. "You may think that what the pope says and does should not matter to us," he whispered. "But if the pope does come to rule princes, then I fear that one day it could matter to the Jews. One day it could matter a great deal."

twenty-two

Judah's heart was chilled by Salomon's warning, and his disquiet increased when he entered the sickroom. His first thought was that they were too late, that Joseph was already dead. The once portly man was skin and bones, except for his distended belly, and his skin was a bizarre shade of yellow. As the men gathered around the bed and Joseph opened his eyes, Judah tried not to stare. For what should have been the whites of the dying man's eyes, and Judah had no doubt that Joseph was a dying man, were yellow as a sunflower.

Isaac haParnas cleared his throat. "I appreciate you making time for my son during these short, busy winter days."

With Moses's help, Joseph struggled to sit up. "Salomon, you warned me to marry a woman my own age, not a young virgin, and I should have followed your advice." He sighed. "Now, when I die, there will not be enough to pay my wife's *ketubah*, let alone leave anything to my son Samson."

"Most of our family's capital belongs to me," Isaac said quickly. "Joseph and I share the income, but by himself my son does not have the one hundred livres that Fleur's *ketubah* obligates his estate to pay her." Isaac fought back tears at the word "estate."

Evidently Isaac had no intention of providing that one hundred livres himself, Judah realized, or none of them would be here now. At least Joseph was well enough to explain his problem clearly; whatever decision he made, Judah could honestly declare that the man was of sound mind at the time.

"I need your help," Joseph said. "I cannot allow everything I own to go to Fleur, leaving my little boy penniless."

"Why should a woman you married only two years ago deprive your helpless orphan of the fruit of your labors?" Shemayah demanded. "A young childless woman like Fleur will surely marry again and secure another *ketubah* payment."

Meir challenged this. "None of that matters. The law is clear. A woman's *ketubah* supports her if her husband dies or divorces her. She always has the first claim on his estate."

Judah had to admit that each side had merit.

Salomon stopped stroking his beard and addressed the room. "Only a man's real property is mortgaged to his wife's *ketubah*. Certainly he may make a gift of his personal property to anyone."

"Even if it would impoverish his widow?" Meir asked.

"Fleur will not be impoverished," Joseph said bitterly. "Even if I give Samson every moveable item I own, she still inherits my house."

It was clear what Joseph wanted. "Surely all would agree that Johanna's jewelry and other belongings should be given to her son," Judah said slowly. "And that Joseph may give little Samson his books."

Shemayah frowned. "He should also give the boy his clothes, shoes, and furs. Fleur's next husband shouldn't have them."

"I think it would be wise to leave some personal property for Fleur, perhaps the household furnishings," Meir suggested. "We don't want people to say your son is robbing her."

Joseph was nearing exhaustion when he finished naming the property that would be valuable to Samson and whose loss was unlikely to outrage Fleur's family. But he motioned for the men to remain.

"One more thing." Joseph looked up at Salomon, tears in his eyes. "It was my wife's wish that our two families should be related. Give my son one of your granddaughters for his bride. I'm sure my father will make it worth your while. Let me die knowing that my little boy's future is assured."

Salomon walked over and clasped Joseph on the shoulder. "I'm sorry, my friend, but I cannot betroth my granddaughters. Only their father can do that."

All eyes turned to Meir, whose gaze darted around the room, looking for an escape. "I can't make that kind of decision now. Our children are too young."

"But when my daughter Zipporah was just an infant, you agreed that Isaac would marry her," Shemayah said.

The color drained from Meir's face. "Our situation is different, Shemayah, entirely different." He looked sadly at the dying man. "Joseph, you must realize that my daughter must marry a *talmid chacham*. Samson seems a capable child, but . . ."

Joseph slumped in his bed. "I understand." Then hope lit his eyes. "But what about a tentative arrangement, that you'll consider Samson as a future son-in-law, if he proves worthy?"

"I take no oaths." Meir paused to choose his words. "But be assured that when the time comes to choose husbands for my daughters, I will give Samson's suit full consideration."

Moses haCohen now stepped forward. "My patient has had enough excitement for today." In an obvious dismissal, he picked up Joseph's wrist and concentrated on the sick man's pulse.

For weeks, every time Meir returned to Ramerupt his stomach knotted in dread as he waited for Joheved's reaction to Shemayah publicly announcing their children's future marriage. Meir knew it was cowardly, but he'd only told Joheved about Joseph's desire for a match between little Samson and Hannah or Leah. And he made it clear that no agreement had been reached.

Only when Joseph died a month later, did Meir breathe a sigh of relief. With Fleur's family complaining loudly about Joseph's deathbed gifts, people in Troyes could speak of little else. If Shemayah's words had not reached Joheved by now, each passing day made it less likely that they would.

So when Meir got off his horse in Ramerupt and Joheved turned aside from his customary kiss, he thought she was upset because he had left Isaac and Shmuel in Troyes.

"Don't be angry at the boys," he explained as they walked toward the barn. "Everyone wants to celebrate with Elisha and his friends before they leave for Worms tomorrow." Meir had to smile as he imagined Judah chaperoning the high-spirited students to their fellow's wedding.

But the smile froze on his face when Joheved said, in a voice as hard as steel, "Francesca came to visit today, and she congratulated me on the excellent matches my children have made—Samson with Hannah and Isaac's engagement to Zipporah."

Meir's heart began to pound. "But there isn't anything definite between Joseph's son and either of our daughters. You know that. I told you exactly what I said to him."

"I'm not talking about our daughters." Joheved's eyes narrowed. "I was led to believe that you and Shemayah were going to keep your agreement to yourselves, and now I hear that half the town knows about it."

He couldn't deny what had been said. "The only people who heard Shemayah were Moses, Judah, your father, Joseph, and Isaac haParnas. Not half the town."

"Just the most influential men in town then."

"Just members of our family and our closest friends, who have every right to know about our decision."

Joheved put her hands on her hips and glared at him. "Not our decision, your decision."

"A decision I'm not going to change."

"Not when you have such a powerful beit din as witnesses."

Meir grabbed Joheved's arms and forced her to face him. "I thought that you'd accepted my authority in this matter."

His anger grew as her eyes blazed defiance. "Ever since I told you, you've been plotting how to prevent it, haven't you?" He pulled her closer, so their faces were just a handbreadth apart. "Well, I won't stand for it. Isaac is going to marry Zipporah, and you're not going to do anything to stop them. I may even decide to betroth Shmuel to Shemayah's new daughter as well."

Joheved wrenched herself from his grasp. "If you love Shemayah so much, why don't you go sleep with him?"

"What did you say?"

"Since you're so fond of Shemayah, you can get on your horse and ride back to your precious study partner right now." She practically spat the words at him.

"All right—I will!" He grabbed his horse's reins and started for the barn door. "And don't expect me to come groveling back to you."

"Just get out of my sight." She picked up a horseshoe and threw it at him, but Meir was already outside and it bounced harmlessly off the door behind him.

That night Joheved was too angry to get much sleep, and the next night, even with both Hannah and Leah in bed with her, she was too lonely and dejected. She managed to fall asleep eventually, only to wake at dawn with an unfamiliar wetness between her legs.

"Oh *non*." Joheved nearly started crying at the sight of the stained sheets.

"What's the matter, Mama?" Hannah stared fearfully at the blood running down her mother's legs. "You're hurt."

"I'm perfectly fine." Joheved grabbed some of Leah's swaddling and shoved it between her legs while she rummaged through the chest. *Where the devil is my sinar?*

"But you're bleeding," Hannah insisted.

"It's nothing. All women bleed from time to time. You will too when you're older." Joheved cleaned up and settled back to nurse her youngest child. How could she have her flowers again so soon? Leah was only eighteen months old.

The next day Miriam arrived with Yom Tov and Shimson, to help with the lambing, and, despite her flowers, Joheved was disappointed when the sun set on Friday with no sign of Meir and her own sons. Miriam said nothing about his absence, yet she must have noticed that something was amiss.

As the week wore on, Joheved's anxiety grew. Meir never stayed away so long unless the weather made riding impossible. Yet if anything had happened to him or one of the boys, somebody would have ridden out to tell her. Was he still so upset over their argument? Was he already announcing at the synagogue that she was a *moredet*, a rebellious woman who refused to cohabit with her husband? *Non*, that wasn't possible—Papa would have come and spoken to her.

Often Joheved could feel Miriam's penetrating gaze, and while she longed for advice, she was ashamed to approach her. It was only after Meir didn't come home for a second Shabbat that Joheved's misery overcame her embarrassment. Still, Miriam had to make the first move.

"It's not like Meir to be away so long without letting us know," Miriam said as they inspected the neatly pruned vineyard.

"Oh, Miriam, we had the most awful fight." Tears began to well in Joheved's eyes. "You must have heard that Shemayah announced Isaac and Zipporah's engagement."

Miriam nodded. *So that's what this is about.* "Francesca told me."

"Now Meir is committed to the match more than ever," Joheved said with a sniff. "It's a terrible mistake, yet there's nothing I can do."

Miriam held Joheved as she sobbed. Joheved wouldn't like it, but there was one thing she could do. "You know it's a woman's duty to obey her husband."

"I know that having Adam rule over her was one of Eve's punishments, and so it is for all women. I have no choice."

"You do have a choice."

Joheved looked at Miriam in surprise. "I do?"

"You can accept how the Holy One created you, count your many blessings, and give in gracefully. Or you can continue to thwart your husband's will and become increasingly unhappy and bitter." Among Miriam's clients were far too many of the latter.

Joheved knew her sister was right. Besides, she couldn't stand another day wondering if Meir was going to ride through the manor gates or not. "Tomorrow is my seventh clean day," she said, her cheeks coloring. "If we leave after Hannah's nap, we can be in Troyes before sunset."

The next morning dawned cloudy and cold, and by midday the smell of snow was in the air. Miriam and Joheved hurriedly bundled their children in furs and set out for Troyes.

"So you heard the news from Francesca," Joheved said as they rode into the forest. "I'm surprised Judah didn't tell you."

Miriam pulled Yom Tov's arms tighter around her waist. It was easier with him sitting behind her and Shimson in her lap, but she wished she could see him. "There was so much to do before Judah left for Worms that he probably forgot."

"He won't be home for Passover?" Joheved asked in surprise. In all his years studying in Allemagne, their father had always spent the festivals in Troyes.

"Judah and Elisha have become quite devoted to one another since Elisha came back at the Cold Fair," Miriam said. "When we heard he was betrothed, I suggested that Judah go to Worms for the wedding. But Judah will be at Uncle Isaac's in Mayence for Passover, and I've asked him to visit Catharina's family while he's there."

Joheved stared at the dark clouds and urged her horse to go faster. "I hope Judah gave you a conditional *get*."

"Of course. After what happened to Eliezer's father and brother, Papa insisted on it."

Jewish husbands were expected to give their wives a conditional bill of divorce when they went on a journey; it prevented her from becoming *agunah*, "chained to him," and unable to remarry should he disappear or die without witnesses. The usual clause, as in the *get* Judah wrote before he left, said she could accept the divorce if he hadn't returned after six months.

Miriam smiled. "Judah is so happy to have a friend here. I think he envies Meir and Shemayah's special relationship."

Joheved grimaced at the trouble that special friendship had caused her. "I didn't realize Judah and Elisha were that close."

"I love to sit with them when they study together," Miriam said. "You can feel the affection between them."

"You sound like you've grown fond of Elisha yourself."

"*Oui*, he is a sweet boy." Miriam thought back to how she'd agonized about Elisha last summer. They didn't need to worry about him killing himself now.

"So besides Judah and Elisha becoming best friends, what else have I missed this winter?" Joheved asked.

"There's the problem of Joseph dying without leaving Fleur enough money to pay her *ketubah*."

"I know, Francesca told me. Finally our town has something to argue about other than you doing circumcisions."

Miriam tightened her grip on Shimson as her horse sped up to match Joheved's pace. "I think Avram may have me do a full *milah* this spring. Several of my patients want me to perform the circumcision if they have boys."

"You sound excited."

"I am. I've been preparing for so long, I'm ready."

Joheved chuckled. "I guess I'll have to come into town for every *brit milah*, no matter how many lamb buyers we have. I'm not going to miss your first one."

Her laughter died and she grew silent as they rode out of the forest, past the newly plowed fields and toward the city walls. *What am I going to say to Meir when I see him?*

Their mother ran into the courtyard when the gate closed behind them. "Joheved, what are you doing here? Is everything all right in Ramerupt?"

"There's nothing wrong in Ramerupt." Joheved exchanged glances with Miriam. "I need to use the *mikvah*."

Rivka hustled her grandchildren into the warm house. "I'd better put some clean sheets on your bed."

"Joheved, is that you?" Aunt Sarah stood at the foot of the stairs, peering up at them. "It sounds like you."

"*Oui*, Aunt Sarah. I just arrived."

"Aren't you here early?"

Joheved tried not to frown. *Will I need to explain my presence to everyone?* "All the lambs are born and we've finished pruning the vineyard, so I thought I'd spend a few days in town before Passover."

"Where is everyone?" Miriam asked.

"Your father has them out in the vineyard, trying to finish the pruning before it starts snowing," Rivka said.

"Not everyone," Sarah interrupted. "Shmuel is napping."

"I know you'll excuse me to go see my son." Joheved gave her mother a hurried kiss and made for the stairs.

But Shmuel had already heard her voice. "Mama!" He ran and jumped into her arms. "Papa said we wouldn't see you until Passover."

Joheved smiled at Miriam. At least Meir had been planning to return to Ramerupt for the festival. But what would he say when he saw her? She managed to fight her panic until she heard men's voices outside. Then her heart started to pound as Shmuel flew out the door, yelling, "Papa, Papa! Mama's here."

Before she could compose herself, Meir was silhouetted in the doorframe. "There's nothing wrong at home, is there?" he asked, taking several steps in her direction. "My mother . . ."

"Marona is well and our daughters are fine too. In fact the girls are here with me."

As Meir approached her, Joheved had no choice but to back away. She was still *niddah*.

Meir couldn't hide his pain and rejection. "So what brings you to Troyes?" he asked, his voice heavy with suspicion.

Joheved swallowed hard to ease the tightness in her throat. "I need to use the *mikvah* tonight and it's too cold to go in the river." Not that the *mikvah* was much warmer, but in Troyes she could take a hot bath afterward.

Meir's face lit up immediately. "You got here just in time. It's almost sunset, and it's starting to snow."

"I'd better head for the stews," Joheved said, giving him a shy smile.

"I'll go with you," Meir said. "I could use a bath too."

They walked to the bathhouse in silence, partly because the softly falling snow was beautiful to watch and partly because Joheved still wasn't sure how to explain her change of heart.

She remained tongue-tied even after their baths. They had nearly reached the synagogue when Meir started clearing his throat. "Joheved . . . uh." He hesitated and motioned her into a doorway where the snowfall wasn't so heavy.

He coughed a couple times while she looked up at him expectantly.

"Before you immerse, I want you to know that you're not going to seduce me into changing my mind about Isaac and Zipporah."

"I know," she said softly. "I have no intention of trying to change your mind, or anything else about you."

"You accept my decision?" His eyes widened in surprise. "You accept my authority?"

While she'd been bathing, Joheved carefully composed how she'd reply to Meir when he asked her this question. "*Oui*, I do." Then she quickly added, "But more important, I accept the Holy One's authority, as I'm sure you do as well."

She tried to keep her voice steady. "If Isaac and Zipporah are truly *bashert*, then there's nothing I can or should do to prevent their marriage. And if they aren't *bashert*, then there's nothing I need to do to prevent it either."

"An answer worthy of a *talmid chacham*."

Was he praising her or being sarcastic? Well, if she were going to be a dutiful wife, she'd better sound like one. "Meir, I am truly sorry about what I said to you in the barn. Can you forgive me?" The snow was gently swirling around them and she took at step toward him. "I missed you."

"I missed you too."

She closed the distance between them so that they were nearly touching. "I'd much rather have you sleep in my bed than in Shemayah's."

He leaned down to whisper in her ear, and she could feel his warm breath on her neck. "Soon, *chérie*, very soon."

A roar of laughter from the inn's dining room yanked Judah back to consciousness. How many times had he nearly fallen asleep tonight, only to be thwarted by the raucous prewedding party downstairs? Not that he begrudged his students their fun. Tomorrow they'd ride into Worms, where he'd admonished them that their yeshiva's reputation depended on their behavior.

Judah pulled the covers tighter over his ears.

When Miriam first declared it shameful if Elisha didn't have any friends standing up for him at his wedding, Judah had fought to control his enthusiasm. The thought of spending several weeks, day and night, in Elisha's company, just when he had resigned himself to their separation, set his pulse racing. It still warmed his heart to recall the look on Elisha's face when he heard the suggestion that Judah accompany him. Filled with pleasurable memories, Judah drifted back to sleep.

The next time it wasn't the festivities below that woke him. Somebody was moving stealthily in his room.

Judah sat up and fumbled for his knife. "Who's there?"

"I'm sorry, Judah." Elisha's words were slightly slurred. "I was trying not to wake you."

Judah relaxed back into his pillow. "It's all right."

Elisha sat down on the bed next to him, and immediately there were two thumps as a pair of boots hit the floor. More movement and then Elisha tumbled into bed beside him.

"Could you move over a little?" Elisha shivered. "My side of the bed is freezing."

Judah happily obliged. "Next time you can go to bed first and warm it up for me."

The room was silent for so long that Judah thought his companion had fallen asleep. He was savoring their closeness when Elisha spoke again.

"Judah." Elisha sounded worried. "The next time we share a bed will be on our way back. I'll be married then."

"*Oui.*" The room remained quiet, but Judah was certain that Elisha was still awake.

"Judah," Elisha whispered. "I'm afraid."

"Don't worry about demons. I'm sure your father won't let you sleep alone tomorrow night, not the night before—"

"I'm not afraid of sleeping alone," Elisha interrupted him. "I'm afraid of . . . of sleeping with a woman. Well, not of sleeping with her. I mean . . . I'm afraid I won't be able to . . . you know."

Judah sighed. *So that's the problem.* "But you know what to do. We've studied all the Arayot."

"That doesn't mean I can do it." Elisha's voice was trembling. "I don't know what's wrong with me, but the thought of lying with a woman doesn't excite me, it terrifies me."

"There's nothing wrong with you, Elisha. I think it's perfectly normal to feel nervous about using the bed for the first time." As much as Judah wanted to give Elisha a reassuring hug, he forced his arm to remain still.

"You do?"

"Of course. Now listen, you don't have to do it the first night if that's the way you feel. After all, your wife will probably be just as frightened as you, maybe more."

"But she'll think there's something wrong with me."

"Not if you explain that you're waiting for her to feel comfortable with you." Judah took a deep breath. "You're the only one I've told this, but Miriam and I didn't use the bed the first night."

"You didn't?" Elisha sounded more impressed than shocked.

"*Non.* Miriam was a widow, still mourning her first husband, and I didn't want her thinking of him instead of me. She was grateful for the delay." Judah chuckled. "She was almost as grateful as I was. So you're not as unusual as you think."

"I thought everyone used the bed on their wedding night," Elisha said slowly. He was obviously trying to adjust to this new information.

Judah yawned and remained quiet. With any luck he'd soon be so fast asleep that even the other students coming up to bed wouldn't wake him.

"Judah . . ." Elisha still sounded worried. "We won't have much time together once we get to Worms, so I want to tell you how much I . . ." There was a very long pause before the words came out in a rush, "How much I admire you. You're a good teacher and a good friend."

It took every bit of self-control Judah had to keep from taking Elisha in his arms and hugging him. "*Merci*, Elisha. I think you're a good student and a good friend."

"*Bonne nuit*, Judah." Elisha made no effort to move back to his side of the bed and indeed snuggled closer to Judah.

Judah could almost taste the wine on Elisha's breath, and the desire he'd been fighting exploded in him. Heart pounding, he lay still, his *yetzer tov* terrified that Elisha would reach to embrace him and his *yetzer hara* eager for it. He didn't dare face Elisha. If their naked bodies brushed against each other frontally, Elisha would recognize his aroused state. And especially since Elisha acknowledged having a carnal relationship with a man. *Then Satan only knows what would happen.*

"*Bonne nuit*, Elisha. Try to get a good night's sleep tonight," he whispered. Sleeping on his stomach in this condition was impossible, so, trying not to touch Elisha, Judah rolled over so his back was toward him.

And waited. All of Judah's senses were attuned to the warm body lying next to him. What would he do if he felt Elisha's hand on his flesh? Would his *yetzer tov* be strong enough to resist? Or would his *yetzer hara* take over?

twenty-three

hree nights later, with another three wedding banquets still to attend in as many days, Judah despaired of ever catching up on his sleep while in Worms. He took a slow drink of ale and searched the crowded salon for Elisha. Two students were gambling at a corner table, one was flirting with the bride's cousin, and the rest were dancing. *But where is the groom?*

In the last seventy-two whirlwind hours, Judah had exchanged less than a dozen words with his friend. A few stolen moments while dancing earlier were enough for Judah to learn that Elisha and his bride were still virgins, but then someone had cut in, leaving Judah to return to his cup of ale.

Judah sighed. Was Elisha ignoring him, or was the boy's family trying to keep them apart? Maybe he should leave for Mayence tomorrow. Uncle Isaac expected him for the seder, but it wouldn't hurt to get there early. Then he would have time to visit with Shmuli's family and deliver Miriam's greetings to Catharina and Samson.

Judah had just drained his cup and stood up when an unfamiliar masculine voice called out, "Judah." Most likely the man was addressing someone else, but Judah turned around.

"Judah ben Natan, it is you." The owner of the voice was coming closer. "What good fortune brings you to Worms after all these years?"

Judah barely had time to recognize this apparition from the past, when he was the recipient of an enthusiastic embrace.

"Reuben, *Baruch ata Adonai*... Who resurrects the dead." Judah took a step back, and the two men surveyed each other. "You're looking well, Reuben."

"You're looking even better than when we first met." Reuben's eyes glinted with desire as his gaze traveled over Judah's body. When Judah didn't respond in kind, his expression quickly reverted to that of a long-lost friend. "So tell me, what have you been doing all these years?" Reuben pulled Judah back down to the table and signaled for more drinks.

An hour and several cups of ale later, Judah concluded his story. "The Holy One has truly blessed me."

Reuben grinned. "I can't wait to tell Natan."

"Is he here?" Judah looked around in alarm.

"Of course not. He spends Passover in Prague." The music changed to a lively tune and Reuben jumped up. "Come dance with me. This is your student's wedding. You should be celebrating."

Judah couldn't see a polite way to refuse. The steps were simple, but he was relieved when the song ended.

Reuben sat down next to him, put his arm around his shoulder, and whispered, "So you never learned to play the game?"

"No. I've never lain with anyone except my wife."

Reuben sighed. "I envy you. My *yetzer hara* has mastered me. I don't even try to fight it anymore."

"Torah study keeps me too busy to indulge my *yetzer hara*," Judah replied. There was no one sitting nearby, but he lowered his voice and added, "Though some here might say that the way I study Talmud is worse than playing the game."

"How can that be?"

"Don't tell anyone, but Rabbenu Salomon, my father-in-law, is writing a commentary on the Talmud." Judah sat up a little straighter. "And I'm helping him."

Reuben's eyes opened wide. "You mean explaining the Gemara so a man won't need a teacher?"

"Of course he'll need a teacher." Judah's anger flared. "Papa's commentary is for after he's studied the Talmud, so he'll remember his learning."

"I don't understand."

"If you promise not to tell anyone, I can show you. I have notes on Tractate Kiddushin in my room, to help Elisha prepare his wedding *drash*."

"This I have to see. Let's go."

"Now? In the middle of the banquet?"

"The feasting will continue for hours." Reuben tugged on Judah's sleeve. "Nobody will miss us."

That was probably true. Judah made his way outside, Reuben following discreetly. His hosts, Elisha's cousins, were unlikely to return home anytime soon, so Judah spread out Salomon's *kuntres* on their dining table. They began with the Mishnah.

> All the mitzvot of the son on the father, men are obligated and women are exempt. The mitzvot of the father on the son, men and women are obligated.

"I never could get it straight whether 'all the mitzvot of the son on the father' meant what a son does for his father or the other way around," Reuben said, scratching his head.

"The Gemara has the same problem," Judah replied. "See:

> If this says all mitzvot a son performs for his father, how can women be exempt? We know that when the Torah says 'you shall revere your mother and father,' this means both of you because the verb for 'you shall' is plural."

Judah continued, "Papa says that both sons and daughters must revere their parents, and thus 'mitzvot of the father on the son' are those a child performs for a parent, regardless of gender."

"This is amazing." Reuben ran his finger over the words, trying to memorize what he'd read.

"Here is another Baraita to support this interpretation." Judah pointed out the text. "These mitzvot are clearly performed by the father for the son":

All mitzvot of the son on the father, these he must do for a son; men
are obligated and women are exempt . . . to circumcise him, redeem
him if firstborn, teach him Torah, take a wife for him, and teach him
a trade. Some say to teach him to swim.

"I assume that when it says women are exempt, this means that the
mother is not obligated to do these mitzvot for her son, especially since
it mentions circumcision," Reuben said slowly. "Yet it could also mean
that a parent does not perform any of them for daughters."

"Actually both meanings are correct, as we will see. A mother is not
obligated to perform these mitzvot for her son, and neither parent performs them for a daughter," Judah said. "You should have heard Elisha
explain this section before the wedding. His father looked so swollen
with pride, I thought he was going to burst." Judah had been nearly as
proud himself.

"You chose a good text for a wedding." Reuben scanned several more
pages. "I can't believe it. Your father-in-law seems to know just what
questions I'm about to ask, and he answers them without so much as an
extra word."

"When Papa started writing his *kuntres* he was too poor to afford
parchment, so he had to write succinctly," Judah explained. "Now he
does it out of habit."

"You must let me copy these. I won't show them to anyone."

"All right." Judah couldn't refuse Reuben; he owed the man his life.
"But only the texts that we study together. I must know that you understand them properly."

"What are we waiting for? We can study until sunset." Reuben
chuckled and turned to Judah, "No wonder you don't play the game.
Between writing these Talmud commentaries and your wife being a
mohelet, your life in Troyes is scandalous enough."

The two men returned to the texts, and only when it was too dark to
read without a lamp did they rejoin the wedding party. Judah had no
sooner filled his plate than Elisha took it from his hand and laid it on the
table.

"Your *souper* can wait. Come dance with me."

Astonished, Judah followed him. Luckily the dance was the same one that Reuben had just taught him, so he didn't need to think about the steps. "You've been married three days now, Elisha. How are things going?"

"Things are fine," Elisha replied with a scowl. "But where have you been all afternoon?"

"I met an old study partner from my yeshiva days, and the two of us decided to study some Talmud."

"In the middle of a wedding banquet, you go off to study Talmud?" One of Elisha's older relatives tried to cut in, but Elisha shrugged him off.

"Reuben—that's his name by the way—wanted to see Papa's *kuntres*, so we went to my lodgings and studied there."

Elisha's scowl deepened. "I know his name is Reuben. The man's notorious for *mishkav zachur*, for lying with other men," he hissed. "I can't believe you just spent several hours alone with him in your room."

Now it was Judah's turn to get angry. "I can't believe that you, of all people, would repeat that kind of gossip."

At least Elisha had the decency to blush. "You and Reuben were study partners?"

Before Judah could answer, Elisha's mother interrupted them. "Elisha, come and eat. Your food's getting cold."

"In a moment, Mama. Let me finish this dance." When she'd moved out of hearing range, Elisha repeated his question.

"We weren't study partners like you and I are," Judah replied. "I was at the yeshiva in Mayence, and when Reuben had business there, we'd study together."

Elisha appeared somewhat mollified. "Please don't study with him alone, not with his reputation."

"We have to study alone. I can't risk strangers finding out about Papa's *kuntres*."

This time Elisha's father came between them. In a tone that brooked no argument, he said, "Elisha, your bride is lonely waiting for you."

Then he took Elisha firmly by the arm and led him away, leaving Judah standing alone among the dancers.

Back at the table where he'd left his plate, Reuben was waiting. "So, your jealous friend couldn't wait to dance with you," Reuben said with a knowing smile.

"Jealous? You're imagining things."

"Calm down and have something to eat. The fish is excellent." When Judah's mouth was full, Reuben continued, "I saw the look on Elisha's face when we returned together. Don't tell me he didn't ask about us?"

Elisha jealous? Judah sampled several dishes while he considered Reuben's statement. "He did ask where I'd been with you for so long."

"See, I was right."

"He also said that you were notorious for *mishkav zachur.*" Judah waited for Reuben's reaction.

Surprisingly, Reuben broke into laughter. "And he was right, too. It takes one to know one."

Judah looked Reuben in the eye. "Elisha hasn't done *mishkav zachur,* and whoever says otherwise is a liar."

"All right, maybe your student doesn't play the game . . . yet, but his old study partner told me that their relationship was more intimate than just friends." Reuben winked.

Judah did not want to hear how well Reuben knew Elisha's old study partner. "Elisha warned me not to be alone with you."

Reuben sighed. "He's probably right about that. I don't want to soil your reputation."

"I'm more worried about Rabbenu Salomon's reputation."

The two men ate in silence until Reuben suddenly slapped the table. "I have it. There's a synagogue nearby that's popular with the yeshiva students. Since they're home for Passover, the place should be practically empty. We can study there."

"What if somebody sees us?"

"They'll think we're studying Talmud, which we are. Nobody is going to examine your texts to see if they're kosher."

There was a fanfare from the musicians as bride and groom rose to leave the party. Judah tried to meet his friend's eye, but Elisha seemed determined to ignore him.

When Elisha disappeared from sight, Judah sat down and addressed Reuben. "Very well. Show me where this place is and I'll meet you there tomorrow."

The rooster in Salomon's courtyard crowed again, but Miriam didn't move, savoring the few moments she had left until the nausea began. The cathedral bells began to toll, and Miriam reached for the matzah on the chest near her bed. The unleavened bread was one of the few foods she could tolerate these days. She sat up slowly and took a small bite. As much as she felt like vomiting, nothing happened. She cautiously finished a whole piece, and when that stayed down, she got up and dressed.

Breakfast was a lukewarm dish of stirabout, sans raisins, and lemon balm tisane with Aunt Sarah, who ate hurriedly before leaving on a case with Elizabeth, her favorite of the Edomite midwives. Aunt Sarah often worried aloud about how Miriam would manage by herself in the future. Until this pregnancy laid her low, Miriam thought she would manage just fine, but now she was relieved that Aunt Sarah was consulting with their Notzrim counterparts.

Miriam sadly surveyed the empty dining room as she drank her second cup of lemon balm. Naturally Yom Tov and Shimson preferred to break their fast at their grandparents', where the fare was too savory for Miriam's disposition. Only Shimson still sat with her at synagogue, his brother having abandoned her for the older boys in the men's section.

Services had barely begun when Miriam felt the familiar ache in her stomach. *Please Mon Dieu, just let me last through the Tefillah; don't let me shame myself and throw up here.* But when the time came she could barely stand, and only managed to finish the prayer by supporting herself on the balcony's edge. She was attempting to swallow away the sour taste in her throat when Rivka whispered to her.

"Miriam, you're as white as snow." Rivka took her elbow. "Come, let's get you home."

"Go on now." Francesca's voice was soft with compassion. "We can follow the rest of the service ourselves."

Other sympathetic voices agreed, and with Rivka holding Shimson, Miriam negotiated the stairs. She leaned against the wall outside as a wave of dizziness rushed over her, but when her stomach retained its contents, she took her mother's arm and began the slow walk home.

They had gone a couple of blocks when Shimson began squirming to get down. He pointed to the street and yelled, "Look, there's Papa."

Rivka grasped him tightly and frowned. "It can't be your Papa. It's too early in the morning for travelers to arrive."

Miriam squinted at the road, but it was too crowded with horses, carts, and shoppers to identify anyone. Shimson was still trying to escape his grandmother's arms so she explained to him, "Anyone who was that close to Troyes last night would have ridden the short distance into town then and spent the night in his own bed."

"But it is Papa. I saw him." Shimson gave a jerk and before Rivka could grab him, he ran across the street.

Rivka bolted after him while Miriam tried to keep up, but she was too light-headed and her stomach hurt. She came to an intersection and stopped to look around, but there was no sign of her son or mother. Please, she prayed, protect my son; don't let him be trampled by a horse or run over by a cart. Before she could decide which way to go, an upstairs window opened and a waste bucket emptied into the dirt in front of her. The stench was overpowering, and the next moment her own vomit was mingling with the slop at her feet.

Miriam staggered away, desperate for a place to sit down. Just before her legs buckled, a strong arm appeared around her waist, supporting her and leading her toward the nearby square.

Shimson, straddling his father's shoulders, called down at her, "I told you Papa was here."

Miriam sank gratefully onto a bench near the well. "Judah, I wasn't expecting you so soon."

"You shouldn't . . . be out . . . on the street," he said, trying to catch his breath. "You're not well."

"Your wife, may Heaven protect her, is perfectly healthy," Rivka said as she strode up, breathing heavily. She lowered her voice. "Her indigestion will likely only last another few months." As Judah's expression transformed from confused to joyous, she pumped water into a cup and held it out to Miriam. "Here, rinse your mouth."

With the vile taste gone, Miriam was almost feeling normal by the time they reached the courtyard gate. Rivka remembered some shopping she needed to do and left the couple alone.

"You're sure you don't need to rest?" Judah asked. "I can take Shimson back to synagogue with me."

"*Non*, I'm much better now," she said. Judah seemed reluctant to leave, so she asked him, "Did you have a good trip? How was the wedding? Where's Elisha?"

"The trip and the wedding were fine." Inexplicably, Judah blushed. "Elisha and the others are probably still sleeping at the inn we stayed at last night. They wanted one last night to celebrate, but I . . ."

"Missed your family and wanted to hurry home." Miriam smiled and completed his sentence.

Judah's blush deepened. He could have ridden home the previous evening, and his *yetzer tov* had pressed him to do so, but his *yetzer hara* had tantalized him with thoughts of a final night with Elisha. And though they again shared a bed, their relationship remained platonic. Like the night outside Worms, Judah spent several sleepless hours both worrying and hoping that Elisha would approach him. When he woke early the next morning, he felt so ashamed for imagining that Elisha would do such a thing that he left immediately.

"Do you mind if I tell you about my trip later, when Papa's there too?" he asked.

"Of course not. We should wait until your students get here." She smiled again. It felt so good when the nausea was gone. "Did you get to see Catharina in Mayence?" she whispered.

"*Oui*, she's doing well," Judah replied. "Her parchment work is getting such a reputation that even Uncle Isaac's yeshiva sends manuscripts to her for repairs." He smiled. "She's expecting another child."

Miriam gave silent thanks that Catharina's abortion hadn't affected her fertility. "Speaking of children, it's been three days since the *brit* of Yvette's son. I think I'll check on them."

"You're going out again so soon?" Judah looked shocked.

"Don't worry, I'm feeling fine now," she said. "Why don't you take Shimson with you to synagogue? I'm sure you're eager to see Yom Tov and Papa."

"Very well, but let me walk with you to Yvette's first." Judah could never understand why pregnant women felt better after throwing up, but Miriam always did. "Wait a moment, did you do your first *brit milah* and I missed it?"

Her face fell. "I was too ill to even attend that morning."

"But it may be months until you don't feel nauseous in the morning."

"I know. It's so frustrating," she said. "Now they'll have another reason why women shouldn't do circumcisions, just when I thought everyone had stopped talking about it."

Shimson squirmed to get down, and Judah gently lowered their son to walk between them. "People have accepted you?"

"Everyone is so busy choosing sides between Joseph and Fleur that they've stopping discussing me," Miriam said.

Judah shook his head in dismay. "Papa must have anticipated this. He had me bring a letter to your uncle about the case."

"What did Uncle Isaac say?"

"He agreed with Papa completely, of course. Only a man's real property is mortgaged to his wife's *ketubah*; he may give gifts of personal property to anyone he chooses, whenever he wants, deathbed or not." Judah paused and then added, "I could tell that Uncle Isaac wasn't pleased giving his answer, but he had no choice. The law is the law."

"Fleur's family isn't going to be pleased with his answer either," she said as they approached Yvette's house.

"Maybe this letter will give people one more thing to talk about." Judah lifted Shimson up for Miriam to kiss, and the two of them headed for the synagogue.

Miriam watched until Shimson had stopped waving. Once inside Yvette's house, which like her own was one of three surrounding a spacious courtyard, Miriam changed the new baby's *haluk* and made sure both mother and son were recovering well.

"Your son continues to wet his swaddling without difficulty?" Miriam asked. A baby was watched to make sure he urinated within three to four hours after his circumcision, as well as regularly after that.

Yvette laughed. "He certainly does." She offered some bread and cheese to Miriam, who reluctantly declined. "I was worried when you missed the *brit*. I was hoping that you'd be the one to do it."

"*Merci*, it's nice to know that somebody besides my family has confidence in me."

Yvette sighed. "Most of the women do, but it's not easy to convince our husbands."

"I doubt I'll be doing many circumcisions anyway in the next few months," Miriam said with a smile. It wouldn't be long before everyone recognized why she was constantly sick to her stomach. She might as well acknowledge it. "Not until I stop feeling so ill in the morning."

"That's too bad." Yvette was quiet for a moment. "Oh, I mean congratulations."

Appreciating Judah's safe return as she walked home, Miriam couldn't help but compare her marriage with her sisters'. Joheved had fought bitterly with Meir, but their reconciliation afterward had obviously been a sweet one. And look at Rachel's refusal to stay behind while Eliezer traveled.

Miriam had missed Judah after he'd left, but what exactly had she missed about him? Their conversations? Talmud study? Using the bed? Or just the snuggling and kissing? And did she actually miss him, or was she merely feeling lonely? Would she still have missed him if Joheved and Rachel had been there? And where was Rachel; didn't she say she'd be back for Passover?

The more Miriam pondered these questions about her marriage, the less certain she was of her answers. Unbidden came the thought that she would certainly have missed Benjamin if he had been gone so long. *Why did he have to die in that stupid accident?* She fought back angry tears and began to walk faster. Ten years now since he died; why did she still keep thinking about him?

Even as she asked it, she had the answer to her question. In only a few weeks the grapevines would begin to blossom, bringing bittersweet memories along with their sweet scent. It was still difficult to work in the vineyard without remembering him. But autumn was the worst, when it was impossible to tread the grapes without visualizing Benjamin's unconscious face, slowly sinking into the bubbling must until the last of his brown curls disappeared.

Stop it! Judah was an excellent husband; they had two fine sons and another child on the way. So why couldn't she feel the same for him as she had for Benjamin?

A week later Rachel slammed the courtyard gate behind her and called out, "Mama, Miriam. I'm home." When this was greeted with silence, her voice rose with annoyance. "Where is everyone?"

Miriam lifted herself up from the bed, where she had been resting while the men were at afternoon services. She took a bite of matzah and waited for her stomach to settle. Then she leaned out the window and greeted her sister.

"Welcome home. I'll be right down."

Rachel took a step back and surveyed her older sibling once the two women finished hugging. "Good Heavens. You always were the thin one, but now you're nothing but skin and bones."

Miriam pulled her *bliaut* tight across her belly so her sister could see the unmistakable bulge. "These days I'm lucky if I can find any food that doesn't make me want to retch."

"I see. When are you due?"

"After Sukkot, I think."

"It's a shame that you have to get so sick, but you'll probably be feeling better soon."

Before Miriam could inform her that Joheved was pregnant as well, a cart arrived with Rachel and Eliezer's baggage.

"Look at these." Rachel held up some small knives whose handles gleamed with precious gems. "Aren't they exquisite? You'll never guess how little we paid. You see, we buy the blades here in Troyes—everyone agrees that our local steel is strongest—and then we have the hilts made in Kairouan. As soon as Countess Adelaide starts cutting her meat with one of these beauties, every noble in Champagne will want one."

After the jeweled daggers, Rachel displayed some elaborate necklaces, followed by a goodly number of brooches and earrings. By the time everything was stored away, Miriam had heard about watching silk weavers in Palermo, surviving the storm that nearly sank their ship off the Barbary Coast, and visiting the most magnificent synagogues in Toledo, along with several other adventures her sister had experienced during the last six months.

"Honestly," Rachel said, "if it weren't that I missed our Talmud study, I'd be traveling all the time. Seeing new places, discovering new merchandise, meeting new people and making deals with them—I love it." Her face shone with excitement. "And you should see their expressions when they find out that I know Talmud."

Miriam thought that, with the exception of seeing new places, you could do these things just as well in Troyes.

"I almost forgot," Rachel said. "I brought back some spices for you. Why should you buy them here when I can get them so much cheaper?"

"What did you get me?" Miriam couldn't hide her skepticism. When had Rachel learned about midwife's herbs?

"Pepper, of course." Rachel pulled a wax tablet from a small chest and consulted it. "Let me see: nutmeg to mix with feverfew in ale to prevent childbed fever, spikenard for fluxes of the womb . . . whatever those are, cumin to seal the cord and for the *haluk*." She smiled smugly at Miriam's awed expression.

"*Merci beaucoup.*" Miriam threw her arms around her sister and hugged her anew. "How did you know what to buy?"

"I had a local midwife make me a list, and I also asked the spice merchants for recommendations," she replied. "Ah, here's one you might want to use, ginger. As a tisane, it's said to be excellent for upset stomachs."

"Ginger?" Miriam gulped. "But ginger is too hot and dry for a pregnant woman."

"But everyone told me that a ginger tisane cures even the most persistent nausea of pregnancy."

"Well, I might try a cup and see if it helps. Do you know how much to use?"

Rachel shrugged her shoulders. "I thought you knew all these things. By the way, what tractate is Papa going to teach this summer?"

"Kiddushin. Judah's been working on it for months."

The cathedral's bells sounded the first note of Vespers. The cathedral, the bishop's church, had the right to speak first, before the count's chapel or the abbey of Notre-Dame-aux-Nonnains—the precedence conceded to Bishop Hugues after an acrimonious debate. The men would be finishing their evening prayers and arriving home soon.

The front door opened and Rivka burst in. "Rachel! Anna told me you were here." She looked up and began addressing the ceiling. "How did I raise such an inconsiderate child? Gone for over six months, and she sits here chatting for who knows how long without letting her poor mother know she's home."

Rachel gave her mother a hug. "I'm sorry, Mama. I did call out for you when I arrived, and when you didn't answer I assumed you were at services with Papa. I haven't been here that long; I'd only just arrived when the bells started chiming."

"At least you could have sent word in advance so I could have prepared a better meal." Before Rivka could continue chastising her youngest daughter, they could hear men's voices at the gate and Rachel bolted for the door.

Miriam slowly followed her and surveyed the scene outside. Mama looked like she'd drunk a cup of vinegar as Papa embraced Rachel and swung her around as if she were still a child. Judah and Eliezer were walking arm in arm, as Elisha followed with the other students, a sour expression on his face as well.

Miriam sighed. Elisha would likely feel better after some time with his wife when he returned to Worms for Shavuot, but Mama would always resent Papa's affection for Rachel.

twenty-four

Troyes
Early Summer 4847 (1087 CE)

iriam and Judah were preparing for bed when they heard the insistent knocking at the door that opened to the street.

Miriam slipped her *bliaut* on again and hurried downstairs. "Who's there?" she called out, wondering which of her patients needed her.

"It's Elisha."

Judah poked his head over the landing and the next moment the two men were embracing like brothers.

"I had to see you." Elisha, grinning widely, kept his arm around Judah's shoulder. "I couldn't wait to tell you the news."

Miriam came closer. "What is it?"

"My wife is with child, may the Holy One protect them both." He stepped back so he could see their faces light up.

Miriam was the first to react. "That's wonderful."

Judah's jaw dropped. Elisha had obviously impregnated his wife during the wedding week, yet he'd been so reticent on the subject during their trip back to Troyes that Judah wasn't sure the couple had performed the holy deed.

Miriam and Elisha were waiting for his reaction, so Judah cleared his throat and patted Elisha's back. "See, you were worried over nothing."

Elisha stepped back, a sober expression replacing the happy one. "But now that I'll have a family, my father says that I've got to start supporting them." Elisha's chin began to quiver. "This will be my last year at the yeshiva."

326

"Oh dear," Miriam said. Judah remained speechless, more stunned than when Elisha announced his wife's pregnancy.

"During the Hot Fair I'll have to spend the afternoons, and maybe some of the evenings, meeting other merchants and finding a business partner," Elisha said.

Elisha leaving the yeshiva—no, this isn't happening. Judah finally found his voice. "You mean this coming year will be your last?"

"*Non*, this past year was my last." Elisha shrank under Judah's stricken gaze. "It's not my decision."

Miriam stepped between them. "Judah, no student stays in the yeshiva forever." She put her hand on his arm. "Unless he marries the rosh yeshiva's daughter."

"It's not like we'll never see each other again," Elisha said. "I'll be back twice a year at fair time."

"Thank Heaven," Judah said.

Tears filled Elisha's eyes. "I owe you two so much . . ." He paused and then said solemnly, "If my child is a boy, I'd like to name him Judah. And if it's a girl, Miriam."

Miriam began to cry too. "That's too much honor. You should name your first child after someone in your family."

"My sisters have children named for family. I want to name this child after someone who treated me kindly, to seal our friendship."

"Friendship is a mutual relationship," Judah said. "If Miriam is carrying a boy, we should call him Elisha."

Miriam stared at her husband in surprise. Three sons and none of them named after Judah's father or her own. Still, if that's what he wanted . . . she slowly nodded.

Judah gazed at her with thanks, and then Elisha, realizing that she had consented, threw his arms around Judah with even more enthusiasm than when he'd first arrived. "You would name a son after me?" His voice was filled with awe.

"You have been like a younger brother to us." Then Miriam's voice dropped. "But enough on this subject. We don't want to tempt the Evil Eye."

The next two weeks were like old times. Judah and Elisha woke early to study with the Eastern merchants, shared meals, and studied together with Eliezer late into the night. While Elisha and his father attended to business after *disner*, Judah worked with his younger students on that day's lesson.

Joheved's family arrived for the summer, so the three sisters were finally able to study together again. Like their husbands, they were discussing Tractate Kiddushin, except that their hands were busy spinning wool.

"This Mishnah in the fourth chapter doesn't seem right," Joheved said with a frown.

> "An unmarried man does not teach young children and a woman does not teach young children.

Yet Miriam teaches our sons almost every day, and Meir taught Aunt Sarah's grandchildren in Mayence when he boarded there."

Rachel pointed to the text with her spindle. "Papa says in his *kuntres* that the Gemara will explain it."

"The Mishnah's short," Miriam said. "Let's finish it and then get to the Gemara.

> Rav Yehuda says: Two unmarried men may not sleep under one blanket. The Sages permit this."

She paused to find their father's comments. "Papa says the two men may be drawn to *mishkav zachur*."

"That's possible," Rachel said with a shrug. "Especially if they're young and naked under that blanket."

"But everyone sleeps naked, and you don't see all the yeshiva students lying with each other," Joheved protested.

"Of course you don't see them." Rachel's voice was heavy with sarcasm.

"Enough," Miriam said. "I want to know what the Gemara says about women teaching." She continued to read.

> "What is the reason? If you say because of the boys, it is taught in a Baraita: We do not suspect Israel of *mishkav zachur*. Rather, an unmarried man, it is because of their mothers, and a woman, because of their fathers."

Joheved nodded. "So that's why the Sages permit unmarried men to sleep together—they don't suspect them of *mishkav zachur*."

"Papa says an unmarried man might become attracted to the mothers who bring their sons to him every day." Rachel frowned. "The author of this Mishnah clearly thinks that bachelors have no control whatsoever, that they'll sin with their students and with the mothers of their students."

Joheved shook her head. "You'd think so too if you knew some of Count André's knights and squires."

"Not that married men are any better," Rachel said.

Miriam could only imagine the unwanted attention her beautiful sister had attracted on her travels. "If a woman can't teach young children because of their fathers, then shouldn't I be permitted to teach the children in my family?"

"You may also teach Samson," Joheved said, adding more wool to her distaff. "He's an orphan."

"Of course you're allowed to teach them. Otherwise Papa would have stopped you," Rachel said. "I wonder why the Sages don't suspect Israel of *mishkav zachur*. Papa skips that line."

"Jewish men don't lie with each other because it's a serious sin," Joheved said.

Rachel rolled her eyes. "Just like they don't commit adultery either."

"It doesn't say that Jews don't lie with other men," Miriam reminded them. "Only that we don't suspect them of it. And our Mishnah certainly suspects them of adultery."

"Maybe we're not supposed to suspect Jews of *mishkav zachur* because we don't want them even thinking about it," Joheved said.

Rachel nodded. "A man who keeps wondering who's doing *mishkav zachur* might be inclined to seek out one of them to do it himself."

"We don't suspect Jews, especially scholars, of *mishkav zachur* because we always want to believe the best of them," Miriam said, thinking of Elisha. "We presume that they are law-abiding."

The cloth fair had been open for a week when Eliezer came in late for *disner*, accompanied by a swarthy young man whose bushy moustache couldn't quite conceal a pronounced overbite.

"Meet Giuseppe." Eliezer redid the place settings to make a spot at the table next to Elisha. "He's from Lucca, where his family owns some merchant ships. He's here to find business opportunities for them." Eliezer elbowed Elisha at the words "business opportunities."

"Welcome to Troyes, Giuseppe," Elisha said. "Or would you prefer to be called Joseph?"

"Giuseppe is the name I'm used to . . ." He hesitated as Miriam set out a wine cup for him. "There's no need to honor me with my own cup. I'm not a *talmid chacham* like the other merchants who dine here."

"You should join my husband and his students for Talmud study while you're in Troyes," Miriam said. Lucca was known for its Talmud academy; this young man was probably being modest.

"Oh no." Giuseppe's blush deepened. "I've only studied a little Mishnah."

Elisha smiled at the stranger. "So listen to us study."

Judah bristled at the eagerness in Elisha's voice, until he realized that the sooner Elisha found a business partner, the sooner he could stop wasting time looking for one.

"*Oui*, listen and ask questions," Judah said. "Papa says that beginning students have the best questions."

Salomon confirmed Judah's words. "As it says in Pirke Avot,

Who is wise? One who learns from everyone.

Which means especially those who are lesser than him, both in years and in knowledge."

Despite this encouragement, Giuseppe remained silent as the others discussed that morning's lesson. Yet his face communicated his feelings—enjoyment as Judah helped the students sort out the various arguments, awe as Elisha and Eliezer debated a particularly convoluted passage, and astonishment whenever one of Salomon's daughters asked a question or added her interpretation.

As the meal continued, Miriam noticed Giuseppe looking confused, so she poked her sister in the ribs and asked him, "What goods did you bring to sell?" *Maybe he has jewelry.*

Rachel understood that she should also engage their guest on the subject. "If I remember properly, Lucca imports silk from Palermo. Am I correct, Giuseppe?"

The young man looked startled at being addressed, but he quickly recovered. "My wife's family is in the silk business there," Giuseppe said. "But on this first trip I only brought pepper and cinnamon, which I've already sold."

"So what are you going to do for the rest of the fair?" Rachel asked.

"I'd planned to spend my time at the fairgrounds, observing the procedures and trying to meet Ashkenazi merchants. Then, once I found a business partner, we'd decide together which goods to take back to Lucca." Giuseppe looked around the room uncertainly. "But I didn't realize everyone here spent so much time studying Torah. I must appear ignorant in comparison."

Miriam wanted to say something to console him, but he was right. Most merchants preferred dealing with a *chacham*. A Talmud scholar, thoroughly versed in commercial and tort law, was assumed to be both intelligent and trustworthy.

"All the more reason why you should join us," Eliezer said.

When Joheved returned to Ramerupt for the wheat harvest, Miriam and Rachel continued to study Talmud together in the morning and evening. In the afternoon, when Miriam's nausea diminished, they did business with a constant stream of women who wanted to buy jewelry, sell jewelry, pawn jewelry, or any combination of these. Alvina had sent word that, instead of attending the Hot Fair, she would come for the Cold Fair and see her new grandchild.

One morning Miriam talked Rachel into weeding her herb garden while they worked on memorizing the latest piece of Gemara and their young sons played in the mud by the well. Expecting no interruptions, Miriam was surprise to see a man in a white robe hesitantly enter the courtyard. He had very short blond hair and was beardless, which was a shame because he had such a weak chin.

As soon as he saw them, his hesitancy disappeared. "*Bonjour*, I am Guy de Dampierre. I would like to buy some of your best wine for my Uncle Hugues, bishop of Troyes."

Miriam knew that Papa would never want his wine used in the cathedral's idolatrous rites. "I'm sorry, but it's all we can do to satisfy our Jewish customers until the fall harvest." The bishop of Troyes was a powerful lord; she needed a plausible excuse for refusing him.

"Why are you wearing a white robe?" Rachel asked. "Are you a monk?" The brown-robed Benedictines were a familiar sight. The monks from Montier-la-Celle delivered grapes every fall, and occasionally one stopped by with a letter from Papa's old friend, Robert, abbot of Molesme.

"I'm a canon at the cathedral's school." Guy ignored their dismissal. "Canons are church scholars, but unlike monks we do not practice poverty and chastity. A more important difference, however, is that we believe scholarship is equally important as contemplation and prayer."

He continued with a small smile, "If your best wine is not available, perhaps I could taste another cask and see if it meets my uncle's standards?"

Miriam and Rachel exchanged worried looks, each wondering how they could rid themselves of this cleric without insulting him. Neither made any move toward the cellar.

Rachel broke the silence. Giving the canon her sweetest smile, she acted disappointed. "Please don't be offended, but we cannot sell the bishop any wine. Our father would be very upset if his wine were used for church ceremonies."

Miriam waited for Guy's angry response, but he started laughing. "Use your excellent wine in the church! I'd sooner water the garden with it." He chuckled and added, "I'm sure you don't remember me, but I attended the banquet for your nephew in Ramerupt a few years ago. I still recall the fine vintage I tasted there."

Guy then made an incredible offer. "As payment for wine for his personal table, Uncle Hugues will supply your household with bread from his mills."

Miriam took a sharp intake of breath. All wheat grown in Champagne had to be ground in Count Thibault's mills, with a tithe going to the ruler. Many churches and abbeys were endowed with produce from these mills, and of course the Cathedral of Peter and Paul, the count's personal church, received this benefice.

"We have a large household," Rachel said slowly. "My father's academy has twenty students who board with us."

Miriam stood up and brushed the soil off her hands. "Why don't you let the canon taste some of our wine while I get Shimson washed up?" she said. "Then we can bring his offer to Papa and let him decide."

Rachel could never understand why her sister bathed Shimson personally; that's what maidservants were for. So she called for Jeanne when Miriam headed for the well.

Miriam knew Rachel thought she was silly, but she picked up Shimson and gently lowered him into the washtub that she'd filled earlier, guaranteeing that the cold well water would be tepid when she needed it. He squealed and giggled as she splashed and washed him, and only reluctantly gave up his place in the tub to his younger cousin when Jeanne brought out the towels.

Upon exiting the cellar, Rachel rolled her eyes at Miriam's damp hair and *bliaut*. But Guy grinned as she expertly dried her squirming son. "I still remember your father's lesson on Noah's ark," he said. "I wasn't expecting such erudition at a banquet. I look forward to meeting him."

Guy not only talked Salomon into selling wine to the bishop, but he wangled an invitation for *disner*. There he made a creditable showing in their discussion of that day's Torah portion. And when Salomon discovered that the canon, after studying in Paris, had been appointed to improve the quality of Troyes' cathedral school, the conversation turned to methods of teaching and motivating students.

After that, Guy made an effort to dine with them once a week, and occasionally he accompanied Salomon into the vineyard to continue their discussions. How do we reconcile revelation with reason in such a way that faith is strengthened? Shouldn't guilt reflect the intention of the sin rather than its outcome, thus making contrition and confession more important than restitution? How should the deeper or mystical meanings of scripture be understood without ignoring the plain sense of the text?

Sometimes Salomon busied himself in the vineyard while Guy demonstrated how grammar, rhetoric, and logic were taught in the cathedral schools, but usually it was Guy who listened as Salomon explained the intricacies of interpreting scripture. In any case, it was clear to Miriam that her father was pleased to find a replacement for Robert, who had no time to visit now that he headed his own abbey.

While Guy limited his visits to Salomon's to Monday or Thursday, the days Torah was read in synagogue, Giuseppe ate all his meals at Judah's table, where the subject was Talmud. He smiled and nodded while following the students' debates, but he never interrupted them. He conducted business in the afternoon, and as often as not returned for *souper* accompanied by Elisha.

One evening in early August, the two young men burst into the dining room, both grinning widely.

"Judah, I'm so happy," Elisha said. "Giuseppe and I have been discussing a partnership agreement, and today I introduced him to my father."

Judah returned his smile. "It doesn't take a *talmid chacham* to determine that your father approved."

"We'll work out the details during the fair and then travel to Lucca to present the offer to my family," Giuseppe said.

"But Elisha, what about your baby?" Miriam asked. "Don't you want to be there when your wife gives birth?"

"We won't stay in Lucca long." Elisha threw his arm around his new partner's shoulders. "Giuseppe and I will be back in Worms in plenty of time. And once my child is safely born, we'll come back for the Cold Fair."

Judah fought the envy building in him as Elisha and Giuseppe enthusiastically shared their plans for the future—sailing the Mediterranean together, from one fascinating city to the next. His envy grew when, instead of returning home with Judah after the evening Talmud session, Elisha stayed out later with Giuseppe—so late that he still wasn't back when Judah left before dawn to study with the Eastern scholars. It didn't help that one of Miriam's pregnant clients had needed her in the middle of the night, leaving him alone in bed.

So Judah couldn't resist goading Elisha after morning services. "I was worried when I didn't see you at breakfast."

"I'm sorry, but Giuseppe and I wanted to celebrate," Elisha said with a sheepish grin. "I ended up drinking so much that I fell asleep at the tavern."

Giuseppe laughingly added, "He may look small, but he was such a dead weight last night that it took two men to carry him to bed."

The students at Judah's table joined in the laughter, and Elisha blushed crimson. Judah didn't even try to hide his irritation when he admonished the class not to waste time from their Talmud studies on gossip.

Chagrined, the discussion returned to Tractate Kiddushin. The section was difficult, with a debate so complicated that there were over thirty steps in the argument. Each step had to be thrashed out until Judah was certain that all the students understood it. Then they continued with the next one.

Giuseppe seemed to be following along, and Judah was peevishly considering asking the young man to explain one of the steps, when Giuseppe hesitatingly said, "Excuse me . . ."

Every head turned toward him.

"*Oui?*" Judah asked. "Do you have a question?"

"There's something I don't understand," Giuseppe said softly. "Probably I missed the explanation when you gave it earlier."

"Nobody remembers everything they hear the first time they hear it," Judah said. He gazed sternly at the other students, silently warning them not to laugh or otherwise ridicule Giuseppe's question.

"I know I haven't studied much Talmud, but I don't understand why the Gemara says women are exempt from Torah study because of what is written in Deuteronomy," he began.

"You shall teach them diligently to your *benaichem* (sons)."

Giuseppe cleared his throat. "After all, in our Mishnah, when the rabbis discuss the obligations of the *ben* (son) and the *av* (father) to each other, it's clear that *ben* refers to both sons and daughters and that *av* includes both father and mother."

Giuseppe's voice, which had started out quite softly, was louder now as he concluded, "From what I've heard this summer, *benaichem* usually means 'children,' both boys and girls. So why in the case of Torah study, does *benaichem* mean only 'sons' and thus exclude daughters?"

Judah stared at Giuseppe. He needed to think. He'd been taught that this was the text's meaning, but it never occurred to him to ask why.

The room was silent until Eliezer slapped the table and burst out laughing. "What a question!" He punched Giuseppe's arm. "I only know the answer because my wife told me."

He turned to address the stunned class. "Belle Assez, I mean Rachel, said that when she and Miriam were studying this section, she asked her father the same question." He paused to heighten the suspense. "Of course they got into a row over it, until Salomon admitted that the interpretation of *benaichem* as sons, not daughters, is actually *miSinai*."

"MiSinai is what the Holy One told Moses on Mount Sinai when He gave him the Oral Law," Judah explained. *MiSinai* was the explanation for an otherwise inexplicable law, the answer that ended all debate.

"Salomon promised Rachel that he would add that to his *kuntres*, in case anyone else wondered about it," Eliezer said.

Giuseppe, who wasn't sure whether he'd asked a brilliant question or a stupid one, started to look proud of himself. "So there is no logical reason, no supporting proof text," he said. "The Holy One told Moses that in this verse *benaichem* meant sons only, not sons and daughters."

Elisha squeezed Giuseppe's shoulder. "Rav Salomon was right when he told us that wise men learn from everyone, especially those with less knowledge."

Jeanne was clearing the dishes when Miriam rushed in, her face lit up with joy. "Blanche had a boy," she announced, throwing her arms around Judah. "I'm so excited."

Six days later, when Obadiah arrived at synagogue alone and mentioned that Avram wasn't feeling well, Miriam's heart began beating so hard she was sure everyone could hear it. This was the signal she'd been waiting for; tomorrow she would circumcise Blanche's new son. The women in the gallery began whispering to each other and several of them smiled encouragingly at her.

Miriam was trying so hard not to be distracted from the prayer service that she didn't notice when the commotion began downstairs. Only when Rachel nudged her arm did she stop and look below.

Fleur's father was standing up and waving his arm. "I demand that everyone hear my complaint," he shouted.

"Oh *non*," Rachel groaned as the other women hurried to the gallery's edge to watch the proceedings.

Interrupting services was a time-honored tradition in the Jewish community. Anyone with an unresolved grievance had the privilege of interrupting services until he received a public promise of redress. It was not a privilege to be taken lightly, so most people went to the beit din with their quarrels before they risked antagonizing the community this way.

"We have tolerated a woman training to do *brit milah* only because no men would do it, but that is no longer the case." He gestured for a young man nearby to stand. "My cousin Ishaiah here is a mohel. If Avram is unable to perform the *brit* tomorrow, Ishaiah is the most expert mohel present, which means he must do it."

Miriam reached out for Rachel's hand. Who, if anyone, would defend her? To her surprise, it was Obadiah.

"How do we know this man is an expert mohel?" he asked. "Let me see his hands."

Ishaiah held up his hands, which did have the requisite pointed thumbnails, but they were as pale as Miriam's, not thick and yellow with experience like Avram's. "I admit I haven't done a *brit* in many months," Ishaiah said. "I've been traveling to Troyes and occupied at the fair."

Then Fleur's cousin Leontin addressed the crowd. "Many of you have told me how shameful it is for Troyes to have a woman mohel instead of a man as the Holy One intended. Now we have a man who is willing to move to Troyes for this purpose."

There was so much conversation in the room that no one voice stood out except Blanche's husband. "I will not have some stranger with dubious credentials circumcise my son," he yelled. "Ishaiah will not be my agent tomorrow."

Several people shouted back that only men should do circumcisions. Then Judah stood and began to speak. Immediately the room quieted.

"In our learned community it is not enough that the mohel be technically competent." He turned to confront Ishaiah. "The final chapter of Tractate Shabbat deals with *milah*, indeed that is the chapter's title. Can you tell us what Rabban Gamliel teaches us there?"

Ishaiah didn't reply, so Judah added, "I'll give you a hint. It's a Baraita that comes just after the first Mishnah."

When Ishaiah remained silent, Judah looked up at the women's gallery. "I expect that my wife is familiar with this text."

Rachel gasped and clutched her sister's hand, but Miriam felt strangely calm. Of course she knew the Baraita; she always studied this Gemara the week before a *brit*. Besides, the people below were her community; surely they knew she studied Talmud.

She focused her attention on Judah and recited the text.

"Rabban Shimon ben Gamliel says: all commandments Israel took on themselves with gladness, like *milah*—as it is written in

Psalms, 'I rejoice over Your word as one who obtains great spoils,' they still perform with gladness. And all commandments Israel took on themselves with strife, like forbidden marriages—as it is written, 'Moses heard the people weeping, every family,' they still observe with strife. For there is no marriage contract where they do not argue."

She concluded with the explanation Papa gave in his *kuntres*. " 'Your word,' in the singular, means the commandment that is binding on Israel above all other, the one given to Abraham first, which is *milah*."

Before anyone could comment, Eliezer began to laugh. "Very clever, Judah. This Baraita makes it clear that the attempt to foist this unknown mohel on us is not motivated by love of mitzvot, but for revenge by Fleur's family now that Joseph's deathbed gift has been validated in Mayence."

The room buzzed with voices until Moses haCohen waved for the right to speak. "Never mind that. What is this fellow's occupation that he can perform a *brit* at short notice?"

The room quieted as Ishaiah replied, "Don't worry, I'm not a doctor. I'm a moneylender." But it became even noisier when he sat down.

Miriam could hear men arguing that they would never give coveted residence in Troyes to someone in competition with them all, that a man who loaned on interest but sold no merchandise would give them a bad name among the Edomites. Then Cresslin said that Fleur was lucky to get as much money as she did, marrying an older man for his wealth, causing Leontin to overturn several benches to lunge for him. Miriam watched openmouthed, sure they would come to blows, but others with cooler heads restrained them.

Now people were shushing others, saying that services had been interrupted long enough. That's when Isaac haParnas stood up. "The decision of admitting new residents to Troyes belongs to our community council," he said calmly. "I suggest that Ishaiah apply for residency as any other candidate would do."

The hazzan began praying again where he'd left off, and to Miriam's relief, the congregation joined him.

hat night Elisha stayed out late again, returning only as Judah was leaving for his early morning study session. When he complained to Miriam at breakfast that Elisha's mind didn't seem as focused as before, she patted his hand and reminded him that this was a difficult time for the youth.

"Elisha is beginning a new life; soon he'll be a merchant and a father instead of a student," she said, helping herself to another slice of cheese. "It's probably more difficult for him to leave us than for us to lose him. After all, we'll have many more students, but you'll be his last teacher."

Judah sighed. Miriam was undoubtedly correct, but her words didn't comfort him.

"I want to thank you for yesterday." She smiled. "What made you think to ask Ishaiah about Tractate Shabbat?"

"He hasn't attended a single one of Papa's lectures, so I guessed that he wouldn't know Talmud very well."

"That was very astute." Miriam scooped up a large dollop of strawberry preserves with her piece of bread.

"I'm glad to see you're eating better."

"Everyone kept telling me I ought to drink more ginger tisane, that it would soothe my stomach so I could eat more."

"But you said that ginger was too hot and dry, that it might hurt the baby."

"I had Moses suggest some foods that were cold and damp, to balance the ginger." Miriam took another bite of bread and jam. "That's why I'm trying to eat more fish and less meat." She smiled up at her hus-band and added, "And why I'm eating so much strawberry jam."

"Whatever you're doing, it seems to be working." Judah had almost said something about how much better Miriam looked these days, but caught himself in time. Heaven forbid that she imagine an insult over how bad she looked before.

"It doesn't seem to be hurting the baby." She placed a hand on her belly. "He, or she, is as active as ever—may the Holy One protect him or her."

"I was sure that you'd have done a *brit milah* by now, but perhaps it's *bashert* that your first one be our own son."

"It was good of Avram to let me know that he feels better this morn-ing," she said. "I suppose I won't be doing my first *milah* until Ishaiah has left Troyes."

Judah grinned. "You don't think he'll be settling here anytime soon either."

She smiled back at him. "I think our merchants would rather have an idolater do circumcisions here than share their clients with Ishaiah."

"If you've finally finished eating, we'd better get the boys ready for services," he said. "You may not do the actual *milah*, but Avram will probably have you do everything else."

Judah could tell by the fullness of his bladder that the night was nearly over, and this was confirmed when he peeked out the window and saw the nearly full moon low in the sky. He slipped on his chemise and went downstairs to use the privy. The Hot Fair was in its final week, and on such a balmy night there was no need to foul the air in the bedroom by using the chamber pot. A quick glance while passing the upstairs bedroom was enough to ascertain that Elisha still hadn't come home.

Judah stepped onto the porch and drew a deep breath. The world seemed so peaceful in those few hours before dawn. As he walked to the privy, he again wondered where Elisha was, what was keeping him up so late these days. Of course the privy was empty, and relatively odorless as well, two advantages of being the first to use it this morning. The disad-vantage was that nobody had collected any fresh moss yet, so Judah had to make do with straw.

He had nearly finished when he heard the courtyard gate close. *Is that Elisha at last?* Through the privy's small window he saw two men heading toward his house, but they continued past it and stopped just beyond the wall. Here they were invisible to the courtyard's residents, but from the privy, Judah had a clear view of them.

It was Giuseppe and Elisha. Judah reached for the straw, but when he glanced through the window again, the moonlit sight rooted him to the spot. The two men were kissing—and not just a friendly peck good night. Their arms wound around each other and they were kissing like . . . well, like Eliezer and Rachel.

Judah took a sharp intake of breath; he felt as if he were suffocating. His *yetzer hara* wanted to rage out of the privy and confront them, but instead he exited silently and sank back against the closed door. He peeked around the side for another look. Maybe he'd been imagining things; maybe the Sheyd shel haBetkisey demon had sent him this tortuous vision.

Elisha and Giuseppe were still there. Judah's *yetzer tov* told him to avert his eyes, to slam the privy door loudly and then walk back to the house and greet Elisha as usual, but his *yetzer hara* wouldn't let him tear his eyes away. So he took it all in—Giuseppe's mouth hungry on Elisha's lips, Elisha's hands gripping Giuseppe's derriere, their torsos straining against each other.

It was astonishing actually, that two men would kiss the same way a man and a woman did. Somehow Judah assumed that when two men lay together it would be a hurried, sordid thing with no preliminaries, just a quick coupling before each man went on his way. But men as lovers? Unthinkable—except for the evidence before his eyes.

After what seemed like an eternity, a rooster crowed and the two men sprang apart. A few kisses followed, but it was obviously in preparation for parting. It was only when Giuseppe closed the courtyard gate behind him and Elisha headed for the privy that Judah realized his own predicament. Heaven forbid Elisha should encounter him outside. Judah quietly circled the privy, remaining on the opposite side from Elisha, and then sprinted home.

Once inside, his heart was pounding, and as clearly as he heard his *yetzer tov* telling him to say nothing and avoid a confrontation, Judah knew he would ignore this advice. He convinced himself that he would be doing Elisha a service, warning him that he and Giuseppe should be more circumspect in the future. Judah waited until he heard Elisha on the porch and then stepped outside.

The youth stopped in his tracks and then a smile of recognition lit his face. "*Bonjour*, Judah. I know it's late, but Giuseppe and I still have things to arrange before the fair ends."

Judah was filled with disgust at the obvious lie. "Don't say any more, Elisha. I just saw you and Giuseppe together, between my house and Eliezer's."

Elisha looked stricken. He opened his mouth, closed it again, and finally choked out, "But—" before Judah interrupted.

"The spot you chose would have served you well had I been indoors or at the gate, but I was in the privy."

Elisha closed his eyes and let out a groan. "Please, Judah. I beg you, don't tell anyone." He tried to grab Judah's arm, but Judah shrugged him off. "Don't expel me. The fair's almost over but I'll leave the yeshiva today. I'll do anything you ask, only don't tell my father."

Elisha was sinking to his knees when Judah stopped him. "I have no intention of telling anyone what I saw, and certainly not your father."

"You're not?" Hope filled his eyes.

"*Non*. First of all, accusations of this nature need two witnesses. Secondly, you're not my student anymore." Upon hearing this, Elisha's chin began to quiver and Judah sighed. "I mean you're a merchant now, not a young yeshiva student. You're responsible for your own behavior. But you're still my friend, and so I must tell you to be careful. Someone else may see you who isn't so discreet as I am."

"*Merci*, Judah, *merci*." Elisha grabbed Judah's hands and began to kiss them. "I don't deserve a friend as true as you."

Judah pulled his hands away. "And is Giuseppe a true friend as well?" *What demon made me ask that?*

Elisha's expression became wistful. "How can I explain about Giuseppe?"

Judah led Elisha into the courtyard. "We shouldn't discuss Giuseppe here. Come take a walk with me."

The sky was beginning to lighten when they reached the towpath that Judah and Miriam had walked years before. A good place for confessions, Judah thought, as Elisha explained how he and Giuseppe had become more than friends.

"I know it's an *averah*, but I can't help it. My *yetzer hara* desires men more than women." Elisha drew a deep breath. "Forgive me, Judah, but I can't keep any more secrets from you. The first few times I laid with my wife, I could only get aroused by imagining that I was in bed with you."

Judah knew he ought to feel insulted, but he didn't. "You certainly intend to test the limits of my friendship this morning." He shook his head. "To think that Miriam and I were convinced that you didn't do *mishkav zachur*, even after you told me about your old study partner."

"Giuseppe and I don't do *mishkav zachur*." Elisha hesitated at Judah's skeptical expression. "We do . . . other things."

Judah's *yetzer hara* wanted to ask, "what other things," but instead he said, "Whether you do these other things or you do *mishkav zachur*, it is still a sin. You know what it says in Tractate Sukkot:

> Such is the *yetzer hara*: one day it bids a man 'do this,' and the next
> day 'do that,' and finally it tells him 'go worship idols' and he goes
> and worships them."

"I'm not going to go and worship idols," Elisha said. "Besides, no man is without sin, and I assure you that Giuseppe and I will be honest merchants, that no one will have to ask us twice to give charity, and that we will scrupulously observe the Sabbath." Elisha added with a grin, "And I can guarantee you that I will never commit adultery. I can barely find the desire for my own wife, never mind another man's."

"The sins that you don't commit do not justify the sins you do," Judah replied. "You may think your sin isn't that serious but remember what Rav Assi says:

> At first your *yetzer hara* is as thin as a spider's web, but in the end it
> is as thick as a rope."

"I know," said Elisha sadly and quoted a word play from Tractate Berachot.

> "Rav Simeon ben Passi said: Woe to me because of Him who formed me (*yotzeri*) and woe to me from my evil impulse (*yitzri*)."

Poor Elisha, Judah thought. The Holy One would punish him for giving in to temptation, yet his *yetzer hara* would make him suffer when he tried to defy its demands. "Yom Kippur is less than a month away. How will you repent?"

"I will pray that the Holy One forgives me, that He will understand that my *yetzer hara* is too powerful to fight.

> Who is strong? He who subdues his *yetzer hara*."

Elisha quoted Pirke Avot and sighed. "I am not strong enough to give up Giuseppe."

"You're still young," Judah said, remembering Reuben. "Think about what Rav Avin says:

> If a man indulges his *yetzer hara* in his youth, it will be his master in his old age.

You don't have to give up your friendship with Giuseppe, just stop the carnal acts."

"I cannot." At least Elisha had the decency to look ashamed. "I love him more than any friend, even more than a brother."

"I see how little my friendship means to you."

"Don't be bitter, Judah. At least I was able to fight my *yetzer hara* where you were concerned. You have no idea how difficult it was for me during our travels for my wedding, sleeping in the same bed as you every night. You can't imagine how much I wanted you."

"Enough!" Judah held up his hands to stop Elisha's words. The sun had risen and the bells pealing Prime began echoing around them. "I need to go back to my studies, and I imagine that you need to get some sleep."

The two of them walked silently through the increasingly busy streets. The wheat harvest was not yet finished and day laborers headed toward the city gates, their threshing tools over their shoulders. Farmers on their way to market passed them in the other direction, carts laden with fruits, vegetables, and crates of squawking chickens. Servants carrying buckets gathered at the city wells, and a line was forming at the bakery.

"There's one more thing I must say," Elisha added as they approached Salomon's gate.

Judah waited.

"When Yom Kippur comes I'll be in Lucca, so I have to ask you now. However I may have injured or offended you, will you forgive me?"

"Of course I'll forgive you." Judah fought back tears. How could he not? At Yom Kippur it was a mitzvah to forgive all who asked for forgiveness. "You're my friend. And how many friends would any of us have if we insisted that they be free from sin?"

"I still intend to call my first son Judah, but I release you from your pledge to name Miriam's child after me."

Judah didn't know what to say. It might be bad luck to name a child after such a sinner, but how could he choose a different name without explaining the change to Miriam? Well, he didn't have to decide now— and maybe the baby would be a girl.

The next few days were torture for Judah. As much as he tried to avoid them, his attention continually strayed to the pair. Did they have to be so obvious in their affection, always standing too close together and sharing private conversations? What was Giuseppe saying that just made Elisha smile? Naturally the Lombard found Elisha attractive, but whatever did Elisha see in such an uneducated man?

The lump in Judah's throat and the tightness in his belly worsened until it was nearly impossible to eat at the same table with them. He couldn't wait for the day when he would no longer be confronted by their presence. But once Elisha was gone and Judah tried to focus his attention on the impending Days of Awe, he was overcome with sadness.

The ache in Judah's heart was one he hadn't felt since Daniel left.

And there was another feeling, one that mortified him. He knew it was Satan's voice he heard, but he couldn't shut it out, especially at night. That's when Satan would remind him of all those nights when Elisha had wanted him on their journey between Troyes and Worms, and against his will, Judah would become aroused.

When he turned to Miriam for relief, consoling himself that the holy deed was good for both mother and child in the last three months of pregnancy, Satan would send the image of Elisha and Giuseppe kissing in the courtyard. But if he tried to restrain his urges, his frustrated *yetzer hara* made him more miserable.

He empathized with poor Rav Simeon ben Passi's suffering, and he prayed again and again Psalm 130, long associated with the Days of Awe.

> Out of the depths I call to You . . . listen to my cry.
> Let your ears be attentive to my plea for mercy.
> If You kept account of sins, who could stand tall?
> Yours is the power to forgive . . . I await Your word.

When Rosh Hashanah arrived, one after another, the *vidui* prayers for repentance assailed him.

> What shall we say before You who dwells on high? You know the secrets of all living; You search the innermost chambers of our hearts and examine our deepest thoughts . . . subdue our *yetzer hara*, submit us to Your service that we may return to You.

In previous years Judah had prayed the Al Chet, the great confession, with confidence, knowing that he personally had committed few, if any, of the long list of communal sins. He'd recited them all, smugly aware that congregants around him were being stung by the lash of recognizing their own sins on their lips. But this year the lash's pain was his.

> For the sin we have committed against You openly or in secret.
> For the sin we have committed against You by impure thoughts of the heart.

For the sin we have committed against You by the *yetzer hara.*

For all these, God of forgiveness, forgive us, pardon us, grant us atonement.

All week Satan taunted him at night, and when Judah prayed the *vidui* on Erev Yom Kippur, he knew exactly how the Accuser would prosecute him before the Heavenly Court. But how could anyone defend him before the One who knew his hidden thoughts? Would he wake up to discover that he'd had an emission of semen during the night, a sure sign that he'd been written down for death in the New Year?

Judah nearly wept with relief when he woke up in a clean bed, and when they reached the afternoon service, with its Torah portion from Leviticus about sexual sins, Judah knew what he would have to do to repent. If he only studied individually with Miriam or Eliezer, if he never made another yeshiva student his study partner, then he wouldn't have the opportunity to become overly fond of one of them.

But that meant he would never share that special study-partner relationship again. So while the rest of the Jewish community celebrated Sukkot, the season of gladness, Judah mourned his loss.

The Jews of Troyes were not only celebrating Sukkot, but had joined the rest of the city in excitement about the tournament that Count Thibault was hosting in honor of his son Eudes' knighthood. Although some gossiped that he was really celebrating the death of Guillaume the Bastard, which elevated his eldest son, Étienne, who was married to the king's daughter Adèle, one step closer to the English throne.

"Mama, can I go to the tournament tomorrow?" The cellar echoed with boys' voices. "Can he go with us, Aunt Miriam?"

Miriam finished opening the clerestory windows, letting in cold air to slow down the fermentation process. Turning to confront her questioners, she was not surprised to see Shmuel and Samson in addition to her own two sons, but Isaac was there too.

"Please let me go, Mama," Yom Tov asked. "Shmuel and Samson are going."

"Papa arranged a safe place for us to watch," Isaac said.

Miriam shook her head. "I doubt there's any safe place to watch a tournament that's still close enough to see the melee."

"We will be safe." Joheved cautiously made her way down the cellar stairs. "Count André has arranged for ladies and children to watch from a raised platform in back of the *lices*."

Miriam looked at her sister with astonishment. "You're going to the tournament in your condition?"

"I am perfectly well. In fact, Meir and I are both attending. The tournament field is located between Troyes and Ramerupt, and André expects his vassals to honor Thibault and young Eudes. Besides, Alain will be fighting and we want to cheer for him."

"Alain?" Miriam asked. *Wasn't he one of the squires who had rescued Benjamin in the forest?*

"*Oui*. Alain squired for us for several years, and now he's one of the knights we provide for Count André. Shouting encouragement for a few hours is the least we can do for him."

"How do you know you'll be safe behind the *lices*?" Miriam asked. She wasn't going to show her lack of sophistication by asking what the *lices* were, but Samson had no such reticence.

"What are the *lices*?" he said.

"*Lices* are neutral ground, where the captured knights, horses, and booty are kept," Joheved explained. "We'll certainly be safe. In addition to Thibault's men, Count Robert of Flanders and his knights will observe and guard the *lices*."

She walked to the nearest window and began to close it. "It's so chilly in the cellar, Miriam. Are you trying to make *vin diable*?"

"Joheved." Miriam grabbed her sister's arm. "I just now finished opening the windows because it was too warm."

Joheved stopped, and Miriam wondered if she was going to call for Papa or Rachel to verify her claim that the cellar was too cold.

But Joheved continued talking about the tournament. "I assure you that Papa and Meir will not let the boys leave the platform area until the melee is over."

"Papa is going?" Miriam began to reconsider. Perhaps watching the tournament wasn't as dangerous as she'd been led to believe. Still, many in town worried about the havoc that all these armed men on horseback could create if allowed to roam at will. Fields trampled, women assaulted, brawls in every tavern, horses racing through the streets. "Is Mama going?"

"*Non*, Mama is staying home to care for my girls. She's also watching little Shemiah so Eliezer and Rachel can come."

"Please let me go with everyone, Mama," Yom Tov said. "It's Sukkot, when we're commanded to be happy."

Miriam found it difficult to resist her sons' pleas until she remembered the sad fate of Emeline's brother. "You think watching knights fight each other, injure each other, maybe even kill each other, would make you happy?"

"Nobody's going to be killed . . . or at least hardly anyone." Joheved sounded like she was talking to children, which for the most part, she was. "The point of a tournament is to capture the opposing side's knights and hold them for ransom, which a dead man obviously can't pay."

Miriam forced herself to think logically and not keep her son home just because she was annoyed with Joheved. "I suppose Yom Tov may go if Judah agrees. But Shimson is too young."

Since Papa was going, Judah had no objections. That was all he'd said; not one question. Judah always became more serious and taciturn as Yom Kippur approached, but this year he was more gloomy than ever. After the Hot Fair closed, he'd spent every waking hour either at prayer or working on Papa's *kuntres*. Even the festival of Sukkot hadn't lifted his spirits.

A day with cheerful company tempted Miriam. And if her sister could attend this tournament while seven months pregnant, so could she. Didn't she owe Alain a debt of gratitude? Never mind that his service had only given Benjamin a few more months of life.

twenty-six

hen the next day dawned as sunny and brisk as only an autumn day can be, Miriam decided that Yom Tov was right. It was Sukkot, the season of happiness. How often did she spend a day at leisure with her father and both her sisters? But she couldn't help swallowing anxiously when Thibault's men-at-arms barred the city gates behind them.

"He'll open them at sunset, when the tournament's over," Meir explained. "Combatants are supposed to stay on the tournament field, but if any defeated knights try to escape, the victors will pursue them, as in a real war."

"It's just as well that our vineyard is on the far side of Troyes," Salomon added.

"If all the knights are from Champagne, how does anyone know who his opponents are?" Isaac asked.

"Thibault has them divided by geography," Meir said. "One side from castles north of Troyes, like Ramerupt, Vitry, and Meaux, and the other from the south, like Ervy and Bar-sur-Aube. Each side wears its own colors."

They could hear the tournament's hubbub long before they reached an opening in the forest that provided a view of the cleared fields below. Trees fringed one long side of the arena, and at each end a raised platform stood shaded by canopies. There were two fenced-off holding areas, which Miriam assumed were the *lices*, on each side of the arena.

The perimeter was surrounded by men. There were the participants of course, knights on horseback, squires, men-at-arms on foot, but many were spectators, peasant and town dweller alike. Miriam identified a few women, most of whom were selling ale or foodstuffs.

Yom Tov was jumping up and down to see better. "Look at all the men, Mama. Have you ever seen so many in one place?"

"This is considered a small tournament, only thirty or forty knights on each side, nearly all from Champagne," said a familiar voice. "I've heard that grand tournaments can involve hundreds of knights, some from as far away as Provence and Angleterre."

"Moses haCohen." Meir embraced the doctor. "I hoped we'd find you here."

Moses smiled when he saw Miriam. "I am pleased to see you looking so well. Are you following the diet I prescribed?"

"My nausea is nearly gone, so I only drink one cup of ginger tisane in the morning," she said. "But I can't resist apples from our tree."

Moses wagged his finger at her. "You shouldn't eat raw fruit; it's too cold and moist, especially for a woman. Promise me you'll only eat baked apples until the baby comes. We don't want your child to be born with too much phlegm."

Miriam wanted to ask the doctor about Judah's melancholy, but Joheved called out, "Miriam, look who's here."

Standing next to Joheved was a tall blond woman, her mouth in a thin smile. Her pale blue, close-set eyes peered anxiously at Miriam, who recognized her at once.

"Emeline. It's good to see you again. How are you?" Emeline had aged well. Though she'd put on weight, her hair hadn't darkened, and she held herself with authority, not timidity.

"*Merci*, I am very well. And yourself?"

"I have seldom felt better." Miriam was thankful that her appearance no longer reflected her previous indisposition.

"I rarely come along when Hugh competes in tournaments," Emeline said with a grimace. "But Joheved wrote that she hoped to attend." She smiled broadly. "I didn't expect to find both of you here."

"Is Gila with you?" Miriam asked, although Emeline's happiness seemed proof that her mother-in-law was still in Plancy.

Emeline laughed out loud at this. "Oh *non*. These days her back bothers so much that she seldom leaves her bed."

Joheved gave her a hug at this news. "So you are the baroness of Plancy at last."

"*Oui*. With time as my ally, her defeat was inevitable."

The noise from the crowd increased, and Rachel waved at them. "Come quickly, it's starting."

The knights lined up at opposite ends of the recently harvested wheat field, their horses munching on the stubble. His face hidden beneath a pointed helmet, each knight held a lance in one arm and a shield in the other. Miriam barely had time to ask Joheved which one was Alain, when the heralds sounded their trumpets, and the two bands of horsemen charged at each other.

It was mayhem. Men yelling, horses neighing, metal clanging against metal, the crowd cheering. Miriam tried to follow Alain, but the swirling dust made it difficult to tell one knight from another. The primary tactic was obviously to knock an opponent off his horse, seize the animal, and gallop off to the *lices*, where the prize was handed to the waiting squires. If the unhorsed opponent was dazed or injured, the knight attempted to deliver him to the *lices* as well, by enlisting the help of his comrades on the ground with swords or clubs. But the opponent had men-at-arms too, and the resulting hand-to-hand combat continued until he was either rescued or captured.

Yom Tov was better at following Alain's exploits than Miriam. Again and again he pointed out the young knight, whose strategy was to cut an opponent's stirrups and then secure the horse once the rider fell off. He elicited screams of glee from Yom Tov whenever he was successful.

There were other maneuvers that drew loud cheers from the crowd. Emeline pointed out an enterprising fellow whose tactic was to ride as fast as he could into the fray and grab the reins of an opponent's horse. Then he would race on, holding the reins just out of reach of the man's sword, thus capturing both horse and rider. One time, however, he rode too close to the forest's edge, and his captive, to the crowd's delight, reached up, grasped a low-hanging branch, and swung himself out of the saddle.

But these exciting events were rare, and by midday Miriam had seen enough. She had little sympathy for the injured knights. Most were landless younger sons eager to risk life and limb to win booty, although those who possessed prowess and luck might win the hand of an heiress as well.

It distressed her to watch the young squires face danger on the battlefield, protected only by heavy leather instead of the chain mail that knights wore from head to knee. A knight was relatively safe on his mount, and if he were unhorsed, his armor would shield him until he got back on again. Should he be captured, he spent the rest of the day lounging in the *lices*, drinking ale and gambling with his comrades. The squires, however, stayed on the field continuously, and each time they defended a fallen knight or attacked a downed opponent, they were in peril of being stabbed or clubbed themselves.

Miriam couldn't help but cringe as she watched the smallest squires scurry between rampaging horses to recover the riderless mounts, at the same time looking to retrieve fallen weapons. Some of them were no older than her nephew Isaac.

Her escape came when Yom Tov announced, "I'm tired of all this fighting, Mama. When can we go home?"

She hadn't a chance to tell him it was dangerous to leave before the tournament ended, when Salomon motioned for them to join him.

"Tell me, Yom Tov," Salomon said. "What happens to Moses in the Torah portion we'll be reading on Simchat Torah?"

"Moses dies, Grandpapa."

"And what happens to the Israelites after that?"

Yom Tov answered without hesitation. "They cross the Jordan into Canaan, to settle the land the Holy One promised them."

Clearly he was proud of his knowledge, and Miriam felt herself filling with pride as well. She had been the one to teach him Torah.

"But do the Canaanites allow them to do this?" Salomon asked next.

"*Non*, Grandpapa. The Israelites have to fight them."

"Aha." Salomon raised his eyebrows and nodded at his grandsons, for by this time, Shmuel had come to see what the discussion was about. "Didn't you wonder why I decided to attend this tournament instead of working on my *kuntres*?"

The boys looked at him blankly, but Miriam smiled and said, "I certainly did."

"I have lived a peaceful life, never once seeing a battle—thank Heaven." Salomon stroked his beard and sighed. "But the Israelites were not so lucky. They fought many wars, against the Canaanites, the Amorites, the Philistines, and others, as your mother has so capably taught you. So when Meir told me about this tournament, I realized that I would see real fighting, to have an idea of what the Israelites went through."

"Oh." Yom Tov looked up at his grandfather with awe. "So when you watch the knights, which side do you see as Israel?"

"Neither. I watch the men on the ground; the Israelites didn't have horses. I think that for the men on the field, battles today aren't that different from those in Moses's time."

"Except that the Israelites and their enemies fought to the death," Miriam whispered to her father after the boys turned their attention back to the field.

"As men do today, if this weren't a mock battle," he replied. "One good thing about this pope, his Truce of God seems to be working. Who would think that he could make the knights limit their warfare to three days a week?"

When Salomon went back to the platform's edge, where his grandsons were standing, Miriam decided to join Joheved and Emeline. The two women's features were surprisingly similar. Joheved's hair was brunette, while Emeline's was blond, but both were tall and full-figured, with blue eyes and small mouths.

As Miriam drew closer, she was struck with the realization that their true similarity was in their bearing. These were women of the nobility, unintimidated by the presence of so many lords and knights, who in the midst of discussing the challenges of estate management, would tell one of André's servants to bring her more smoked fish, cheese, or bread with the assurance that her request would be immediately obeyed.

Joheved and Emeline were discussing some cases that had come to their manor courts.

"I don't understand it," Emeline said. "At least half my alewives pay the fines rather than wait for the official ale tasting."

Joheved shrugged her shoulders. "If she knows she's going to be fined anyway for selling weak ale, she may as well get fined for selling before it's been tasted."

"You're probably right. But why do so many villeins default on the demesne plow work when they know they'll be fined? It's not that they're lazy; they labor hard enough on their own land."

"It's the same with us," Joheved said. "Industrious villeins can earn more money from their own crops than what it costs them in fines. But our steward says their fines more than cover our costs to hire day laborers."

"It's easy for you to hire day laborers," Emeline said. "Half the men in Troyes are runaway villeins needing work."

Joheved nodded. "I suppose that's why we never have trouble hiring workers, even at the height of the summer harvest."

"I expect your steward doesn't have any trouble collecting *merchet*, *leirwite*, *tallage*, or *heriot* fees either," Emeline said.

Miriam had no idea what these were, and as much as she didn't want to expose her ignorance, this time there was no child to ask for her. So far she'd been listening quietly, amazed at how Joheved seemed to have become a completely new person. At home, studying Talmud or helping with the vintage, Joheved might try to boss her younger sisters around, but mostly they were equals. Here, in the presence of Emeline, she wasn't merely another woman, she was Lady Joheved of Ramerupt-sur-Aube.

Before Miriam could ask, Joheved began explaining the mysterious terms. "Those are words you won't find in the Talmud. *Tallage* is the annual rent a villein pays for his land, *merchet* is the fee he pays when his daughter gets married, *leirwite* is the amount she pays if she gets caught lying with a man before she's married, and *heriot* is what his family pays when he dies. Because our estate is so small, only one village, it's impossible to hide these from our steward and reeve."

The poor villeins, Miriam thought. Paying rent was one thing, but Meir's villagers also had to pay him when they married or died.

"With all the villages we have, and all the incompetent people Gila had running them, I doubt these fees were collected or turned over to us." Emeline shook her head with disgust.

Then her expression softened. "I rarely have to check on things in Méry-sur-Seine anymore, not since your Pierre has taken over as steward there. I've heard that all the stewards you train are as capable, which brings me to a favor I want to ask you."

Joheved looked surprised, but she answered, "I can't imagine what favor you could need from me, but I will do it if I can."

"I told you about the boy Hugh fathered with his mistress?"

Both Joheved and Miriam nodded.

"His name is Milo and he's already learned to read and write," Emeline said. "I'd like to continue his education at your manor, so that he may be as fine a steward as Pierre."

Joheved remained silent, and Miriam said what surely was on her sister's mind. "I understand your desire to remove this youth from your midst, but won't his mother object?"

Emeline shook her head. "You misunderstand me. Milo's mother died a few years ago, in childbirth, and out of pity I began teaching him his letters. He has shown surprising intelligence and I've become fond of him."

"Why not send him into the Church?"

"My husband expects one of our younger sons to go into the Church, where a baron's legitimate son can attain a higher office than an illegitimate one."

Joheved knew the Edomites rarely educated more than one son for the Church. "Since you recommend his son, I'm sure we can train him. But we must have Hugh's permission."

"I wanted to have your approval before I went to him with the idea," Emeline said. "But of course Hugh will agree. Why wouldn't he want Milo to have a future beyond that of a landless *juvene*, fighting in one tournament after another?"

As Joheved and Emeline discussed the details that needed to be settled before Milo could become a squire, Miriam remembered that she wanted to consult Moses haCohen about Judah.

She found him standing next to Meir near the platform's edge. "I need some medical advice," she said.

Moses walked with her toward the back, where they could have some privacy. "How can I help you?"

"Judah, my husband . . ." Miriam hesitated, unsure how to describe her concerns.

The doctor waited for her to continue, and she finally decided simply to say what she thought. "I believe he suffers from melancholy."

To Miriam's surprise, Moses didn't question her about Judah's symptoms. Instead he asked, "Doesn't Judah's normal temperament tend toward the melancholic?"

"*Oui*, but he seems to be more gloomy than usual."

"Autumn is the season associated with black bile, so people often feel sad at this time of year," he said. "In fact, extra black bile in autumn can be helpful for the Days of Awe because it brings on confession and penance."

Miriam frowned. "So I should just wait until spring and then he'll be better?"

"Not at all," Moses replied. "Satan can be connected to the black bile, because he finds in it a disposition for great damage; for example, persuading men to hang themselves and despair of God's mercy, or torturing them with strange imaginations. Don't worry, I will speak with Judah when I return to Troyes for Simchat Torah. And if he complains of melancholy, I will prescribe an appropriate regimen to rid him of his excess black bile."

Thus reassured, Miriam's interest in medicine claimed her attention. "You said that black bile is related to autumn, but I would have thought it was more appropriate to winter."

Apparently Moses was also bored with the tournament, because he continued by telling her all sorts of fascinating things about the four humors.

"Each humor is associated with a certain personality, as well as with a specific element, planet, season, and organ of the body. For example, excess black bile makes a man too dry and cold, thus causing melancholy, which is actually the Latin word for black bile," he said. "The person with excess blood is too warm and moist, too sanguine, while extra yellow bile makes him choleric, too hot and dry. Finally, too much moist and cold phlegm makes a man phlegmatic."

Miriam smiled at the doctor. "So phlegm is the humor of winter."

"Indeed, as blood is the humor of spring and yellow bile the humor of summer." He smiled and asked her, "I recall telling you which humor goes with which element, but do you know which one comes from which organ?"

"Let me think," Miriam said. "Phlegm is clearly made by the lungs, and I believe blood is made in the liver."

"Correct." Moses nodded.

"But I don't know where yellow and black bile come from."

"Yellow bile is produced in the gallbladder and black bile in the spleen."

"I didn't know the planets were paired with humors." Miriam gestured toward the battlefield behind them. "However I would guess that choleric yellow bile is attached to Mars, which influences man to anger and war."

"Correct again." The doctor smiled broadly. "Blood is under Jupiter's influence, while phlegm is under the moon's, which is perhaps why people do such foolish things when the moon is full. Black bile is the humor of Saturn—do you know if Judah was born on the Sabbath? That sometimes predisposes a man to melancholy."

"I doubt it," she said. "Papa once told us that he was born on Shabbat, and though Judah's mother was with us, she didn't say that Judah was born that day as well."

"I wouldn't have thought that Salomon was born under Saturn's influence, although another planet dominant at the hour of his birth probably mitigated Saturn's effects." Moses looked pensive. "Certainly the influence of Saturn would explain his deliberativeness."

Miriam wanted to know more about how the planets affected everyone, but suddenly shouts and noises coming from the tournament grew so loud that further conversation was impossible. Miriam, along with everyone else on the platform, ran to the edge to see what had caused such excitement so late in the afternoon.

When Miriam began speaking with Moses, it seemed that the tournament would drag on until every last man had been captured or dropped from exhaustion. But now there were fresh knights riding into battle, men whose colors were neither those of the northern nor the southern Champagnois.

Several shouts rang out. "It's Count Robert's men!"

"That's not fair," other men began yelling. "They're supposed to be guarding the *lices*, not fighting."

Miriam turned to Emeline. "Are they allowed to do this?"

"Who's going to stop them?" Emeline shrugged her shoulders. "The only rule enforced in a tournament is that no one may attack men in the *lices*. Knights aren't supposed to chase each other through village streets, but they do. And they aren't supposed to keep fighting after sunset, but they do."

Indeed, Count Thibault's men merely watched as the Flemish knights swept onto the field, snatching up prisoners at random. The few remaining local knights were too exhausted to put up much of a fight, and those with their wits about them, including Alain, fled into the forest. In less than an hour, it was over.

To Miriam's surprise, nearly everyone considered the Flemish maneuver a clever tactic, not an unfair one. As Salomon reminded her, "Tournaments are preparation for warfare, and it makes sense for captains to deliberately keep some men back from the battle at first so they'll have fresh troops later."

True to his word, Moses haCohen invited Miriam and Judah to *disner* the day after Simchat Torah. When Francesca excused herself to nurse the baby, Miriam exchanged looks with Moses and left with her. But Miriam had barely finished sharing Emeline's story when the doctor asked her to return to the salon.

Judah spoke as soon as he saw her. "I want you to hear the advice Moses has given me, since it involves hanging some herbs in our bedroom and putting me on a special diet."

Miriam turned to Moses. "What do you want me to do?"

"Judah and I agree that he mostly likely suffers from *tristitia*, which is a temporary sadness, rather than *acedia*, a long-term melancholia," Moses said. "So we will begin with a gentle regimen and see how he feels in two months."

In two months Elisha would be back, Judah thought. He'd better be cured if he was going to see Elisha and Giuseppe together every day without crying.

"Judah tells me that he has never undergone therapeutic bloodletting." The doctor's voice was disapproving. "So I'm going to bleed him twice a month, every other Sunday at the beginning of the ninth hour, when Saturn is ascending. At that time we are likely to draw off the highest concentration of black bile."

Miriam nodded, and Moses turned to Judah. "Even when you feel better, I want you to continue with monthly bloodletting on Sunday afternoons. Men need to remove corrupt humors from their bodies since they don't bleed regularly like women do."

"You mentioned a special diet," Miriam said. She hoped the necessary ingredients wouldn't be too difficult to find.

"It's a simple thing, and since these foods tend to make people cheerful, your whole family can eat them. First, I recommend small cakes made with nutmeg and cinnamon, both of which are hot and warm. Judah may eat as many as he likes, but he should eat at least two a day, morning and night."

"That's easy enough. What else?"

"Rue and fennel are also helpful for this condition."

"I could put them in my bread dough," she suggested.

Moses nodded and addressed Judah again. "You should avoid fish and roasted meat, unless they are served with a spicy sauce. Try to eat more boiled meats and stews. Also, because of the cold, dry nature of black bile, your body has become so desiccated that you will need regular baths."

Judah blushed with shame. Had Miriam told Moses that since Elisha left, Judah had stopped going to the stews on Friday afternoon? The only time Judah had bathed recently was with Papa, just before Rosh Hashanah.

"Are there any other foods Judah should avoid, other than plain fish and roasted meat?" Miriam asked. So far, Judah's special diet was a simple one.

"Dill can increase melancholy, but other than that, he may eat any other herb or spice."

Miriam rose to return to Francesca's chamber, but the doctor had something else to say. "Normally I would suggest hanging some sweet-smelling herbs in a melancholy person's bedroom, but I don't want to encourage your child to be born too soon, under Saturn's influence."

Like most midwives, Miriam understood that Saturn ruled the eighth month of pregnancy, with the result that babies born that early rarely survived. But she was close to starting her ninth month, the one ruled by Jupiter, and if the baby came then it would be a relief. So she hung basil and sweet lemon balm in the bedroom, prepared the pre-scribed diet for Judah, and prayed that the Merciful One would soon heal him.

And three weeks later, when their third son was born after a quick and uneventful delivery, Judah's mood had improved. Miriam suspected that, while this event certainly cheered him, the cause of his better spir-its was not the special diet or sweet spices, nor the baths and bloodlet-tings, but that Papa had asked Judah to study Tractate Sanhedrin with him in preparation for the Cold Fair. Not to mention the anticipation that, after five years of training, Miriam was finally going to perform her first *brit milah*—on their own son.

Each time she changed her new son's swaddling, Miriam carefully stretched his foreskin forward and then pushed it back as she cleaned him. Every Jewish mother did this for her newborn son to make his foreskin easier for the mohel to cut. With her first two boys Miriam had cleaned them without thinking about it, but this child was different. She would be doing the circumcision herself.

She was trying to decide if she had softened the foreskin sufficiently when she heard a familiar voice downstairs calling, "Miriam, I'm com-ing up. I can't wait to see your new baby." It sounded like Rachel, but shouldn't she be in Barbary?

"What are you doing here?" Miriam said as her younger sister came in. "Is anything wrong?"

"Everything is fine. I kept thinking that if you had a boy this would be your first *brit*, and I couldn't bear missing it. So we decided to travel to Kiev with Samson and buy furs."

"I'm glad you're here in time." Miriam placed her son in his cradle so she could hug her sister. "How long will you be home?"

"Two months at least. The Cold Fair has the best armor and weapons, so we'll get some to sell in Sepharad this spring."

Rachel peered down at her newest nephew and then winked at Miriam. "He's an ugly little brute, but then what can you expect from such a father?"

Miriam smiled back. *He is an attractive baby.* "My labor was so fast that his head didn't have a chance to get deformed."

"You may have difficult pregnancies, but you always manage to have an easy birth." Rachel sat down on the bed. "How is Joheved?"

"Her child hasn't turned over yet, so I think I'll have her stay in Troyes after the *brit*." If Joheved's baby were breech, it would be best to deliver in a town with experienced midwives.

A flicker of fear crossed Rachel's face, but then she brightened. "This will be her fifth child. Surely everything will be fine as usual."

"It's so good to see you. I'm glad you decided to deal in furs and steel this winter." Miriam put her arm around her sister. "I missed you."

Rachel basked in the unexpected attention. "I've missed you too, but we're also here because of Eliezer." She sighed. "My husband is getting better at buying and selling, but his heart wishes he was still in the yeshiva."

"Judah will be glad to have his old study partner back again," Miriam said. "And so will I."

Rachel's expression became thoughtful. "Mama said you're doing the *brit* tomorrow, but you don't seem nervous."

"I've been training for so long, I just want to get on with it already," Miriam said, pleased that she was hiding her anxiety so well.

twenty-seven

iriam was not so reticent when Judah remarked on her surprising calmness that night. "Now I understand the tradition of having an apprentice do his first *milah* at the last moment, when the mohel is indisposed," she said. "Having to wait and worry for eight days is awful."

Judah set up the cot next to their marital bed, as he would continue to do until forty days after the baby's birth. "I'm sure you'll do an excellent job."

Miriam peeked once more at the sleeping form in the cradle and then blew out the lamp. "You said it was *bashert* for my first *milah* to be our son."

Twice that night, Miriam got up to nurse, and each time Judah sat up with her and explained the Gemara he and Papa were working on. It was good of him to try to distract her, but she still spent much of the night worrying.

When it was light enough to see, she crept out of bed and, for the last time, checked that her mohel's kit was complete. *Oui*, the oil and cumin that she'd prepared yesterday had not spilled, the *haluk* had no hanging threads, and the small container of Papa's strongest wine remained sealed.

Then she took out her *azmil* to test its sharpness. Steel blades naturally form a burr during sharpening, so she gently slid her fingertip from one side of the blade over the edge, feeling for a burr dragging against her skin. Next, Miriam pressed the edge lightly against her thumbnail. If it cut into her nail it was sharp enough, if it slipped it was dull, and the sharper the blade the smaller the angle she could make before it slipped. Another reason experienced mohels have such ugly thumbnails, she thought, as she tested both sides of the knife.

Satisfied, she took her *azmil* outside, where the sun was rising over the courtyard wall. Papa had taught her how a good sharpener can see a dull edge. For her final test, she held the blade up with its edge in line with the sun and then moved it slightly, looking for the glint that re- flected off a dull edge or a burr. She sighed with relief at finding none.

By now the rest of the household was awake, and Judah called down that their new son was hungry. Miriam took a deep breath and went back upstairs. Lying in bed, baby at her breast, she realized that the next time she nursed him would be after his circumcision.

At synagogue it was a good thing that Joheved had agreed to lead the women in her stead, because Miriam kept losing her place in the service. Judah had made her his agent for the *brit,* but to be sure, Avram had stayed home, complaining of a headache. When Judah refused, terrified that he might move at the crucial moment, Papa had agreed to hold the boy on his lap during the circumcision.

As the time for her son's *brit milah* approached, the congregation's prayers grew quieter, and when Miriam carried her new son downstairs to give to Judah, the entire room was silent. He made the father's invoca- tion, handed the boy to Papa, and it was as if everyone were holding their breath. Miriam placed the wine-soaked cloth in her son's mouth, picked up the *azmil,* and, for the first time, said the mohel's blessing, "*Baruch ata Adonai* . . . Who commands us concerning *milah.*"

Then, as she had seen Avram do so many times, she focused her *kava- nah* on the tiny penis in front of her, pulled the foreskin tight, and sliced it off. Little Elisha barely whimpered, and the sound of hundreds of people breathing at once was like gusts of wind blowing inside. Miriam realized that she had been holding her breath as well, and sighed with pleasure that there were no shreds left; she had made a perfect cut. Tears ran down her cheeks as she bandaged her son, while Judah made the fa- ther's blessing and Papa led the prayers for her health and the baby's.

Then, her newly circumcised son content in her arms, she returned Judah's smile as Papa announced, "May this child, named in the House of Israel, Elisha ben Judah, become great. Even as he has entered into the covenant, so may he enter into Torah, the marriage canopy, and the practice of good deeds."

Three hours later little Elisha had wet his swaddling twice. Three days later Avram came by to check the boy's health and offer congratulations. And three weeks later, just as her family was leaving for morning services, Joheved's water broke.

The baby had remained breech, but as Miriam trimmed her nails, she prayed that Joheved's labor wouldn't last too long. And while Rachel collected all the family's tefillin, spread fennel among the rushes in their old bedroom, and chalked the floor and walls against Lillit, Miriam kept reminding herself of the many breech lambs she'd delivered safely.

Papa and Judah came back from synagogue with a Torah scroll and a minyan to pray psalms, just as Meir returned from Ramerupt with Marona. By sunset Joheved's womb was completely open, but something kept Miriam from announcing that the child would be born that evening. Instead she asked Meir to bring the Torah scroll into Joheved's bedroom and for the men to go home to get some sleep. A new minyan from the evening service would replace them and stay all night if necessary.

It was necessary. The baby was buttocks down, and even with Joheved clutching Countess Adelaide's ruby, it took Miriam and Sarah most of the night to get the child's feet out. The rest of the baby should have quickly followed, but nothing happened. After twenty-four hours of labor, enough of the baby had emerged to know that it was a boy, but his head remained firmly lodged, no matter how many times one of them whispered the verse from Exodus in Joheved's ear,

> Get you out and the people that follow you;
> After that I will go out. And he went out.

When Rachel came downstairs and said she was going to fetch Elizabeth, Meir, who had stood up hopefully when he saw her on the stairs, sank back into his seat. Shemayah gently laid his hand on Meir's shoulder and suggested that perhaps they should get some rest. Meir shook his head, and Shemayah sat down again.

Elizabeth soon arrived, and her expression became grave upon learning that the baby's progress had stopped. "The fennel and basil smell nice, but we need something stronger."

"We're sending Rachel to buy fresh agrimony at the fair," Sarah said. "She could get rose oil for Joheved's thighs; that would also help entice the baby out."

Miriam couldn't hide her anxiety. "Even with both of us pulling his legs for hours, he hasn't budged."

Elizabeth began examining the patient. "Perhaps we can manipulate the womb to open further."

"I've tried several times, but I can try again." Miriam turned to her sister. "I know this hurts, Joheved, but if you can relax, it will be easier."

Joheved closed her eyes and stifled her moans as Miriam tried, to no avail, to get her hand past the baby's head.

"It's still early, but if we need to, we can take him out in pieces," Elizabeth whispered.

Miriam grimaced. Only twice had she been forced to remove, piece by piece, a baby who'd refused to be born. And one of those times the mother had died anyway.

"Don't kill him," Joheved pleaded. "I can still push."

"That's not the problem," Sarah explained. "If the child is stuck, you could push too hard and rupture your womb."

The three midwives exchanged somber glances. They had all treated women whose obstructed labor had ripped an opening from her womb into her bladder or rectum, leaving her with excrement that leaked continuously and made her smell like a privy.

"I have an idea," Elizabeth said. "If I can get my hands on top of the child's shoulders, I can push down while one of you pulls on his legs and the other gets some sleep."

Sarah nodded. "If we do it slowly and continuously, the baby's head may compress enough to get through."

"I slept some when I nursed Elisha," Miriam said. "I can stay here while Aunt Sarah rests."

Once Joheved's thighs were smeared with rose oil, and the fresh agrimony was tied there, root down, Elizabeth oiled her hands and slid them up into her patient's birth canal. Then, when the next contraction came, Elizabeth pushed while Miriam pulled. It was an awkward position, and the oily baby was so slippery that his legs kept sliding out of her grasp.

It seemed to Miriam that they had made some progress when Marona poked her head in a few hours later. "Miriam, your own baby is crying for you, and you should have some *disner* as well. Sarah's still asleep, so show me what to do."

Downstairs all eyes were on Miriam as she downed her chicken stew and bread. She knew how badly her family wanted a progress report, but she forced her face to remain impassive. She hoped that nobody would question her, but she wasn't surprised when Meir followed as she headed upstairs to where Mama was surely pacing her room with hungry little Elisha.

Meir's face was ashen, and his voice shook as he spoke. "I know you'd tell us if there was any good news. But you've got to tell me something. At least give me reason to hope."

Miriam sighed. *Is it better to raise his hopes only to dash them later or to tell him truthfully how little chance there is?* "I don't know, Meir. Your son is breech, and we're trying to pull him out, but he doesn't want to be born."

Meir's face seemed to crumple, and tears began pooling in his eyes. "If it's a choice between Joheved's life and the baby's, don't even think about it. Save my wife."

"Of course."

"And if . . ." His voice sank to a whisper. "If the worst should happen, I want to see her while she still lives."

"Things aren't that bad," Miriam said as she reached the top of the stairs. "After all, how many women in labor have the protection of seven pairs of tefillin?"

As Mama tucked her and little Elisha into bed, Miriam could hear the children downstairs crying and Judah trying to pacify them. Then Mama closed the door and all was quiet.

Miriam woke to the sound of her baby whimpering next to her and the smell of swaddling that needed changing, but when she opened her eyes she couldn't see anything. The sun had set some time ago. She jumped up, grabbed her son, and raced for her former bedroom, her heart beating wildly. Downstairs, the continual murmur of prayers was encouraging.

She opened the door to the sound of her mother's voice. "My hand is cramping up, Sarah. I can't pull any longer."

Aunt Sarah was just standing up when she saw her niece. "Elizabeth's idea is working. It's slow going, but the boy's head is definitely further out than before."

"Thank Heaven." Miriam sat down and put her now-crying son to her breast. "How are you feeling, Joheved? I can help as soon as Elisha finishes."

Joheved's eyes flickered open and she moaned softly. "If pain could kill, I'd be dead already . . . now I'm just tired of pushing . . . I just want everything . . . the pain, the pushing, everything . . . to be over."

Marona wiped the sweat from her daughter-in-law's forehead. "Just a little longer, dear."

As Miriam fed her baby, she observed her older sister—the unfocused gaze, straggly hair, grey-tinged skin, and labored breathing. When he was done, she leaned over and gently removed the ruby from Joheved's fist. "Mama, could you bring me a cup of warm wine and a mortar and pestle?"

Rachel gasped, and then nobody made a sound as Miriam ground the small ruby into pieces, dumped them into the wine, and recited an incantation over the cup. The gem was hers to do with as she wished. "I conjure you, Armisael, angel who governs the womb, that you help this woman and the child in her body to life and peace. Amen."

And they all followed, "Amen, amen."

Miriam took Elizabeth's place, and the older midwife stretched her arms out and wiggled her fingers gratefully. "What do you think? Have we made enough progress that Marona can go downstairs and give her son some comfort?"

"You've done wonderfully. I can feel his ears." Miriam made no attempt to hold back her tears of relief. Surely Joheved's child would be born before dawn.

"I'll change Elisha's swaddling and put him to bed," Rivka said. "Then I'll try to persuade my stubborn husband to join us."

Rachel added her strength to the midwives', but it took most of the night for the child's skull to mold to fit through Joheved's birth canal. Joheved was nearly unconscious by then, but the sound of her son's birth cries, feeble as they were, roused her to open her eyes and make sure that all his parts were as they should be.

"His head looks so odd," she whispered.

Miriam couldn't remember if she had ever seen a baby with such a large head before. "Your son's head was constricted as we pulled him out," she replied. "It should change to a more normal shape as he grows."

When Meir came in with Salomon, Sarah confidently assured them that, while it might take several months, the boy's head would eventually be round like other babies'. Meir thanked her gratefully, then collapsed into the chair near the bed and fell asleep. Salomon sat down next to him and began to study.

Two days later Joheved's temperature started climbing, and she complained that her belly hurt. The next morning Miriam soberly advised Meir to call his students back to pray for his wife's health, and to hire a wet nurse.

"Is there no medicine that will help?" he asked.

Thinking of poor Rosaline, Miriam slowly shook her head. She had gone to visit the young woman at Notre-Dame-aux-Nonnains later, but the nuns told her that Rosaline had died.

"I've already been giving her nutmeg mixed with feverfew in ale, which is supposed to prevent childbed fever, but clearly they are not enough to vanquish Lillit and her demons. That requires divine intercession and mercy."

"I understand," Meir replied. It was time for prayer, fasting, and giving charity.

Yet by the morning of little Salomon's *brit milah*, for that was the name she and Meir had chosen, Joheved was so ill that the ritual was again performed on the grandfather's lap, not the mother's, and little Salomon was whisked off to his wet nurse almost immediately. Miriam's mind was so concerned with her sister's failing health that she did the cutting by rote, as if it had been her hundredth circumcision instead of her second.

Meir couldn't wait to go back upstairs to where Joheved lay. Since the birth he had been forbidden to touch her, but now the eight days of her impurity from childbirth were complete. He took the damp cloth from Anna and began wiping the sweat from his wife's face and neck. Each time he dipped it in fresh water and wrung it out, he recited one of the biblical verses that wielded the power of the Holy Name against the fever demons. First, from Deuteronomy:

> Adonai will keep off from you all sickness; He will not bring upon
> you any of the dreadful diseases of Egypt.

And then from Numbers:

> Moses cried out to Adonai, saying, "O God, please heal her."

Exhausted, Meir stripped down to his chemise and got under the covers. Tears running down his cheeks, he held Joheved's burning body close and prayed the verses against fever again and again. Lying limply in his arms, she seemed oblivious to his presence, but as long as he could feel her chest rise and fall, Meir had hope.

There was a soft knock on the door. "Meir?" Shemayah asked from the hall. "I have the Torah scroll from the synagogue."

Meir reluctantly got up and opened the door. Together they placed the holy scroll near the bed.

"I don't suppose you're interested in rejoining the feast," Shemayah said. "Even though you are the host."

When Meir shook his head, his friend continued, "I thought as much, so I also brought along my copy of Tractate Sanhedrin."

It wasn't long before their study was interrupted by another knock. This time it was Miriam at the door, followed by Judah, Salomon and Rivka, and Rachel and Eliezer, all wearing somber expressions.

Miriam sniffed the air, alert for the slightest hint of the stench that had pervaded Rosaline's sickroom. "Meir, your efforts alone may not be sufficient to save Joheved."

"You know how dangerous pairs are," Rivka whispered. "Of course there's nothing you could have done to prevent it, but two sisters each giving birth to a baby boy, so close together—certainly this has provoked the Evil Eye."

Judah nodded. "Especially their being daughters of a *talmid chacham*, and married to scholars themselves."

"Our entire family must help," Miriam said. "Papa says he knows of no one with Ben Yochai's store of wisdom, but surely there are scholars at the Cold Fair who know spells to fight Lillit and the Evil Eye."

"I want all of you to also try to remember anything you've studied on this subject," Salomon said.

Miriam turned to Rachel. "Talk to our clients. Ask them what methods they've heard of."

"I'm sure I'll find out something. Women know things about childbirth that men don't."

Rivka suddenly gave a gasp. "Our mezuzah is the same one since Salomon and I married. Maybe there are spiders nesting in it or insects have eaten some of it." She turned anxiously to her husband. "When was the last time you checked it?"

"It was all right the last time I looked." Salomon evaded her question. "But in case some of the letters have faded, I shall get a new one."

"See if you can find Mordecai," Miriam said. "He made Rachel's birth amulet at the Cold Fair two years ago."

"You'll have to do that tomorrow morning," Judah said. "Or wait until Monday."

"What?" Miriam stared at him in surprise.

"A mezuzah must be written on Thursday in the fourth hour, ruled by Venus and the angel Anael," Judah explained. "Or during the fifth hour on Monday, when the sun and the angel Raphael rule."

"Tomorrow at the fourth hour then." Salomon stood up. "I will look for this Mordecai immediately, so he'll be ready."

Judah was the next to leave. "The Eastern merchants I study with may have some esoteric knowledge."

"Remember those two men speaking Arabic on the caravan with us from Arles?" Rachel asked Eliezer. "They're still in town; I saw them at Shabbat services."

"I'll question them."

The next morning Salomon headed for the fairgrounds, accompanied by his two healthy daughters. Mordecai the scribe was ready when they arrived at his stall. He squinted at Miriam and Rachel for a moment and then his face lit up in recognition.

"I originally had another client scheduled for today, but since your case is urgent I told him to come back next week," he said. "It's well that amulets may be written on both the twelfth and the sixteenth day of the month. For if, Heaven forbid, the new mother is not better by Thursday, I will write another mezuzah for the sickroom door."

At their surprised expressions he explained, "Some pious folk hang one on every door in their house. I know a rabbi in Rothenburg who was tormented by an evil spirit whenever he took an afternoon nap, but not after he put a mezuzah at his study door."

The scribe took out a small sundial and aligned it on the counter. "It's almost the fourth hour. Let's begin." He reached below and took out a cow's horn full of ink, a goose quill, and a small piece of parchment.

Then, staring at these, he chanted, "*Baruch ata Adonai*, King of the World, Who has sanctified Your great name and revealed it to the pious ones, to invoke Your power and Your might by means of Your name and Your words."

Miriam glanced at Rachel, who nodded in return. Mordecai had said the same prayer before writing Rachel's birth amulet.

He held up the parchment. "This *klaf* is made of deerskin."

"I thought it looked different from the sheep parchment we made." Salomon held out his hand. "May I examine it?"

"Not unless you immersed in the *mikvah* this morning and can assure me that you've touched nothing impure since," Mordecai replied.

Salomon withdrew his hand and then leaned closer as the scribe spread out the *klaf* and wrote "Shaddai" in the middle of it.

"The letters of this holy name also stand for 'guardian of the dwellings of Israel,' and when it's done I shall roll the *klaf* in such a way that you can read 'Shaddai' through a hole in the mezuzah case," Mordecai explained.

He turned the *klaf* around and wrote three strange words, "Kozu Bemochsaz Kozu," at the very bottom. "This is a powerful, secret name for the Holy One," he whispered. "If you take each Hebrew word and replace its letters with the next one in the alphabet, you get . . ."

"Adonai Eloheinu Adonai," Rachel interrupted, her eyes wide. "The three names for God in the Shema—"

"Which is the first line written on a mezuzah," Miriam finished for her.

"'Kozu Bemochsaz Kozu' must be written on the exact place where 'Adonai Eloheinu Adonai' appears on the reverse side," Mordecai said as he drew several bizarre figures at the bottom of the *klaf*. Then, in one smooth motion, he blew on the ink to dry it, turned the *klaf* over, and proceeded to scratch twenty-two parallel lines into the blank parchment with an empty quill. "Now comes the actual text from Deuteronomy."

The three observers stood as close as they could without blocking the sunlight. Miriam was astonished to see that Mordecai was writing more than just the biblical text. At the end of the first line, he wrote "Yah," one of the Holy names, and below that a pentagram. The last letter in the third line had a little circle under it, and under the pentagram he wrote the archangel's name, Michael.

Miriam had always assumed that the only words on a mezuzah were those from the Torah. Obviously this wasn't so; every line was followed by holy names and esoteric symbols. But who had decided this and why?

Papa must have been thinking the same thing, because no sooner had Mordecai finished the sixth line than he asked, "What are those extra words and figures on the left?"

"And why do you draw those little circles between some of the words?" Miriam asked. It seemed sacrilegious to add these doodles in the middle of the holy text.

Mordecai continued to work as he answered Salomon. "My learned teacher taught me that along the left side we write the names of seven angels, as well as five holy names of God. I don't know the purpose of all the figures, but the ten pentagrams represent the Ten Commandments."

Then he told Miriam, "Some say that the circles, which will number ten in all, also correspond to the Ten Commandments, while others say they indicate the ten elements of a man's body. As to why we use these additional names and symbols, and why they go in certain positions on the *klaf*. . ." Mordecai paused for a moment to consider the question. "I was taught that they make a mezuzah more powerful."

Miriam couldn't object to that. Every Jew had to trust that the mezuzah scribe followed the correct procedure.

"Can a woman write a mezuzah?" Rachel asked.

"I don't know of any who do," the scribe admitted.

Salomon stroked his beard. "Since women are obligated in the mitzvah of mezuzah the same as men, it would seem that, once she's been to the *mikvah*, a woman could write one just as a man does," he said slowly. "After all, the reward of mezuzah is to increase our days. If we talk about long life for a man, doesn't a woman deserve a long life too?"

They silently thought of Joheved, for whom this mezuzah would hopefully bring a long life.

Mordecai held up the finished mezuzah for them to inspect, and Rachel couldn't help herself. The letters were pale grey, not black. "The color is so light," she complained.

The scribe smiled at her. "A well-prepared ink will darken to an intense purplish black, and its marks will adhere so firmly to the *klaf* that, unlike other inks, they cannot be erased by rubbing or washing, only by scraping off the writing surface itself." His voice rang with pride.

"Where do you get your ink?" Salomon bought ink from the same merchants every summer, but perhaps the scribe had a less expensive source.

"I make it myself." Mordecai blew on the *klaf* to dry it. "It's not difficult. First add some crushed oak galls to water, then boil the mixture for several hours. After it cools, mix in some green vitriol along with gum arabic, which thickens the ink and makes it flow properly from the quill. Some people allow the gall nuts to ferment in water for a few weeks rather than boil it, but I find that boiling yields a deeper black."

"I see." Salomon nodded and decided to continue buying ink from his usual vendors, no matter what the cost.

Miriam took the rolled up mezuzah scroll and gently placed it in her sleeve, awed that such an innocuous-looking thing could wield such tremendous power against evil. She walked home cautiously, lest some misstep damage the scroll and bring her family bad luck.

twenty-eight

hat evening at *souper*, with Joheved no better, her family shared the advice they'd received for healing her. If Meir weren't already doing so, he should say his morning and evening Shema at Joheved's bedside, loud enough that she could hear it, especially the anti-demonic Ninety-first Psalm.

Salomon immediately hung the new mezuzah at the front door. "I intend to immerse on Thursday and then help Mordecai make another mezuzah. I will write the lines starting with:

> Inscribe them on the doorposts of your home and on your gates—
> that your life and your children's lives will be prolonged."

Everyone nodded in approval. A mezuzah Salomon wrote himself should be more protective of his family than one done by a stranger.

Rachel was eager to share what she had learned. "When a woman in Sepharad has childbed fever, they pray the Twentieth Psalm in her ear nine times every day at the ninth hour."

"Aunt Sarah once told me about that psalm helping a woman in labor," Miriam said. "Maybe it will heal a new mother as well."

Judah had consulted the Eastern merchants. "I was hoping they could recommend some of the fever remedies in Tractate Shabbat, but they'd never heard of any of them curing childbed fever."

Every face at the table fell with disappointment, until Judah continued, "But one man knew of an incantation against Lillit's fever demon, Ochnotinos: A pious man, while still fasting in the morning, spits three times and then says, 'Ochnotinos, notinos, otinos, tinos, inos, nos, os.' The fellow said this was from the Talmud, but I've never heard of it."

Judah looked questioningly at Salomon, who stroked his beard for a while before answering. "I recall something like that from Tractate Avodah Zarah. The evil spirit shrinks and finally vanishes as he hears his name decreasing."

"My wife was correct," Eliezer said proudly. "One of the men on our caravan has studied the hidden Torah and knew a spell effective against fever demons."

"Which is?" Meir looked hopeful now that Judah's spell had been verified by the Talmud.

"Take a new knife and draw a circle around the fevered area nine times," Eliezer replied. "Do this every day and the patient will either be cured in nine days or . . ." He didn't need to say what would happen otherwise.

"Did you find out anything, Mama?" Miriam asked. Her mother was always battling evil spirits; she must have some remedy.

Rivka did. "I've also heard about making circles with a new knife, although I learned that you make three circles, not nine," she said. "Of course, every woman knows that the best cure for fever is chicken broth well seasoned with garlic."

"I say we try them all." Miriam wished she could consult her aunt, but Aunt Sarah had gone to bed early, complaining of fever herself.

"I'm already fasting from meat on Monday and Thursday," Meir said. "But for the next nine days, I will not eat meat except on the Sabbath."

"Nor will I," added Salomon.

Judah could see that Miriam was about to join them. "Miriam is nursing, she cannot fast," he said. "So I will fast in her place."

"You don't need to buy a new knife, Papa," Rachel said, for it was clear that he should be the one to perform the two spells. "Eliezer and I have several for you to choose from." Then she turned to her husband and they nodded at each other. "And we will also avoid meat for nine days."

As Joheved's fever continued to rage, her family settled into an awkward routine. Normally Salomon, Meir, and Judah spent nearly all day with the scholars at synagogue or teaching at home once the Cold Fair opened. But now Salomon woke early to perform the healing spells, after which the family prayed the morning service together in the salon. Only then did the men head for synagogue. On the way home Meir visited his new son at the wet nurse's, and after *disner* he studied Talmud with Shemayah upstairs in the sickroom, while Salomon and Judah worked with the yeshiva students below.

Alvina took care of Miriam and Rachel's clients so they could sit with Joheved and study while the men were away and say the Twentieth Psalm nine times when the bells tolled None in midafternoon. Since Miriam already got up several times a night to nurse, she slept in her old bedroom so she could easily recite the healing psalm in Joheved's ear at Lauds, the ninth hour after sunset. She alternated between relief when all she could smell in Joheved's room was Mama's garlic chicken soup, and despair as days passed without any improvement in her sister's condition.

Saturday night Meir wanted to stay up late praying and studying, but his eyes kept closing before he could complete a page. The third time his head started to droop, Shemayah took the manuscript out of his hands and closed it. "Meir, you're exhausted. Go to bed; I'll continue downstairs with the others."

Meir tried to protest, but he was yawning too much, and Shemayah was out the door before he could reply. So he undressed and got into bed with his wife. It had been six days since they'd begun their regimen against Lillit's fever demons, and still Joheved's body felt so hot. Nine days, he thought, the spell was supposed to work by nine days.

"*Shema Israel Adonai Eloheinu Adonai Echad,*" he began the bedtime prayer, making sure to pronounce each word loudly and clearly. He was so sleepy, but he forced himself to say the Ninety-first Psalm without yawning, changing "him" to "her" at the end.

> "I say of Adonai, my refuge and stronghold . . .
> He will save you from the destructive plague . . .
> His fidelity is an encircling shield
> You need not fear terror by night or arrow that flies by day
> Plague that stalks in darkness or scourge that ravages by noon . . .
> Because you took Adonai as your haven
> No harm will befall you, no disease will touch your tent
> He will order His angels to guard you wherever you go . . .
> I Adonai will deliver her, keep her safe
> I will be with her in distress, I will rescue her . . .
> I will make her honored, let her live to a ripe old age
> And show her My salvation."

Dawn was breaking when Meir woke up shivering, entangled in damp sheets. Panic gripped him as he reached for Joheved's cold and clammy body, but he relaxed when he felt her chest rise and fall. *Mon Dieu, has her fever finally broken?*

Meir forced down his exaltation and concentrated on gently moving Joheved toward his side of the bed, where the sheets weren't soggy. She murmured something about not wanting to get up yet, that it was still dark.

He had to tell the others, so he threw on his chemise and bounded down the stairs, pausing to reach up and touch the new mezuzah on the bedroom doorpost. Salomon was at the first step, the new knife in his hand, and Miriam peeked out her bedroom door, little Elisha in her arms.

"Joheved sweated a river last night," Meir said, his eyes shining with happiness. "We need to change her sheets."

"Her fever?" Miriam whispered as she headed for the sickroom.

"I think it's gone."

"*Baruch ata Adonai* . . . Who heals the sick," Salomon said as the others joined him.

By the time the bells had finished chiming Prime, Joheved was propped up in bed, dipping pieces of freshly baked bread into a large bowl of chicken soup, and asking about her baby.

"How soon can I see him?" she asked, once assured that little Salomon was doing well at the wet nurse's.

"Your fever just broke last night. I think we should wait a couple of days before we bring him to visit you." Miriam wagged her finger at her sister. "I must insist that you stay indoors and rest for another week at least."

"What about Hanukkah?" Salomon asked. "We will be toasting the new vintage in ten days."

"Erev Hanukkah is six days away; we'll see how she's doing then." Miriam stared at them sternly. "We don't want a relapse."

The following week Miriam and Joheved stood in Salomon's courtyard, scanning the sky for the three stars whose appearance would herald the Sabbath's end. The weather was fair for the end of November, and Joheved rejoiced in her first day out of her father's house. That morning she had taken her new son to synagogue and said the *gomel* prayer thanking God for her escape from danger.

Standing opposite her older sister in the Havdalah circle, Miriam wasn't quite as joyful. She knew better than anyone, except maybe Aunt Sarah, how precarious Joheved's recovery was, how much rest those recuperating from childbed fever needed, and would need for many weeks to come. Aunt Sarah was still bedridden with the fever she had caught when Joheved became ill.

"Think of it as an extra-long Hanukkah vacation," Miriam told Joheved. "Many women take the whole festival week off, and now you can make up for all the years when you worked during it."

She couldn't help but smile as their father adjudicated Yom Tov and Shmuel's argument over who got to hold the spice box.

"Shmuel had it last week," Yom Tov protested.

"But you live in Troyes," his cousin pointed out. "You get to hold it all the time."

"I do not. Your family comes here for Shabbat."

"Not in the winter. Once it starts snowing we'll be stuck in Ram-erupt."

Years ago she and Joheved had squabbled like that over whose turn it was to wash first.

But Papa didn't lose his temper. "Who can tell me why we smell the sweet spices during Havdalah?"

Both boys stared at their feet.

Isaac stepped forward. "Grandpapa, doesn't it have to do with the *mazikim*?"

Salomon agreed and the children crowded around him. "You know that we're forbidden to light a fire on the Sabbath."

He waited until his small audience nodded. "So it is that the fires of Gehenna are extinguished on Friday at sunset and not lit again until it is time for Havdalah. And what do you think happens to all the evil spirits there when the fire goes out on Shabbat?"

"They stop getting burned?" Yom Tov replied hesitantly.

"Not only that," Salomon replied. "On Shabbat the *mazikim* are released from Gehenna entirely."

"That's why it's so dangerous to travel on Saturday night," Isaac said. "Because they're not all back in Gehenna yet."

"Not only are the *mazikim* still abroad in our world, but they're angry because they have to return to Gehenna and start getting burned again," Salomon explained. "Which makes them particularly eager to attack travelers."

"But what does this have to do with the spices?" Shmuel couldn't let his brother have all the attention.

"Have you ever smelled burnt hair?"

When the children grimaced at this, Salomon smiled and said, "Once the fires in Gehenna are relit on Saturday night, the smell is a thousand times worse."

"Which is why we need the Havdalah spices, to mask that terrible stench," Isaac haParnas concluded.

Salomon embraced his business partner. "I didn't expect you and little Samson until later, when we start to celebrate the new vintage." He reached down and ruffled the orphan's hair. "But since you're in time for

Havdalah, perhaps you could take the wine cup while Samson holds the spice box."

Positioned between her mother and grandmother, Hannah lifted the Havdalah candle high for Salomon to light, flinching slightly as a drop of hot wax landed on her hand. Meir stood proudly in the midst of his family, his left arm supporting Joheved, his right hand holding his daughter Leah's. Despite his wife's apparent good health, he insisted on spending the afternoons at her bedside studying with Shemayah, and though Joheved often appeared to be napping, Meir could tell by her questions later that she had followed their discussions. He wasn't worried about neglecting his students; they were doing fine with Judah, who managed to juggle the beginning and intermediate Talmud classes in addition to his own studies with Eliezer.

Judah took a sip of the wine and then took a little on his fingertip before passing the cup to Eliezer who did the same. Then both men touched their wet fingertips to their eyelids, to give them insight. Eliezer also touched his finger to his empty purse, as did Isaac haParnas when the wine cup reached him again, so that their business might prosper in the coming week. They finished Havdalah with the incantation against Potach, Prince of Forgetfulness, and then it was time to light the Hanukkah menorah.

The musicians arrived when the five small flames were nearly gutted, signaling bedtime for the younger children. While Miriam checked on Aunt Sarah, Judah tried to get his weeping middle son ready for bed.

"But I'm not sleepy yet." Shimson struggled as Judah removed his shoes and hose. "Yom Tov doesn't have to leave."

"Yom Tov is older," Judah responded calmly. "When he was your age we put him to bed even earlier, as soon as we lit the menorah."

"Just let me stay up tonight . . . please, Papa. I'll go to bed early tomorrow."

Judah pulled off his son's *bliaut* and chemise, stifling his protests. "If you go to sleep without a fuss tonight, I'll let you stay up as late as Grandmama Alvina on the eighth night." That was too easy. His mother usually went to bed as soon as the menorah flames were extinguished.

"Sit with me until I fall asleep," Shimson pleaded.

"I'll sit with you and we can say the Shema together, but I have to go help your grandpapa open the new wine. Now use the chamber pot like a good boy and get under the covers."

By the time Judah had finished saying the bedtime prayers, Shimson was asleep. He tiptoed down the stairs only to stop in consternation at the bottom.

Elisha, still wearing traveler's clothes, rushed forward to embrace him. "Judah. It's so good to see you again."

Elisha had returned to Troyes as though nothing had changed. But for Judah the blade that used to be sharp enough to cut was dull with disuse. The fire that had blazed hot enough to burn him last summer was now reduced to coals.

Judah stepped back as soon as he could without hurting Elisha's feelings. "Congratulations on your new son."

Elisha smiled and shook his head in disbelief. "Who could have imagined last year that I would be the father of Judah ben Elisha and you the father of Elisha ben Judah?"

"Miriam is done nursing your namesake. Would you like to see him?"

"I'd prefer to get something to eat," Elisha said. "I haven't eaten since *disner.*"

"You were riding on the Sabbath?" Judah's voice was heavy with disapproval. "I thought you weren't going to commit any other sins."

"We spent the Sabbath at that inn just east of Troyes," Elisha said. "I left Giuseppe there with our merchandise as soon as the sun set."

Judah felt flattered that Elisha had abandoned his new lover for him, at least for one night. He was wondering what to say when he heard Miriam on the stairs.

"Shame on you Elisha. You know how dangerous it is to ride alone by yourself on Saturday night? Especially when there's no moon." She scowled at him. "You're a father now, aren't you? You should be more responsible."

Elisha was immediately contrite. "You're right, Miriam. I'll be more careful in the future."

Judah took Elisha by the arm and led him to the door. "You picked the right time to be hungry. There's probably enough food in our court-yard to feed the whole city."

They stepped outside into the hubbub of people eating, talking, and laughing. Boys raced back and forth, stopping only long enough to wolf down some food from the long tables laden with plates and dishes. A few people were dancing, but most were milling around, eager for the mo-ment when Salomon and Isaac haParnas would open the wine casks now sitting next to the cellar doors.

"There you are, Miriam," Rachel called to her. "Papa's waiting for you."

The sisters made their way through the crowd to where their parents stood with Isaac haParnas. Joheved sat on a bench next to them, her sleep-ing baby in her arms. When Salomon saw them, he held up his cup, made the blessing over the wine, and took a drink. He smiled and gave the cup to Rivka, who tasted it and passed it on to Joheved.

"It's not bad," Joheved declared, handing the cup to Miriam. "But we've had better."

"And we've had worse," Miriam said.

"I don't have as much experience as you two." Rachel licked her lips. "But I think it tastes pretty good."

Salomon had a satisfied expression on his face. "It's not our finest vintage, but our customers will be content."

The celebration grew louder as jugs of wine began making their way around the courtyard. Miriam saw Judah and Elisha go inside to study, and she half expected Eliezer or Meir to follow them. But her two brothers-in-law headed for the dancing. Before she could decide whether to join her husband in study, Rachel seized her hand and pulled her into a circle of dancing women.

"Our nephew's *brit* was no fun at all," Rachel said. "Now we can finally celebrate . . . and I intend to."

"Meir must feel the same way," Miriam said as she watched him swing Salomon around.

Rachel lifted her skirt and twirled. "We can dance as long as we like. Judah will find you when your baby gets hungry."

"I hope Joheved doesn't get up to dance." Miriam craned her neck to see what her older sister was doing. "She shouldn't attempt anything too exhausting yet."

But Joheved was satisfied just to sit and hold her son until he needed to go back to his wet nurse. So Miriam took Rachel's hand and gave herself over to the music's joyous rhythms. She was alive, Joheved was alive, their two babies were alive—and she had successfully circumcised both of them.

The Cold Fair closed on a Friday, and the following Sunday was a snowy Christmas Day, giving Miriam an extra week to enjoy her sisters' company. For Monday and Wednesday, the second and fourth days of the week, were obviously unlucky days to begin traveling, and nobody departed on Tuesday under the malevolent influence of Mars.

Some merchants did start out on Sunday morning, ignoring the Notzrim holiday, but Eliezer preferred to wait, since the most auspicious time to begin a journey was on Thursday just after dawn, when the planet Jupiter ruled both the day and hour. Thus Salomon's courtyard was lit by torchlight that morning as Rachel loaded the last of her luggage on the cart and said a tearful good-bye to her family.

Hugs, kisses, promises to see each other again at the Hot Fair, and then they were gone. A gust of cold blew around Miriam's legs, and, shivering, she ran back inside to don her tefillin and say her morning prayers.

"Before I go back to Ramerupt I want to thank you for all you did for me while I was ill," Joheved said, taking her hand as they walked home after services. "I asked Rachel to find you another ruby, to replace the one I drank."

Miriam took a deep breath. "You may not feel thankful when you hear what I'm going to say."

Joheved looked Miriam in the eye. "I can't have any more children, is that it?" She didn't wait for an answer, adding, "It's all right; five healthy children, may the Holy One protect them, is more than enough. And with two boys and two girls, Meir has fulfilled his mitzvah to procreate no matter whose standard he uses."

Miriam shook her head. "Your labor was difficult, but I see no reason why you won't be able to have more children—eventually. However, Aunt Sarah and I agree that for your own safety, you shouldn't get pregnant again until next year."

"So, since I'm not nursing I'll have to do something to prevent it," Joheved said.

"I strongly recommend that as soon as you're healed, you start using a *mokh*." The *mokh*, a wad of wool smeared with mint oil and inserted into the woman, was the most effective contraceptive Miriam knew, but it required more diligence than drinking some herb-laced wine. It was also not as unobtrusive; so some husbands didn't like it.

"I thought the Talmud restricts who can use a *mokh*."

"I've studied that Baraita carefully," Miriam replied. "And the interpretation is ambiguous. Here's what it says:

> Three women use the *mokh*: a minor, a pregnant woman and a nursing woman. The minor, because she might become pregnant and die; the pregnant one, because her fetus might become deformed; the nursing one, because she might have to wean her child early and he would die . . . This is the opinion of Rabbi Meir. The Sages say: this one and the other have relations as usual and mercy will come from Heaven."

Joheved's forehead creased with worry. "Does this apply only to these three women or to any woman whose pregnancy is a danger to herself or her other children?"

"It depends on what Rabbi Meir means," Miriam said. "Does he intend that these three women *must* use the *mokh*, in which case the Sages say that they, and other women, *may* use it? Or that the three *may* use the *mokh*, in which case the Sages say that they, and other women, *may not*?"

"How does Papa explain it?" Joheved asked.

Miriam shook her head. "He says that 'use the *mokh*' means they are permitted to use it to avoid pregnancy, but the Sages prohibit this because the man would be wasting seed."

"But that can't be right." Joheved's voice rose. "Women aren't commanded to procreate; surely the Sages wouldn't forbid a woman whose life is in danger from using a *mokh*."

"I agree with you." Miriam's voice was firm. "I believe the Baraita is concerned with these three women because none of them are likely to get pregnant."

Joheved paused to consider this interpretation. "So they can safely rely on Heaven's mercy."

Miriam nodded. "Thus Rabbi Meir says that, although pregnancy is unlikely, they either must or may use a *mokh*; while the Sages say that, since pregnancy is unlikely, they needn't or shouldn't use one."

"Therefore a woman in true danger may certainly use a *mokh*." Joheved sighed with relief.

"And Rabbi Meir might require her to do so," Miriam added.

"But what about the man wasting seed?" Joheved asked. "If he's wasting seed when she uses a *mokh*, wouldn't he be wasting seed when she uses a sterilizing potion or they turn over the table?"

"Yet both of those are permitted," Miriam finished her sister's thought. "Do you think Papa is wrong?"

"If he means that an ordinary woman may not prevent pregnancy, no matter how dangerous it is for her, then I believe he's wrong."

"So do I," Miriam said with determination. "And I will recommend every option to my patients who must avoid pregnancy. Which reminds me—I also have some herbs for you to take."

Joheved gave her sister a hug. "I still want to thank you, for everything. I know it must have been difficult, what with Alvina visiting, Aunt Sarah being sick, and your own new baby too. At least nobody else is due to deliver until spring."

Miriam blushed. She didn't deserve any thanks; she was a midwife and Joheved was her sister. "It was difficult . . . sometimes, especially with Aunt Sarah taking so long to recover. Alvina does help with the children, but sometimes they're too much for her. I have the feeling that the Cold Fair may be Alvina's final visit to Troyes."

Joheved shrugged. "So you and Judah will take the children to Paris to see her. It's not that far."

"I suppose so. If we leave on a Sunday we can get there before Shabbat."

"I'm glad Rachel stayed until Thursday, even though Sunday ought to be the best day to start a journey," Joheved said. "When you leave on Thursday you have to stop for Shabbat after only two days of traveling."

"Sunday may be more convenient, but considering how dangerous a long trip is, I think most people would prefer to begin one when the stars are the most favorable."

Joheved sighed. "I wonder what day Eliezer's father and brother started their last journey." Miriam tried to remember what day Benjamin had left Troyes for the last time, but she couldn't recall. She did know that it wasn't a Thursday; he had departed with plenty of time to get to Rheims before the Sabbath.

twenty-nine

Troyes
Early Summer 4848 (1088 CE)

ntil Miriam became Avram's apprentice and began checking the babies three days after he circumcised them, she had no idea that so many Jews lived only a short ride away from Troyes. The women obviously used a local Edomite midwife but sent to the city for a mohel.

She usually rode past her family's vineyard without a second thought, but now it was in bloom. She'd avoided subjecting herself to the blossoms' scent on her ride to Payns, but when heading home she wondered if it was time to test her feelings. Ten years ago Benjamin had died, and only when she smelled the flowering vineyard would her deepest emotions be exposed. It would be like picking off a scab; once removed, the sore would either open up again or reveal unblemished skin.

So when the vineyard came into view, Miriam slowed her mare and allowed the heady fragrance to take her back in time. Tears welled in her eyes as she recalled that warm afternoon when Benjamin first kissed her, and with a sigh of resignation, she accepted that this wound would never fully heal.

Yet to her surprise, another memory came flooding back—her wedding night, when she and Judah had thrown the grape blossoms decorating their room out the window and spent the rest of the evening studying Talmud. She had to admit that she was proud of marrying Judah. He was a fine scholar, a very handsome man, and he treated her with respect and kindness. Heaven knows how her marriage to Benjamin would have turned out. Probably her children wouldn't be nearly such good scholars, or so good-looking. Miriam smiled and sighed again as she thought of them. Judah

390

had given her three wonderful sons, the lights of her life. Just thinking of them made her breasts ache, and Miriam realized with a start how low the sun was in the sky. It was almost time to nurse little Elisha.

She rode back to Troyes, still sorting out her feelings. Her reverie ended abruptly when one of the guards at the Prés Gate motioned her toward him.

"*Bonjour*, Mistress," he greeted her. "I haven't seen your father coming through my gate recently. I hope all is well."

"All is well," Miriam replied. "The vineyard is blossoming and we don't work in it during this time." *How odd that the guard suddenly wants to converse with me.* For years her family had been passing through this gate every day on their way to the vineyard, and he had never said more than *bonjour*.

"Since you're here today, maybe you could help us with this fellow." He indicated a dark-haired young man fidgeting nearby.

The youth's clothes, while finely made, were clearly not of the local style, and a saddlebag lay at his feet. His swarthy complexion further proclaimed his foreignness.

"It's unusual for a stranger to arrive alone at this gate, especially with a saddlebag and no horse," the guard said, scowling at his prisoner. Merchants usually came in caravan, entering through one of the western or southern gates that led to the fairgrounds.

"And he doesn't have any merchandise, only his clothes and some books." The guard showed one of them to Miriam.

The young man protested vigorously in some unfamiliar language as she opened the book, and he stared at her in shock when she addressed him in Hebrew. "Don't worry, you're safe now. I'll take you to the synagogue."

She turned back to the guard. "He's one of my father's new students. *Merci* for finding him for us."

The guard nodded for the young man to go. As he left with Miriam, she heard the guard saying, "Her father, the vintner—you'd never know it to look at him, but merchants come from all over to study with him."

"Shalom aleichem. What's your name?" Miriam asked the foreign youth as they walked.

"Aleichem shalom. My name is Aaron ben Isaac."

"By the way, this year we're studying Tractate Sanhedrin, not Kiddushin." She waited to see his reaction.

"I also have Sanhedrin . . ." He stopped short and stared at her. "You recognized my book?"

"I'm Miriam, Salomon ben Isaac's daughter." She smiled at his consternation. "He taught me Talmud, along with my two sisters, and I assume you're here to study with him as well."

Aaron looked at her with suspicion. "Where I come from nobody teaches girls Talmud."

"And where do you come from?" Miriam asked coldly.

"My family lives in Sepharad, in Cordoba."

"You came all that way alone? Not speaking our language?" Her opinion of the stranger softened.

"I traveled with merchants to Provins, but they stopped there to attend the fair," he said. "Then my horse came up lame, so I had to leave him at a village nearby. The blacksmith said he wouldn't be healed for weeks."

"That must have been quite a journey."

Aaron grinned widely, displaying a missing tooth whose gap made him look like a mischievous child. "I managed."

Miriam began to reassess her judgment of Aaron. Of course he was surprised that she studied Talmud; he was from Sepharad, where they considered teaching one's daughter Torah like teaching her lechery.

"You heard about Papa's yeshiva all the way in Cordoba? He'll be pleased."

"Everyone said the Talmud masters were in Ashkenaz, but on the way I heard about the yeshiva in Troyes, and I was quite relieved not to travel all the way to Mayence."

As Aaron continued to talk about the Talmud academies he'd studied at—he'd even spent a year in Damascus—and how they compared to each other, Miriam surreptitiously scrutinized him. *Was it the hot weather that caused men from the south to dress so flamboyantly?*

His chemise's neckline was cut so deeply that his chest hair was exposed above it. And while young men usually wore their *bliauts* knee length or above, Aaron's was so short that his *braises* were clearly visible. Miriam tried not to stare, but what were they made of?

"Pardon me, Aaron." Miriam had to say it twice to get his attention. "I've never seen *braises* like yours. Are they common in Cordoba?"

Aaron lifted up his *bliaut* to better display his *braises*, which were either dark brown or black. "They're leather, but made from a thinner part of the hide than shoes. They're very comfortable for riding. Most men in Cordoba have them."

Miriam quickly averted her gaze from the skintight material encasing Aaron's thighs. Leather *braises* would be difficult to clean, but maybe men in Cordoba wore regular linen *braises* underneath. She certainly wasn't going to ask him and turned her mind to more practical matters. Aaron hadn't mentioned knowing anyone is Troyes, and with the Hot Fair approaching he'd be hard-pressed to find lodgings. Well, there was always room for another student in the attic.

"You must be hungry," she said. "We'll go to our house first, and then to the synagogue."

By the time the Hot Fair began, Aaron was at home in the attic and in the yeshiva. The other students doted on stories of life in Sepharad, especially his married life, since he'd been wed for a year. Salomon was thrilled with Aaron's knowledge of Talmud, interpretations gleaned from years of study with Sephardic scholars.

Miriam, along with her mother and her sisters, found Aaron charming. He complimented their clothes and their cooking, and Rachel found his opinions helpful in determining which pieces of jewelry would be popular with which clients. Miriam thought that Aaron would make a perfect study partner for her husband, but Judah surprised her by remaining with Eliezer, even though the two were no longer equal in knowledge. So Papa asked Elisha to study with Aaron for the summer.

To Miriam's dismay, Judah seemed to take an immediate dislike to the fellow. He not only avoided sitting next to Aaron, but he chose a seat as far away from the new student as possible. Like Papa, Judah always tried to praise his pupils when they asked clever questions and to make sure he answered them completely. But Judah treated Aaron's queries dismissively, with replies so curt that they almost stung. Other students challenged Judah if they disagreed with him, but when Aaron did this, Judah chastised him to respect his teacher.

And so Aaron became two different people. In the large synagogue class with the merchants, his knowledge and enthusiasm merited him a seat at the front. There, Aaron was garrulous, asking questions and provoking discussions, but in their salon, he restrained himself. Judah's students usually took their meals at his table, but Aaron ate at Salomon's. Miriam couldn't understand what had come over her husband; surely he wasn't jealous of the attention Papa had lavished on the newcomer.

Judah had no idea that his wife was aware of his efforts to distance himself from Aaron. But from the moment they'd met, when Judah recognized the frank appraisal in Aaron's eyes and felt himself responding in kind, Judah understood the danger. And so he refused to be the young man's study partner rather than risk another bout of the pain he'd suffered with Elisha.

But the stars had mocked his sacrifice, arranging for Aaron to study with Elisha and denying him the company of both men. As if that weren't bad enough, fate brought Natan ben Abraham to Troyes' yeshiva.

"Shalom aleichem, Judah." That silky smooth voice sounded nearly the same as ten years ago. "You're even more handsome than when I last saw you."

Judah looked around to see who might be listening, but the students were gathered around Salomon. "Aleichem shalom, Natan. So our Hot Fair has brought you all the way from Prague."

Natan's hair was now silvery white, his belly was a bit larger, and he wore a sapphire ring in addition to the emerald and black pearl rings he'd had before. "I've heard about the Troyes fairs, and when Reuben mentioned seeing you, I decided to pay your city a visit."

Natan still had his old charisma, but Judah observed his lecherous smile and felt his insides curdle at how he'd almost sinned with this man. "Then he must have told you that I don't play the game."

"He did," Natan said cheerfully, ignoring Judah's coldness. "But there are plenty of other men here who do."

Judah searched for a new topic of conversation. "You've studied at every Rhineland yeshiva. How does ours compare?"

"I don't know how it is when the merchants are gone, but now it's more than adequate. It's interesting to study with so many foreign scholars. Some of their knowledge is unique."

They discussed the texts that Salomon had been teaching in Troyes and compared them with the ones that Natan had studied recently in Mayence and Worms. Judah was almost feeling comfortable when Aaron walked by, paused, and then kept going.

Natan threw his arm around Judah's shoulders and began to laugh. "You don't fool me. You may not play the game, but it's not because you don't want to. That Sephardic fellow would be in your bed in a moment if you'd say the word."

Judah threw off Natan's embrace. "How dare you?"

Still chuckling, Natan shook his head. "Ah well, your loss may be my gain."

Judah watched with horror as Natan hurried after Aaron. At *disner*, every time someone entered who wasn't Aaron, his anxiety and anger grew. Only when the meal was finished did Aaron and Elisha arrive, talking and laughing together, leaving Judah not knowing which he wanted to do, hit Aaron or kiss him. In his consternation he knocked over his wine cup, earning him a penetrating stare from Miriam.

Ah, Miriam. What would his wife think if she knew that he went to sleep terrified lest Lillit visit him in Aaron's form? Or that he came to Miriam at night aroused to the point of madness from imagining Natan and Aaron together. Did Miriam suspect anything? She was fond of Aaron; all the women were. And so, Heaven help him, was he.

Thus the miserable summer passed. Judah stayed up late and woke early to study, argued furiously with Eliezer over every interpretation of the passages they studied, and snapped at his sons when they needed his help. He kept a covert watch on Aaron's comings and goings, yet he avoided Aaron as much as it was possible for a teacher to avoid his own student. That is, until it was time for the wine harvest and he found himself treading grapes one night in the same vat as Aaron.

It was early in the process, when the grapes needed continuous treading. As usual, Miriam, Joheved, and Anna spent mornings and afternoons in one vat, while members of the congregation rotated among the others. Most merchants and students had gone home for Rosh Hashanah, so until the initial *bouillage* phase of fermentation was finished, Judah treaded for one of the lengthy night shifts as well as during the day.

Many in the community enjoyed the camaraderie, but jumping around half-naked in the fizzing grape juice, the woody stems flogging his exposed lower limbs, was an ordeal for Judah. So when Salomon woke him at midnight for another turn in the vats, Judah was in a foul mood. Groggy from lack of sleep, his arms and legs sore from the unaccustomed physical labor, Judah threw on his stained chemise and trudged downstairs to the moonlit courtyard. He tied on his linen boots and lowered himself into the fizzing half wine, almost cursing when the acid liquid stung a cut he'd received on his leg earlier. Then he looked up and his jaw dropped.

Aaron was standing opposite him, struggling to turn over the raft of grapes and stems with his paddle—stark naked.

Judah looked away immediately, but the vision of droplets of grape juice dripping through Aaron's chest hair and further down his torso was already seared in his memory. Most of the students preferred to work naked in the vats at night, another reason treading the vintage was a trying experience for Judah. Not that he could argue with them. Why should they ruin their chemises when there were no women present and it was too dark for anyone inside to see them?

Judah took up his paddle, resigned to the situation by his duty to Salomon. The lewd songs and raucous laughter coming from the other vats made him grimace. Nighttime treading was a giant party for the students, and Salomon encouraged them to enjoy themselves as long as they kept the grapes roiling.

Judah forced himself to concentrate on digging his paddle as deep as he could into the tangled raft before hauling it up, turning it over, and treading it back in. Each hour would seem an eternity, but he would get through it, and from now on he'd look to see who was in the vat before he got in.

"Judah." Aaron's voice broke his concentration.

"What?" Judah made no attempt to hide his irritation.

"Would you please tell me what I've done this summer to anger you?"

"I'm not angry at you." *Why is Aaron choosing this moment to ask about my feelings?*

"Then why do you treat me so badly?"

"I treat you the same as all my students," Judah said, uneasy about where the conversation might lead.

"*Non*, you don't. You usually ignore my questions, and when you do deign to answer them you act like I've said something stupid or obscene."

"You're too sensitive, you've imagined things." *Have I really been so unkind?* He hadn't meant to hurt Aaron, never that.

They trod the grapes silently for a while, with Judah hopeful that his shift would end without further conversation.

"One thing I haven't imagined," Aaron said. "You never look at me when you talk to me."

It was true. Looking at Aaron filled Judah with a painful longing. Still, he had no choice now but to face Aaron and let his emotions take the consequences.

"I'm looking at you now. And if you have any Talmud questions you think I haven't answered properly, feel free to ask them." Judah continued to stare at Aaron, determined that he would not be the one to look away.

"I'll need a little time to think of them all," Aaron replied, locking eyes with Judah.

They kept each other in view as they moved around the vat, until suddenly Aaron started to look embarrassed. He averted his gaze from Judah, turned around, and kept his back to Judah as much as possible. Judah couldn't imagine what had caused this furtive behavior until Aaron lifted up a paddle full of grapes and stems, causing the liquid level to fall.

Aaron had an erection.

Judah immediately scooped up a large section of the raft and dumped it between them. Aaron's state wasn't unusual; students got erections in the vats occasionally, prompting a round of jokes and teasing.

But to his horror, Judah felt himself growing aroused. Now he was trapped. Any moment the raft would shift position and expose him. But if he attempted to get out of the vat, his condition would be obvious to Aaron, and perhaps even to the nearby students. In desperation Judah drove his paddle into his injured leg. The pain caused him to lose his balance, and Aaron hurried to catch him before he was completely submerged. They gazed at each other, nose to nose.

"Now you know how I feel about you," Aaron said, his eyes full of regret. "I wish it could have been different between us."

Before Judah could find a response, the church bells began to chime None, signaling the end of their shift. The treaders vacated the vats and headed for the well to wash. If they hurried to bed, they might manage three hours of sleep before dawn brought another day of working on the vintage.

"Judah, wake up."

"What's wrong?" Miriam wouldn't have woken him up unless it was an emergency.

"You've got to talk to Aaron. He's leaving."

Judah was too groggy to comprehend. "Where's he going?"

"I don't know whether he's going to Mayence or back to Sepharad. He told me he can't study Talmud in Troyes anymore." Miriam was near tears. "You must stop him. He's our first student from Sepharad. We can't let him leave and tell everyone how awful our yeshiva is."

"Papa should talk to him, not me."

"It's your fault that he's leaving, not Papa's."

Judah was wide-awake now. "What are you talking about?"

"I don't know why you dislike Aaron, but I'm sure he doesn't deserve it." Miriam grabbed Judah's arm and pulled him out of bed. "It's a sin to keep someone from studying Torah. So if Aaron goes before you ask him to forgive you, you'll never see him again and even Yom Kippur won't atone for the damage you've done."

Judah pulled on his clothes and raced out the front door, Miriam at his heels. Maybe Aaron was still in the courtyard.

Miriam hurried to the gate and peered outside into the predawn gloom. "He's gone." She leaned against the doorway and began to cry.

"*Non*," Judah shouted. "He has to get his horse from the stables."

"Take your mantle if you're going out on the street," she called after him, but it was too late. Judah had disappeared around the corner.

Judah was running too hard to worry about the cold. He dashed through the muddy streets, leaving a trail of cursing servants in his wake, until he came to the road where the stables were located. The sun was just rising, but it was light enough to provide a clear view down the street, a street without a single person on horseback.

Judah let out a sigh of relief and slowed to a walk as the morning bells began to ring. Most folks didn't get up until Prime, so stable hands would need even more time to prepare a horse if they didn't know about it the night before. Aaron was likely to still be there. But what was Judah going to say to him? The truth?

The voices complaining inside quieted as Judah walked through the stable gates. Two boys were trying to saddle a dappled horse that obviously wanted to eat instead, but there was no sign of Aaron.

"Excuse me," Judah asked the older boy. "Can you tell me where this horse's owner is? He forgot some of his things."

"He's at the inn next door," came the surly reply. "I'm not surprised he forgot something, he was in such a hurry. But you can't hurry horses, no sir. Folks who want to leave at first light need to inform us in advance." The litany of complaints continued as Judah edged his way toward the doorway.

Suddenly the gate swung open and in marched Aaron. "How much longer until my horse is ready?" he demanded.

"He'll be ready when he's ready," the boy replied. Aaron turned to stalk out and nearly ran into Judah. They stared wordlessly at each other until Aaron said, "What the devil are you doing here?"

"I came to ask you not to leave." Aaron's expression hardened, and Judah quickly added, "I want to apologize to you. You were right. I did treat you badly."

"You're too late. As soon as my horse is saddled, I'm going."

Judah fought his rising panic. "It's almost Yom Kippur. At least listen to me first."

"I'm listening." Aaron put his hands on his hips.

Judah looked Aaron straight in the eye. "I don't want you to go. I want you to stay and study with me . . . very much." Then he held his breath, waiting for the stars to seal his fate. The heat his body had generated while running was finally gone and he began to shiver.

The stable boy called out, "Are you leaving this morning or not?"

Aaron's expression relaxed. He opened his mantle and flung it around both their shoulders. "You can apologize indoors, where it's warmer." He tossed the boy a coin. "Just feed my horse for now. If I want him saddled, I'll let you know."

"Whatever you say, milord."

As soon as they shut the inn's sturdy wooden door behind them, the pungent smell and sizzling sound of bacon cooking took Judah back to his early yeshiva days, when he and Azariel stayed overnight at so many inns like this.

Aaron led him to a table next to the hearth, where the innkeeper soon brought them a platter of food and two steaming mugs of ale.

"No bacon for us," Aaron said, waving that serving dish away. "But we'll have some eggs and cheese."

The fragrance of fresh bread made Judah realize that he was famished from all his work on the vintage. But he couldn't relax and eat until he'd heard Aaron forgive him.

"I've never disliked you," Judah began. "If anything, I liked you too much."

Aaron smiled. "You had an odd way of showing it."

"I didn't mean to be cruel to you, but I was so focused on fighting my *yetzer hara* that I never considered how my behavior would affect you. I hope you can forgive me."

"You were fighting your *yetzer hara*?" Aaron squinted up at him. "I don't understand."

Judah took a deep breath and slowly let it out. "Please don't tell anyone, but a couple of years ago I became overly fond of one of my students. When he left the yeshiva, as all students do eventually, the pain of losing him was almost more than I could bear." Judah could feel the tears forming.

"I'm sorry." Aaron reached across the table and squeezed Judah's hand.

Judah didn't pull his hand away. "I promised myself to never let it happen again, and then you showed up. You're smart and charming, and I've been struggling with my *yetzer hara* all summer."

"I thought you hated me."

"I think I hated how you made me feel," Judah said. "Now that you know, I hope you won't still want to leave Troyes. But if you do, I ask you to forgive me first."

Aaron began to chuckle. "After what you just told me, the last thing I want to do is leave Troyes." Then his expression grew serious. "There's no need to ask for my forgiveness. I was leaving this morning because I was sure you'd inform Rav Salomon about my behavior in the vat. Elisha told me what happened to him in Mayence, and I didn't want to wait around to be expelled."

Judah almost told Aaron about his own reaction in the vat, but said instead, "Trying to protect myself is no excuse for how I mistreated you. Will you forgive me?"

Aaron squeezed Judah's hand again. "Of course I forgive you. You're rather smart and charming yourself," he said with a grin. "And don't worry. It will be many years before I must choose between the yeshiva and my family's business."

Judah gently pulled his hand away. "Aaron, I will study with you and be your friend, but you must understand that I will never engage in any sinful carnal actions with you." He lowered his voice but still said firmly, "Don't even think about it."

Aaron nodded. "So we will be like the study partners in Avot de Rabbi Natan.

> A man should get a companion to eat with him, drink with him, read Torah with him, study Mishnah with him, sleep with him and share all his secrets with him—secrets of Torah and secrets of worldly matters.

Except, of course, that we won't sleep together." Then he added, "But don't expect me not to think about it."

Judah sighed. He'd be thinking about it too.

"Since you've just shared your secrets with me, I have one to share with you," Aaron said. "That student you cared for so much before—was it Elisha?"

"How did you know?"

"I was Elisha's study partner all summer. In addition to Talmud, we discussed you."

"Does he know how I felt about him?"

"Don't worry. He has no idea that you ever wanted him as badly as he wanted you."

"That's a relief." Judah sighed. "He seems happy with the arrangement he and Giuseppe have now . . . although I don't understand what he sees in someone so uneducated."

Aaron shrugged. "Giuseppe adores him."

"Enough eating, drinking, and telling secrets." Judah wiped his hands on the tablecloth and stood up. "It's time to go back and start studying Torah." Miriam would be waiting anxiously for him to return with Aaron.

That night in the wine vat with Aaron, Judah couldn't believe how much had changed in twenty-four hours. Miriam had been nearly ecstatic in her relief when they returned, hugging both of them. When Salomon heard that Aaron had decided to study in Troyes permanently and that Judah had agreed to be his study partner, he asked them to work on his Talmud commentaries together, to make sure that both Ashkenaz and Sephardic interpretations were considered.

"This is truly sharing secrets of Torah," Aaron exclaimed when he saw the extent of Salomon's *kuntres*. "Promise me that when I finally have to leave Troyes, I can take a copy with me so I'll never forget my learning." Aaron gazed up at Judah and added, "Or you."

Judah's spirits soared. "We will harness our passion for each other and use it for Torah study."

"Just like Rav Yohanan and Reish Lakish. You can be Rav Yohanan, my beautiful, beardless teacher . . ."

"And you will be Reish Lakish, my strong, bandit student?" Judah asked, flattered and amused at Aaron's comparison. Then he grew serious. "Except we won't let any misunderstandings ruin our friendship."

"In Sepharad we have a saying about men as beautiful as you," Aaron whispered. "In his youth he seduces men away from their wives, and in maturity he seduces women away from their husbands."

"Don't say that, not even in a whisper. You'll tempt the Evil Eye. It's enough to be likened to Rav Yohanan, a great teacher who fathered ten sons."

Miriam insisted that it was dangerous for Aaron to sleep alone in the attic now that the students had gone, and she arranged for him to share Yom Tov and Shimson's room. Which meant that he and Judah were in each other's company from early in the morning, when they came downstairs together, to late at night, when they said *bonne nuit* in the hall before disappearing into their adjoining rooms. During the day they edited Salomon's commentaries, falling into the familiar intimacy of Talmud study.

As the vintage continued night after night, they shared their life stories, talking about their families, childhoods, and how they had come to be scholars. Eventually they spoke of deeper things, and, finally, of the difficulties of yeshiva life with a *yetzer hara* that became attracted to other students.

Aaron rarely spoke of his wife (he had yet to mention her name), but Judah was proud to explain how he had come to marry such an exemplary women as Miriam, the rosh yeshiva's daughter, a *mohelet*, and a scholar in her own right.

"It is because of her that I am able to control my *yetzer hara*." Judah silently gave thanks that he had followed Reuben's earlier advice. "You must find it difficult to only visit your wife once a year, at Passover."

Aaron shrugged. "Such a thing is common in Sepharad; the merchants who travel to India may be away from home for years."

"Men like me and Meir are unusual," Judah said, thinking of how

Miriam had come to be the mohel's apprentice. "When Papa was a student he only came home for the three festivals, and traders in Troyes often travel for months at a time as well."

"Some men don't mind being away from their wives. Look at Elisha and Giuseppe; they have the perfect arrangement."

The wistful tone of Aaron's voice made Judah certain that Aaron was one of those men. He was about to say how much he enjoyed being with his sons every day, watching them grow up. Little Elisha was walking now, and Miriam had started teaching Shimson to read Torah. Yom Tov was already more advanced in Mishnah than Judah had been at that age. But Aaron was unlikely to have the same opportunity, assuming he had any sons, and Judah saw no reason to remind him of this.

By the time the Cold Fair began, Salomon was so pleased with the progress Judah and Aaron were making on his *kuntres* that he asked Shemayah to teach the advanced students, freeing Judah to continue editing. Judah was happy to oblige, so happy that he began to fear that others would discover, and condemn, his newfound source of happiness.

Merchants like Natan and Levi would surely recognize how his relationship with Aaron differed from that of study partners like Meir and Shemayah. No matter how platonic their behavior, or how carefully he guarded himself, someone might see something, or hear something, that would give them away. The gossip would start and before he knew it, Fleur's relatives would be interrupting services to denounce him and Aaron. The Troyes yeshiva would be rocked with scandal, Papa's reputation ruined.

Judah saw no choice but to distance himself from Aaron to avoid suspicion, at least during the Cold Fair. It took several days to muster the courage to discuss his worries with the object of his affection, but to his relief, Aaron understood. They agreed that for the fair's duration, when so many eyes might be watching, Aaron would spend his evenings with the Sephardic merchants or other advanced students. Judah easily kept Salomon company at night, but it was not so easy to keep from dwelling on where Aaron was or why he came home so late.

iriam was too worried about her aunt to notice her husband's changing moods. Aunt Sarah, her mentor and friend, who had been almost a second mother to her, was dying. The elderly midwife never fully recovered from her illness the previous winter, and then the Hot Fair brought some new pestilence to Troyes. By Hanukkah her family acknowledged the inevitable.

They kept the lamp in Sarah's room burning and never left her alone. Nearly every Jewish woman in town came to visit and settle any quarrels they might have had during her lifetime; the exception being those named Sarah themselves. Heaven forbid the Angel of Death should arrive for the invalid and claim another with the same name.

Sarah's last days presented a challenge to her family. They wanted her death to be peaceful, which meant preventing a painful battle between the *mazikim* and her soul at the final moment. On the other hand, the Angel of Death must be permitted to perform its ultimate assignment and the spirits of recent dead allowed to welcome her to the next world. Thus Sarah's visitors were careful to keep her limbs within the confines of her bed, so demons couldn't grab them, but they didn't recite the usual anti-demonic prayers, such as Psalm 91.

Instead Miriam chanted from the thirtieth chapter of Exodus twice a day when she recited the Shema:

Adonai said to Moses: Take the herbs stacte, onycha and galbanum, together with pure frankincense . . . Beat this into a powder and put it before the Ark in the Tent of Meeting, where I will meet with you.

Everyone knew that merely the description of preparing incense for the Holy Temple could evoke its power to repel the *mazikim* responsible for a person's death agony. And with the daily repetition of these verses, Miriam came to accept that her source of midwife lore and advice would soon be gone.

Rivka and her guests kept Sarah company during the daytime, leaving Joheved and Miriam to sit with her at night while their husbands studied at the synagogue. It was an opportunity to study without their children interrupting and, once Aunt Sarah was asleep, to discuss subjects that required privacy.

"Is it safe to stop taking the sterilizing herbs?" Joheved asked. Without looking she pulled a strand of wool from her distaff, twisted it into thread, and wound it onto her spindle.

"I think you've waited long enough," Miriam replied. "As long as it doesn't bother you to use the bed."

Joheved shook her head. "It did at first, but now it feels like it did before. We haven't overturned the table in months."

"We just studied an interesting text in Sanhedrin about that," Miriam said.

"Can you teach it to me?"

"I can teach it to you tonight. It's not very long; one line of Mishnah, then the Gemara on it:

These are to be stoned . . . one who lies with a male. How do we derive this?"

"Obviously from the Arayot in Leviticus," Joheved answered and quoted the passage.

"A man who lies with a male, the layings of a woman . . . they shall be put to death."

Miriam smiled. "I thought that was the text too, but it's not." She quoted the Gemara:

> "'The layings of a woman'—this plural teaches that there are two ways to lie with women. R. Yishmael says that this text is not about men; it is teaching about prohibited relations with women."

"Really?" Joheved stared at Miriam with surprise.

"Papa says the two kinds of lying with women are natural and unnatural, that is, turning over the table. Whoever lies with a woman forbidden to him is liable no matter which way he does it."

"I see. A man who thinks he's not committing adultery because they're turning over the table . . ." Joheved began.

"Has indeed committed the sin if the woman is married to someone else," Miriam concluded.

"Meir told me that turning over the table is permitted so that a man won't do *mishkav zachur*," Joheved said.

"Perhaps." Miriam paused to consider this. "Remember what Yalta told her husband in Tractate Chullin:

> All that the Merciful One prohibited to us, He permitted us something similar. Blood is forbidden, but liver is permitted. Laying with a *niddah* is forbidden, but permitted with a virgin or a woman after childbirth. Pork is forbidden, but the fish *shibuta* is permitted. It is forbidden to lay with a married woman, but permitted to lie with a divorcée while her husband is alive."

Joheved smiled at Miriam. "We're so lucky to have each other to study with. I miss this so much when I'm in Ramerupt."

Miriam smiled in return. "So do I."

"I didn't think it would work out, but Meir has been study partners with Shemayah for over ten years," Joheved said. "I don't know what he'd do without him."

"I thought you didn't like Shemayah."

"I've changed my mind." Joheved sighed. "He was so faithful while I was ill last year, sitting with Meir all day and into the night as well."

"Have you changed your mind about his daughter?"

Joheved nodded. "Let me tell you what I intend to do about her." She leaned forward and lowered her voice. "I heard that many children have died of the pox in Prague and cases are starting to appear in Allemagne. So it's only a matter of time before we have the pox in Troyes."

Miriam shuddered. "I have heard this." Though she tried to keep the gruesome images out of her mind, sometimes she couldn't help but imagine her precious sons covered with sores.

"The air in the country is better than in the city, so I'm inviting Zipporah to stay with us. She can start learning how to manage the estate, which she'll need to do as Isaac's wife, and hopefully she'll be protected from the pox." Joheved sounded confident. "Isaac and Shmuel were in Ramerupt for the last epidemic and barely got sick at all."

"I'll send my boys to you too," Miriam said. *But will country air really protect against the pox?* She couldn't shake the fear that, after several mild epidemics, the pox was gathering strength for the coming attack. And then no place would be safe for her sons.

But Joheved wasn't concerned with the pox. "I'm going to start teaching Zipporah Torah, as well as how to spin wool properly," she said. "As much as I miss having my baby with me, keeping little Salomon in Troyes with his wet nurse has given me time to teach Hannah and Leah their letters. Zipporah can study along with my daughters; it doesn't matter that she's older."

Joheved paused and frowned. "But I'll have to ask Isaac to tutor Milo in Hebrew once Zipporah is here. That boy is too handsome and clever to study with her."

"Milo is learning Hebrew? Whatever for?" Miriam asked.

"He was learning how to keep our estate's accounts with Hebrew letters, and he said our way is much easier than with Roman numerals," Joheved replied. "Then he wanted to learn to read Hebrew, to understand Jewish business contracts. It wasn't difficult to teach him along with the girls; he already knows the Bible in Latin."

"So having Milo squire for you hasn't been a problem."

"Not at all. Emeline was right about how good a student he is. The only problem is that the village girls, and some of the ladies at Count André's court, can't seem to leave him alone."

"You don't worry that he'll be a bad influence on Isaac?"

Joheved smiled. "Isaac will be a good influence on Milo."

The two sisters fell silent. Miriam chastised herself for not asking about little Salomon once her sister mentioned him, something Joheved rarely did. She felt guilty that her baby, only a month older than his cousin, was doing so much better. It was painful for Miriam to watch them together; it must be far more so for Joheved. Elisha was not only walking, he was usually running around, while little Salomon could barely sit up. Elisha was constantly babbling, yet his cousin was silent.

Miriam sighed at another opportunity lost. And now the pox was coming. Maybe Joheved was right. The last two times the pox struck Troyes weren't so terrible; hopefully it would be like that this year. But country air hadn't protected Meir's siblings and neighbors. She remembered his sister's *tahara*, when Marona told them how every woman in Ramerupt had buried children during a pox epidemic, some losing all of them.

Soon they would be doing *tahara* again. Tears stung Miriam's eyes as she thought about Aunt Sarah and all she'd taught her. She recalled their many outings in the forest, gathering herbs and learning her family's history, until her thoughts were interrupted by a dog howling outside, followed by another and then another throughout the neighborhood.

Joheved frowned. "Why do dogs have to whine like that, all together?" Then her eyes opened wide and she jumped up, her spindle and distaff falling to the floor.

Nobody understood why some animals were sensitive to the presence of *mazikim*, but a dog's disconsolate howl was a sure sign that the Angel of Death was roaming nearby.

Miriam immediately joined her sister at Aunt Sarah's side. While Joheved listened at their aunt's chest, Miriam felt for a pulse, and at the same moment that she realized there was none Joheved stood up and slowly shook her head.

They embraced, tears running silently down their cheeks, until Joheved let go, saying, "*Baruch Dayan Emet.* Shall I go dump this water or do you want to?" One of them would have to remain with the corpse.

"You do it. I don't mind staying here for a while."

Joheved carefully picked up the bowl of water sitting near the bedside. The Angel of Death, its mission fulfilled, was supposed to dip its poisoned sword in the nearest container of water, but as a precaution they would discard every drop of water in the house. Some said to discard the water lest the deceased's soul drown in it, while others said the soul bathes in it upon leaving for the next world.

Miriam didn't know which of these were true, but it didn't matter. Mama would see to it that all the water in the house was removed. Aunt Sarah's eyes were already closed, and her limbs were nowhere near the edge of the bed, so the only thing Miriam needed to do was arrange the corpse's fingers to form the holy name Shaddai. Then she resumed her spinning and began reciting psalms, satisfied that their efforts had made Aunt Sarah's death so easy that she and Joheved weren't aware of anything amiss when it happened.

No one at morning services was surprised to hear about Sarah's funeral that afternoon. There were funerals in Troyes every day now, and some of the gravediggers wanted to prepare two graves simultaneously to save time. But a grave left open after sunset would only tempt the Angel of Death to fill it as soon as possible, and thus, no matter how severe a pestilence hit the city, graves were only dug for those who needed them.

Sarah's status as the rosh yeshiva's unmarried sister-in-law ensured that most merchant-scholars would attend the funeral and at least one of the seven days of shiva. Judah tried to hide his discomfort when Natan showed up each morning to pray with the mourners; after all, the man was performing a mitzvah.

But did Natan have to keep staring at him and Aaron? And did anyone else, especially someone from Fleur's family, think Aaron was acting too sympathetic over Judah's loss? As much as he wanted Aaron's comfort, Judah forced himself to avoid any overt signs of affection between them.

"I will be going back to the Rhineland once the fair ends," Natan said to Miriam. "I would consider it an honor to deliver a message to your cousin in Speyer."

"That's not necessary," Judah said immediately.

Miriam looked at her husband in surprise. Why should he object to the offer?

Judah realized he had spoken too quickly. "I'm sure you're in a hurry to attend to your business in Mayence."

"I will gladly wait to fulfill such a mitzvah." Natan bowed and headed toward a group of merchants chatting together softly, one that included Aaron and several men Judah recognized as playing the game.

"Why were you so rude to that man Natan?" Miriam asked him later. "He's doing us a big favor to take the news and Aunt Sarah's things to Cousin Eleazar."

Aunt Sarah had left her house and furnishings to Miriam and Judah, in gratitude for caring for her during her old age, but her jewelry and money would go to her son. To Miriam's relief, there were no debts. Sarah had invested her *ketubah* money in many business partnerships, providing capital for merchants to buy goods at the Troyes fairs that they later sold for profit far away. The amount of her money on credit with the fair accountants would help assuage Eleazar's sadness when he learned of his mother's death.

Despite Judah's misgivings, Miriam found that Natan was uniformly regarded as reliable in his business dealings. And if he had difficulty resisting a handsome youth, well, there were worse sins in the world. Even Isaac haParnas recommended him.

Thus, the first Thursday after the Cold Fair ended, Judah entrusted Natan with a box containing Sarah's jewelry and letters of credit. As they shook hands, Judah couldn't help but notice that Natan's one piece of tasteful jewelry, the black pearl ring, had been replaced with one containing a garish orange topaz. Natan's embrace good-bye was both too long and too tight, but Judah thankfully felt no pleasure from it.

Between the continued pestilence that sickened so many of the elderly and the first cases of pox among the city's children, the Jews of Troyes found it difficult to anticipate a joyous Purim. And not just

Troyes but all the towns in Champagne were affected. Marona fell ill in mid-January and succumbed before the month was over, forcing Joheved and Meir into mourning at the height of the lambing season.

Judah and Shemayah took Meir's students to Ramerupt to make a minyan for the first seven days of mourning, while Miriam stayed in Troyes. She felt guilty knowing Joheved was observing shiva without her or their parents, but Salomon had become feverish the week before, followed by Rivka a few days later. Miriam was so busy caring for them that she almost regretted sending Yom Tov to Ramerupt with his cousins; he at least could have kept Shimson occupied.

She woke Saturday morning determined to attend synagogue for the first time that week. But there were scarcely any women to lead services for; apparently most of them were tending other invalids or were ill themselves. Suddenly realizing that Meir had been gone over a week, Miriam hurried to visit little Salomon.

The wet nurse began to weep as soon as Miriam entered her small home. "Thank Heaven you're here. I've been so worried. I went to Lord Meir's house twice but they told me he was away, to come back next week."

Miriam's stomach tightened with fear. "What's the matter?"

"See for yourself," she said, leading Miriam to the cradle by the hearth.

Miriam thought her heart would break when she saw her poor little nephew lying there limply, his face and arms covered with the pox's bright red pustules. "Oh, *non*. Meir hasn't been to visit because his mother just died," she explained, fighting back tears. "This will devastate them."

The woman shook her head and blew her nose on her sleeve. "There's not much hope for the little fellow. The sores in his mouth are so bad that he won't nurse, and it's all I can do to get some broth into him."

"I can't ride to Ramerupt today, it's our Sabbath," Miriam said, trying not to gag.

Even if she sent an Edomite with a message, Joheved and Meir were forbidden to interrupt shiva for his mother, so the news would only cause them unnecessary pain. A child this sick couldn't be moved.

"I've been paid until the end of the month," the wet nurse said. "So I don't mind keeping the poor babe a while longer."

"They'll be done mourning tomorrow, and if Meir isn't here by noon, I'll send a message to him."

Miriam wasn't usually squeamish, but she couldn't wait to get outside and away from the horrific scene. She trudged onto the street, the vision of little Salomon's poxy body seared in her mind, and vomited into the mud.

How long before her own little Elisha lay in his cradle, suffering similar sores? How long before all her sons were covered with them? When she got home she hugged Elisha so tightly he complained she was hurting him.

The next morning Meir arrived to find that his youngest son had died during the night, bringing him the dreadful task of transporting the small body back to Ramerupt for another funeral and another seven days of mourning. Miriam held her weeping sister's hand during the funeral and wept with her, but the next day a message came that Rivka's fever was spiking, sending Miriam and Judah anxiously hurrying back to Troyes. Purim was less than three weeks away.

As the festival grew closer, Miriam understood that Meir and Joheved, still mourning for Marona and baby Salomon, would not come into town for Purim. Papa had little enthusiasm about the holiday; he'd been ill for a month and the vineyard pruning was badly behind schedule. Mama, still weak and mourning her sister, was in no mood to host the feast that usually took place in their courtyard. She clutched her amulet and prayed that none of her remaining grandchildren would fall victim to the pox, even as she knew that the odds were against her.

For Miriam, it was thoughts of the months following Purim that filled her with fear. She was enceinte again, which wasn't surprising considering how often Judah wanted to use the bed during the Cold Fair, but this time her nausea started almost as soon as she missed her flowers. Each of her pregnancies had sickened her worse than the one preceding it; how could she endure this one until autumn?

Yet that was better than worrying about her children. Each time she touched the new mezuzah at her front door, she agonized over when they would get the pox, how badly they might suffer, and how she was going to care for them if she were ill herself. Little Salomon's death racked her with guilt, and she began to have nightmares in which one of her or Joheved's children died.

But it was Judah who dreaded Purim the most. This was the holiday, based on the biblical book of Esther, that celebrated the Persian Jews' escape from destruction at the hands of the evil Haman—the holiday about which the sage Rava said:

> On Purim a man must drink wine until he cannot tell the difference between "blessed is Mordecai" and "cursed is Haman."

Judah thought of that Simchat Torah night when Yom Tov had been conceived, the one he still couldn't remember. How could he possibly control his *yetzer hara* during those twenty-four hours when it was a mitzvah to get utterly drunk?

Once the Cold Fair ended, despite his dread of discovery, he was increasingly tempted to put his arm around Aaron's shoulders or to press his thigh against Aaron's while they were studying. And Aaron was finding excuses for his body to touch Judah's. More and more, Judah caught himself gazing at Aaron's face instead of concentrating on the text before them.

When the twin funerals in Ramerupt and mourning with Meir's family did nothing to dampen his emotions, Judah feared that his downfall was coming, that he would sin with Aaron or somebody would denounce them, or both. But Judah's apprehension reached new heights when Salomon approached him privately.

"I need to talk with you." Salomon's face was an unreadable mask. "About Aaron."

Judah said nothing as he followed Salomon upstairs, but his heart was pounding. *Who had found them out and exposed them?*

"A rosh yeshiva has more responsibilities to his students than educating them in Torah," Salomon said, shutting the bedroom door behind them. "One of them is being aware of potentially improper relationships and intervening if necessary. Students have strong *yetzers*, and with the intimacy of a study-partner relationship, this can make them vulnerable."

"True," Judah said, trying to hide his growing panic.

"It is also common for students to become infatuated with their teachers; especially our most enthusiastic pupils," Salomon said. "The attachment usually runs its course without incident, as did Elisha's love for you."

Judah nearly choked. *How many others know about Elisha's feelings for me?*

Salomon shook his head sadly. "But when a teacher returns a student's affection, that presents a problem." He stroked his beard and hesitated. "Do you think you've become too fond of your friend Aaron? He clearly cares a great deal for you."

Judah tried desperately to think of something, anything, he could say to defend himself. He wanted to scream a denial, protest his innocence, but that would mean lying to Salomon.

He sighed in resignation. "My *yetzer hara* is aroused by men as well as by women." Judah included both even though it wasn't women causing him trouble.

"And?" Salomon waited.

Judah took a deep breath. "And by my study partner." *There, I've admitted it. Now comes my punishment.*

Salomon sighed. Aaron being attracted to Judah was understandable. But Judah was no hot-blooded youth; he was almost thirty, and married. "You've been able to control your *yetzer hara* so far?"

Judah nodded, his eyes lowered with shame. "I've been using the bed with my wife more often. But Miriam's condition will soon preclude this solution."

"Let me remind you of Abaye's problem with his *yetzer hara*, from Tractate Sukkot," Salomon said.

> "Abaye, hearing a certain man say to a woman, 'Let us travel to-gether,' decided to follow them, to keep them from sinning. When

the couple parted, the man said, 'Your company was pleasant and now the way is long.' Abaye thought, if I had been in his place, I could not have restrained myself, and he fell into despair. An old man (Elijah the prophet) came and taught him: the greater the man, the greater his *yetzer hara*."

That his teacher was neither angry nor ashamed of him, and even considered him capable of greatness, only made Judah feel more unworthy. "I don't know what to do. Help me."

Salomon remembered a conversation he'd had years ago with the monk Robert. It was during those depressing early days when he had almost envied the monks, men able to devote themselves fully to holy matters instead of supporting a family.

"Doesn't your vow of chastity bother you?" he had asked. "The Holy One created us with strong urges, so we will marry and have children."

"I have chosen to be holy in both body and soul, to forgo carnal pleasures in exchange for spiritual ones," Robert replied. "For as Eve corrupted Adam, the lust women inspire lures men to imperil their immortal souls."

"But what about the lust that men inspire in each other?" Salomon responded, aware of the many songs and jokes about lecherous monks and novices.

"That's why we have St. Benedict's rule to avoid favorites. But when that is not possible, the two are exhorted to take their mutual ardor and turn it toward love of God . . ."

As if reading his thoughts, Judah burst out, "We've tried to channel our passion for each other into passion for Torah study." He could see that Salomon was about to speak and quickly added, "Aaron shouldn't have to stop his studies here because of my *yetzer hara*."

Thinking about Robert gave Salomon an idea. "Before we even think about Aaron leaving Troyes, I want you to consult Guy de Dampierre."

"The canon at the cathedral school? You want me to confide in one of the Notzrim?"

"*Oui*. Notzrim expect their monks and canons to spend their lives studying with other men, yet remain unmarried."

Salomon watched sadly as Judah closed the door behind him. Ah, the greater the scholar, the greater his *yetzer hara*. If only Judah could restrain himself with Aaron until Yom Kippur, surely this infatuation would fade with time.

thirty-one

With great trepidation, Judah left the next afternoon to meet with Guy at Pierre's Cave, a tavern near the cathedral. As soon as Judah opened the door, he knew it was a place frequented by men who played the game. Their stares displayed more than casual curiosity and there wasn't a woman in sight. Judah turned to walk out, but Guy waved to him from a corner table.

"Why did you pick this tavern?" It was bad enough that Salomon expected him to reveal his most shameful secret to this stranger, but to meet in such a place . . .

"I needed to see your reaction," Guy said as Judah reluctantly took his seat. "You recognized the type of men who frequent this tavern, yet you ignored their interest in you. So you are no innocent, but neither are you attracted to those who want a meaningless tryst."

"Salomon told you about me."

"*Oui.* And also that he has great confidence in you."

Judah didn't want to tell his story again, he wanted answers. "So what did you do the first time you felt carnal desire for another student?"

Guy smiled. "Nothing. Nothing that is, except think lustful thoughts and wallow in guilt."

Judah couldn't help but smile back. "How did it end?"

"Eventually I was distracted by someone new, a woman I think."

"Women don't distract me. I enjoy lying with my wife, but it doesn't make me desire my friend any less."

"No reason why it should," Guy said amicably. "Desire is not ours to command. Some we are attracted to against our will, while toward others we can never experience it."

"But lying with men is a sin."

"For us, lying with anyone we're not married to is a sin."

"I thought clergy didn't marry."

"That's what Pope Gregory wants, which is causing great turmoil in the Church." Guy shook his head. "Some clerics do marry, and they complain that they are vilified while sodomite priests suffer few penalties. Certainly some of the reformers are Ganymedes who rush to remove the married clergy because they themselves have no interest in the pleasures of women."

"Ganymedes?"

Guy looked at Judah in surprise. "You aren't familiar with the Roman gods?"

"Of course not."

"But you do know the names of the planets?"

When Judah nodded, Guy continued, "According to the Roman pagans, some of their gods are the seven planets."

"That's probably why we call idolatry *avodah zarah*, 'worshipping the stars,'" Judah said.

"The king of the Roman gods is Jupiter, and one of their legends has him carrying off a beautiful prince named Ganymede. The two loved each other so passionately that Jupiter set Ganymede in the heavens to be his cupbearer for eternity."

"Thus men who love each other are Ganymedes?"

"It's better than being called a sodomite," Guy said. "Not that all Ganymedes are sodomites. Some men, particularly those in monasteries, manage to love each other without sinning. They are blessed to enjoy a spiritual friendship that is more intimate and passionate than any carnal relationship."

"How do they resist sinning?" Judah asked.

"The best way to avoid temptation is to never be alone together."

"What about using your love for each other to serve God?"

Guy sighed with nostalgia. "It is a great consolation to be so united that you join heart with heart, soul with soul, so that the sweetness of the Holy Spirit flows over you."

Judah also sighed. Studying Talmud with Aaron felt like that sometimes, but his *yetzer hara* interfered too often now.

As if reading his thoughts, Guy continued, "But Satan is just waiting to trap you, so, to be safe, always study with other people around. And never go out drinking together."

Judah looked up in alarm. *How can I avoid drinking with Aaron at Purim?*

"That was my downfall. We were studying at a tavern much like this one, drinking and touching each other under the table. Before I knew it, we were in a room together upstairs."

"What happened?"

"Of course, it was common knowledge the next day. I was so mortified that I left school for another town," Guy said. "Which reminds me, if you realize Satan has won and you're going to sin, at least be discreet."

"The Talmudic Sages teach us the same thing," Judah said.

> "Rav Ilai the Elder said: if a man sees that his evil urge will overwhelm him, he should go to where they will not recognize him, dress in black with a black cloak, and then do as his heart desires. He should not desecrate the Name of Heaven and sin openly."

"Your Sages are wise men," said Guy.

"How long does this love usually last?"

"A year or two at most. If you can avoid sinning that long, your love can resolve into a great friendship." Guy paused and smiled. "It's been over ten years now that Bonidoine, Countess Adelaide's chaplain, and I have been the closest of confidants."

"And what if you do sin; can the friendship survive?" Judah's stomach knotted with fear.

"That depends on several things," Guy replied. "How guilty you each feel, if one wanted to continue sinning and the other didn't, and if the sin was kept secret or not."

The tavern was growing crowded as men stopped in after work. "I've got to go," Judah said. "I thank you for your good advice."

"Here's another piece of advice, one I usually offer to Christian clergy," Guy said as they walked up the stairs. "Confession can be powerful if you truly wish to avoid sin."

On his way home, Judah mulled over Guy's words. Confession was powerful for Jews too, but Judah's daily confession to the Holy One had clearly lost its effectiveness. Admitting his guilt to Papa hadn't helped conquer his desire to sin either. But he had to do something. He was lucky that thus far only Papa had found him out; next time it wouldn't be someone so sympathetic.

Confess to Miriam, his *yetzer tov* urged him, and his blood ran cold at the idea. She would be as ashamed as he was, perhaps more, and she would be hurt. He hadn't made her cry since their wedding night and Heaven forbid he should repeat the experience.

Worse yet—she would probably be angry. What if she demanded a divorce?

As Purim loomed ever closer, Judah's compulsion to confess to Miriam only grew, but he could never find the right moment. He didn't want to upset her when she wasn't feeling well, but that seemed to be almost all the time. Yet he had to tell her before it was too late.

Aaron was pushing for them to go to the bathhouse together, and each time Judah found it more difficult to decline. Several times a day Aaron put his hand on Judah's thigh, and when Judah, sometimes with some delay, pulled that hand away, Aaron would smile and squeeze his hand in return. And despite it being completely foreign to his temperament, Judah let Aaron talk him into performing a Purim parody together in front of the community while wearing identical costumes.

But when Aaron began teasing him about how the two of them would enjoy themselves so much on Purim that they'd have to be careful not to get too drunk or otherwise they wouldn't remember what happened—Judah decided to confess that night.

"Miriam, I need to speak with you," Judah said after she put their sons to bed. "It's important."

She followed him into their room and lay down while he paced back and forth. She was so tired. Hopefully Judah's talk wouldn't take long. He certainly seemed nervous.

Judah sat down on the bed. "Lately I've been worried . . ." He hesitated and then stood up.

"What's the matter?" she asked as he paced the room again. He must be anxious about their children getting the pox. Several families they knew had lost children already. Maybe they should send the boys to Ramerupt before Purim?

Judah took a deep breath. "I'm worried about Aaron."

"Why? Aaron looks fine to me."

"I'm worried about *me* and Aaron, about what I feel for him."

A knot of fear began to form in Miriam's belly, making her nausea even worse. "What do you mean?"

Judah sat down on the bed again, but he couldn't look at her. "Forgive me, but I've become too fond of Aaron . . . so fond that I've begun to feel a carnal attraction toward him."

Before she could stop them, tears were flowing down Miriam's cheeks.

"But we haven't done anything carnal." He grabbed her hand. "I swear it." *Why did I have to tell her? I knew this was going to happen.*

She only wept harder. "I know Talmud study excites you. If I had offered to overturn the table with you, then maybe I could have satisfied your needs and you wouldn't want a man."

"This has nothing to do with overturning the table. Which I do not particularly desire, not with you or with Aaron."

Judah had no idea what he ultimately wanted to do with Aaron. His fantasies hadn't progressed beyond the two of them finally being alone together, embracing without fear or shame. But his fantasies must remain that, nothing more.

"I don't understand." Miriam blinked back her tears. Here she was, barely able to keep down any food, terrified that her children would die of the pox like Shemayah's younger daughter or Moses haCohen's son, and now her husband was confessing his desire for his study partner. *What have I done to deserve this?*

Judah couldn't bear watching Miriam cry. His overwhelming need to confess compelled him to tell her all about Aaron, and about Elisha as well. He even shared his conversation with Guy de Dampierre. "You've got to help me. I don't want to sin with Aaron, I just want to study with him."

Miriam lay back in bed, stunned by his revelations. But this was no time for recriminations. After all, Judah hadn't sinned and betrayed her—yet. And would he have confessed like this if he hadn't been desperate? But what could she do?

The answer was obvious. "I will do my best to keep a close eye on you and Aaron, unless my sickness gets worse . . ."

When he heard Miriam's sorrow give way to determination, Judah nearly cried with relief. "You are truly a woman of valor," he quoted Proverbs. "I don't deserve you."

Miriam patted his hand. "You must be strong. Didn't Guy say these infatuations usually last about a year?"

"*Oui*. It was just over a year with Elisha."

"You were so miserable when he left at the end of the Hot Fair, but you were better at the Cold Fair."

Judah blushed with shame as his wife reminded him of another painful secret. But that was part of his penance. "If only it were Yom Kippur already."

Miriam sat up straight, a look of triumph on her face. "I have an idea. Do you think it was your separation from Elisha that helped you get over him?"

"Perhaps." Judah's throat tightened with anxiety.

"If our sons stay in Troyes, they're sure to get the pox. But if they were far away, the pox might not be so strong there. And if you went with them, your feelings for Aaron could cool while you're apart."

"I suppose we could visit my mother for Passover." Judah spoke without enthusiasm. "And come back for the Hot Fair."

"Excellent." Then she locked eyes with him. "Although it might be best if you also spent the summer in Paris."

He knew Miriam was right. For instead of thinking of the danger to his sons, how happy Alvina would be to see him and her grandchildren, or how he'd worry about Miriam's fragile health while he was gone, his heart had nearly broken knowing that he wouldn't see Aaron again for six months. And if he didn't return until the fall, Aaron might desert him for one of the Ganymede merchants at the Hot Fair, as Elisha had.

"I'll leave the day after Purim," he said, trying to hide his despair. "It's a Thursday."

The pain in Judah's eyes tore at Miriam's heart. All the more reason why, until the day after Purim, she would have to watch him and Aaron like a hawk.

"I think it's best not to announce your plans for Paris until just before Purim," she said. "We don't want to alert the *mazikim* or to overexcite the children."

Judah agonized over when to tell Aaron, who would rightly feel abandoned, and delayed until the day before Purim. That was the day the community observed Taanit Esther, the fast commemorating how the Jews of Persia abstained from food in solidarity with Queen Esther as she prepared to entreat the king to save her people. Aaron argued that Taanit Esther was not mournful, unlike other fasts in the Jewish calendar. But Judah agreed with Salomon that praying Selichot was necessary, just as Esther needed mercy from Heaven before risking her life by approaching the king without permission. At the same time, Judah felt as if he too were waiting to speak about a matter of life and death.

Waiting until they were walking home from morning services, Judah told Aaron that he would be taking the children to Paris for Passover and staying with his mother until the pox was gone from Troyes. Judah had prepared himself for shock, for anger, for tears even, but Aaron only smiled and continued their discussion by asking whether Taanit Esther was a rabbinic obligation or merely a custom.

That evening, after the Megillah was read, Aaron was more affectionate than ever and Judah allowed himself to reciprocate. *Who cares if anyone sees us? It's Purim and I'm leaving in two days.* They spent most of the night dancing in the moonlight with the men, where the more Aaron drank the more provocatively he danced. Judah was careful never to be alone with him, except for a few moments at the top of the landing, when they shared a lengthy hug before heading to their separate rooms.

The next afternoon Judah drank just enough wine that he was too drunk to feel nervous about his upcoming performance, but not drunk enough to forget his lines. Miriam gave him a kiss for luck and then there was a drum roll, followed by the jongleur's announcement that two of the yeshiva's finest scholars would now debate an important matter.

Miriam sat down and took another sip of her ginger tisane. It was her third cup today, but she was determined to keep an eye on her husband, no matter how queasy the many different food odors made her feel. She joined the cheers and catcalls that greeted Aaron and Judah as they climbed unsteadily atop one of the tables. Despite the terrible epidemics that threatened Troyes, or perhaps because of them, the crowd seemed even more raucous than usual for Purim.

The two were wearing identical black leather *braises* and low-cut silk chemises, the latter nearly transparent and belted provocatively short. Those clothes had to belong to Aaron, who was smaller, because no tailor in Troyes would deliberately create clothes so tight. Miriam shook her head. Judah must be infatuated with Aaron, as well as inebriated, to agree to wear such a flamboyant outfit, although he certainly looked handsome in it.

Judah began by proclaiming that he intended to prove that the gambler trespasses every one of the Ten Commandments, after which his adversary would attempt to refute him. He waited until he had the attention of even the men playing dice in the back.

"Friends, the first two commandments warn against idolatry, yet when the gambler loses, he blames everything on his unlucky stars. As regards the third, 'not taking the name of the Holy One in vain,' it is evident that, at every discrepancy between players, gamblers will swear innumerable oaths."

He's actually good at this, Miriam thought in surprise, as the crowd burst out laughing.

"And how easily is the commandment to observe the Sabbath broken," Judah continued, catching one man's eye and then another. "Playing at dusk on Sabbath eve, the loser, hoping to win back what he has lost, and the winner, whose greed is not satisfied, suddenly find that the Sabbath has overtaken them."

People pointed fingers at each other and roared with mirth.

"Honoring of father and mother is equally jeopardized. When parents chastise their son who is steeped in gambling, he gives them no ear and answers them harshly. Furthermore, when a man loses his money, hatred burns within him against the winner. He calls him a scoundrel, the other retorts, and each draws his sword, so that one of them is killed. Thus the sixth commandment is transgressed."

Miriam smiled with pride as Judah wagged his finger at the men in the back. "The gambler mixes with immoral women, and it is clear that the prohibition against adultery will easily be broken. And when his vice leaves him destitute, he will brood on how he may steal secretly, to make up his losses."

Judah shook his head in disapproval. "It may happen that he and his friend agree to share their gambling profits; a dispute arises and an arbitrator is called in. Then what becomes of the commandment against bearing false witness?"

The entire courtyard seemed entranced as Judah paused before his last statement. "It stands to reason that if a man is not particular regarding the law of stealing, he will certainly ignore the prohibition, 'You shall not covet.'" Judah raised his fist. "Consider the evil of this wicked pastime—surely one who indulges in it cannot go unpunished!"

He bowed to the cheering audience and grinning broadly, embraced Aaron before sitting down next to Miriam. Immediately Aaron downed his wine, wiped his mouth, and saluted the crowd with the empty cup. A jug was passed up to him and he took a swig from it. Holding the vessel aloft, he began his rebuttal.

"Gentlefolk, I will be brief." This drew several guffaws. He turned to Judah. "You, my pious friend, have employed many words to condemn this sport, but all you have said might concern every human pursuit. I know a man who deals in grain who, upon hearing news that wheat had depreciated in value, swore the most fearsome blasphemies." Aaron put his hands over his ears and pretended to swoon in horror.

Though unsteady on his feet, he strutted back and forth on the bench, pointing to different men as he caught their eyes. "And where will you find the occasion for more profanity than among merchants, which they employ during the course of buying and selling?" Aaron emphasized the word "merchants" as if shocked at their behavior, causing several in the crowd to shout out their agreement.

"Regarding the violation of the Sabbath, this may apply to the tailor, silversmith, and every businessman who desires to increase his profits." This time Aaron indicated some of the wealthier men in the crowd, while the rest chortled with glee.

"And there are many diversions that lead to dishonoring parents or to the commission of murder and adultery. It is the same with stealing, which any fellow in tight circumstances may justify." Aaron turned out his empty purse, inspected his bare sleeves, and shook his head sadly.

"False swearing may occur in any form of partnership, and covetousness is known to reside naturally in the heart of man." He jumped off the bench and with a greedy look, pulled Bonfils' ermine-lined cloak off him and tried it on. When Bonfils snatched it back, the crowd erupted with laughter.

Aaron drained his cup and saluted the courtyard. "To sum up the matter: a righteous person will be as upright in commercial pursuits as in sport or anything else, while a sinful one will act just as wickedly in one matter as in the other."

The audience burst out in applause, yelling and stamping their feet. Aaron helped Judah back onto the table and the two were showered with praise. While both men were clearly showing the wine's effect, Miriam wasn't sure if their exaggerated efforts to keep from falling off the table were real or playacting. One woman after another sought her out to say how clever, and how good-looking, Judah was and how nice it was to see him so outgoing for a change.

Miriam tired as afternoon turned into evening. Judah and Aaron had remained in plain view, and she wanted to put her boys to bed herself on their second to last night home. She accompanied them upstairs with the firm determination to come down immediately after the children fell asleep. But it was too tempting to lie down on the bed with them while she retold the Purim story, and she soon nodded off.

When the church bells finished chiming Compline and Miriam hadn't reappeared, Aaron took Judah's hand and pulled him away from the party. Together they stumbled until they were behind the house, out of view of the revelers in the courtyard. Judah's *yetzer tov* was afraid, and his *yetzer hara* hopeful, that Aaron intended to kiss him, but instead Aaron threw his arms around Judah and said, "You are brilliant. I had nearly despaired of ever sharing our passion for each other, and now you've arranged for us to be together in Paris. The city is so huge that almost no one will know you, and nobody knows me there at all, so we'll be free to do whatever we want even if we don't wear black cloaks."

Judah tried to focus on Aaron's face, less than a handbreadth away from his own. Lust glittered in Aaron's eyes and Judah felt his body responding. Aaron put his hands on Judah's derriere and pulled him closer. Through the tight leather, they strained against each other.

Finally Judah's *yetzer hara* vanquished his *yetzer tov*. "How will you find me in Paris? You must be discreet."

"There's an inn outside the Jewish Quarter called Jacques' Watering Hole." Aaron's breathing was heavy. "Leave word for me there."

Judah began to laugh.

"What's so funny?"

"All those taverns and inns for men who play the game; I just realized why they're all called so-and-so's cavern or cave or hole." Judah continued to chuckle. "That's how the Ganymedes find each other."

"So you know about Ganymede and playing the game. And I thought you were so pious and innocent."

"I am pious and innocent." But Judah's chuckles belied his words.

"Not for long."

Judah's heart was pounding and his body ached with desire. "How soon will you get to Paris?"

"I'll pretend I'm going home for Passover. Then it depends on the merchants I travel with." He looked longingly at Judah. "If some are going to Sepharad, I'll have to go with them. It will look suspicious if

I don't." He caressed Judah's buttocks and sighed. "Probably we'll have to wait until after the festival."

"I've waited this long; I can wait a little longer." Judah lingered in Aaron's arms until they heard someone staggering in their direction. They quickly separated, Aaron heading for the privy and Judah returning to the dancers.

When Miriam woke up the next morning in her sons' bed, she nearly knocked over the baby's cradle in her hurry to see where Aaron had spent the night. She nearly cried with relief to see Judah alone in their marital bed, and then her nausea hit her with such force that she barely made it to the chamber pot in time. Judah slept on, oblivious, and Miriam quietly went downstairs. Aaron lay snoring on the salon floor, along with the other students who had drunk too much to navigate the ladder to the attic.

The servants were still asleep, so Miriam stoked the fire in the kitchen hearth and prepared her first cup of ginger tisane. She'd bought all the ginger in stock locally, and at this rate she would run out well before the spice merchants arrived for the Hot Fair.

Late that afternoon, Judah asked if she still had the conditional *get* he'd written her before Elisha's wedding.

"I think so."

"Could you find it, please?" he asked. "I'd like to make sure that nothing has happened to it."

Miriam opened the chest that held her best clothes and pulled out the piece of parchment for him to examine.

"Good, it's undamaged." Judah rolled up the *get* and returned it to her, a relieved expression on his face. "In case something happens to me."

Miriam gave him a hug. "Nothing's going to happen to you. You'll be at Alvina's in less than a week." She was proud that her husband was so punctilious, so concerned about her being left an *agunah* that he wanted to protect her against the unlikely event of him disappearing or dying without witnesses on such a short trip.

She was further impressed when Judah chose to have *souper* alone with her and their children, while Aaron ate at Salomon's. And later that night he took a good deal of time kissing her and stroking her hair before finally entering her. Miriam would have been content to forgo his attentions and go to sleep early, but the Sages taught that it was a mitzvah for a man to lie with his wife before a journey. So she tried to ignore her queasiness and return his kisses with more enthusiasm than she felt.

Afterward, she heard him weeping softly, so she reached out to stroke his shoulder. "I know you'll miss Aaron while you're gone, but don't worry, you'll see him again soon."

Judah turned over and pulled her close. "*Non*, I'm thinking that I'll miss you."

Guilt flooded through Miriam. She had been thinking only of how much she would miss her children. She leaned over to kiss him and said, "You'll be home soon, Le Bon Dieu willing."

The next morning there was much hugging and crying as her family exited through the Paris Gate, especially little Elisha, who clung to her until Aaron pulled him off and handed him to Judah. On the way home she threw up on the street, and, by the time she returned, she felt so ill that Jeanne had to help her up the stairs and into bed.

Miriam was feeling worse than ever when Aaron came to bid her adieu a few days later. He would have preferred to travel with Jews, but the only people going to Sepharad were some pilgrims Guy had located who were on their way to Santiago de Compostela for Easter.

"I want to thank you for all your hospitality," he said, averting his eyes from hers.

"You're most welcome," Miriam replied. It was odd how he looked excited and happy, yet furtive at the same time. *Of course, he is going to see his wife after nearly a year's absence.* "I'm sure you're looking forward to seeing your family again."

"Most definitely."

Miriam tried to catch his eye, but he refused to meet her gaze. "Have a safe trip. We'll see you in a few months."

"I hope you'll be feeling better soon," he said with a small smile. "Good-bye then."

Miriam pondered their exchange as she watched Aaron carry his saddlebag across the courtyard. His expression didn't seemed right, a strange combination of triumph and pity.

He was lying.

She had enough dealings with liars in the jewelry business to identify one easily. Alvina had taught her and Rachel to ask where a woman had acquired the jewels she wanted to pawn or sell, and not just to avoid stolen merchandise. Noble women with gambling debts and mistresses selling their lovers' tokens of affection often lied at first, until they understood that Miriam needed to know these things to prevent shame for the seller, to make sure that an item wasn't inadvertently resold to someone who would recognize its origin.

Why would Aaron lie to me?

The answer hit her with a shock that pushed her back into the pillow and forced tears from her eyes. Aaron wasn't going home to Sepharad. He intended to go to Paris. That's why he was traveling with Notzrim who didn't know him and wouldn't care when he left their party.

And Judah was expecting him; that's why he was so attentive to her on their final night together. She began to sob in earnest.

Mon Dieu, he's taken the children with him. I might never see them again.

thirty-two

Troyes
Late Spring 4849 (1089 CE)

iriam was dimly aware of a rooster crowing, and the next moment she sensed a flutter of movement within her belly. Somehow she'd survived another night—now she would have to endure another day. Her nausea began to grow, competing with the terrible thirst that was her constant companion.

Papa had found plenty of leftover matzah for her to eat, far more than she could keep down, but her supply of ginger was gone. Too ill to travel even the short distance to Ramerupt, Miriam spent a sorrowful Passover at home with Anna and Baruch, who'd lost both daughters to smallpox.

Despite her own infirmity, Miriam couldn't stay away from their sickroom. Perhaps her sons were at that moment suffering the same symptoms. So she sat and prayed for hours with the girls, as one declined and then the other. The younger took ill first, with a fever and stomachache that Anna hoped might be due to tainted meat. But then the pimples appeared on her face and hands, and by the time they spread to the rest of her body she was screaming and clutching her belly in agony. Helpless to ease this torment, Miriam could offer only the comfort of her presence, and the girl's heartrending cries echoed in Miriam's ears long after she returned home.

By the time the little one died, her older sister's body was covered with the small pimples, which soon grew into vesicles and filled with pus. Miriam tried to be optimistic; she and Joheved had also looked horrible at this stage, yet they had survived. But the girl's pustules, instead of deflating and drying out, began to merge together into larger and larger sheets, until her skin separated from the flesh underneath. When the Angel of Death finally came, Miriam could only weep with relief that the poor child's suffering was over.

Ramerupt had proved no haven from the pox; both of Joheved's daughters had been stricken, as well as Zipporah and Judita, the doctor's daughter, who had also taken refuge there. Joheved couldn't tend to all these youngsters herself, not while recuperating from a miscarriage, so when Passover was over and Papa came home, Mama remained behind.

Now it was Anna and Jeanne who cared for Miriam, who coaxed her to drink what little she could and cleaned up what she couldn't retain. So many nights Miriam dreamed of her sons, covered with sores and crying for her in pain, while she tried desperately to reach them. These nightmarish visions haunted her, and, terrified that she would never see her children again, Miriam began to wish that she too wouldn't wake up the next morning. But Anna was determined to keep the Angel of Death from returning to their courtyard, and it seemed that Miriam's unborn child was equally determined, because somehow Miriam managed to ingest just enough nourishment to sustain them both.

Eyes still closed, Miriam reached for a piece of matzah and instead found a warm cup in her hand. A female voice urged her, "Swallow some of this."

Miriam had to be dreaming, because the drink smelled like ginger tisane and the voice belonged to her younger sister.

"Rachel?" The room was too dark to see who was helping her sit up.

"*Oui*, I got here late last night." She pressed the cup to Miriam's lips.

Miriam let a small amount trickle down her throat. She managed to swallow two more mouthfuls of the tisane, along with another piece of matzah, before the cramps started, but a miracle happened and nothing came back up.

"What are you doing here? The Hot Fair isn't for weeks."

Rachel handed her a cloth dipped in the ginger tisane to suck. "Papa sent a courier to Arles for me."

"That must have cost a fortune."

"Judah can afford it. Papa said to come home immediately and to bring a six months' supply of ginger," Rachel said. "Now what's this about Judah taking the children to Paris?"

At the mention of her children, Miriam began to cry. She'd been keeping her misery dammed up inside for so long that it was impossible to hold back. In between sobs and sips of ginger tisane, she poured out what she knew about Judah and Aaron, what she suspected, and what she feared. "Now Judah's taken my children away; I'll never see them again."

Rachel shook her head. "I can't believe it—not Judah."

Miriam wiped her tears on the sheet. "The way Judah asked about my conditional *get*, I'm afraid he's not coming back."

"Perhaps he didn't go to Paris at all." Rachel jumped up, her hands on her hips. "I'm going to find out."

Miriam's emotions warred within her. While desperate for news of her sons, she wasn't sure how Judah would react to Rachel's presence. "Maybe Judah does intend to return home. Maybe he's just following Rav Ilai's advice and going to a place where no one knows him to commit the sin his heart desires."

"I suppose even pious men like Judah sin sometimes," Rachel said. "But I'm leaving for Paris after the Sabbath. I have some items that I'd like Alvina to sell there, and in return I can bring her merchandise back to the Hot Fair."

"Please wait a little while. You just got here."

"All right. But only because you're so sick."

Now that the room was getting light, Rachel was appalled at Miriam's emaciated appearance. She would have to stay in Troyes at least a week; Heaven forbid that Miriam should die while she was on her way to Paris. And while she was here, she could visit Mama and Joheved in Ramerupt.

Rachel waited for two Sabbaths to pass. Miriam still looked ghastly, and while she ate far less than she should, she managed to keep most of it down. Joheved's daughters seemed to be out of danger as well, although it would be some time before they regained their full health. Thank Heaven the pox had been mild in Arles; little Shemiah had hardly been sick at all. Maybe by the time she returned from Paris, her husband and son would be waiting for her in Troyes.

There was always traffic on the roads once the Champagne fair cycle began, and Rachel had no trouble finding someone to guide her to the Jewish Quarter of Paris. Events began as she anticipated when she knocked on Alvina's door and the astonished woman accepted without question Rachel's explanation for her visit. Judah was also amazed to see her, and Rachel tried not to show how relieved she was to find him in residence.

"Judah," she whispered, preparing to test him. "I would speak with you in private."

Clearly alarmed, he led her into the side room where Alvina saw her clients. "What's the matter?"

"Miriam is gravely ill," Rachel said solemnly. "This pregnancy has been harder than the others, and frankly I don't know how much longer she has to live." She hadn't lied to Judah; who knows how long anyone has to live?

Judah's reaction was all she'd hoped for. The blood drained from his face, and he staggered to the nearest chair as if she'd hit him. "What am I to do? You tell me that my wife is dying, but I can't travel to Troyes while Shimson is so ill."

"What's wrong with Shimson?"

"He has the pox. All three of them do, but Shimson's case is the worst." Judah put his head in his hands, but not before Rachel could see the tears in his eyes. "Why did I ever take them away from home?"

Rachel groaned inwardly. Now she would have to wait until Shimson's illness was resolved, one way or another. She couldn't go back to Miriam with this news and admit that she'd left without knowing what happened to him.

"Judah, shall I stay with the boys tonight so you can get some rest?" How would he react to this idea?

"*Merci*, but *non*. I sleep with them every night," he said. "It comforts them to have me nearby."

Neither of them said it, but both of them had the same thought—*if there is any change, he'll be the first to know.*

At that moment Alvina returned. "Elisha is crying for you, Judah, and Rachel, you must be tired after your long journey."

Rachel was tired, as well as relieved that she could send Miriam a message that Judah and the boys were indeed in Paris. But she was also perplexed. Was Aaron in Paris or not? And if not, had he already been here and left or had something delayed his arrival? Could her sister's suspicions be groundless? She fell asleep impatient to find the answers to her questions.

Lying next to his pox-covered son, sleep eluded Judah completely. First Shimson stricken and now Miriam; this was the Holy One punishing him. How could he have allowed Aaron to believe that they would meet in Paris? How could his desire have so overwhelmed everything he knew was right?

Aaron—his thoughts kept returning to the man even though he tried with all his might to shut them out. *Where is Aaron?* It was over a month since Passover. The first time Judah approached Jacques' Hole, he walked around the block five times before finding the courage to enter. But soon he was stopping in daily to ask about recent visitors, only to leave disappointed.

Had Aaron been in an accident? Or had he met an old love in Sepharad and decided to remain there? Shimson's illness would keep Judah in Paris for another month at least; if Aaron were coming, he'd certainly arrive by then.

What am I thinking? How can I want to prolong my son's sickness to wait for Aaron? No wonder I'm being punished. Mon Dieu, forgive me. Don't make my wife and son suffer for my sin. Don't let them die, I beg you, and if I should see Aaron again, I will send him away immediately. Heal them, please, and I swear that I will never even think carnally about another man.

The guilt was as relentless as the passion that had consumed him for months.

The next morning Rachel attended services with Judah, and when he stayed to assist the rosh yeshiva, she remained behind as well. It didn't take long to ascertain that this was Judah's usual routine, and by the end of the day she learned that he was a man of regular and pious habits, who spent his time either at his mother's home or the Paris yeshiva. His sadness and anxiety were attributed to concern about his sons' illness, feelings that every parent in Paris shared these days. A chat with Yom Tov assured Rachel that neither Aaron, nor anyone else they knew in Troyes, had visited Paris recently.

When Shavuot passed without a sign of Aaron, Rachel decided to return to Troyes. She had long since reconciled Alvina's accounts, and the Hot Fair would be starting in a few weeks. Shimson had survived the pox, and though he was still weak, he'd eventually be well enough to travel. She offered to bring Yom Tov back with her; seeing him might speed Miriam's recovery.

"But Yom Tov demurred," Rachel explained to Miriam a week later. "He said this was the first time he'd spent so much time studying with his father, just the two of them."

Miriam struggled to sit up in bed. "So was I wrong about Judah and Aaron?"

"All I know is that Aaron never came to Paris." Rachel handed Miriam a cup of ginger tisane. "Here, drink some more."

"*Merci*, it's the only remedy that works for my nausea."

Rachel had said nothing about Miriam's skeletal appearance. Thank Heaven her sister was alive. It was just as well that Yom Tov had stayed in Paris; he shouldn't see his mother like this.

"Miriam, haven't you eaten anything besides matzah while I was gone?"

"If your stomach ached all the time, you were too tired to lift a spoon, and everything you tried to eat tasted like vomit, you wouldn't eat much either."

There was a quiet knock on the door. "Mistress Miriam," Jeanne said. "Guy de Dampierre wishes to see you. I told him you weren't receiving visitors, but he says it's important."

"Very well, ask him to wait."

Miriam allowed Rachel to assist her down the steps. Guy stood to greet her, a somber expression on his face.

"Please excuse my untimely visit. I understand that you've been ill, which is why I delayed bringing you this message," he said. "However, your father tells me that your malady is likely to continue through the summer."

Miriam gave him a small smile. "I am strong enough to withstand some bad news."

Guy took a deep breath. "The pilgrims accompanying Judah's friend Aaron have returned. They are sorry to report that he became ill with smallpox during the journey, and they were forced to leave him at a hospice for travelers. On their return trip they learned that he had died there."

Rachel and Miriam looked at each other, gasped, and each reached for the other's hand. "*Baruch Dayan Emet.*"

"Not knowing his family, they brought his belongings back here." Guy handed Miriam a sealed piece of parchment. "Among them was a letter for your husband."

"Poor Aaron," Miriam whispered once Guy was gone. "So that's why he never came to Paris."

"Are you going to open the letter?" Rachel asked. Her sister was holding it at arm's length.

"It's wrong to read someone else's mail. I should send it to Judah."

"Everyone knows that letters sent with travelers aren't private. You should make sure there's nothing shameful inside."

Miriam's resolve began to waver. "Maybe I'll read it first, and then send it to Judah if it's not too bad."

"Read it aloud." Rachel leaned forward, her eyes wide. "I'll help you decide."

Miriam unfolded the parchment and scanned it. "At least Guy and the other travelers didn't read this. It's in Aramaic."

"So Aaron had some need for discretion."

"I suppose you already know too much." Miriam sighed with resignation and began to read. "My beloved Judah . . ."

She paused and they stared at each other in trepidation.

"It is a terrible thing to die alone. Yes, I know I am dying—my skin is turning black and they tell me the whites of my eyes are red with blood. But worse than my physical pain is that of knowing that we will never see each other again. For you will surely go to Gan Eden, while my sins condemn me to Gehenna. I have committed transgressions with many men, and I repent for them. But you must believe that you are the only one I truly loved, and I will never repent for this. We have committed a sin, if it is a sin to love, yet the One who created me in His image made me to love you."

Miriam gulped. "I definitely can't risk someone else seeing this letter."

"Is there anything else?"

Tears welling in her eyes, Miriam began reading again. "To die never having tasted your sweet lips, to have seen you naked in the baths and never felt your flesh against mine—I will burn with unrequited desire forever. Only a few weeks more and you would have been mine, body and soul, but the Holy Judge decreed that you should remain chaste."

"That's a relief," Rachel said. "Although it sounds like your suspicions were correct."

"There's still more," Miriam said. "I never told you, dearest Judah, but I had a seminal emission on Erev Yom Kippur and was thus fated to die this year. That's one reason I was so impatient to consummate our love, my great passion for you being the other. I bequeath you my meager belongings as a remembrance of one who loved you like my own soul and wanted so much to have loved you better."

The room was silent except for the sounds of their breathing. Finally Rachel whispered, "I agree. You don't dare let that letter leave Troyes."

Miriam sniffed a couple of times. "I need to think about it, but right now I'm more sad than angry."

"You always were too kind. If this letter were to my husband, I'd be demanding a divorce."

"But Aaron is dead." And Judah might wish he were too.

Rachel was about to retort, *And what happens when the next Ganymede student comes to Papa's yeshiva?* But she decided that Miriam was upset enough. "So are you going to send word to Judah or make him wait until he gets home?"

"I think I'll wait. I want to be here when he finds out."

"As do I."

"I have to inform Papa of Aaron's death," Miriam said. "But I'm not telling him about the letter. And I'm not going to tell Judah I've read it either."

Rachel took Miriam's hand in hers. "Don't worry, I will never mention Aaron's letter to anyone."

Try as she might, Miriam couldn't work up enough anger toward her errant husband to overcome her sympathy for him. But the strangest feeling she had was envy; if only she'd received a letter like this from Benjamin before he died.

It was the day after Rachel's husband and son arrived in Troyes that a merchant from Paris brought a message from Judah. Shimson had suffered a relapse, and the doctor advised another month of rest. Judah hoped that Miriam's health had improved and that she would tell Aaron not to worry, they'd be studying together again soon. Miriam, whose health had not improved at all, winced when she heard the part for Aaron.

Once the Hot Fair began, Joheved and her family moved to Troyes for the summer, along with Zipporah and Judita, who both came to study with her every morning after services. After the death of her father and younger daughters, Shemayah's wife declared that their house in Provins was cursed. Brunetta insisted on their buying a house in Troyes, one with new mezuzot written by Mordecai, since it was clear that one of his had protected Joheved during labor and another had saved the children under her roof from the Angel of Death.

Shemayah's wife wasn't the only one to notice that no child had died from smallpox in either Joheved or Miriam's home, and Mordecai was besieged with orders for amulets. The pox epidemic was dissipating, but not the one affecting Troyes' elderly. Isaac haParnas died shortly after Shavuot and Count Thibault was also stricken, throwing doubt on the future of the Troyes fairs. The two men had nurtured them and worked diligently to bring about the success they currently enjoyed.

Thibault was so ill that he placed the sovereignty of Blois in the hands of his eldest son, Étienne-Henri, and gave Champagne to Adelaide's son, Eudes. The Jews of Troyes wondered if Bonfils, Isaac's successor, would be as clever and tactful, enabling them to continue enriching both themselves and their sovereign. Would the new *parnas* be strong enough to keep the Jewish community united or would old disagreements and jealousies be allowed to jeopardize their newly won prosperity?

And what of Eudes? Since his knighthood, the young man had shown more interest in hunting, fighting, and whoring than in statecraft. Opinion in town divided between those who hoped he would continue those pursuits and leave ruling Champagne to his mother and her capable advisors, and those who expected him to push his mother aside as soon as Thibault died and squander his inheritance in less time than it took his father to amass it.

The consensus from taverns and merchant stalls throughout Troyes was that Bonfils, while not likely to attain Isaac's stature, would fill his shoes adequately. Salomon had offered no preference concerning who should be the new *parnas*, saying that all of the men on the community council were sufficiently wealthy and prominent.

Yet he would clearly rather not see one of Fleur's cousins assume the position. The feud between Fleur's family and those who supported Joseph's deathbed gift to Samson had cooled once the council voted to deny Ishaiah the mohel permission to settle in Troyes, but it still simmered enough that the council had selected Bonfils as their *parnas*. Bonfils was not quite the richest Jew in town, but he possessed the exemplary trait of having somehow not offended either party to the dispute.

With the others in their family out of danger, Rivka, Joheved, and Rachel turned their attention to Miriam. While most women suffered nausea in early pregnancy, it was unheard of for a woman in her seventh month to vomit daily. There had to be some food besides matzah that Miriam could tolerate.

Joheved, recalling Meir's illness, had the first success with rice cooked in chicken broth, and Rivka soon found that her daughter could keep down mashed turnips and carrots if she seasoned them with nothing except salt. But it was Rachel who triumphed by encouraging a local alewife to concoct a brew with ginger. If Miriam drank this at meals, she was able to eat almost anything with minimal discomfort.

Perhaps it was the ginger beer, but the amount of food Miriam ate increased as the time decreased before she would see her sons again. She hadn't expected Judah to travel over the fast days, so she was shocked when, on the day after Tisha B'Av, Jeanne ran upstairs yelling, "Mistress Miriam, wake up. Master Judah just rode through the gate."

Heart pounding, Miriam rushed to the open window. Papa was cradling a sleepy Elisha as Yom Tov dismounted from one pony, while Judah gently helped Shimson down from the other. Both older boys rushed toward the privy, and Miriam was relieved to see that Shimson ran almost as fast as his brother. She waited only until Papa put a comforting arm around Judah's shoulders before heading downstairs.

Judah's journey week had been a terrible mixture of hope and fear. Hope that he and Aaron would be able to study together as brothers from now on, and fear that as soon as he saw Aaron again the fire of his thwarted passion would be kindled even hotter than before. Or worse, that Aaron would be with Natan ben Abraham, or some such Ganymede, which was why he hadn't come to Paris.

The one thing he did not expect was Salomon, his face heavy with sadness, taking him by the arm and saying, "I'm afraid I have some bad news for you."

Judah closed his eyes and his head slumped. *I am too late. Miriam is dead.* He opened his eyes again and realized that Salomon's *bliaut* and chemise were not torn, as a mourner's would have been. So it wasn't Miriam; but maybe she'd lost the baby. "What happened?"

"Aaron died of smallpox on his way to Sepharad."

Non! "Impossible. Aaron was too old." He stared up at Salomon, his eyes begging for this to be a mistake.

"The pilgrims he traveled with have no reason to lie," Salomon replied gently. "And I have heard that some children miss getting the pox, which makes them especially vulnerable when it comes again."

Salomon waited for Judah's expression to change from denial to resignation, for him to make the blessing that demonstrated his acceptance of Aaron's death. That initial step was often the hardest for a mourner, even more difficult than the funeral itself. Of course, there would be no funeral for Aaron here, no official period of mourning. Judah's loss, no matter how bitter, would be a private thing.

A stubborn, childish part of Judah refused to say the blessing; as long as he remained silent, Aaron would somehow not be dead. But Papa put an arm around his shoulder and was standing there patiently. Judah knew what he was supposed to do, and that only by doing it would Papa let go so he could finally see Miriam.

Judah took a deep breath and let it out slowly. "*Baruch Dayan Emet.*" Blessed is the True Judge. It felt as though he had closed the lid on Aaron's coffin.

Salomon began leading Judah toward the house. "Come, let's go see your wife. She was very ill while you were away, but lately she's been better, may the Holy One protect her."

Miriam had always been a slender woman, and she had lost weight during her previous pregnancy with Elisha, but Judah was unprepared for the gaunt creature sitting at the dining table with their sons. As soon as she saw him, she rose and reached out to him with such a sympathetic expression that he could barely restrain his tears. Seeing her standing up, her swollen belly in such contrast to the rest of her body, Judah winced to realize that he was responsible for her condition.

"Yom Tov, could you watch Elisha?" she asked. "Your father and I need a little time to ourselves before services."

Once she closed the bedroom door behind them, Miriam handed him the letter. "This came with Aaron's things."

Judah only read for a moment before he had to sit down. Soon his hand was shaking so hard he couldn't read the words.

"I'm so very sorry," Miriam said.

He'd wronged her terribly, Judah thought. He ought to be the one asking for forgiveness, but she was the one apologizing. He had managed to hide his grief from his sons, but now there was no stopping his tears, and when Miriam opened her arms he laid his head on her breast and wept.

Miriam rocked her husband as though he were an injured child. Rachel would have been furious with her, would have said she was a fool to offer comfort to the man who had betrayed her, who had returned to her only because his lover hadn't come for him. But she knew what he was suffering; she knew better than anyone.

thirty-three

Miriam couldn't remember such a miserable Sukkot. Count Thibault died on the second day of the festival, so Judah's grief blended into the city's mourning. He rarely spoke unless someone addressed him, and Miriam thought that he was losing weight faster than she was gaining it. He was far more melancholy now than he'd been after Elisha left the yeshiva.

How could I not have seen that he was infatuated with Elisha back then? Even when he and Elisha agreed to name their sons after each other, she'd suspected nothing.

As the Days of Awe approached, Miriam expected Judah to apologize or offer some explanation, but he only made the general plea that he hoped she would forgive him for anything he'd done to injure her in the last year. She had planned to apologize for reading Aaron's letter, but instead she merely asked forgiveness for what she had done to hurt him.

Miriam wished she could talk to Rachel, but her little sister was almost as miserable as Judah. Only after Simchat Torah, when Eliezer left with the other merchants and Rachel remained behind with Shemiah, did Miriam learn of her troubles.

The two of them were walking through the vineyard, untying the shoots from the props that had supported them since spring. "It's not fair," Rachel wailed. "I'm the one who loves to travel and I'm stuck here in Troyes, while Eliezer's the one who wants to study at the yeshiva, but he has to journey to all these faraway places to support our family."

"I thought you were going to travel together," Miriam said.

"That's what I thought too."

Miriam untied the thin piece of straw from the now-leafless vine. "What happened?"

"I didn't want to tell you while you were so ill, but the reason I was in Arles when Papa's courier came was that I was recovering from a miscarriage."

"I'm sorry. Are you all right?"

"I'm fine." Rachel dropped a piece of straw into her linen bag. Because the straw ties tend to harbor pests, each had to be removed and burnt. "In fact I suspect I'm enceinte already."

"It must be difficult traveling when you're pregnant."

Rachel nodded. "That was only part of the problem. Last year we had to leave Shemiah with Eliezer's mother. He kept getting diarrhea from all the strange foods, and it was nearly impossible to do any business with a toddler around." Rachel's chin began to quiver and she paused to control her emotions. "When I got back to Arles, he wouldn't come to me. He didn't recognize his own mother."

Miriam reached out and patted her sister's hand. "I know. When my boys came back from Paris, Elisha wouldn't let Judah leave him alone with me."

Rachel threw her bag of straw ties on the ground, sending up a cloud of dust. "There's nothing I can do except endure it. I hate being separated from Eliezer, even for a few weeks, and now we'll be away from each other more than we're together."

Miriam tried to think of something sympathetic to say, but Rachel continued, "All I can do is wait until his nephews get older. Then they can travel while he stays home."

"At least he'll be here for the fairs and for the Days of Awe," Miriam said.

"But I'll have to celebrate Purim and Passover alone." Rachel picked up her bag and moved to the next row. Every vine needed to be untied before pruning could take place.

Miriam wanted to point out that her sister wouldn't be alone; she'd be with her family. But Rachel was clearly in no mood for consolation. Miriam suspected that this was also not a good time to complain about Judah, who, while not particularly good company, spent every day in her presence.

When Miriam gave birth to a healthy baby girl with her usual minimum of fuss, her reaction was more relief than joy. Elizabeth was a competent midwife, but she wasn't Aunt Sarah. Miriam had been delivering babies by herself for years; but it was only with the birth of her own child that Sarah's death finally became real.

Judah nearly ignored his daughter's birth. He nodded unenthusiastically when Miriam asked if he still wanted to name their daughter Alvina, while she gave secret thanks that they didn't have to choose a boy's name. *What if he'd wanted to name a son Aaron?*

Not that she would have that problem in the future.

A few days after Alvina's birth, Elizabeth had solemnly approached her. "Everyone thinks it's normal for a pregnant woman to be sick to her stomach, but I must warn you that a woman who gets increasingly nauseous with each pregnancy eventually reaches a point when it proves fatal."

Miriam put little Alvina to her shoulder and patted the baby's back. "How many pregnancies does it take?"

"I've only seen a few cases. But I consulted with the other midwives, and we agreed that a woman with this condition never survives five pregnancies. Most succumb during their fourth."

"If my sister hadn't brought back all that ginger for me . . ." Miriam didn't need to finish the sentence.

"You are lucky to be alive today." Elizabeth lowered her voice. "I have several herbal mixtures that can bring on your flowers if they're late. Just in case."

Miriam nodded and helped Alvina find her nipple. She knew these herbs as well. Plus there was always a *mokh*. "At least my husband has fulfilled the commandment to procreate."

"What is that?"

"According to Jewish Law, only a man is obligated to be fruitful and multiply," Miriam explained. "When he has fathered both a son and a daughter, he has discharged that obligation."

That was Hillel's view. Shammai said a man needed two sons, but Miriam wasn't going to discuss the vagaries of Jewish Law. Judah had fulfilled the mitzvah no matter whose rule one accepted.

Elizabeth looked intrigued. "Only a man?"

"*Oui*, a woman is not commanded to procreate. So we are free to avoid pregnancy."

Miriam decided not to tell Judah yet. It would only upset him more, and, besides, she didn't have to worry about it for another two months. Papa taught that, as it was written in the Torah, a woman who gave birth to a daughter was *niddah* for fourteen days and then, even if she was still bleeding, her blood was pure for the next sixty-six days and she was permitted to her husband. Those who preferred to be strict, and Judah was among them, said that she must stay separate from her husband for the entire eighty days.

"Since you're not going to bear any more children, it's a good thing the ones you've got have survived the pox," Elizabeth said as she prepared to leave.

"May the Holy One continue to protect them." Miriam focused her attention on her daughter's hungry mouth at her breast. After Alvina was weaned, Miriam would never again enjoy this wonderful and intimate sensation.

Snow fell nearly every day during the last week of the Cold Fair, and Miriam didn't look forward to using the *mikvah*. She had immersed fourteen days after Alvina was born, but Judah would expect her to do so again on the eightieth day. Just the thought of plunging into that dark, freezing water made her shiver, but it wouldn't be fair to Judah to delay; the poor man hadn't used the bed since Purim.

Maybe she would go to the stews first, luxuriate in a hot bath, and then use the *mikvah*. There were some women who refused to immerse if it was too cold. A warm bath was good enough, they said. Miriam tried to teach them what Jewish Law required, but her efforts were often ignored. It was just as well that so many Jewish men were away during the winter.

Judah never mentioned Aaron during the Cold Fair, rebuffing Giuseppe and Elisha's offers of sympathy. Shemayah continued to teach Judah's old class, and while ostensibly Judah and Eliezer were study partners again, Eliezer spent most of his evenings with Rachel, apparently trying to make up for their upcoming six-month separation. When Miriam suggested that Judah study with her, he invariably found some excuse.

So it was odd when Judah asked her to set aside some time for him after *souper*. Eliezer had left, and Miriam hoped that if she and Rachel began studying again it might lift her sister's spirits. But Judah's firm demeanor made it clear that whatever he wanted to discuss could not be postponed.

Her anxiety increasing, Miriam managed to nurse little Alvina while Judah sat with the boys as they said their bedtime prayers. When he finally joined her in their bedroom and closed the door, her stomach was twisting with dread.

"I don't know how to say this, but I have to tell you before you go to the *mikvah*." His voice was cold and he refused to meet her eyes.

Miriam's fear almost choked her. "Tell me what?"

Judah took a deep breath, hesitated and slowly let it out. "I can't live with you any longer. I want a divorce."

No—this isn't happening. "What have I done? How have I offended you?" Mon Dieu, if he divorced her, he would take the children away. Boys always went with their father.

She fell to the floor and threw her arms around his knees. "Judah, don't do this to me—I beg you. Whatever I've done to displease you, I'll stop. I promise."

Judah tried to step away from her, but she held him fast. "You've done nothing wrong. It's me who has wronged you. You deserve someone better."

"And if I don't want someone better?" How would she find another husband when she couldn't have any more children? And she wanted her own children to raise, not someone else's.

"Miriam, it's no use." There was both sadness and resolve in his voice. "I can no longer be a good husband to you."

"And if I refuse to accept your divorce?"

"Then we would remain married in name only. It doesn't matter to me. I have no desire to remarry."

"I . . . I have to think about it." She'd talk to Rachel tomorrow; her sister would help her decide what to do.

"Take as long as you like. Just understand that I won't be using the bed with you."

Shaking, Miriam got back into bed and averted her eyes while Judah undressed. When he lay down, he turned his back to her as he had done every night since Alvina was born. This time she turned away from him as well. She needed to cry, but the tears wouldn't come. Judah was doing this because of Aaron—he had to be. But it didn't matter why he wanted a divorce; she would never let him take her children away again.

The next morning his wife and daughter were still asleep when Judah woke, and observing them lying together so peacefully, he felt a pang of remorse. Miriam came downstairs in time to see him and the boys off to synagogue, and it was as if nothing untoward had happened the night before.

Judah had almost begun to feel that the worst had passed when, upon entering the courtyard after services, Rachel grabbed his arm and led him into her salon.

She latched the door behind them and turned to face him, her hands on her hips. "You and I are going to talk."

Judah took a seat and waited, although he had a good idea what was coming.

"Miriam told me you want a divorce."

"And since when is this any of your business?"

"My sister's future is my business." Her eyes were blazing. "In case you don't remember, I nursed her back to health from her deathbed last spring while you were waiting for your lover in Paris."

He stood up and headed for the door. "My reasons are my own. I don't have to explain them to you or anyone."

But she blocked his way. "I think you don't have any good reasons to divorce Miriam, and that's why you can't explain them to me or to her. I bet you can't even explain them to yourself."

Judah scowled back at her. She wasn't going to trick him into telling her about Aaron and his vow.

Then her expression softened and she led him back to the table. "Judah, I know that you're what they call a Ganymede. I know that Aaron was one, and other merchants as well, including Elisha and Giuseppe."

He sank onto the bench, his eyes wide. "How did you know?"

Rachel sat down next to him. *He hasn't tried to deny it.* "As far back as I can remember men have undressed me with their eyes. At first I thought that you just hid your desire better than most, but after years traveling with other merchants, I realize that men who look at me without lust are often attracted to other men instead."

"I see."

"I don't know if you can appreciate how safe I feel with Ganymedes, compared to other men, and that's why I've cultivated their business, and their friendships." Her voice hardened. "But I've never known any of them to divorce their wives for another man. To avoid suspicion, they're usually exemplary husbands—as you have been until now."

"I do understand how you feel about men staring at you. I've had to live with both men and women lusting after me."

She was surprised by the empathy she felt for him. "We both know you don't need a divorce to play the game. So why divorce Miriam?" He didn't seem so defensive now; maybe he would tell her the truth.

"Playing the game is a sin. I don't want to be tempted to do it, so I can't stay here and teach in Papa's yeshiva. I'll be attracted to one new student after another. It will be torture."

"So you'd go back to Paris?"

"*Non*, not there." Return to Paris and listen to his mother complain how he'd shamed her by getting a divorce? Heaven forbid.

"Then where would you go?"

"I don't know, maybe to Orléans."

"If you want to avoid temptation, I doubt that city would be a good place for you to live. It's populated by so many Ganymedes that even the archbishop is one."

"You must think I'm being stupid." He couldn't bear to look at her, he felt so ashamed.

"Just not thinking clearly." Maybe Miriam was right to worry about him; what if he didn't have any plans because he intended to commit suicide? It wasn't ethical to divulge her business transactions, but she had to let him know that Aaron wasn't worth killing himself over. "Let me show you something."

She removed a ledger from a nearby cabinet and pointed out several listings. There was the date, Aaron's name on the right, the amount she advanced him, and then a description of the item he'd sold, including its previous owner. He'd pawned quite a few pieces of jewelry during the Hot and Cold fairs, all acquired from different men. Prominent among them was a black pearl ring sold in the summer and a topaz ring in the winter—both obtained from Natan ben Abraham.

Judah knew that Rachel intended him to feel disgust and outrage at Aaron's promiscuity, but his heart sank as despair, not anger, flooded him. So that's what Aaron had been doing on all those late nights. Judah's eyes filled with tears. All those men had enjoyed physical pleasures with Aaron that he would never share, could not even imagine.

Rachel reached out and tilted his head up so their eyes met. "Have another talk with Miriam. Tell her what's in your heart. There must be a solution you two can agree on."

Teeth chattering, Miriam wrapped the towel around her damp hair, pulled her fur-lined mantle tightly around her body, and raced down the street from the synagogue to the bathhouse. The attendant was waiting, and in no time Miriam was enveloped in steaming water, the icy *mikvah* only an unpleasant memory. It was one thing if Judah didn't want to use the bed, but the other consequences of *niddah* made life too awkward: not handing him things directly, not sharing dishes with him, not touching him, even accidentally.

If she continued to avoid those things, people would notice and gossip, speculating that she was a *moredet*, a rebellious wife who refused to use the *mikvah* in order to avoid relations with her husband. So when there was a break between winter storms, she took the opportunity to immerse and get it over with. With any luck, she wouldn't be *niddah* again until Alvina was weaned.

As she soaked in the warm bath, Miriam wondered again how long should she wait for Judah to approach her. Rachel had divulged their conversation, and that she thought Judah was reconsidering. Miriam wanted to be patient; as long as he and the children continued to live with her, no decision was a decision.

No—that would be impossible. She'd wake up every morning worrying that he might leave that day. Tonight she would let him know that she had used the *mikvah*, and then they would talk. Or at least she would.

When she handed Judah a plateful of meat at *souper* and then sat down next to him, his alarmed expression made it clear that he recognized the significance of her actions. In addition, she made a point of scooping stew out of his bowl with her bread, and when she announced that she would be going to bed early, Judah resigned himself to everyone's expectations and said he would join her shortly.

"I have a confession to make," Miriam said once they were alone. "The letter that Aaron wrote to you before he died—I read it. That's why I didn't send it to Paris. Forgive me, but I was afraid someone would read it." *There, that should provoke a response from him.*

"Then you know that Aaron and I never did . . ." Judah hesitated, unsure what word to use.

"But you were planning to, you were waiting for him in Paris." It was half question, half accusation.

"I knew he intended to come to Paris, but, honestly, I don't know what I intended to do." Relief coursed through him at being able to talk about it.

"You weren't planning to run off with him?" Miriam looked at him in surprise. "I thought that's why you asked about my conditional *get* before you left."

"I hadn't planned anything after Paris. I just wanted to be with him.

I know—it was wrong, it was a sin, but . . ." He trailed off helplessly and looked away, but not before she saw the tears in his eyes.

Miriam sighed. How could she be angry with Judah? All he'd done was love someone he shouldn't have, someone who was now dead. She couldn't help remembering Aaron's words: "We have committed a sin, if it is a sin to love, yet the One who created me in His image made me to love you."

She said gently, "But why does this make you want a divorce? He's dead now."

"How could you possibly understand?" Judah's voice began to rise. "I'll never love anyone as much as I loved Aaron, and he died without us consummating our love. I never even kissed him, and I wasn't able to say good-bye to him."

Miriam knew she shouldn't say it, but she did. "I was widowed in *erusin*, remember, from a man I loved more than the world, and even today I miss him and wish that we had laid together before he died, no matter what the consequences."

Judah stared at her in dismay. "You still mourn him after all these years?"

Miriam nodded, tears streaming down her face. "Benjamin died alone too, less than a month before our wedding, and I didn't say good-bye to him either. At least you got that love letter from Aaron; I'd give anything to have one from Benjamin."

She hadn't spoken of him in years and now the words wouldn't stop. "He was treading grapes by himself, and during a stormy *bouillage* the fumes overcame him and he drowned in the vat. How do you think I feel, every year, when I have to help with the vintage, when I must climb into that vat of fermenting grapes? And working in the vineyard holds a hundred memories more."

"I'll never forget Aaron then," he whispered as the enormity of this knowledge sunk in. "Not as long as I study Talmud."

She nodded again, then reached out and took his hand. They would both always be mourners; they should be able to comfort each other. "So you see that in some ways I understand you very well. But what I don't understand is why you want a divorce."

After all they'd shared, he had to tell her the truth. "When Shimson was so ill and Rachel told me that you might be dying too, I swore to the Holy One that if He healed you both, I would never even think carnally about another man." He took a deep breath. "But I can't use the bed with you without thinking about men."

"But that's why we say Kol Nidre at Yom Kippur," she said. "To nullify vows to Him that we can't keep."

"Not a vow with our sons' lives at stake."

"Then ask Papa to convene a beit din. They can annul any kind of vow."

"I can't confess my vow to Papa, Meir, and some other scholar, probably Shemayah."

"But . . ." Miriam tried to think of something else, but he interrupted her.

"Since I can't fulfill my marital duties, you are entitled to a divorce."

"You intend to be celibate for the rest of your life?"

"If the monks can do it, so can I," he replied. "You know what it says in the fifth chapter of Tractate Sukkot, the section that Papa explains as referring to the male organ.

. Rav Yohanan said: A man has a small member—when he starves it,
  it is satisfied, and when he satisfies it, it is starving.

Mine has been starving for almost a year, and it's not hungry anymore. You're a young woman. You need a husband who hasn't taken a vow of celibacy."

But Miriam didn't find great pleasure in using the bed. In fact, chastity was a small price to pay for keeping her children. The knowledge that she would never nurse a baby once little Alvina was weaned saddened her far more than the thought of not lying with a man again. Judah was mourning Aaron, but she was mourning all the children she would never have. Suddenly she had the answer.

"Judah, I have another confession to make, and I apologize for not telling you sooner," she said. "You realize that this last pregnancy almost killed me?"

He nodded and she continued, "Even with ginger tisanes I cannot expect to survive another. I remembered you saying that a scholar should father as many children as he could, so I was afraid to tell you."

"Even if you can't have more children, you shouldn't be celibate." But he didn't sound so sure.

"If nuns can do it, so can I." She threw his words back at him. Aunt Sarah had been celibate for years.

"But how can I stay here, where everything I see reminds me of Aaron?" He didn't want to be like her, where winemaking had made her mourn her beloved for over ten years.

"Unless you give up Talmud, you'll be reminded of him no matter where you go. And here, you won't be alone."

"If I stay, I won't be able to teach in the yeshiva." His expression was heavy with sadness. "I suppose I could work on Papa's *kuntres*, but I won't ever have someone special to study with again."

"I know someone here in Troyes who could be your new study partner, someone who's as learned as you are." Miriam's eyes were shining with excitement. "Someone you won't worry about having an improper relationship with either."

He tried to hide his disappointment. "I appreciate your offer, but I don't think you could attend lectures in the yeshiva with me, not with a new baby."

Miriam began to chuckle. "Not me. I'm not your equal in knowledge. Besides, now that Rachel is living in Troyes all year, I already have someone to study with."

"Then who?"

"Why Papa, of course. He hasn't had a study partner in twenty years because there wasn't anyone here at his level. But I bet he would love to study with you if you asked him."

Study with Salomon? With the rosh yeshiva? But why not? Why shouldn't the rosh yeshiva have a study partner like other scholars did? For the first time since Purim, Judah smiled.

thirty-four

Ramerupt
Spring 4890 (1090 CE)

When the lambing threatened to overwhelm Joheved, Miriam offered her assistance. Judah still slept in his own linens as though she were *niddah*, so why not spend a month or two in Ramerupt? Nobody in Troyes was expecting a baby anytime soon.

The weeks approaching Passover seemed to fly by. Alvina began sleeping through the night, a treat for Miriam after spending an exhausting day with the laboring ewes. Since both Moses and Shemayah's families were invited to spend the festival week in Ramerupt, Joheved asked Zipporah and Judita to come early and help with the lambing as well.

Watching Zipporah and Isaac together at meals, Miriam couldn't help but remember how shy Joheved had been with Meir at first. Like her prospective mother-in-law, Zipporah blushed whenever she encountered Isaac and almost never addressed him, apparently finding it easier to talk to his brother. For his part, Isaac definitely preferred conversing with Judita when the alternative was his little sisters.

Late one morning Miriam had returned to the room she shared with her nieces to change Alvina's swaddling, when she heard Meir and Isaac on the landing.

"You said you needed to talk to me alone." Meir sounded impatient.

The door closed in the bedroom next to her, but Miriam could clearly hear the two voices through the wall.

"Papa, is it true that when you and Mama conceived me, you had some magical device that gave you the *yetzer hara* of a ram?"

"Who the devil told you that?" Meir was angry now.

Isaac stood his ground. "I think I overheard one of the older students talking about it. Is it true?"

Miriam had told Rachel about Joheved's magic mirror, and she'd surely told Eliezer. Apparently the story was still being passed around, a dozen years later.

Meir sighed. "*Oui*, something like that is true."

"Because it would explain why my *yetzer hara* is so strong," Isaac said. "Maybe when I was conceived, I got the *yetzer hara* of a ram too."

"Most boys your age think their *yetzers* are strong."

"Mine is too strong." Isaac sounded scared. "Lillit comes to me at night."

"I know it's difficult for you, but how can I help?"

"Rav Hisda said that if he had married at fourteen, Satan would have had no influence over him. I'll be fourteen next year, Papa. Would you let me get married then?"

Miriam was blushing at the subject of this supposedly private conversation, but she didn't dare leave her room and risk discovery. Now if only Alvina would stay quiet.

Meir was chuckling. "Zipporah is rather young, but since you're so eager, I'll talk to Shemayah about it."

"Uh, Papa. There's another thing." Odd, but Isaac sounded more anxious than before. "I studied in Tractate Kiddushin, that

> Rav Yehuda says in the name of Rav: it is prohibited for a man to betroth a woman until he has seen her, in case he should find her unattractive."

"That's correct." Meir's voice held suspicion.

Isaac's words came so quickly that Miriam could barely understand him. "So I can't marry Zipporah. I don't find her attractive. I want to marry Judita, Moses haCohen's daughter."

For a moment there was silence, then a door banged open. "Joheved," Meir bellowed. "Joheved, where the devil are you?"

There were heavy footsteps on the landing and Meir yelled again,

"Shmuel. Go find your mother and bring her up here immediately. I don't care what she's doing."

Miriam could hear her nephew racing down the stairs, then a little later there were more footsteps coming up and finally Joheved panting, "What's . . . so important . . . that you have . . . to drag me away . . . in the middle of . . . doing the lamb accounts?"

"Isaac just told me that he refuses to marry Zipporah, that he wants to marry the doctor's daughter. You're behind this, Joheved. I know it."

Miriam was safe in her room but she cringed at Meir's fury.

Joheved wasn't cringing. Her defiant voice rang out, "I had nothing to do with it. True, I invited Judita to stay with us, but Zipporah has been here as well."

Meir's voice was equally firm. "I made an agreement with Shemayah, and I will not break it. His daughter is going to marry my son and that's final."

Joheved and Isaac responded almost simultaneously.

"Meir, be reasonable. Isaac and Zipporah will both be miserable if you force him to marry her."

"If you make me marry her, I'll just divorce her."

Miriam could almost see the three of them glaring at each other. Then there was Shmuel speaking, his voice hesitant. "If you want, I'll marry Zipporah. I don't mind being like Grandpapa and having only daughters."

"What did you say?" Miriam couldn't tell if Meir was outraged or astonished.

Shmuel's voice was stronger now. "If you promised Shemayah that your son would marry his daughter, then you wouldn't be breaking your oath if I married her."

"You're sure?" Isaac seemed in awe of his younger brother.

"Quite sure." Shmuel sounded confident now. "And I think you're making a mistake marrying a doctor's daughter when you could marry a scholar's daughter instead."

"This is the Holy One's doing, Meir." Joheved was jubilant. "I told you that if Isaac and Zipporah were *bashert*, there was nothing I could do to prevent their marriage, and if they weren't, then there was nothing I needed to do."

Meir knew when he was beaten. "Very well, I'll speak to Shemayah when he comes up for Passover."

"*Merci*, Papa," came Isaac's grateful voice. "And Shmuel, if there's ever anything you want from me, just ask and it's yours."

But Meir had the last word. "Don't start celebrating yet, Isaac. Only if Shemayah agrees will I speak to Moses, and if Judita is promised to someone else, you may end up with neither girl."

Miriam gave a sigh of relief as the family traipsed downstairs without realizing that she'd been listening. She had no doubt that Shemayah would find Shmuel, a far better student than his brother, an acceptable son-in-law, just as Moses haCohen would find Isaac, heir to the estate of Ramerupt-sur-Aube, more than acceptable.

The evening before Passover began, Salomon watched with pride as his eight grandchildren hunted for *hametz*. Six grandsons and three granddaughters so far—he had certainly fulfilled the mitzvah to be fruitful and multiply. Of course his wife and daughters had already cleaned up every trace of leaven, so several pieces of stale bread had been hidden around the first floor for the children to find, thus performing the commandment to search out and remove all *hametz* from dwellings before Passover. The servants, having grown used to generations of their lord's eccentric religious habits, resigned themselves to eating their bread and stirabout in the steward's house for the next week.

The children had found all but a few crusts when the family was distracted by a commotion in the courtyard. Soon the front door opened and Rachel's husband stood framed in the entryway.

"Eliezer," she shrieked, racing into his outstretched arms. "I thought I wouldn't see you again until June."

Eliezer held her close. "When you're married to the most beautiful woman in France, you don't want to leave her alone for too long," he said with a wink.

Rachel giggled. "Don't say things like that, it tempts the Evil Eye."

"My business in Barcelona concluded more easily than I anticipated," he replied, stroking Rachel's swollen belly. "So I realized that I could get here in time for Passover."

"By the way, Judah." Eliezer reached into his sleeve and pulled out a letter. "I ran into one of your fellow Parisians in Troyes, and he gave me a message for you." When Eliezer saw everyone's looks of alarm, he quickly added, "Don't worry, it's good news. In fact, I believe congratulations are in order."

Yom Tov gave Miriam the bread crusts he'd found and bolted to Judah's side. "What does it say, Papa?"

Judah stared up at Miriam, his eyes wide with astonishment. "It's from the Paris community. Their rosh yeshiva wants to retire and they ask me to take the position."

"Mazel tov, you deserve it." Meir shook Judah's hand. "Imagine, my brother-in-law the rosh yeshiva of Paris."

"Just when I was starting to enjoy having a study partner again after all these years," Salomon said with mock despair.

But Miriam and Rachel exchanged anxious glances. How would this unexpected honor affect Judah's decision?

"Excuse me, Eliezer, but did the man say how long I had to make up my mind?" Judah asked.

"I don't think it occurred to him that you'd need any time to make up your mind," Eliezer replied. "But he's staying in Troyes for the festival, so I suppose you have at least eight days to decide."

Rachel gazed at her husband with loving eyes. "You must be exhausted from your trip. Shall we get ready for bed?"

"Perhaps your son would like to sleep with his cousins tonight?" Joheved asked with a knowing smile.

"I think we should all be going to bed," Salomon said. "We'll need a good night's sleep tonight if we want to stay awake for the entire seder tomorrow."

"Judah, what are you going to do?" Miriam whispered as they walked upstairs to their room.

"I don't know." He shook his head. "I have never wanted to live in

Paris, but this is an honor I cannot easily refuse. At least I have a week to think about it."

"I don't want to go back to Paris," Shimson whined. "I don't have any friends there, and Grandmama is always hugging and kissing me."

Miriam tousled his hair. "I'm sure you'd make new friends in Paris, and your grandmama was just thankful that you weren't sick anymore."

The thought of Shimson nearly dying of the pox made her want to hug and kiss him herself. Not that she wanted to move to Paris either. But everyone would expect her and the children to go with Judah if he accepted the position, despite leaving her community without a midwife. Just when they'd finally begun to accept her as their mohel—and just when Rachel's decision to remain in Troyes meant that she and her sister could be constant study partners. *But maybe this is the excuse Judah needs for us to live separately.*

Miriam tried to overcome her anxiety and enjoy what might well be the last seder she'd spend with her parents. The three sisters and their husbands had celebrated Passover together only once before, and she could scarcely call that a celebration, coming as it did immediately after Eliezer learned of his father and brother's untimely deaths.

Meir had obviously arrived at agreements with both Shemayah and Moses, because with the first cup of wine he toasted the two newly affianced couples. Joheved, of course, beamed with delight, and Miriam couldn't help but wonder if her older sister had found a way to arrange things to her satisfaction.

When little Elisha chanted the four questions perfectly, it was Miriam's turn to glow with pleasure. Papa must have been feeling proud of his children as well, because he made a point of asking them questions concerning women's role in the exodus from Egypt, questions whose answers came from the Talmud.

"Four being an unlucky even number, we would normally never drink four cups of wine at a meal," he said. "But just as the Holy One protected the Israelites from the Angel of Death on the first Passover in Egypt, so are we protected tonight."

All three of his daughters nodded. This was explained in the tenth chapter of Tractate Pesachim.

"Rachel, where do we learn that women are obligated in all the mitzvot of Passover, including the four cups of wine, though they are generally exempt from time-bound positive commandments?"

"It's in the first chapter of Tractate Sotah," she replied.

> "Rav Avira said: Because of the merit of the righteous women of that generation, Israel was redeemed from Egypt."

"And these women were?" Salomon encouraged her to continue.

"First were the midwives, Shifrah and Puah, who refused Pharaoh's order to kill the newborn Hebrew boys." Rachel's voice was confident. "Then there was Batyah, Pharaoh's daughter. She was bathing in the river because she had leprosy, but when she touched the baby Moses, she was healed. So she saved his life and later converted to Judaism. The last is Miriam, who brought Moses's own mother to be his nursemaid." She gazed around the table and added, "In honor of these four righteous women, we drink four cups of wine tonight."

Salomon turned to his middle daughter. "What does this text tell us about the reward the midwife Miriam received when she refused to kill the Israelite baby boys she'd delivered?"

Miriam smiled at him before answering. Of course Papa would ask her a question about the midwife named Miriam.

"Our Sages teach that Shifrah was actually another name for Joheved, Moses's mother, and Puah was another name for Miriam.

> It is written: Because the midwives feared the Holy One, He made houses for them . . . houses of royalty, meaning King David, who descended from Miriam and Caleb."

Now Salomon addressed Joheved, who was anticipating a question about her biblical namesake. "Near the end of Genesis, it is written that seventy descendants of Jacob came down to Egypt. Yet when we count all the people listed, there are only sixty-nine names. How does Tractate Sotah explain this?"

Joheved quoted the text.

> "Rav Chama ben Chanina said the missing person is Joheved, who was conceived en route and born within the walls of Egypt. As it says: 'The name of Amram's wife was Joheved, daughter of Levi, who was born to Levi in Egypt.'"

Then she gave her explanation. "Notice that our verse from Exodus says first that Joheved was a 'daughter of Levi,' and then that she 'was born to Levi in Egypt.' Since there are no superfluous words in the Torah, this apparent duplication is there to teach that, while Joheved's birth occurred in Egypt, her conception did not."

"So she was 130 years old when she gave birth to Moses," Zipporah said as her father's jaw dropped.

"We certainly have no shortage of righteous women in our generation either," Meir said, saluting them with his wine cup.

After the seder was officially concluded, they continued discussing Tractate Sotah's description of Moses's life in Egypt. Rachel and Eliezer went to bed around the time the conversation branched off onto Tractate Pesachim, but Miriam stayed up as late as Judah.

Each night that week, she refused to go bed until he did. He seemed comfortable chatting about their sons or that day's studies, but she waited in vain for him to bring up the subject of Paris. Finally, on the sixth night of Passover, when she left the salon to put Alvina to bed, he yawned and announced that he would join her.

Miriam settled into bed, Alvina at her breast. Judah blew out the lamp, but she could see him clearly in the moonlight. He came to the point immediately.

"Miriam, you're the only person I can be honest with. I need you to convince me why I shouldn't move to Paris and become their rosh yeshiva."

Her heart leaped with hope, and she decided to be forthright as well. "Why *you* shouldn't move to Paris or why *we* shouldn't move to Paris?"

He paused to consider her question. "I already know plenty of reasons why you shouldn't move to Paris. Convince me why I shouldn't be their rosh yeshiva and then neither of us will have to worry about moving there."

"The obvious reasons are that you're a person who isn't impressed by status, you'd hate the politics involved, and you prefer studying to teaching. But most importantly . . ." She hesitated. "As rosh yeshiva you'd be continually tempted by students looking up to you, coming to you for advice, expecting you to mentor them." He said he wanted honesty.

"You're right." Judah nodded his head sadly. "Until I met Aaron I thought I was strong enough to control my *yetzer hara*. But now I know how weak I truly am." He took a deep breath and looked into her eyes. "And it terrifies me."

Miriam reached out and took his hand. "You would be terribly vulnerable as a rosh yeshiva, even in Troyes."

"Maybe with you there I could be stronger; it wouldn't be like before when you didn't know until it was too late." He stood up and addressed the room. "How can I refuse? It's an acknowledgement of my learning and an incredible honor. It would make my mother so happy."

"And it would make you so miserable. You'd have to give up working with Papa on his *kuntres*." She had to convince him to stay in Troyes, not merely to refrain from moving to Paris.

"*Oui*, I would miss him greatly." Judah sighed. His wife understood him, and, despite great provocation, she had never condemned him. How could he have been afraid to talk to her?

"Papa would miss you," Miriam said. "You heard what he said when you first got the letter, about finally having a study partner again."

"And staying here is the only way I'll ever have one again." He sat down and turned to her. "So how can I say no to Paris without offending them?"

"Tell them that Papa is getting old and he needs you to help finish his Torah commentary."

Judah nodded. "After all, they can find another rosh yeshiva, but where will Papa get someone else with my experience to work on his *kuntres*?"

"And your discretion," Miriam added. Papa's Torah commentary was no secret, but his Talmud *kuntres* was another matter.

She handed drowsy Alvina to Judah, who put her in her cradle. Then she waited while he undressed and got into bed. There was one more salvo in her argument. "In Troyes your memories of Aaron are mostly sweet ones," she said. "But in Paris you'll be reminded of worrying and waiting for him, when all the time he was already dead."

The next moment Judah was weeping in her arms with great gulping sobs. "Miriam, I miss him so much."

She held him and cried with him, mourning Benjamin, Aunt Sarah, the additional children she would never bear, and the perfect marriage she'd thought they had. Finally, when all their tears had been shed, she whispered, "So long as we remember them, those we loved will never truly be gone."

Suddenly Judah froze, apparently realizing that they were in each other's arms, naked. But he didn't turn away from her; instead he lay on his back and stared up at the ceiling for a long time. "Do you remember, when I first came to Troyes, how I wanted to be like Ben Azzai?"

"*Oui*," she said. Probably Ben Azzai's *yetzer hara* was also more attracted to men than to women; that's why he preferred Torah study to procreation. And why he was so devoted to Rabbi Akiva, neglecting his wife, Akiva's daughter.

"I think my destiny is to be Ben Azzai to Papa's Akiva, except that I will have fulfilled the mitzvah of procreation."

"I take it that I've convinced you to remain in Troyes," she said. "Do you need me to convince you not to get divorced?"

He stared at the ceiling a while longer. "*Non*, my children need their mother . . . and their father needs her too."

"Our children need both their parents." She was too stunned to acknowledge his need of her.

Judah remained silent, so Miriam pulled the covers up and tried to sort out her feelings. First, there was relief that was almost exaltation. There was also resentment, for all the agony he had put her through.

Yet mixed in was sadness and empathy for the pain he endured. Her love of Benjamin had been sanctioned and celebrated, while his love for Aaron would remain a shameful secret. One day she might tell him these things, but not tonight.

Her thoughts were interrupted when Judah rolled onto his side, facing her, and slipped his arm around her waist. *Has he changed his mind about using the bed, too?* But she didn't have any of the sterilizing herbs prepared.

"I'm glad you decided to go to the *mikvah*," he whispered. "Besides having someone to confide in, another benefit of marriage is sharing a bed, keeping each other warm, and not being alone in the dark. Just because we're not using the bed doesn't mean we can't appreciate each other's company at night."

"I agree," she replied, surprised at how relieved she felt.

"And if I happen to be sleeping with my back to you, you're welcome to put your arm around me."

"I'll remember that."

She was appreciating how much she'd missed the feeling of his warm body nestled against hers when Judah leaned over and kissed her cheek.

"I want you to know that, as much as I loved Aaron, I still love you," he said. "*Bonne nuit.*"

Fate was an ironic thing, Miriam thought. Her two sisters felt such great passion for their husbands, yet Eliezer would be sharing Rachel's bed less than half the year, while Meir sometimes spent several nights a week in Troyes, leaving Joheved alone with their daughters in Ramerupt. Only she seemed destined to sleep with her husband every night. They might live more like brother and sister, but it was love.

"*Bonne nuit,* Judah. I love you, too."

She had relinquished the holy deed, yet she had not lost her husband's affection. Though she would eventually have to give up nursing babies, teaching her children Torah would be an enduring pleasure. And, as a midwife and *mohelet*, babies would always be part of her life. In fact, she would be a far better midwife and *mohelet* now that she wouldn't be incapacitated by future pregnancies.

Miriam snuggled closer to Judah, until she felt his warm breath on her neck, and remembered Papa's favorite quote from Pirke Avot.

> Ben Zoma said: Who is wise? One who learns from everyone.
> Who is strong? One who conquers his *yetzer hara*. Who is rich?
> One who is content with his portion.

She and Judah had made their choices; he to be strong and she to be rich.

Some hours later, Miriam wasn't sure how many because there were no bells in Ramcrupt, there was a soft but insistent knocking at her door.

"Miriam," Joheved whispered loudly. When Miriam cracked open the door, her sister held up a lamp and continued, "Yvette's manservant is here. He says she's in hard labor."

Miriam began to dress. "I hoped that she'd last until after the festival, but at least she didn't interrupt our seder."

"I woke up a stable boy to saddle your mare."

"*Merci.* Yvette's other births didn't take very long, but I'll bring Alvina with me in case I'm delayed."

Miriam grabbed her fur-lined cloak, kissed Judah, and whispered, "I have to ride into Troyes for a birth. I should be back before sunset."

Judah murmured something unintelligible and pulled the covers over his head. But Miriam was already in the hall.

The half-moon gave off sufficient light to follow the road to Troyes, although Miriam was confident that her horse could find the way home even in the dark. The sky was just starting to lighten, illuminating the city walls in the distance. Birds were serenading the approaching dawn, and with her baby snuggled in her lap, Miriam felt that all was well in creation.

All around her the forest's budding leaves were uncurling to meet the springtime sun, and soon Troyes' Jewish Quarter would hear the cry of new life. She hoped it would be a boy.

afterword

THE QUESTION EVERYONE ASKS: what is fact in *Rashi's Daughters* and what is fiction?

Salomon ben Isaac was a real man, whose Torah and Talmud commentaries contain many thousands of words about his life, his community, and his opinions. For him, I made every attempt to be as historically accurate as possible, and when forced to be creative, I used the wealth of information contained in his own writings to stay true to his character as I understood it. The legend that he was named after King Solomon because his *brit milah* coincided with the haftarah reading from First Kings 5:26, however, was too good to pass up.

But I admit it—there is absolutely no evidence, not even the hint of a legend, that Rashi's son-in-law, Judah ben Natan, was physically attracted to men. And there is also no evidence or legend that his daughter Miriam was a midwife or a mohel, or that she was betrothed to another man before marrying Judah. On the other hand, Joheved and Meir's lives on his estate in Ramerupt are described by their son Samuel, so I was more constrained in inventing their story.

While Judah and Miriam are certainly real historical figures, as is everyone in Rashi's immediate family, I created their characters as archetypes. I apologize to those readers who greatly mourned the death of imaginary Benjamin, but it was common in Rashi's time for young men to die in accidents and young women to die in childbirth. Jews who lived past adulthood often had more than one spouse, and I thought that at least one person in Rashi's family should experience that.

The role of the *femme sage*, or midwife, learned in women's medicine, was one I wanted to share with my readers, as well as the role of women merchants/moneylenders. So I chose Miriam to be the midwife and Rachel to be the merchant. When I discovered that women sometimes performed circumcisions in medieval Ashkenaz, I couldn't resist giving Miriam that occupation as well. After all, there's no proof that she wasn't a midwife or mohel, and it's entirely possible that she was.

Once I decided on her profession, I conducted years of research to ensure that my descriptions of medieval midwifery, *brit milah*, and mohel's training were as accurate as possible. The same for Miriam's herbology, Moses haCohen's medical advice, and Jewish women's lives in general.

But what about Judah?

Early in my Talmud studies with Rachel Adler, she pointed out how homosocial the yeshiva environment was, how a student with even the slightest inclination toward homosexuality would be vulnerable to falling in love with his teacher or study partner, and how traumatic this could be. I became intrigued with this phenomenon and decided to make Judah a model of it. Little did I know that ten years later I would become study partners with Rabbi Aaron Katz, who has greatly enlightened me with his personal perspective on the subject.

As I researched the history of homosexuality, I was fascinated to learn that not only is this word of recent origin, but the very concept is recent as well. Until after the Renaissance, as in ancient Greece and Rome, Europeans accepted that men might be sexually attracted to anyone beautiful, both maidens and youths. Lusty young men were assumed to have sex with each other, especially since young women were expected to remain chaste.

Sex with other men, known as "playing the game," was prohibited, but the desire for it was not abnormal. Sexual relations between men were sinful, but love between them was honored. It is clear from songs and jokes of this time that monks were believed to be especially prone to these feelings, and we have many love letters written by medieval clergy to each other that confirm this belief. Apparently the society that was tolerant toward Jews and learned women also tolerated Ganymedes.

But enough about Judah's possible sexual orientation. Since his and

Miriam's only daughter was named Alvina, I chose to call his mother that. Their oldest son, Yom Tov, became a scholar in Paris, so I based Judah's family there. Their other two sons are less well known, so I can only hope the names I found for them are correct. Rachel's husband really was Eliezer ben Shemiah, but his brother Asher is imaginary, as is Aunt Sarah.

Meir's family were clearly feudal lords, as both viticulture and raising sheep required a good deal of land. His son Samuel did marry Shemayah's daughter, and because the couple had only daughters, I got the idea of making her a hemophilia carrier (the disease is described in the Talmud). The scandal of Joseph marrying a young woman and then leaving most of his wealth to his son Samson before dying appears in several responsa, as does the custom of interrupting services. I included this because Samson did end up marrying one of Meir's daughters.

Count Thibault, his wife, Adelaide, and his sons are historical figures, as are Count André of Ramerupt and his wife, Alice. Pope Gregory's battles with King Henry over reform of the Catholic Church are well documented. The twin epidemics of 1089 killed many of the youngest and oldest members of the population, including Count Thibault, although unlike more modern times, smallpox was almost exclusively a disease of children in Rashi's time.

Machzor Vitry (an eight hundred–page anthology of Jewish law, liturgy, and customs compiled by Rashi's students and disciples) was one of my primary sources for knowledge of how his community observed Jewish holidays and life-cycle events. The chapters on *niddah* and *brit milah* were particularly useful, as were those describing Havdalah and Passover. Another amazing source was *Urban Civilization* by Irving Agus, which despite its bland title is a collection of medieval Ashkenaz responsa, translated into English and arranged by subject. It is truly a "Dear Abby" of medieval Jewish life, and the inspiration for many scenes in my novels. The magical and medical remedies I used in *Rashi's Daughters*, as well as the astrology and demonology, came from the Talmud itself or other medieval sources; I could never have invented such bizarre stuff.

Speaking of the Talmud, the passages I quoted are: Bava Metzia 64a (chapter 3), Yevamot 65b and Pesachim 108a (chapter 6), Yevamot 61b (chapter 8), Chagigah 14b (chapter 9), Berachot 62a and Niddah 31b (chapter 10), Niddah 31a (chapter 14), Avoda Zara 27a (chapter 16), Shabbat 133b, Niddah 64b, and Nedarim 20a (chapter 18), Bava Kamma 83b (chapter 20), Kiddushin 29a (chapter 23), Kiddushin 82a, Kiddushin 29a, and Shabbat 130a (chapter 24), Avoda Zara 12b and Yevamot 12b (chapter 28), Sanhedrin 54a and Chullin 109a (chapter 30), and Sotah 11b and Pesachim 108b (chapter 34). You can find the Sages' discussion of lucky and unlucky days in Shabbat 129b. Please note that all translations are my own.

For those readers who are interested in my many sources, a bibliography is located on my website, www.rashisdaughters.com, under "Historical Info."

glossary

Allemagne   Germany

Angleterre   England

Arayot   sections of Talmud dealing with sexual relations

Azmil   special knife used for circumcisions

Beit din   Jewish court

Bima   pulpit, raised platform in synagogue where Torah is read

Bliaut   tunic, outer garment worn over a chemise by both men and women

Braises   men's short pants

Brit milah   ritual circumcision, performed when the baby boy is eight days old

Chacham   Jewish scholar

Denier   silver penny; a chicken costs four deniers

Disner   midday meal, usually the largest meal of the day

Edomite   European non-Jew (Talmudic term for Roman)

Erusin   formal betrothal that cannot be annulled without a divorce but does not allow the couple to live together

Gehenna   hell, populated by evil spirits and souls of the recent dead

Get   Jewish bill of divorce

Havdalah   Saturday evening ceremony that marks the end of the Sabbath

Kavanah   serious intention before praying or performing a mitzvah

Ketubah   Jewish marriage contract given by the groom to the bride specifying his obligations during the marriage and in the event of divorce or his death

Kuntres   notes and commentary explaining the Talmudic text

Lauds   second of seven canonical hours, approximately 3 a.m.

Lillit   demon responsible for killing newborn babies and women in childbirth, Adam's first wife

Livre   a pound, unit of money equal to 240 deniers

Matins   first canonical hour, midnight

Matzah   unleavened bread eaten during Passover

Mazikim   demons, evil spirits

Midrash   genre of rabbinic commentary that expands and explains the biblical text, generally used to refer to non-legal material

Mishkav zachur   sexual relations between men, literally lying with a male

Mikvah   ritual bath used for purification, particularly by women when no longer *niddah*

Mitzvah   (plural *mitzvot*) divine commandment

Mohel   (fem: *mohelet*) one who performs a ritual circumcision

Motzitzin   drawing the blood after circumcision to help heal the wound

Niddah   a menstruating woman

Nisuin   ceremony that completes the marriage, followed by cohabitation

Notzrim   polite Jewish word for Christians; literally those who worship the one from Nazareth

Parnas   leader, or mayor, of Jewish community

Priah   thin membrane between the foreskin and the baby's penis

Prime   dawn, third of seven canonical hours, approximately 6 a.m.

Rosh yeshiva   headmaster of a Talmud academy

Seder   ceremony observed in a Jewish home on the first two nights of Passover

Selichot   prayers for forgiveness, also the special religious service that takes place at midnight on the Saturday night preceding Rosh Hashanah

Sepharad   Spain

Sext   noon

Shiva   seven days of mourning following the death of a relative

Souper   supper, evening meal

Sukkah   booth in which Jews dwell during the harvest festival of Sukkot

Tahara   preparation of the corpse for burial

Talmid chacham   great Jewish scholar

Tefillin   phylacteries, small leather cases containing passages from scripture worn by Jewish men while reciting morning prayers

Trencher   piece of day-old bread used to hold meat (instead of a plate)

Vespers   sixth of seven canonical hours, approximately 6 p.m.

Yeshiva   Talmud academy

Yetzer hara   evil inclination, usually refers to the sexual urge

Yetzer tov   inclination to good